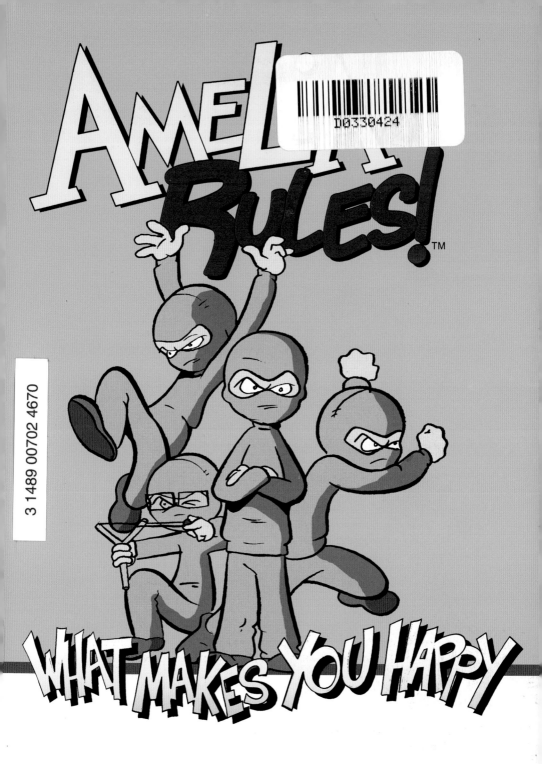

AMELIA RULES!™

WHAT MAKES YOU HAPPY

Atheneum Books for Young Readers
New York   London   Toronto   Sydney

MEET THE GANG

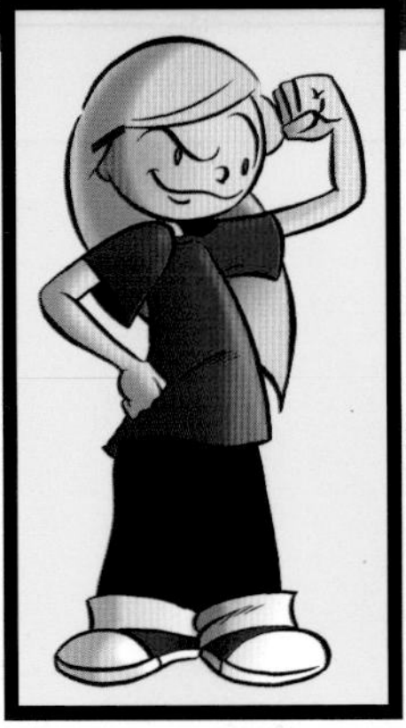

Amelia Louise McBride:
Our heroine. Wise cracking, yet sweet. She spends her time hanging out with friends and her aunt Tanner.

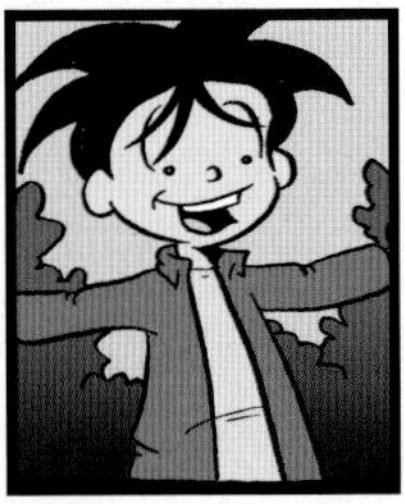

Reggie Grabinsky:
A.k.a. Captain Amazing. Founder of G.A.S.P., which he forces . . . er, encourages, his friends to join.

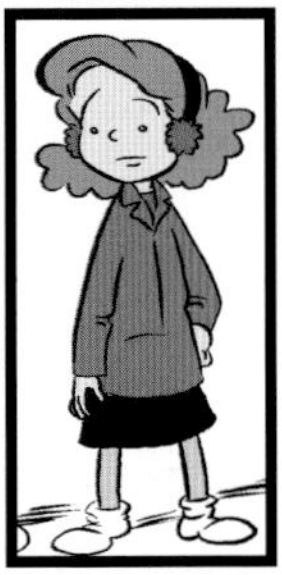

Rhonda Bleenie:
Smart, stubborn, and loud. She wears her heart on her sleeve and it's filled with love for Reggie.

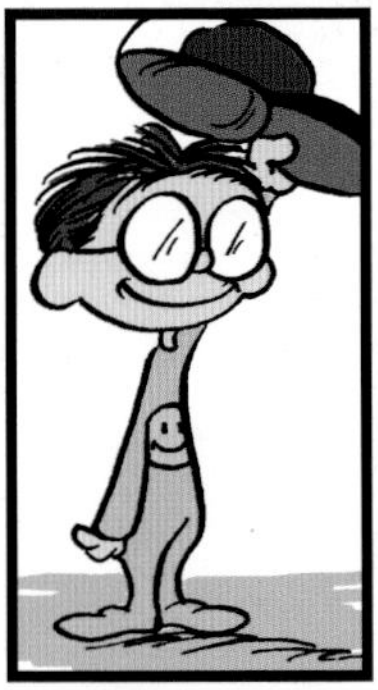

Pajamaman:
Never speaks. Always cool. His feetie jammies tell you what's on his mind.

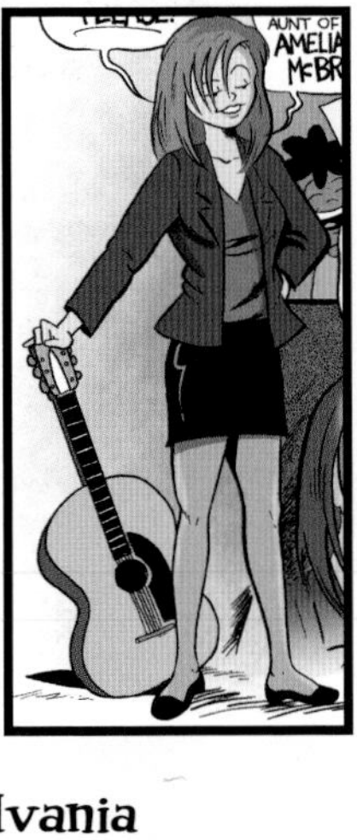
AUNT OF
AMELIA

Tanner:
Amelia's aunt and a former rock 'n' roll superstar.

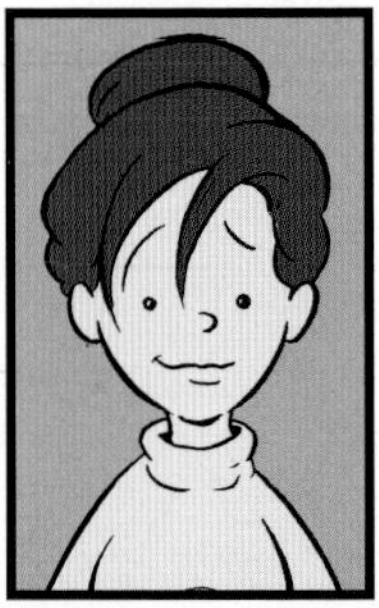

Amelia's Mom (Mary):
Starting a new life in Pennsylvania with Amelia after the divorce.

Amelia's Dad:
Still lives in New York, and misses Amelia terribly.

G.A.S.P.
Gathering Of Awesome Super Pals. The superhero club Reggie founded.

Park View Terrace Ninjas:
Club across town and nemesis to G.A.S.P.

Kyle:
The main ninja. Kind of a jerk but not without charm.

Joan:
Former Park View Terrace Ninja (nemesis of G.A.S.P.), now friends with Amelia and company.

Tweenie Zeenie:
A local kid-run magazine and Web site.

tweeniezeenie.com

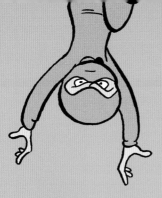

· Special thanks to Michael Cohen ·

ATHENEUM BOOKS FOR YOUNG READERS
An imprint of Simon & Schuster Children's Publishing Division
1230 Avenue of the Americas, New York, New York 10020

Atheneum Books for Young Readers is a
registered trademark of Simon & Schuster, Inc.
For information about special discounts for bulk purchases, please contact
Simon & Schuster Special Sales at 1-866-506-1949
or business@simonandschuster.com.
The Simon & Schuster Speakers Bureau can bring authors to your live event.
For more information or to book an event, contact the Simon & Schuster
Speakers Bureau at 1-866-248-3049
or visit our website at www.simonspeakers.com.

Book design by Jimmy Gownley and Sonia Chaghatzbanian
Manufactured in China
0317 SCP
First Atheneum Books for Young Readers paperback edition August 2009
8 10 9
CIP data for this book is available from the Library of Congress.
ISBN 978-1-4169-8605-8
These comics were originally published individually by Renaissance Press.

To my beautiful girls:
Stella Mary and
Anna Elizabeth,
And to their wonderful mother, Karen.

You're what make ME happy.

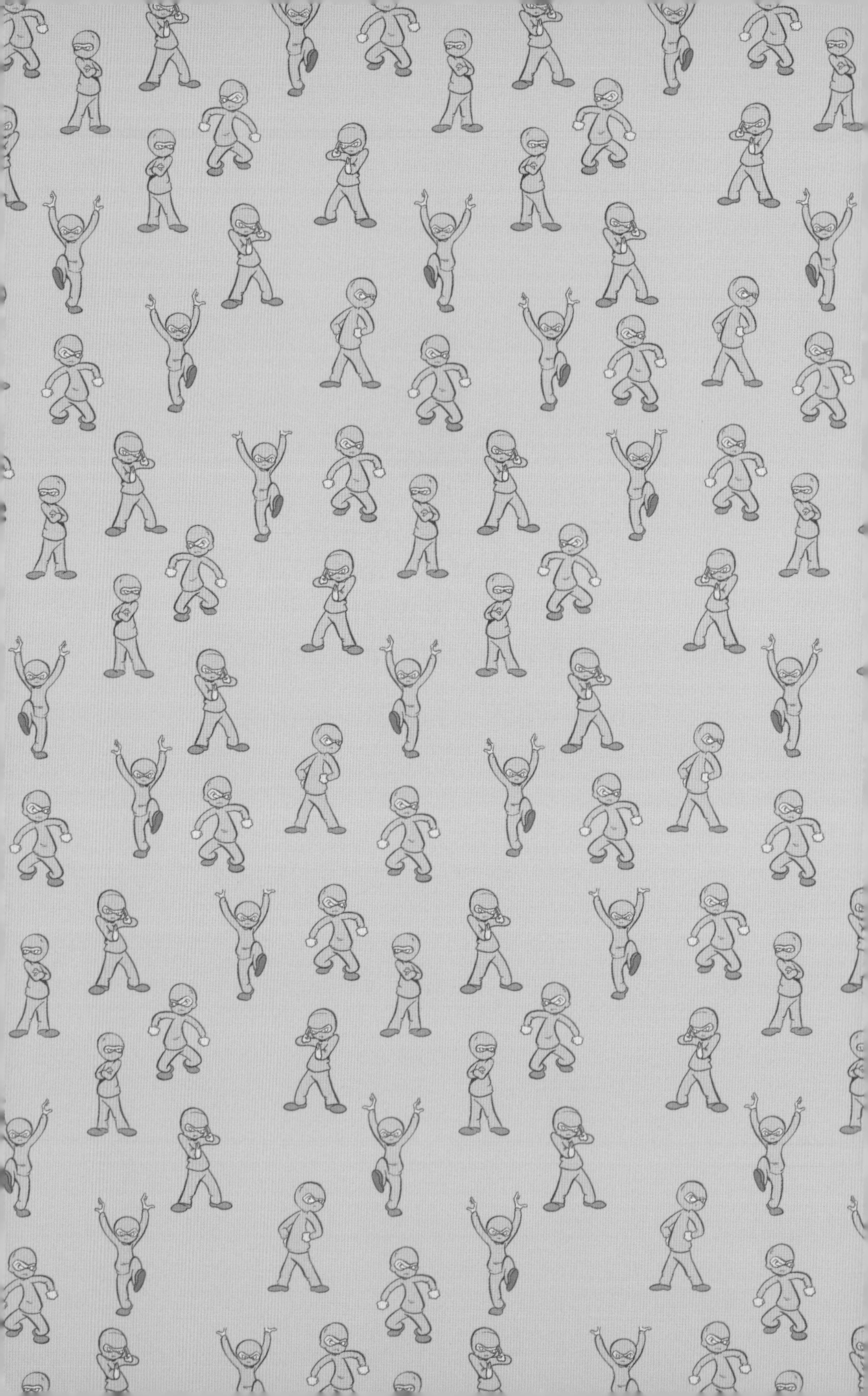

WHAT MAKES YOU HAPPY

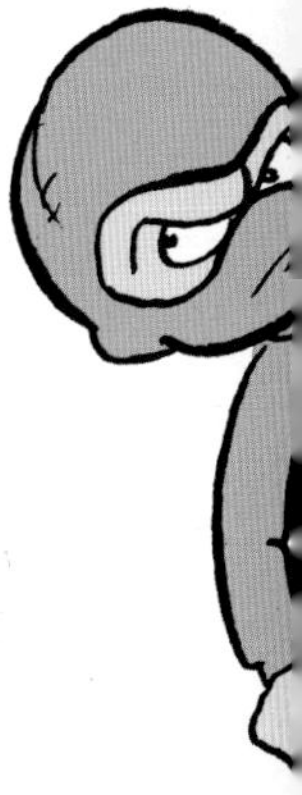

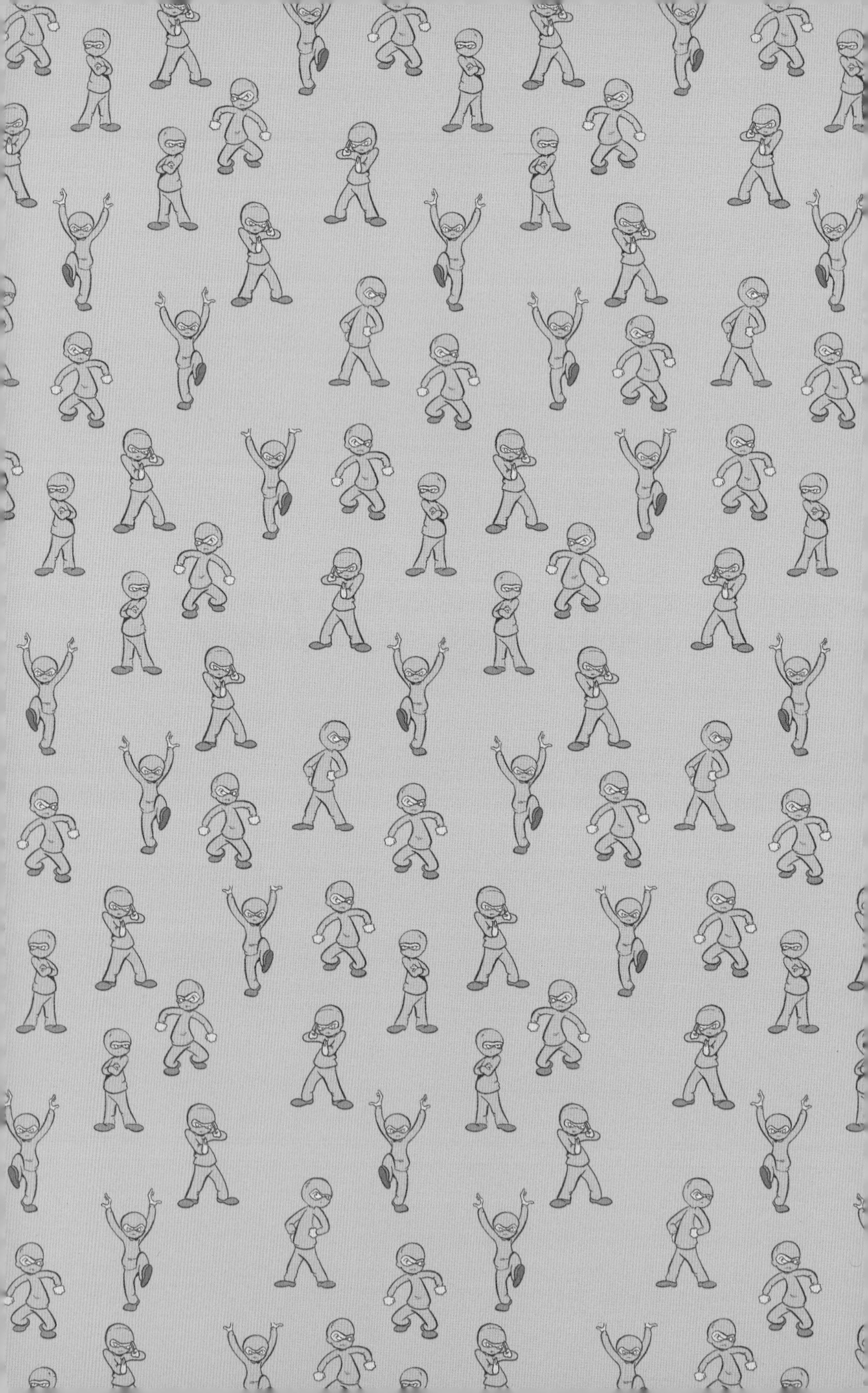

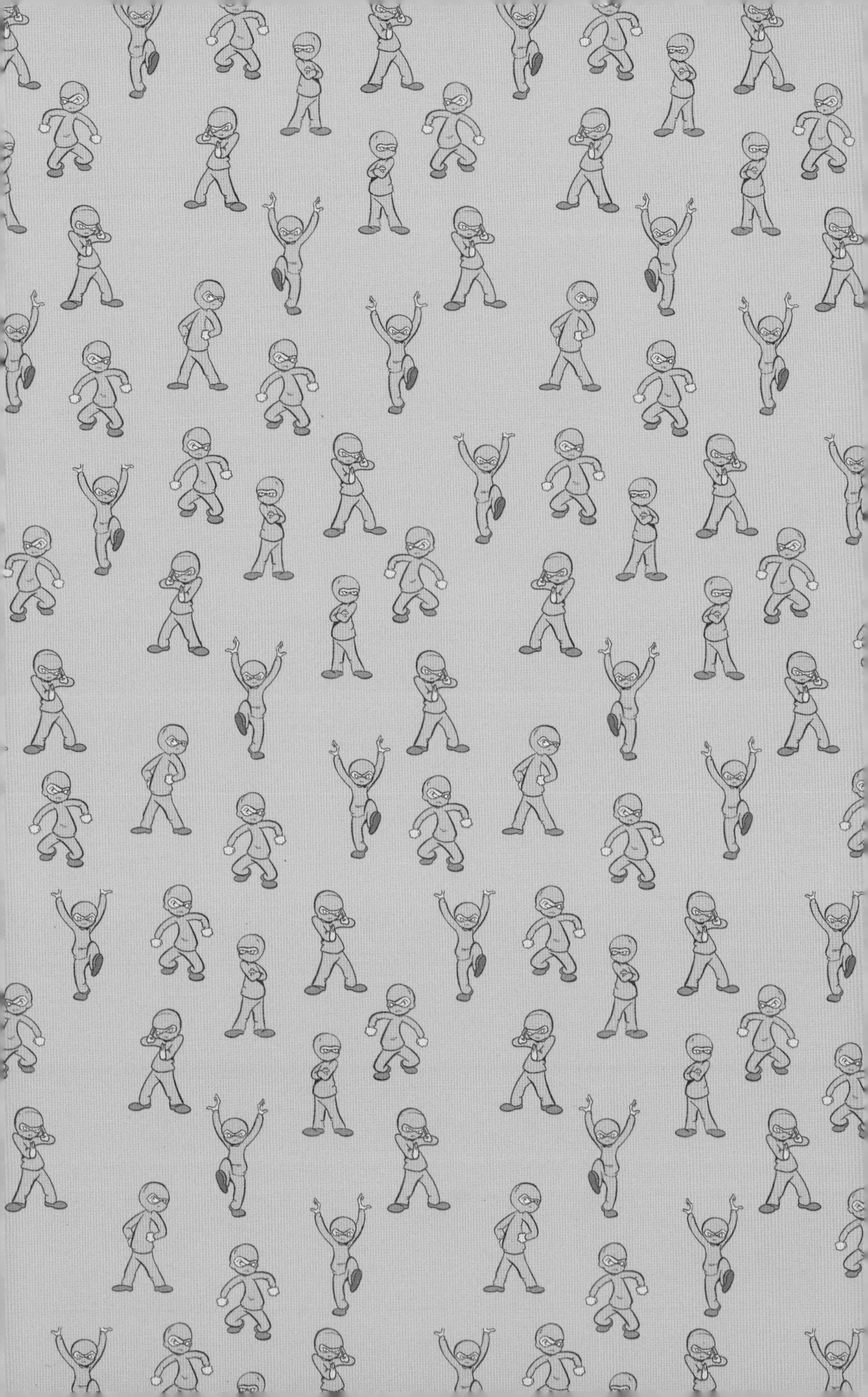

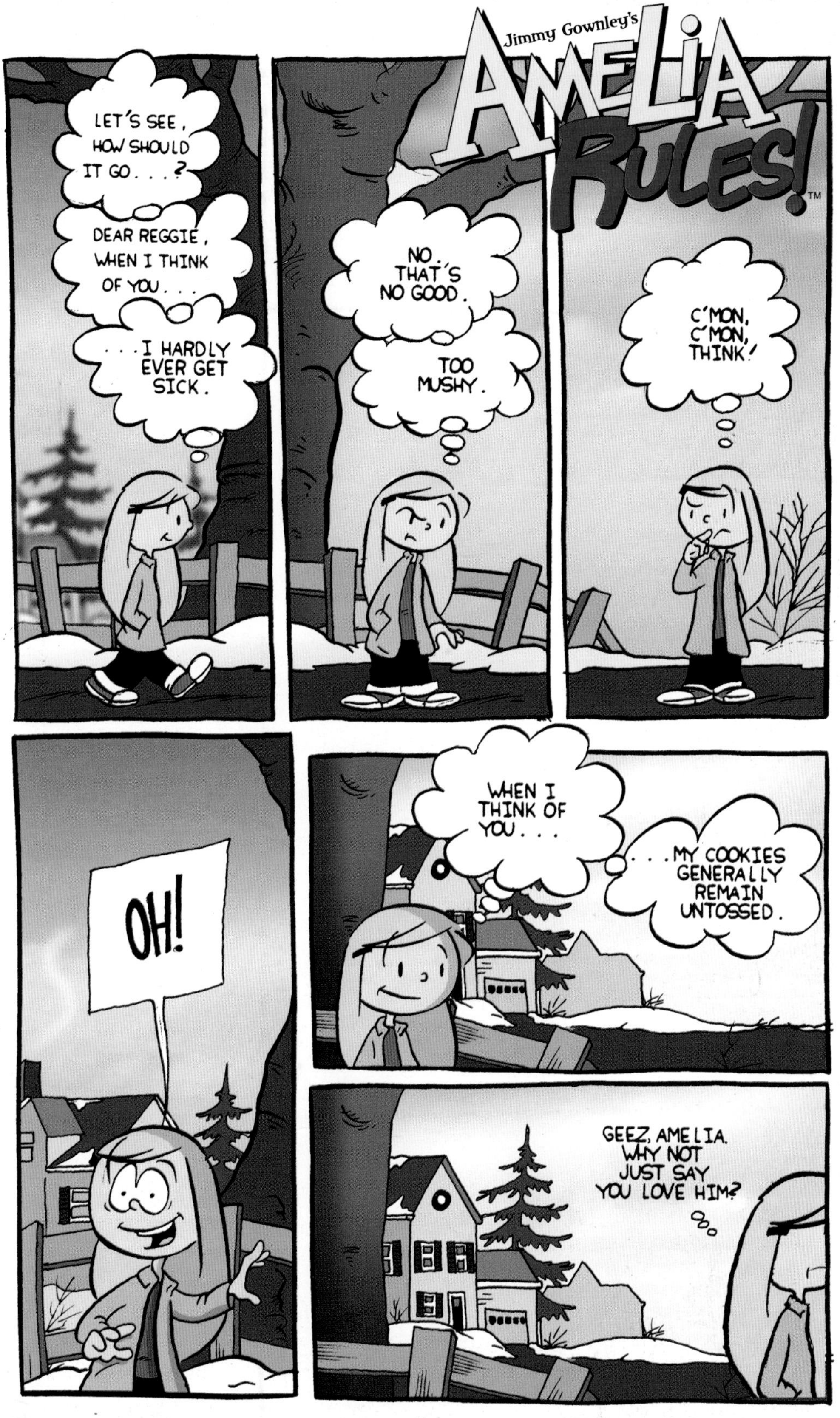
Jimmy Gownley's
AMELIA RULES!™
LET'S SEE, HOW SHOULD IT GO . . . ?
DEAR REGGIE, WHEN I THINK OF YOU . . .
. . . I HARDLY EVER GET SICK.
NO. THAT'S NO GOOD.
TOO MUSHY.
C'MON, C'MON, THINK!
OH!
WHEN I THINK OF YOU . . .
. . . MY COOKIES GENERALLY REMAIN UNTOSSED.
GEEZ, AMELIA. WHY NOT JUST SAY YOU LOVE HIM?

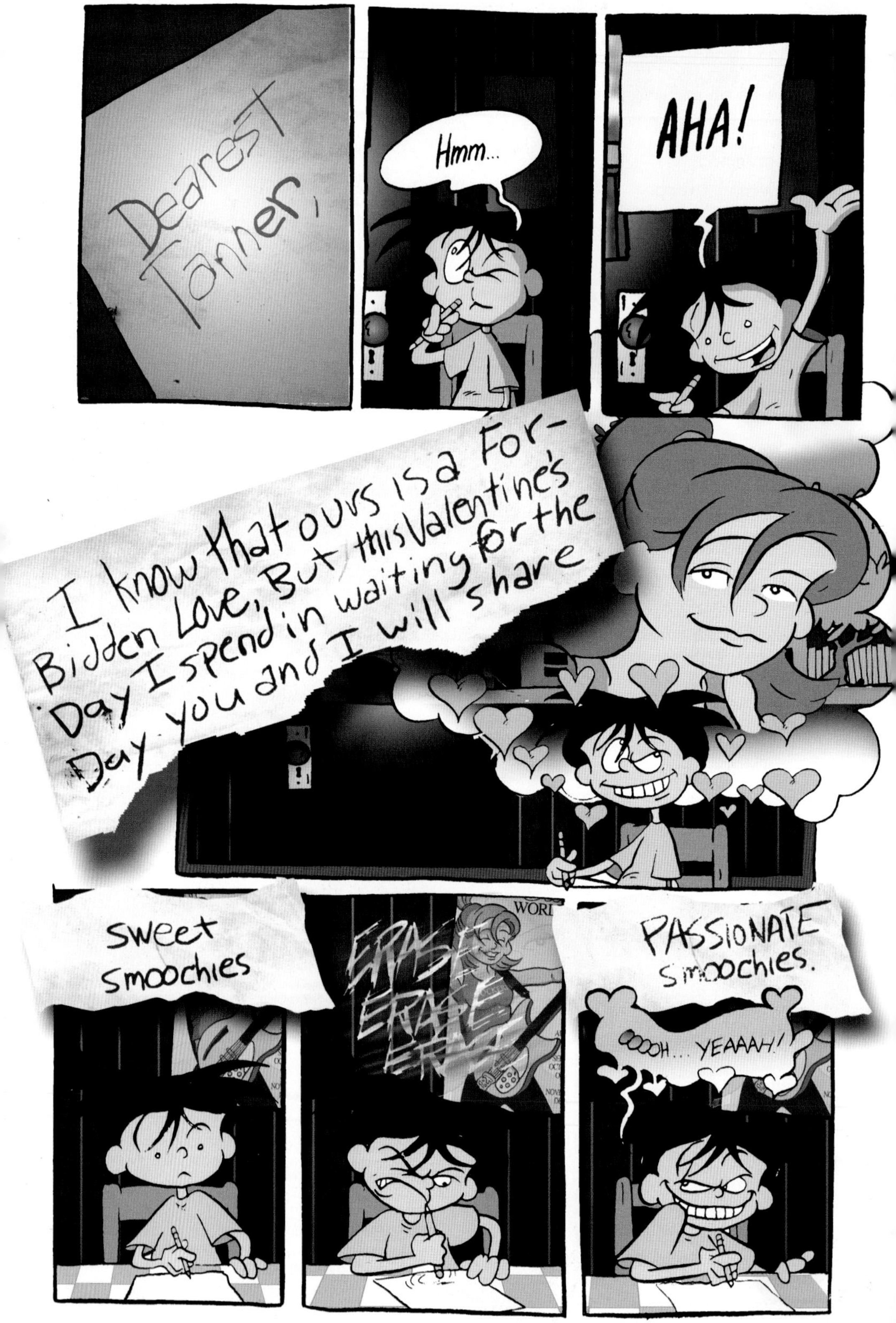

Dearest Tanner,
Hmm...
AHA!
I know that ours is a For-
Bidden Love, But this Valentine's
Day I spend in waiting for the
Day you and I will share
Sweet smoochies
ERASE ERASE ERASE
PASSIONATE smoochies.
OOOOH... YEAAAH!

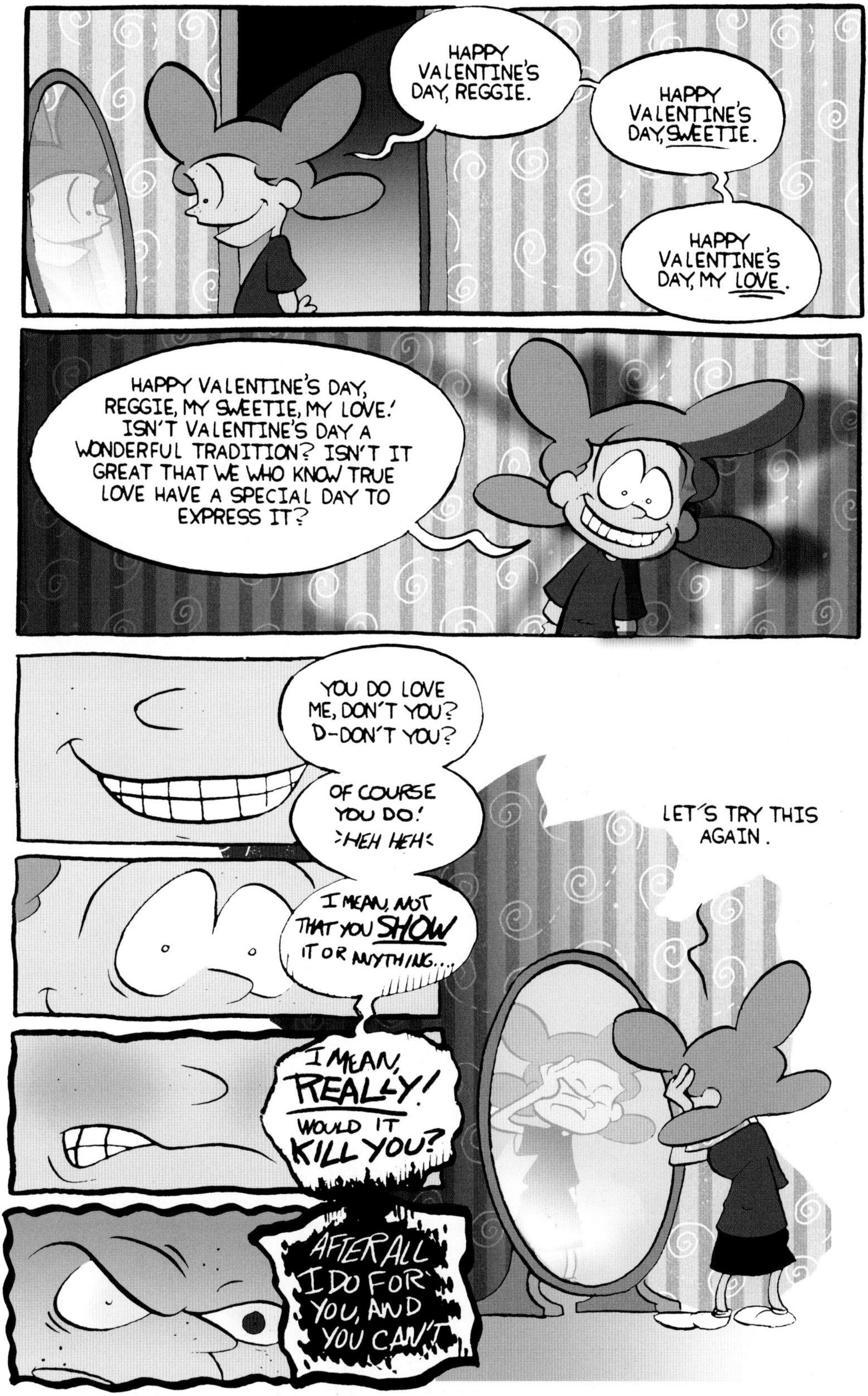
HAPPY VALENTINE'S DAY, REGGIE.
HAPPY VALENTINE'S DAY, SWEETIE.
HAPPY VALENTINE'S DAY, MY LOVE.
HAPPY VALENTINE'S DAY, REGGIE, MY SWEETIE, MY LOVE! ISN'T VALENTINE'S DAY A WONDERFUL TRADITION? ISN'T IT GREAT THAT WE WHO KNOW TRUE LOVE HAVE A SPECIAL DAY TO EXPRESS IT?
YOU DO LOVE ME, DON'T YOU? D-DON'T YOU?
OF COURSE YOU DO! >HEH HEH<
I MEAN, NOT THAT YOU SHOW IT OR ANYTHING...
I MEAN, REALLY! WOULD IT KILL YOU?
AFTER ALL I DO FOR YOU, AND YOU CAN'T
LET'S TRY THIS AGAIN.

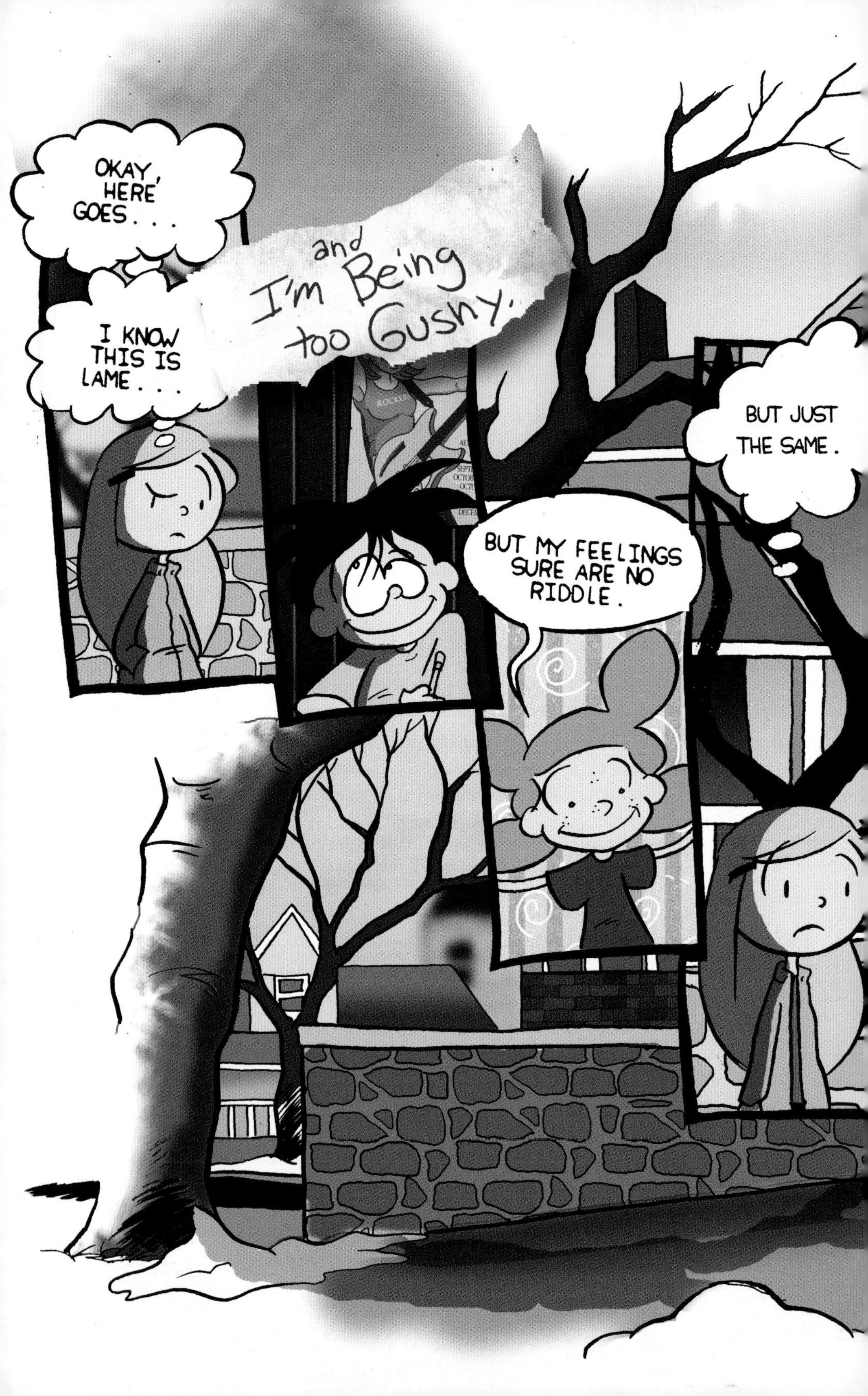
OKAY, HERE GOES. . .
I KNOW THIS IS LAME. . .
and I'm Being too Gushy.
BUT MY FEELINGS SURE ARE NO RIDDLE.
BUT JUST THE SAME.

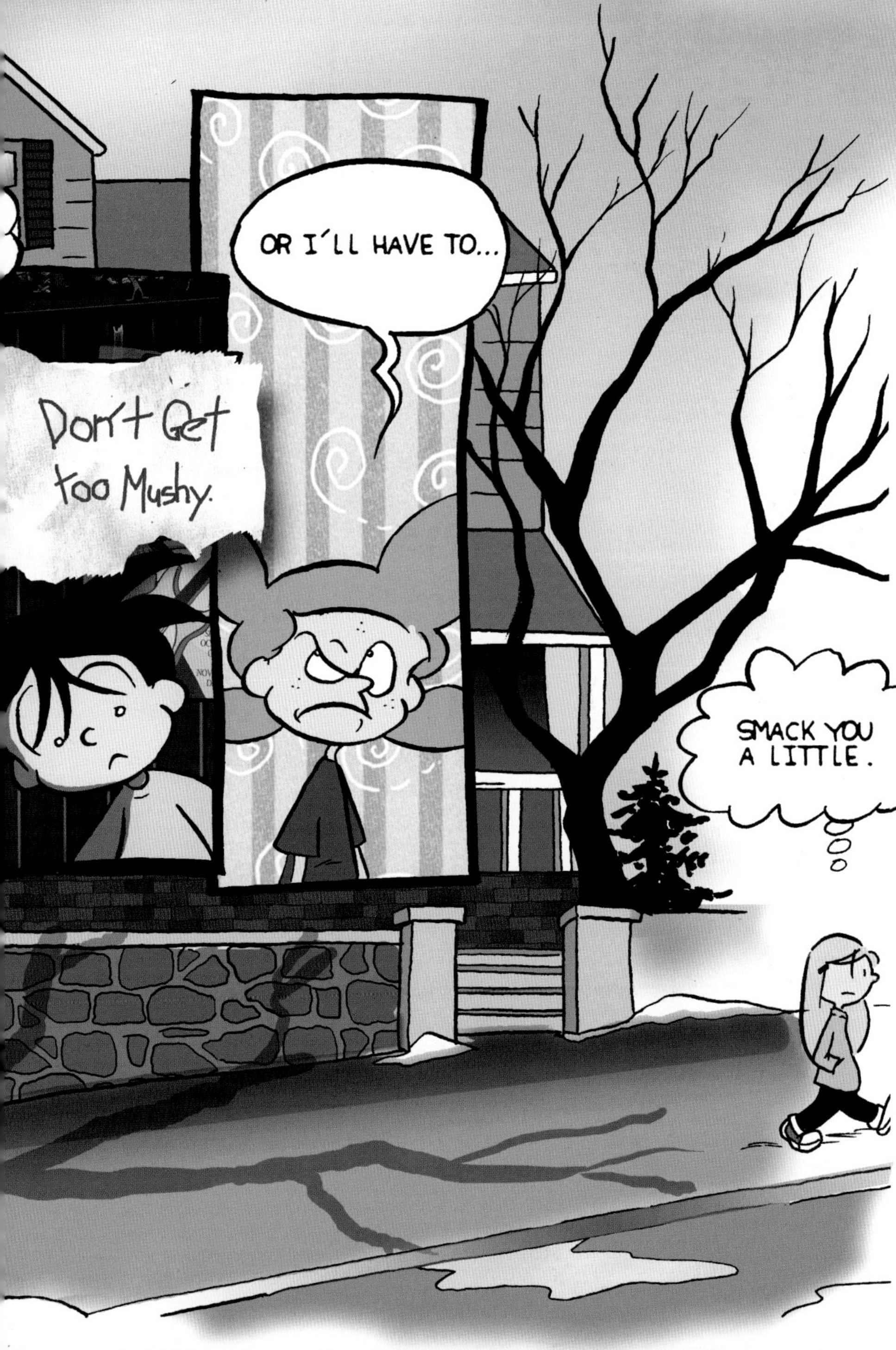
Don't Get too Mushy.
OR I'LL HAVE TO...
SMACK YOU A LITTLE.

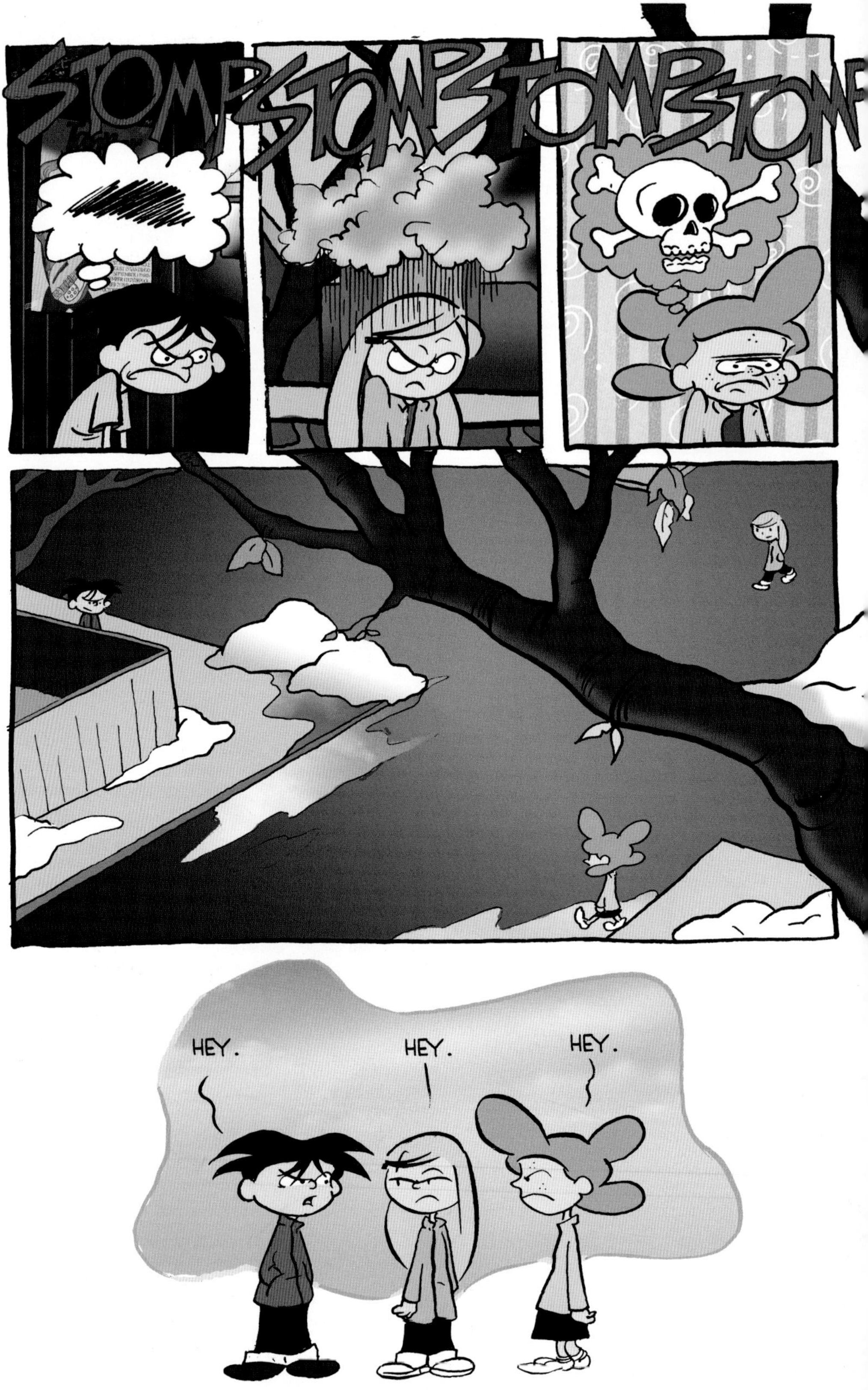
STOMP
STOMP
STOMP
HEY.
HEY.
HEY.

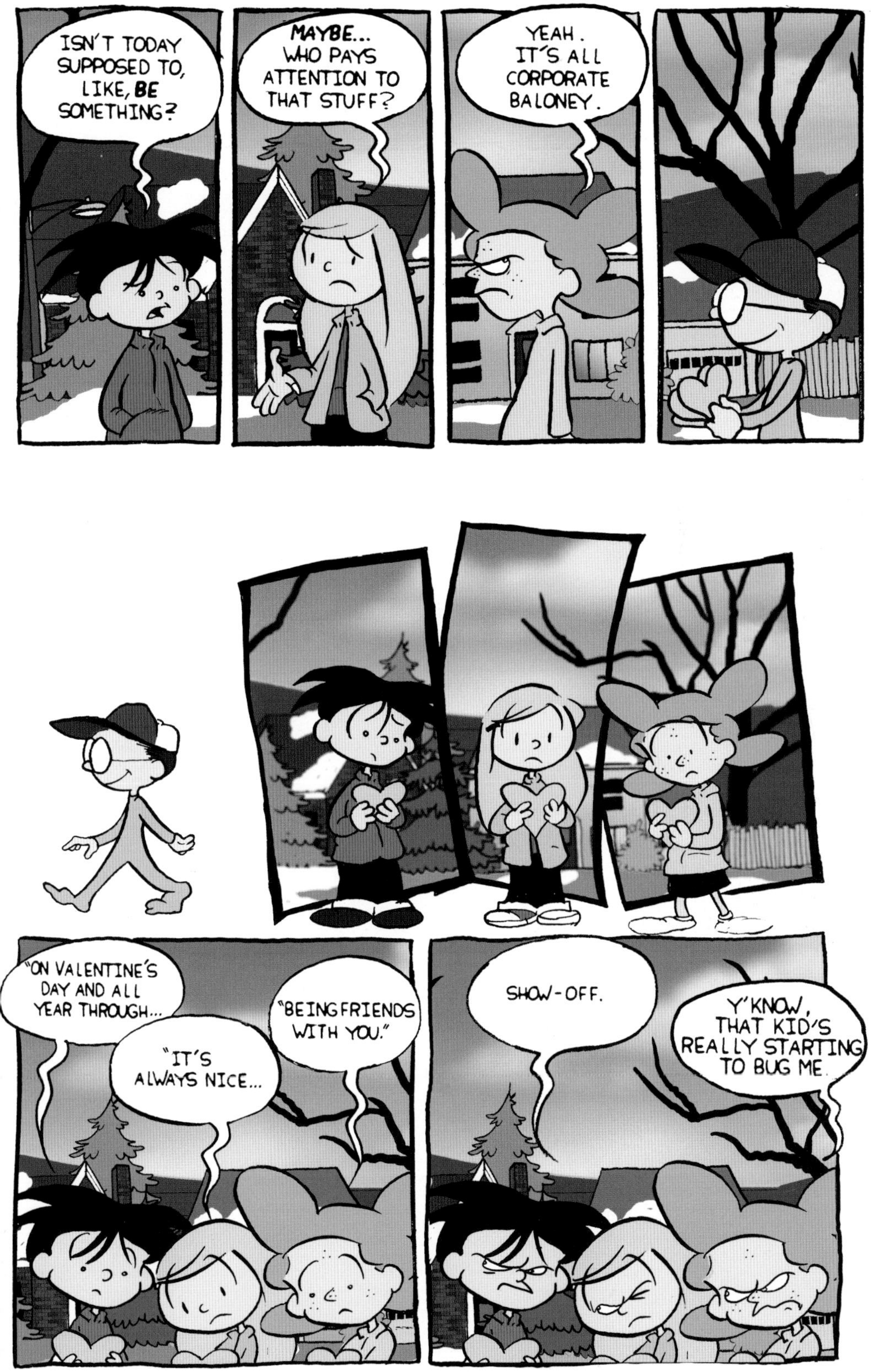
ISN'T TODAY SUPPOSED TO, LIKE, BE SOMETHING?
MAYBE... WHO PAYS ATTENTION TO THAT STUFF?
YEAH. IT'S ALL CORPORATE BALONEY.
"ON VALENTINE'S DAY AND ALL YEAR THROUGH...
"IT'S ALWAYS NICE...
"BEING FRIENDS WITH YOU."
SHOW-OFF.
Y'KNOW, THAT KID'S REALLY STARTING TO BUG ME.

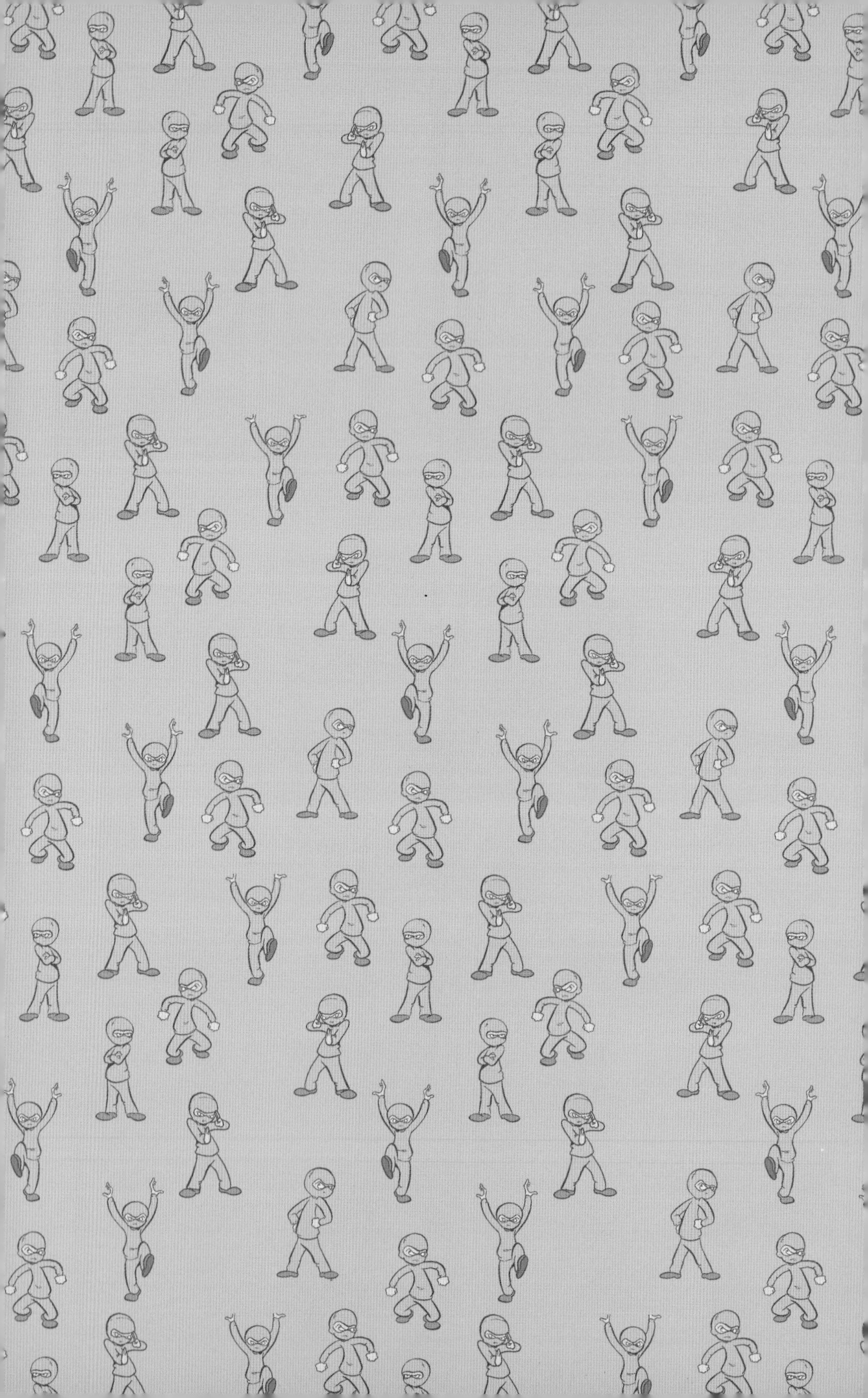

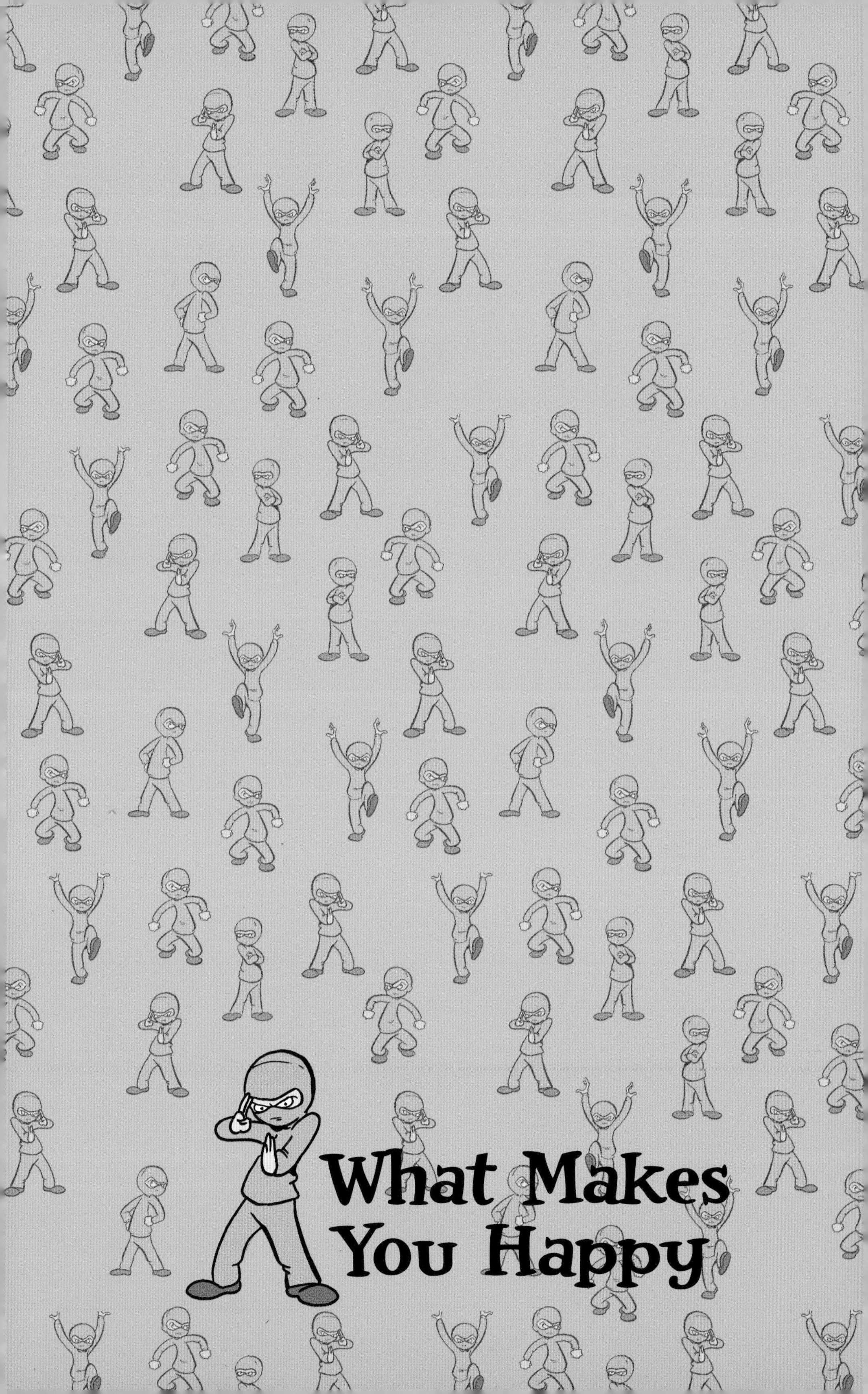

What Makes You Happy

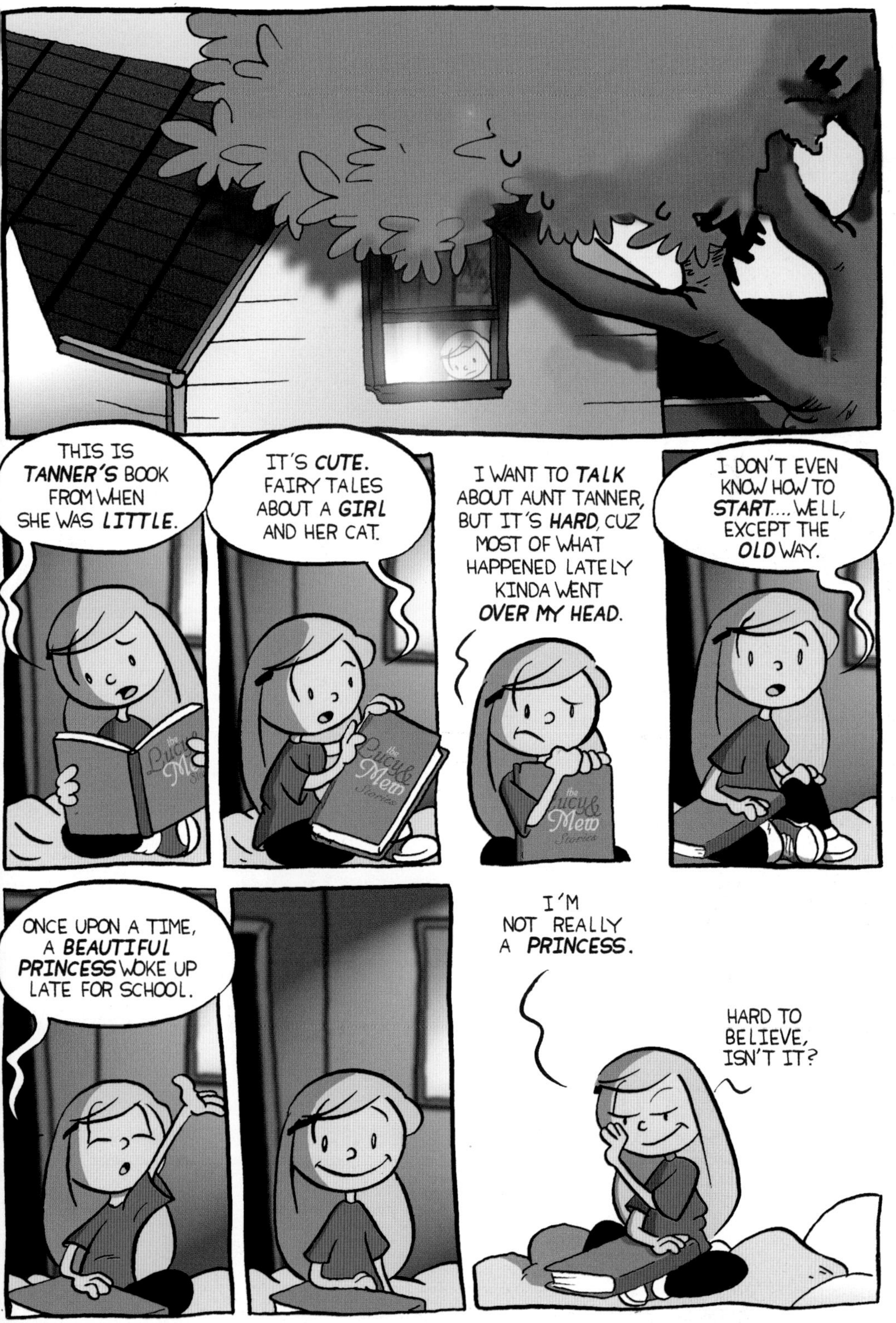
THIS IS TANNER'S BOOK FROM WHEN SHE WAS LITTLE.
IT'S CUTE. FAIRY TALES ABOUT A GIRL AND HER CAT.
the Lucy & Mew Stories
I WANT TO TALK ABOUT AUNT TANNER, BUT IT'S HARD, CUZ MOST OF WHAT HAPPENED LATELY KINDA WENT OVER MY HEAD.
I DON'T EVEN KNOW HOW TO START.... WELL, EXCEPT THE OLD WAY.
ONCE UPON A TIME, A BEAUTIFUL PRINCESS WOKE UP LATE FOR SCHOOL.
I'M NOT REALLY A PRINCESS.
HARD TO BELIEVE, ISN'T IT?

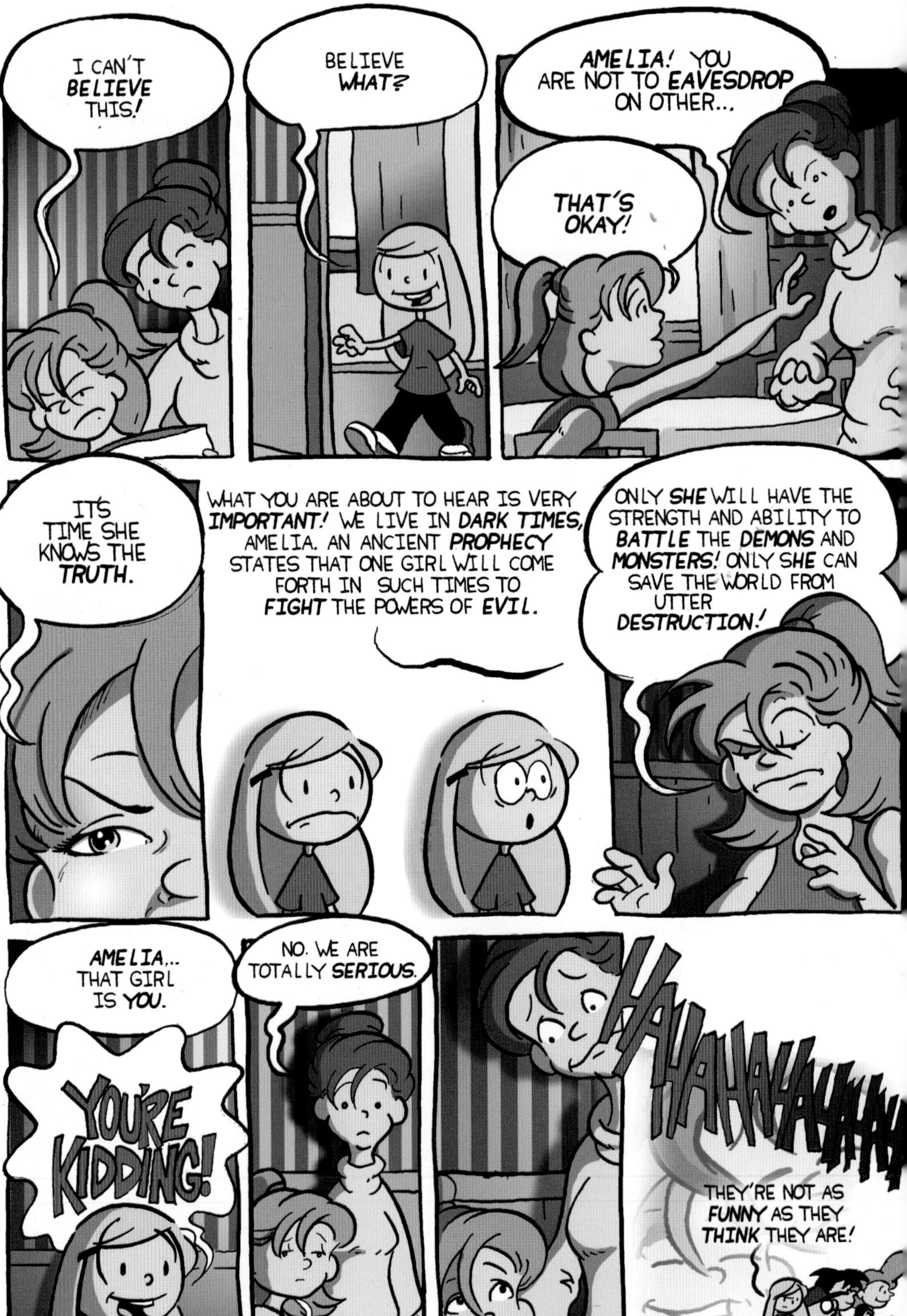
I CAN'T BELIEVE THIS!
BELIEVE WHAT?
AMELIA! YOU ARE NOT TO EAVESDROP ON OTHER...
THAT'S OKAY!
IT'S TIME SHE KNOWS THE TRUTH.
WHAT YOU ARE ABOUT TO HEAR IS VERY IMPORTANT! WE LIVE IN DARK TIMES, AMELIA. AN ANCIENT PROPHECY STATES THAT ONE GIRL WILL COME FORTH IN SUCH TIMES TO FIGHT THE POWERS OF EVIL.
ONLY SHE WILL HAVE THE STRENGTH AND ABILITY TO BATTLE THE DEMONS AND MONSTERS! ONLY SHE CAN SAVE THE WORLD FROM UTTER DESTRUCTION!
AMELIA... THAT GIRL IS YOU.
YOU'RE KIDDING!
NO. WE ARE TOTALLY SERIOUS.
YOUR TRAINING STARTS TODAY.
THEY'RE NOT AS FUNNY AS THEY THINK THEY ARE!

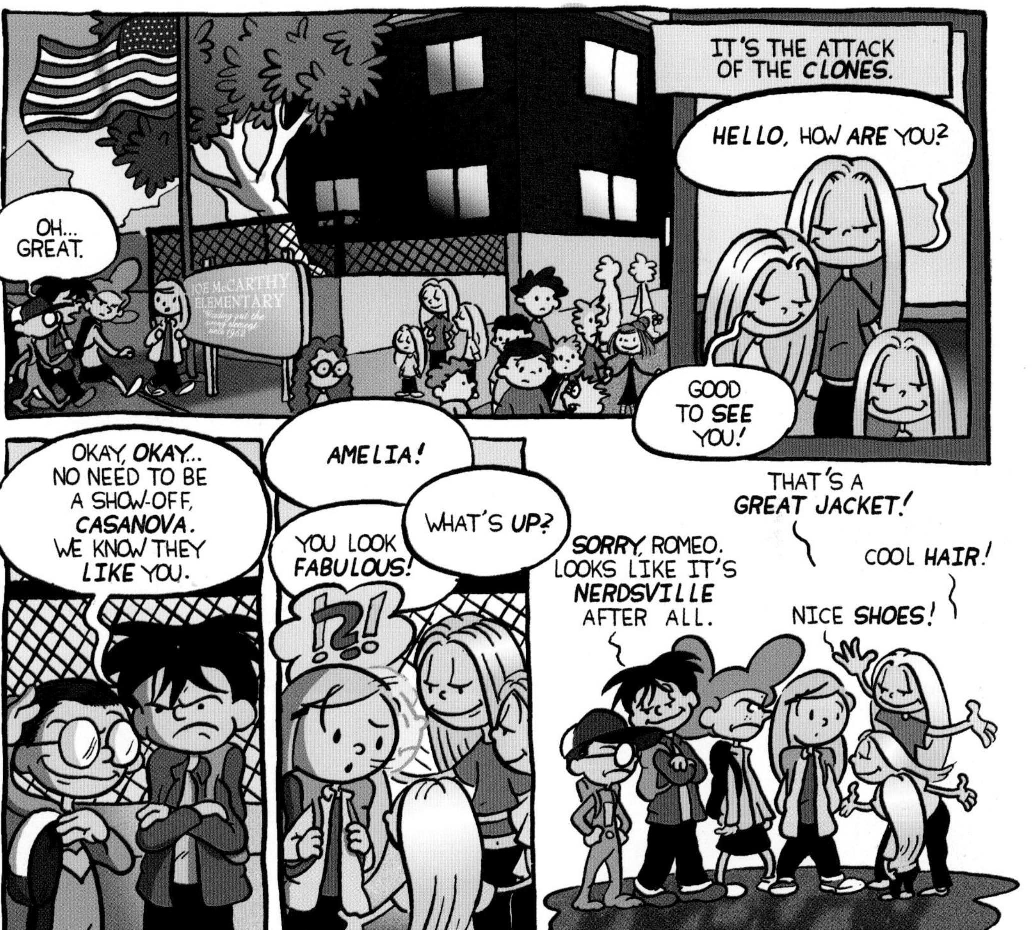

OH... GREAT.
JOE McCARTHY ELEMENTARY
IT'S THE ATTACK OF THE CLONES.
HELLO, HOW ARE YOU?
GOOD TO SEE YOU!
OKAY, OKAY... NO NEED TO BE A SHOW-OFF, CASANOVA. WE KNOW THEY LIKE YOU.
AMELIA!
YOU LOOK FABULOUS!
WHAT'S UP?
?!
SORRY, ROMEO. LOOKS LIKE IT'S NERDSVILLE AFTER ALL.
THAT'S A GREAT JACKET!
COOL HAIR!
NICE SHOES!
WELL...WE SHOULD BE GOING!
WE DON'T WANT TO BOTHER YOU.
YOU AND YOUR FRIENDS MUST BE BUSY.
BUT WE'LL TALK REAL SOON.
HAVE A GREAT DAY!
AND TELL YOUR AUNT WE SAID HI.
UH... SURE!

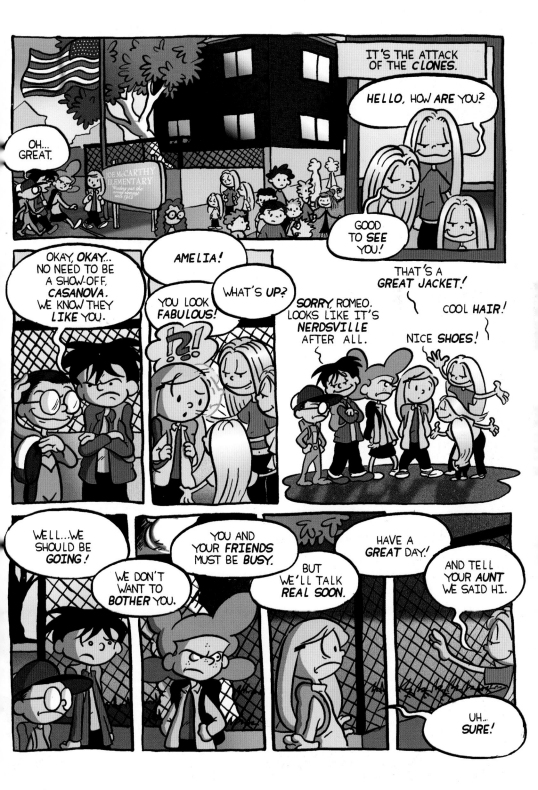

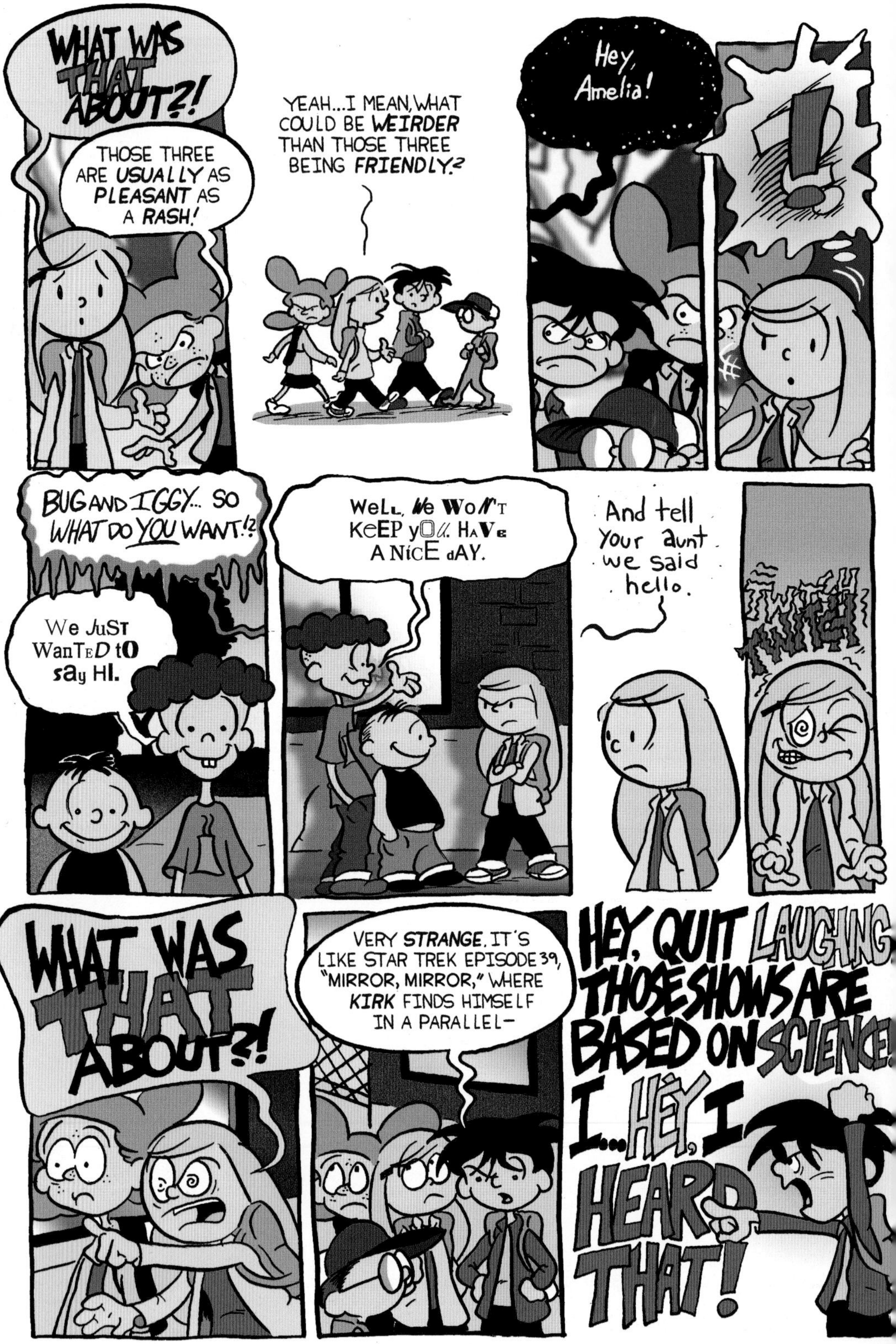
WHAT WAS THAT ABOUT?!
THOSE THREE ARE USUALLY AS PLEASANT AS A RASH!
YEAH...I MEAN, WHAT COULD BE WEIRDER THAN THOSE THREE BEING FRIENDLY?
Hey, Amelia!
!
BUG AND IGGY... SO WHAT DO YOU WANT!?
We JuST WanTeD tO say HI.
WeLL, We WoN'T KeEP yOU. HaVe A NicE dAY.
And tell your aunt we said hello.
TWITCH TWITCH
WHAT WAS THAT ABOUT?!
VERY STRANGE. IT'S LIKE STAR TREK EPISODE 39, "MIRROR, MIRROR," WHERE KIRK FINDS HIMSELF IN A PARALLEL—
HEY, QUIT LAUGHING THOSE SHOWS ARE BASED ON SCIENCE! I...HEY, I HEARD THAT!

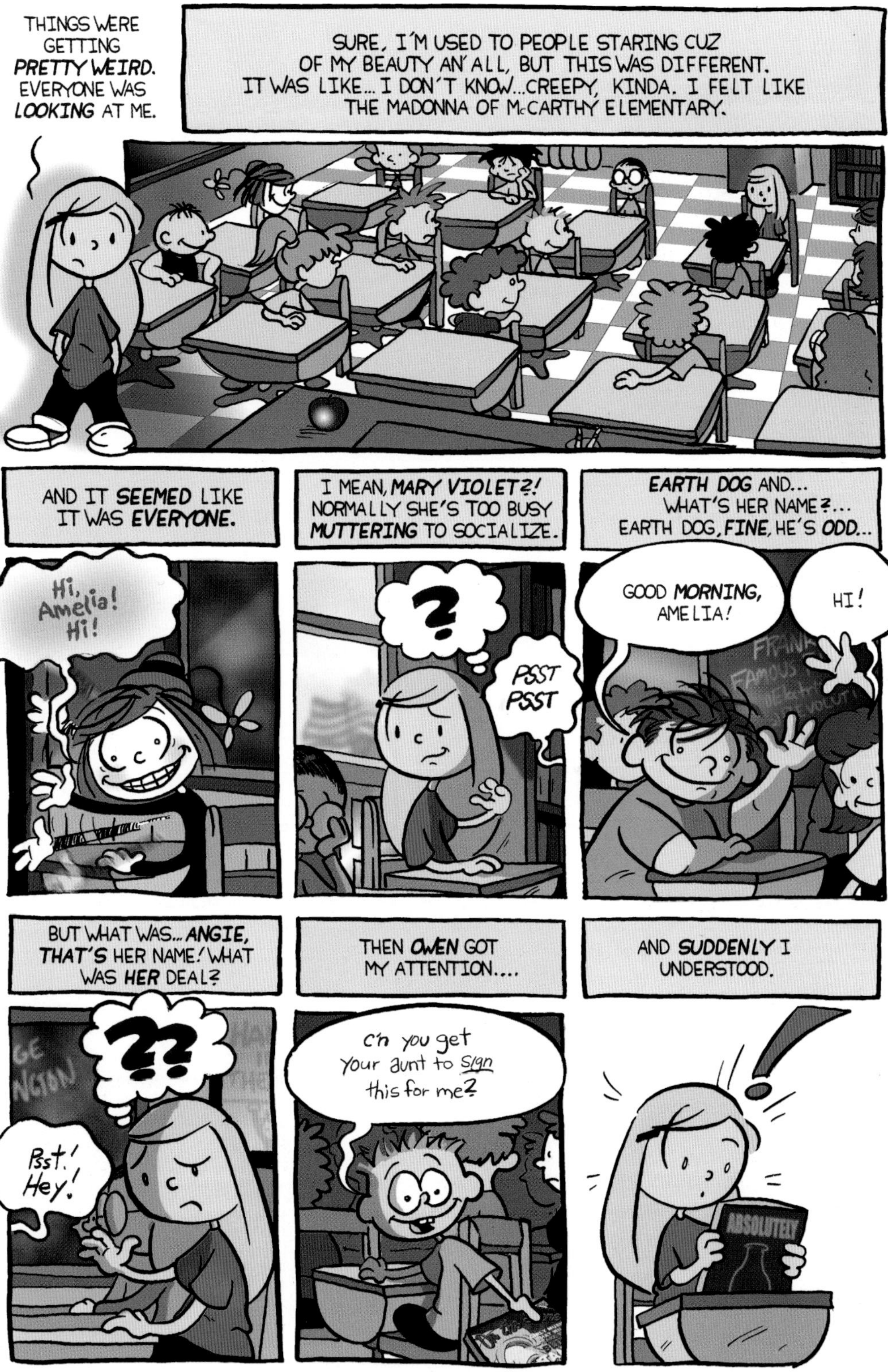
THINGS WERE GETTING PRETTY WEIRD. EVERYONE WAS LOOKING AT ME.
SURE, I'M USED TO PEOPLE STARING CUZ OF MY BEAUTY AN' ALL, BUT THIS WAS DIFFERENT. IT WAS LIKE... I DON'T KNOW...CREEPY, KINDA. I FELT LIKE THE MADONNA OF McCARTHY ELEMENTARY.
AND IT SEEMED LIKE IT WAS EVERYONE.
Hi, Amelia! Hi!
I MEAN, MARY VIOLET?! NORMALLY SHE'S TOO BUSY MUTTERING TO SOCIALIZE.
?
PSST PSST
EARTH DOG AND... WHAT'S HER NAME?... EARTH DOG, FINE, HE'S ODD...
GOOD MORNING, AMELIA!
HI!
BUT WHAT WAS... ANGIE, THAT'S HER NAME! WHAT WAS HER DEAL?
??
Psst! Hey!
THEN OWEN GOT MY ATTENTION....
C'n you get your aunt to sign this for me?
AND SUDDENLY I UNDERSTOOD.
!
ABSOLUTELY

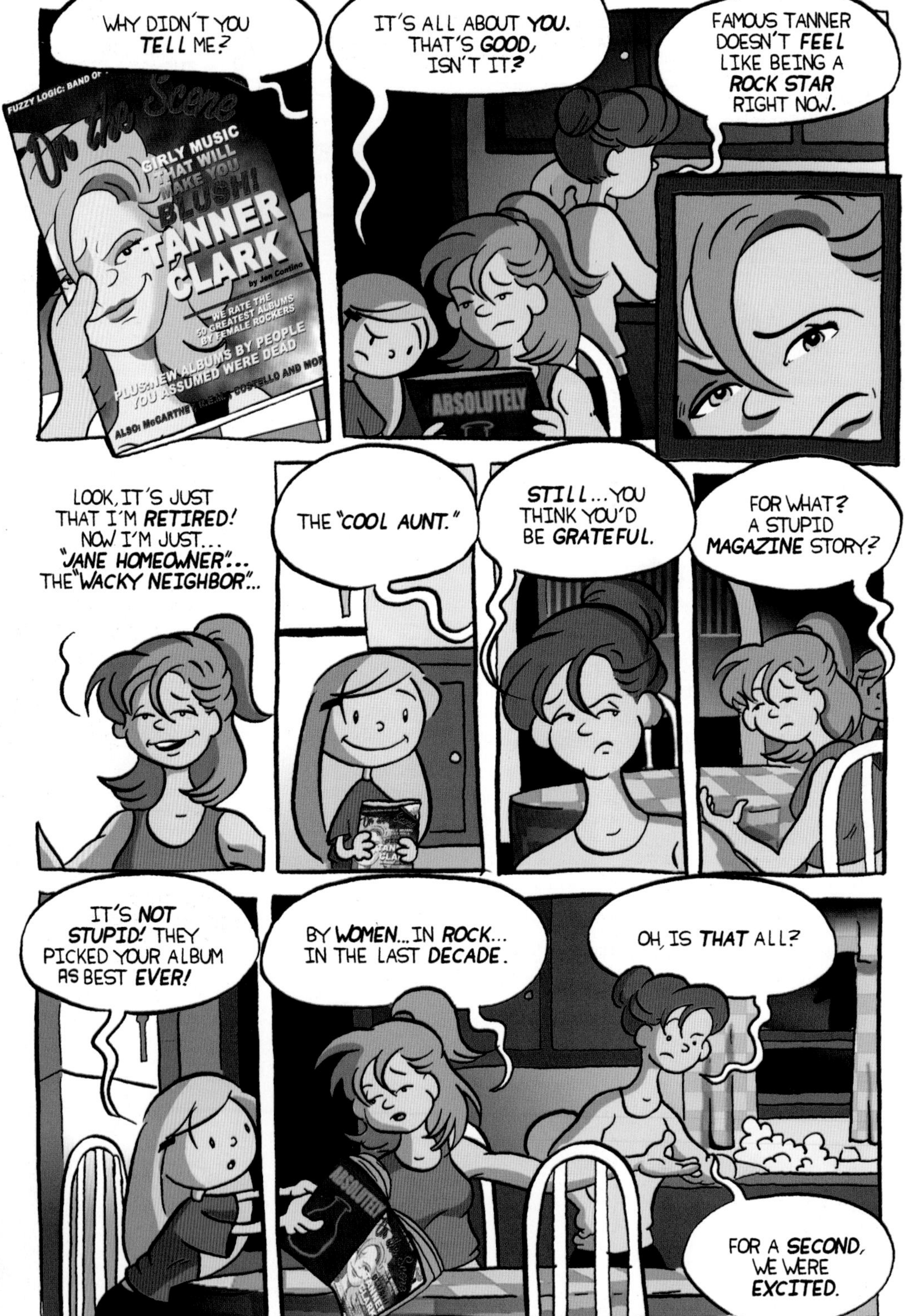
WHY DIDN'T YOU **TELL** ME?
FUZZY LOGIC: BAND OF
On the Scene
GIRLY MUSIC THAT WILL MAKE YOU BLUSH!
TANNER CLARK
by Jen Contino
WE RATE THE 50 GREATEST ALBUMS BY FEMALE ROCKERS
PLUS: NEW ALBUMS BY PEOPLE YOU ASSUMED WERE DEAD
IT'S ALL ABOUT **YOU**. THAT'S **GOOD**, ISN'T IT?
ABSOLUTELY
FAMOUS TANNER DOESN'T **FEEL** LIKE BEING A **ROCK STAR** RIGHT NOW.
LOOK, IT'S JUST THAT I'M **RETIRED**! NOW I'M JUST... **"JANE HOMEOWNER"**... THE **"WACKY NEIGHBOR"**...
THE **"COOL AUNT."**
STILL... YOU THINK YOU'D BE **GRATEFUL**.
FOR WHAT? A STUPID **MAGAZINE** STORY?
IT'S **NOT STUPID**! THEY PICKED YOUR ALBUM AS BEST **EVER**!
BY **WOMEN**... IN **ROCK**... IN THE LAST **DECADE**.
OH, IS **THAT** ALL?
FOR A **SECOND**, WE WERE **EXCITED**.

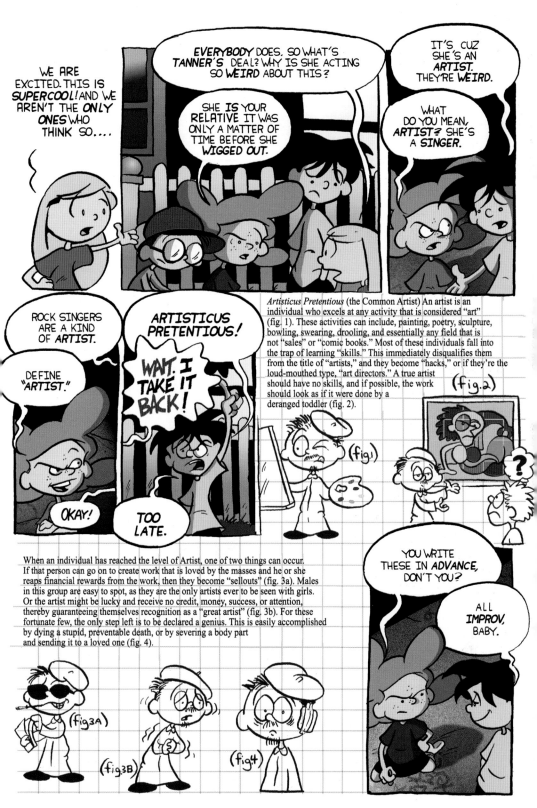

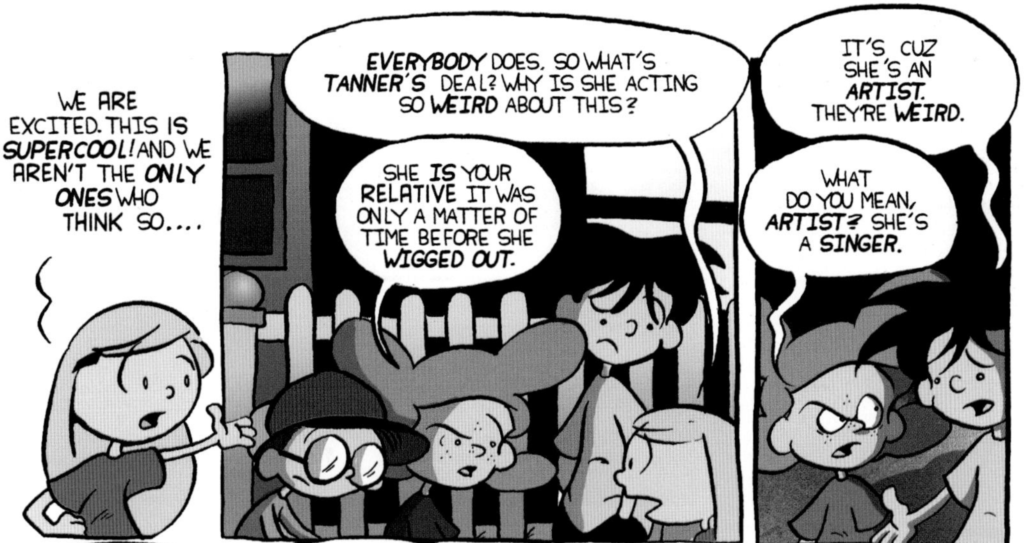
WE ARE EXCITED. THIS IS SUPERCOOL! AND WE AREN'T THE ONLY ONES WHO THINK SO....
EVERYBODY DOES, SO WHAT'S TANNER'S DEAL? WHY IS SHE ACTING SO WEIRD ABOUT THIS?
SHE IS YOUR RELATIVE IT WAS ONLY A MATTER OF TIME BEFORE SHE WIGGED OUT.
IT'S CUZ SHE'S AN ARTIST. THEY'RE WEIRD.
WHAT DO YOU MEAN, ARTIST? SHE'S A SINGER.

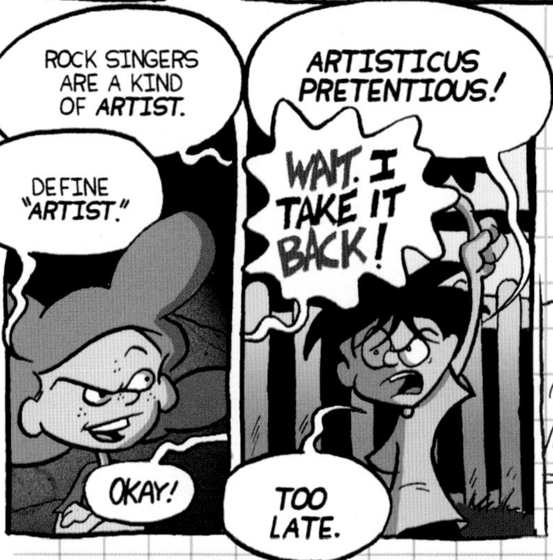
ROCK SINGERS ARE A KIND OF ARTIST.
DEFINE "ARTIST."
OKAY!
ARTISTICUS PRETENTIOUS!
WAIT. I TAKE IT BACK!
TOO LATE.

Artisticus Pretentious (the Common Artist) An artist is an individual who excels at any activity that is considered "art" (fig. 1). These activities can include, painting, poetry, sculpture, bowling, swearing, drooling, and essentially any field that is not "sales" or "comic books." Most of these individuals fall into the trap of learning "skills." This immediately disqualifies them from the title of "artists," and they become "hacks," or if they're the loud-mouthed type, "art directors." A true artist should have no skills, and if possible, the work should look as if it were done by a deranged toddler (fig. 2).

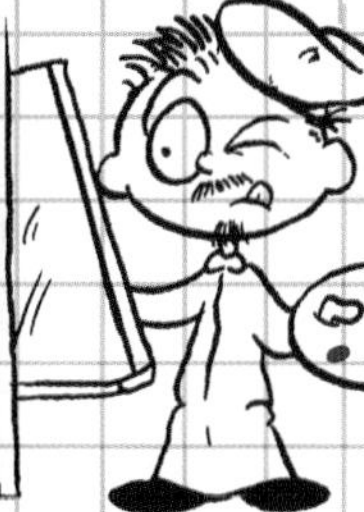
(fig.1)

(fig.2)
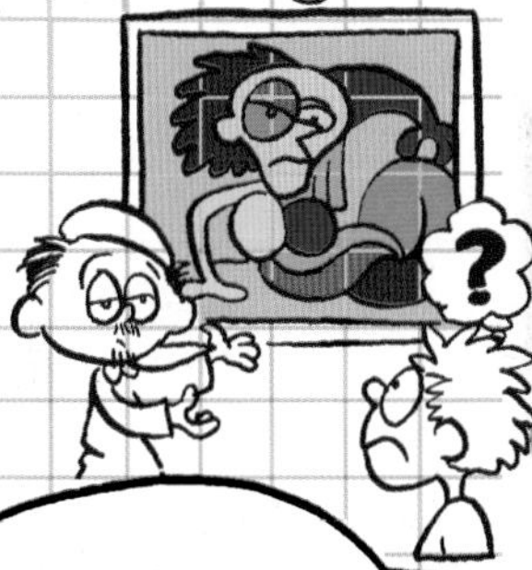
?

When an individual has reached the level of Artist, one of two things can occur. If that person can go on to create work that is loved by the masses and he or she reaps financial rewards from the work, then they become "sellouts" (fig. 3a). Males in this group are easy to spot, as they are the only artists ever to be seen with girls. Or the artist might be lucky and receive no credit, money, success, or attention, thereby guaranteeing themselves recognition as a "great artist" (fig. 3b). For these fortunate few, the only step left is to be declared a genius. This is easily accomplished by dying a stupid, preventable death, or by severing a body part and sending it to a loved one (fig. 4).

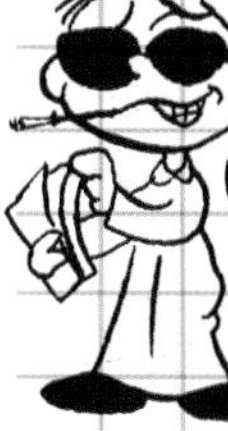
(fig3A)

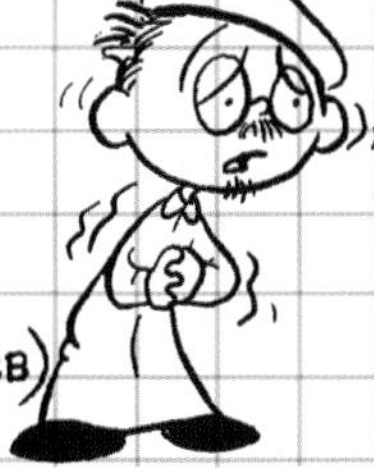
(fig3B)

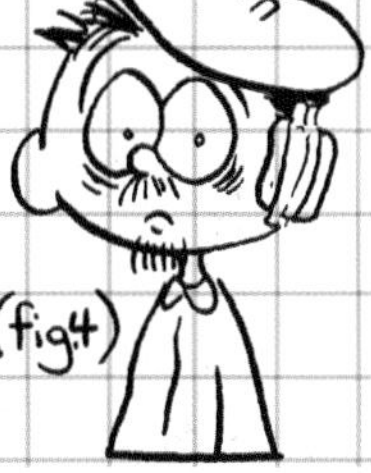
(fig4)

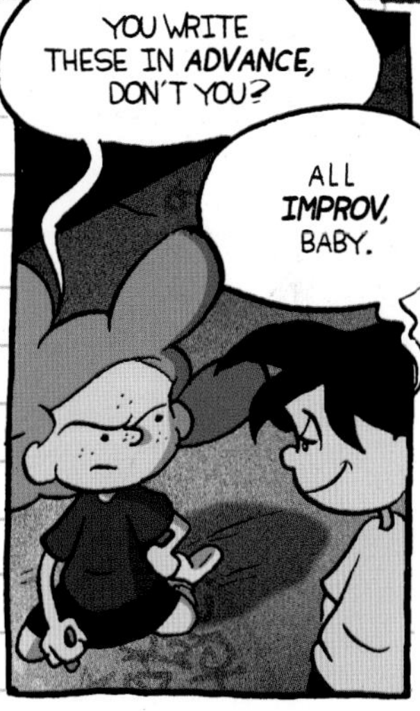
YOU WRITE THESE IN ADVANCE, DON'T YOU?
ALL IMPROV, BABY.

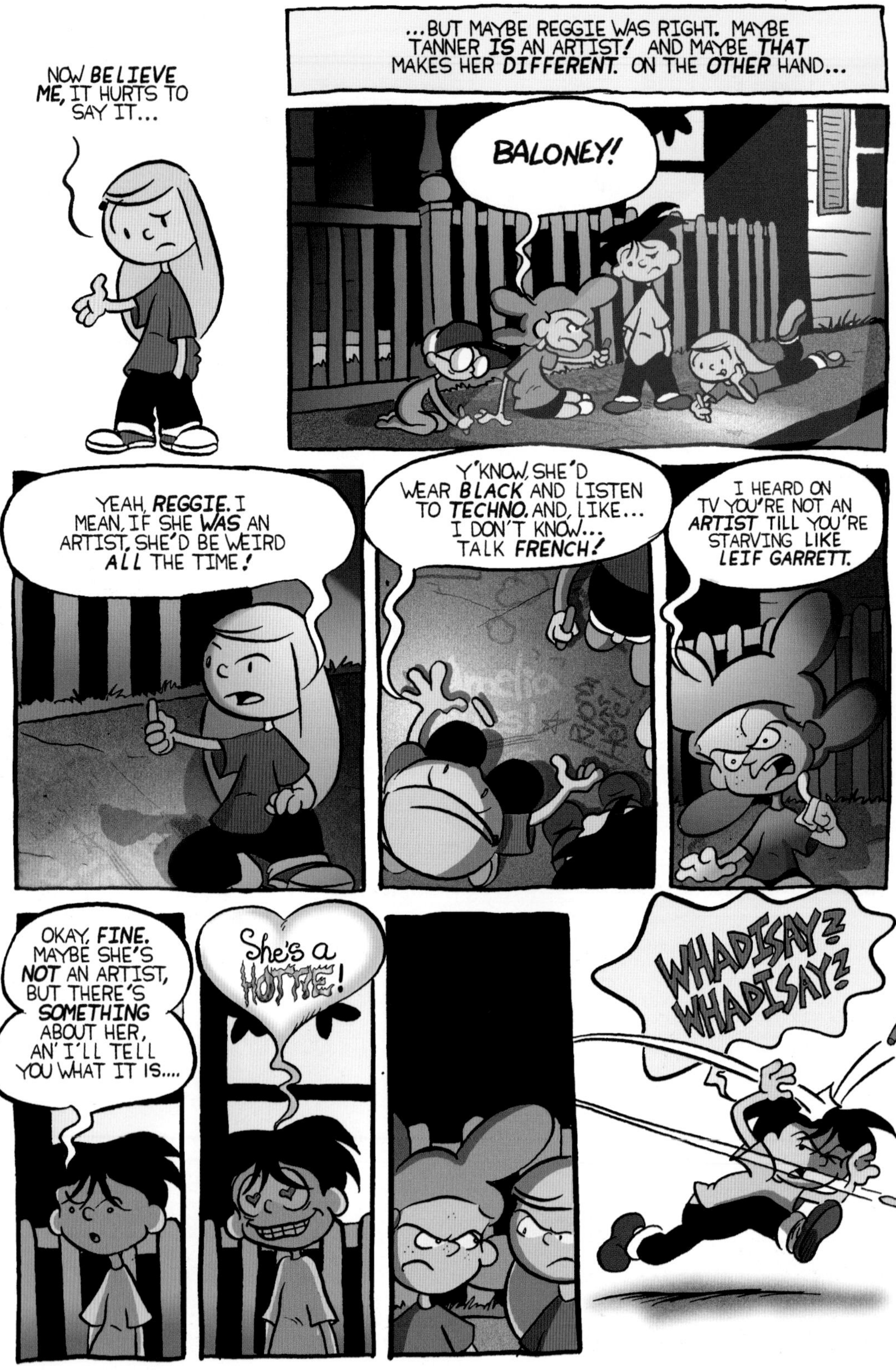
NOW BELIEVE ME, IT HURTS TO SAY IT...
...BUT MAYBE REGGIE WAS RIGHT. MAYBE TANNER IS AN ARTIST! AND MAYBE THAT MAKES HER DIFFERENT. ON THE OTHER HAND...
BALONEY!
YEAH, REGGIE. I MEAN, IF SHE WAS AN ARTIST, SHE'D BE WEIRD ALL THE TIME!
Y'KNOW, SHE'D WEAR BLACK AND LISTEN TO TECHNO. AND, LIKE... I DON'T KNOW... TALK FRENCH!
I HEARD ON TV YOU'RE NOT AN ARTIST TILL YOU'RE STARVING LIKE LEIF GARRETT.
OKAY, FINE. MAYBE SHE'S NOT AN ARTIST, BUT THERE'S SOMETHING ABOUT HER, AN' I'LL TELL YOU WHAT IT IS....
She's a HOTTIE!
WHADISAY? WHADISAY?

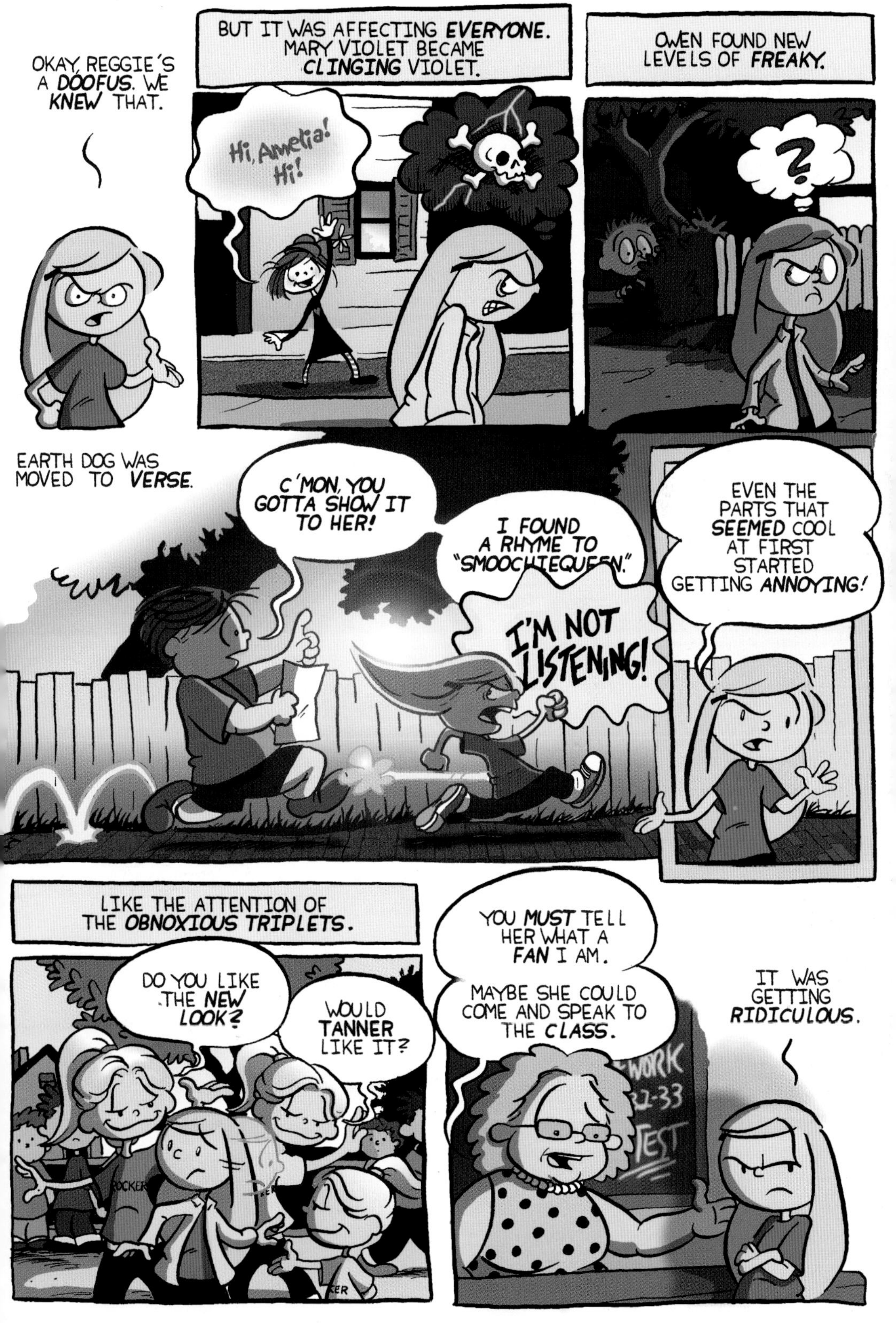
OKAY, REGGIE'S A DOOFUS. WE KNEW THAT.
BUT IT WAS AFFECTING EVERYONE. MARY VIOLET BECAME CLINGING VIOLET.
Hi, Amelia! Hi!
OWEN FOUND NEW LEVELS OF FREAKY.
?
EARTH DOG WAS MOVED TO VERSE.
C'MON, YOU GOTTA SHOW IT TO HER!
I FOUND A RHYME TO "SMOOCHIEQUEEN."
I'M NOT LISTENING!
EVEN THE PARTS THAT SEEMED COOL AT FIRST STARTED GETTING ANNOYING!
LIKE THE ATTENTION OF THE OBNOXIOUS TRIPLETS.
DO YOU LIKE THE NEW LOOK?
WOULD TANNER LIKE IT?
YOU MUST TELL HER WHAT A FAN I AM.
MAYBE SHE COULD COME AND SPEAK TO THE CLASS.
IT WAS GETTING RIDICULOUS.

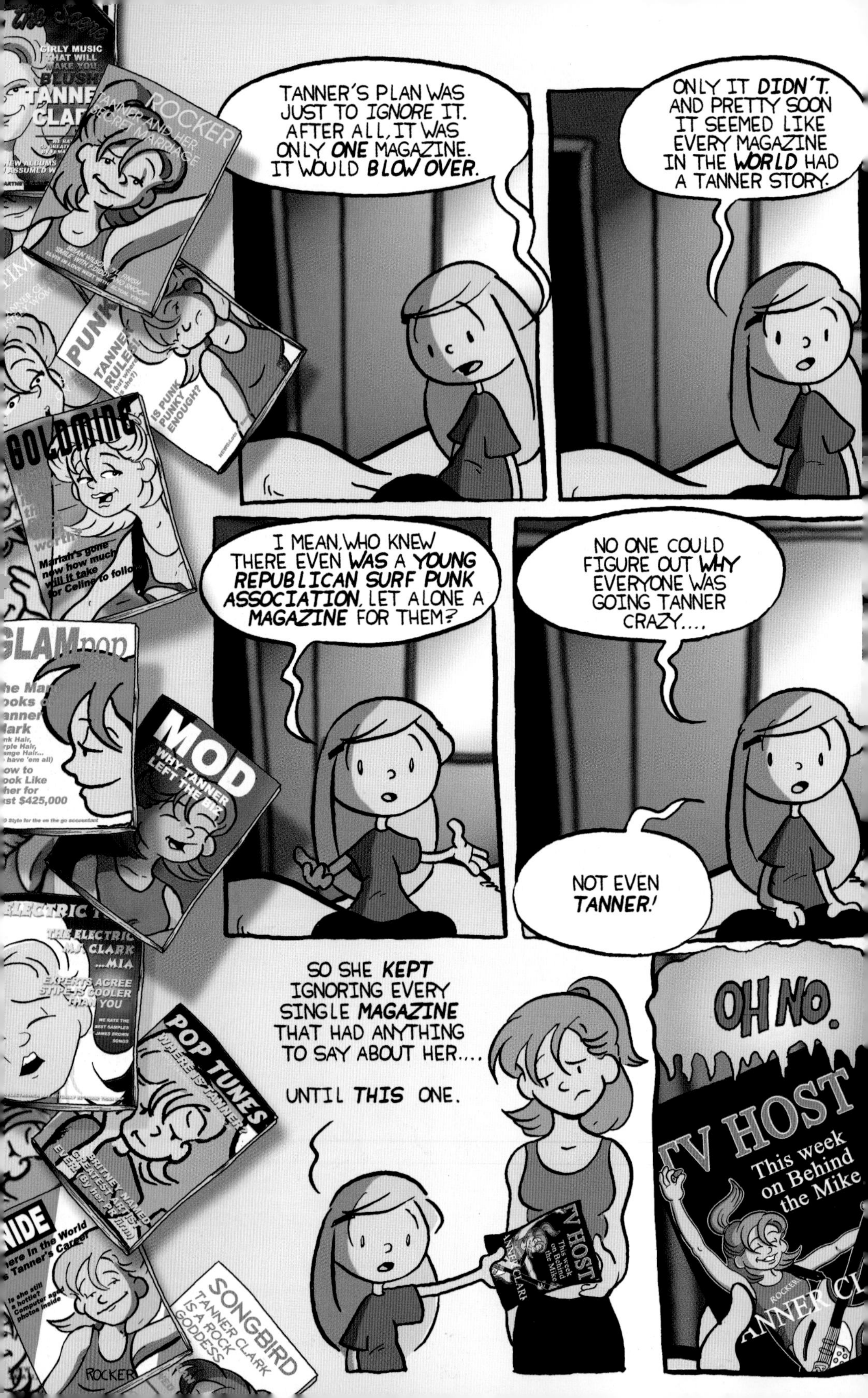

TANNER'S PLAN WAS JUST TO IGNORE IT. AFTER ALL, IT WAS ONLY ONE MAGAZINE. IT WOULD BLOW OVER.
ONLY IT DIDN'T. AND PRETTY SOON IT SEEMED LIKE EVERY MAGAZINE IN THE WORLD HAD A TANNER STORY.
I MEAN, WHO KNEW THERE EVEN WAS A YOUNG REPUBLICAN SURF PUNK ASSOCIATION, LET ALONE A MAGAZINE FOR THEM?
NO ONE COULD FIGURE OUT WHY EVERYONE WAS GOING TANNER CRAZY....
NOT EVEN TANNER!
SO SHE KEPT IGNORING EVERY SINGLE MAGAZINE THAT HAD ANYTHING TO SAY ABOUT HER....
UNTIL THIS ONE.
OH NO.
TV HOST
This week on Behind the Mike
ROCKER
TANNER AND HER SECRET MARRIAGE
GIRLY MUSIC THAT WILL MAKE YOU BLUSH
IS PUNK PUNKY ENOUGH?
GOLDMINE
MOD
WHY TANNER LEFT THE BIZ
GLAMpop
EXPERTS AGREE STIPE IS COOLER THAN YOU
POP TUNES
WHERE IS TANNER?
SONGBIRD
TANNER CLARK IS A ROCK GODDESS

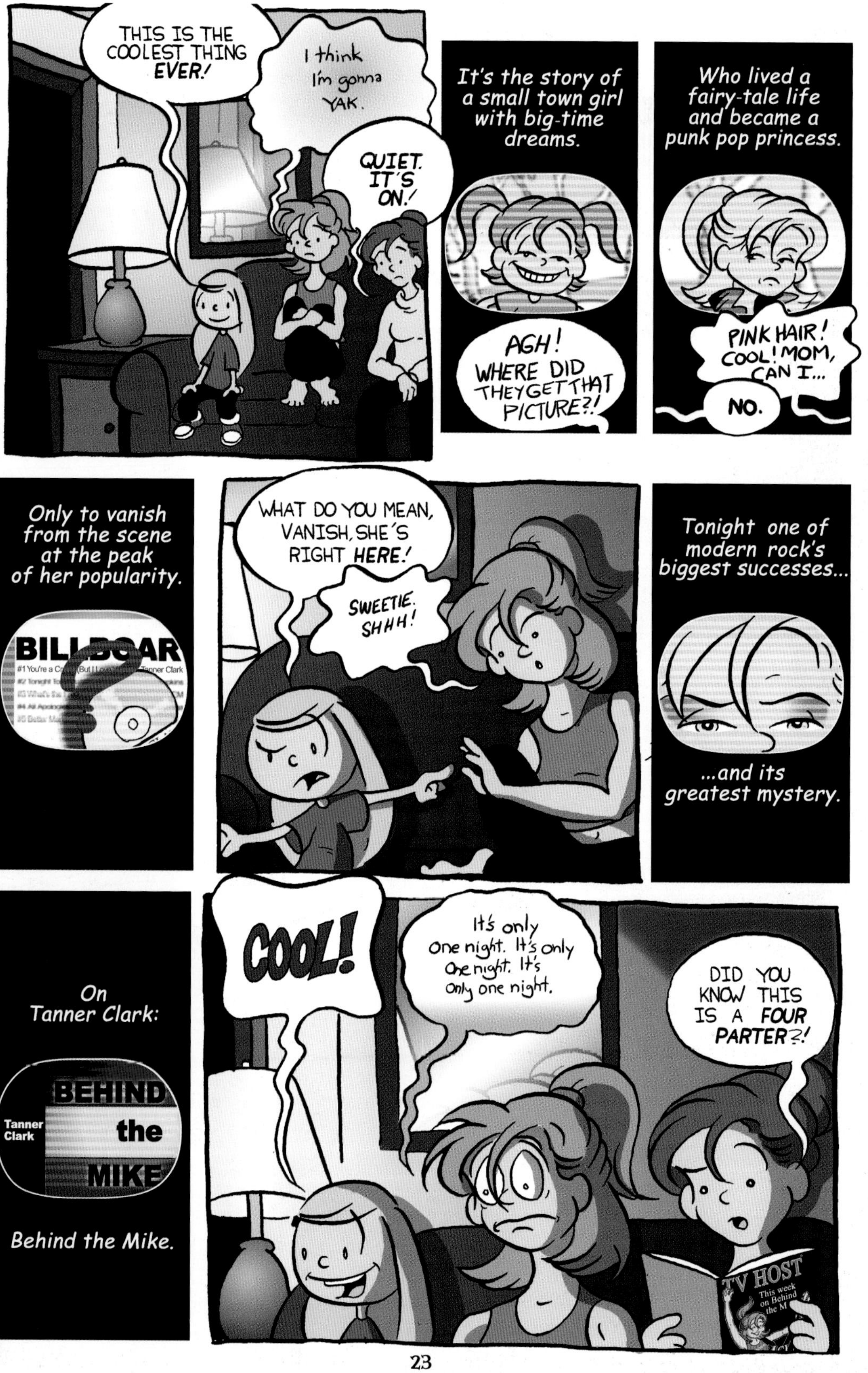
THIS IS THE COOLEST THING EVER!
I think I'm gonna YAK.
QUIET. IT'S ON!
It's the story of a small town girl with big-time dreams.
AGH! WHERE DID THEY GET THAT PICTURE?!
Who lived a fairy-tale life and became a punk pop princess.
PINK HAIR! COOL! MOM, CAN I...
NO.
Only to vanish from the scene at the peak of her popularity.
BILLBOAR
#1 You're a C (But I Love) Tanner Clark
WHAT DO YOU MEAN, VANISH, SHE'S RIGHT HERE!
SWEETIE. SHHH!
Tonight one of modern rock's biggest successes...
...and its greatest mystery.
On Tanner Clark:
BEHIND the MIKE
Tanner Clark
Behind the Mike.
COOL!
It's only one night. It's only one night. It's only one night.
DID YOU KNOW THIS IS A FOUR PARTER?!
TV HOST
This week on Behind the M

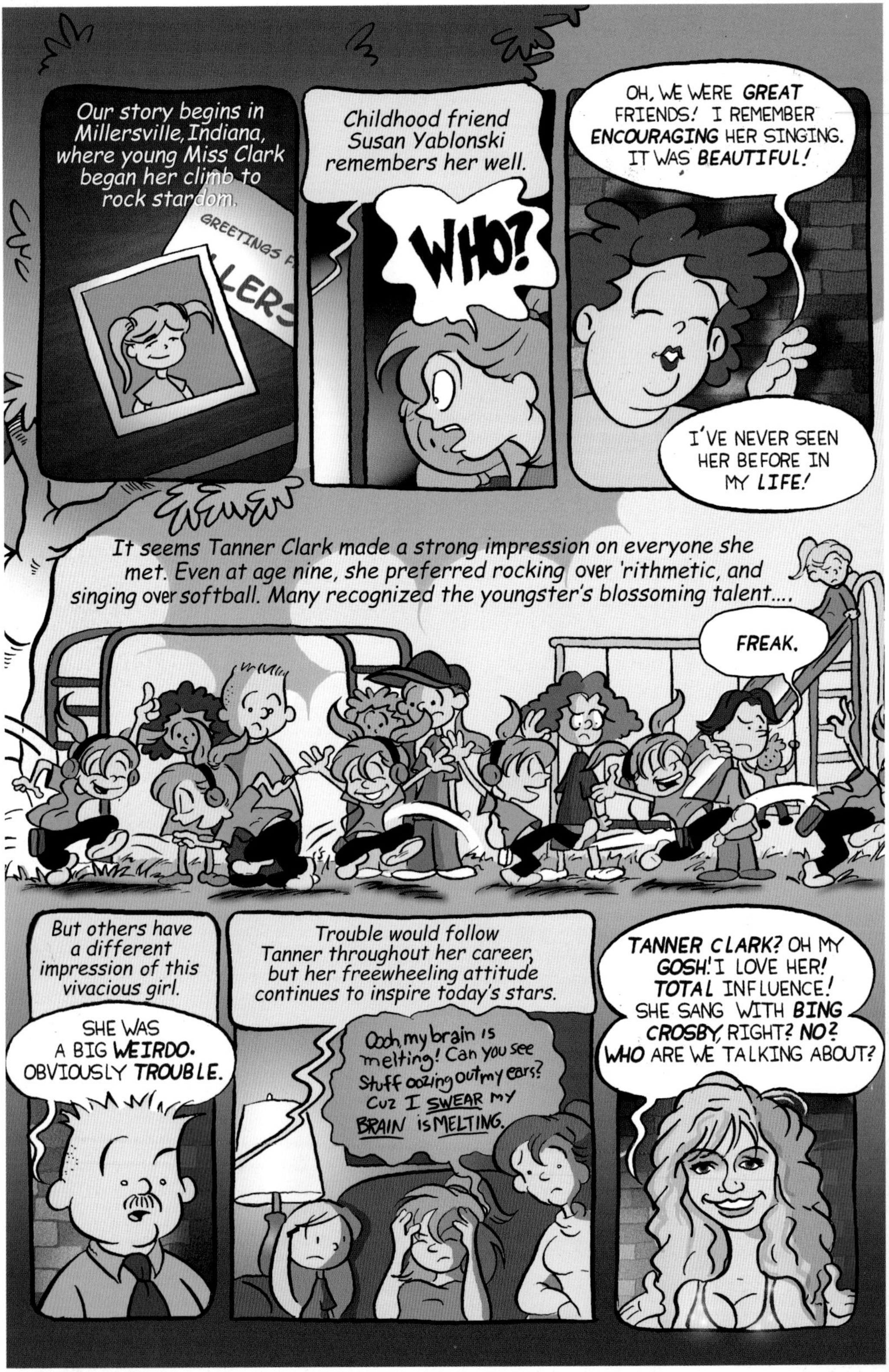
Our story begins in Millersville, Indiana, where young Miss Clark began her climb to rock stardom.
GREETINGS F
LLERS
Childhood friend Susan Yablonski remembers her well.
WHO?
OH, WE WERE GREAT FRIENDS! I REMEMBER ENCOURAGING HER SINGING. IT WAS BEAUTIFUL!
I'VE NEVER SEEN HER BEFORE IN MY LIFE!
It seems Tanner Clark made a strong impression on everyone she met. Even at age nine, she preferred rocking over 'rithmetic, and singing over softball. Many recognized the youngster's blossoming talent....
FREAK.
But others have a different impression of this vivacious girl.
SHE WAS A BIG WEIRDO. OBVIOUSLY TROUBLE.
Trouble would follow Tanner throughout her career, but her freewheeling attitude continues to inspire today's stars.
Oooh, my brain is melting! Can you see stuff oozing out my ears? Cuz I SWEAR my BRAIN is MELTING.
TANNER CLARK? OH MY GOSH! I LOVE HER! TOTAL INFLUENCE! SHE SANG WITH BING CROSBY, RIGHT? NO? WHO ARE WE TALKING ABOUT?

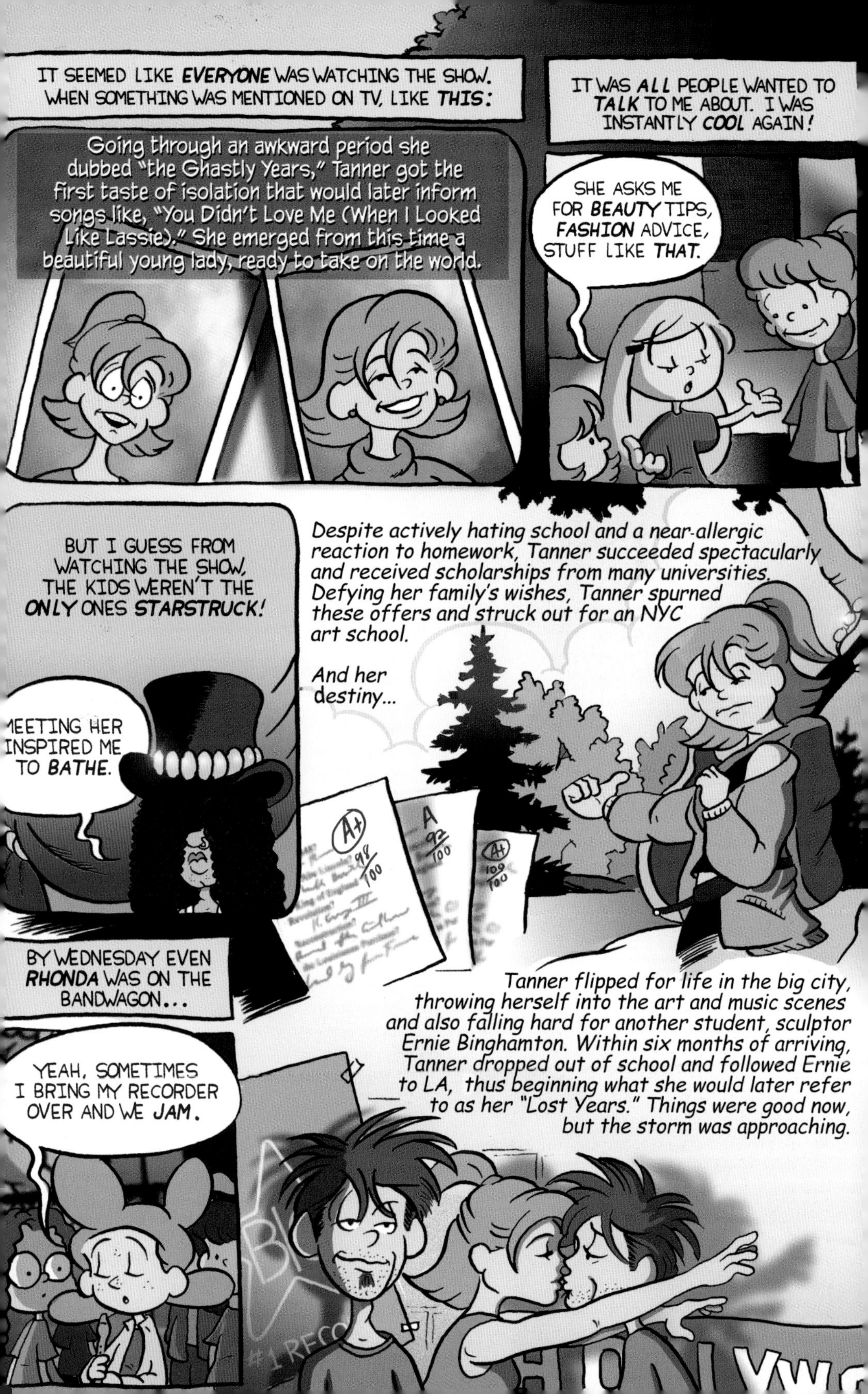
IT SEEMED LIKE EVERYONE WAS WATCHING THE SHOW. WHEN SOMETHING WAS MENTIONED ON TV, LIKE THIS:
Going through an awkward period she dubbed "the Ghastly Years," Tanner got the first taste of isolation that would later inform songs like, "You Didn't Love Me (When I Looked Like Lassie)." She emerged from this time a beautiful young lady, ready to take on the world.
IT WAS ALL PEOPLE WANTED TO TALK TO ME ABOUT. I WAS INSTANTLY COOL AGAIN!
SHE ASKS ME FOR BEAUTY TIPS, FASHION ADVICE, STUFF LIKE THAT.
BUT I GUESS FROM WATCHING THE SHOW, THE KIDS WEREN'T THE ONLY ONES STARSTRUCK!
MEETING HER INSPIRED ME TO BATHE.
Despite actively hating school and a near-allergic reaction to homework, Tanner succeeded spectacularly and received scholarships from many universities. Defying her family's wishes, Tanner spurned these offers and struck out for an NYC art school.
And her destiny...
A+
98/100
A
92/100
A+
109/100
BY WEDNESDAY EVEN RHONDA WAS ON THE BANDWAGON...
YEAH, SOMETIMES I BRING MY RECORDER OVER AND WE JAM.
Tanner flipped for life in the big city, throwing herself into the art and music scenes and also falling hard for another student, sculptor Ernie Binghamton. Within six months of arriving, Tanner dropped out of school and followed Ernie to LA, thus beginning what she would later refer to as her "Lost Years." Things were good now, but the storm was approaching.

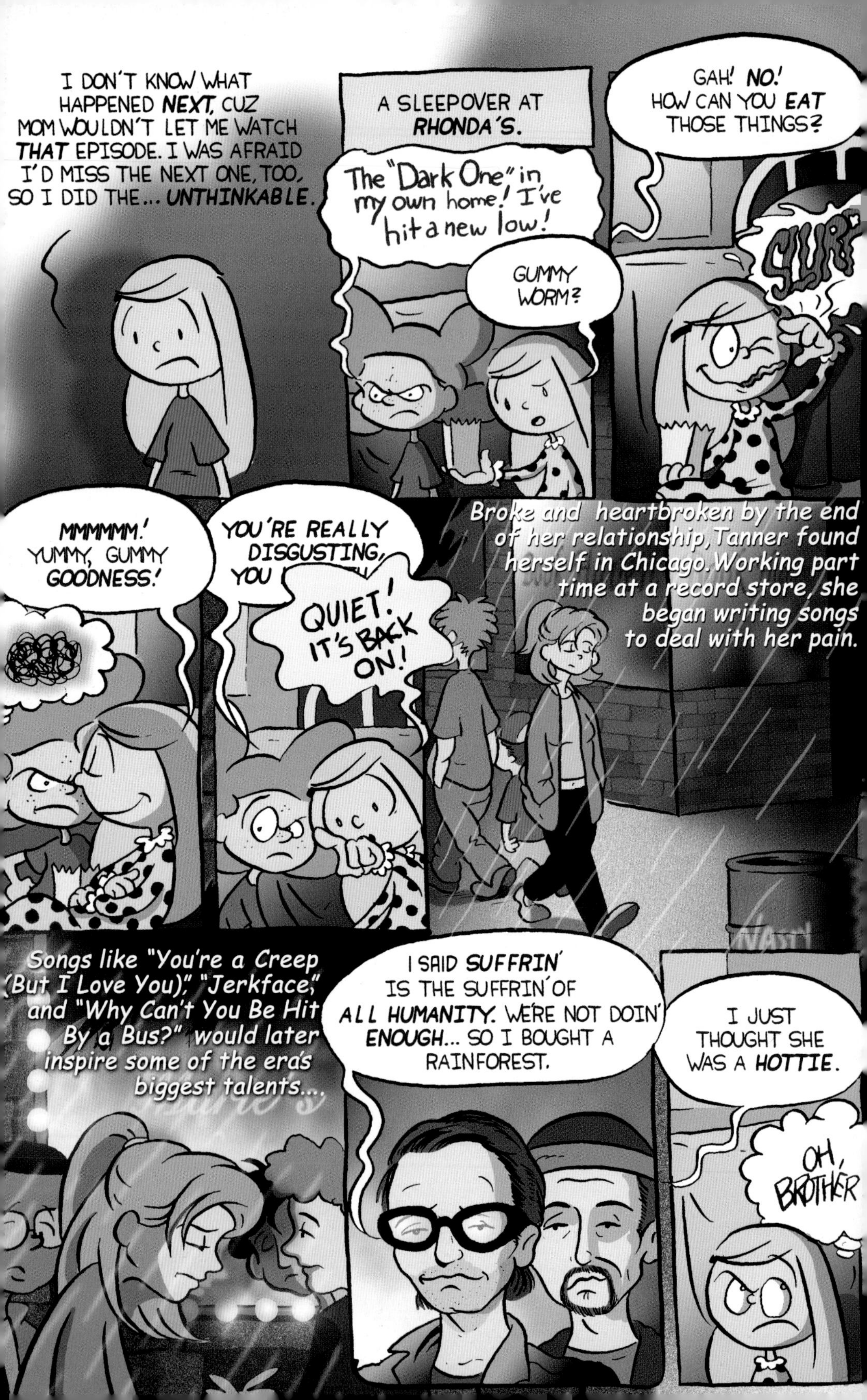

I DON'T KNOW WHAT HAPPENED **NEXT**, CUZ MOM WOULDN'T LET ME WATCH **THAT** EPISODE. I WAS AFRAID I'D MISS THE NEXT ONE, TOO, SO I DID THE... **UNTHINKABLE**.
A SLEEPOVER AT **RHONDA'S.**
The "Dark One" in my own home! I've hit a new low!
GUMMY WORM?
GAH! **NO!** HOW CAN YOU **EAT** THOSE THINGS?
MMMMMM! YUMMY, GUMMY **GOODNESS!**
YOU'RE REALLY DISGUSTING, YOU
QUIET! IT'S BACK ON!
Broke and heartbroken by the end of her relationship, Tanner found herself in Chicago. Working part time at a record store, she began writing songs to deal with her pain.
Songs like "You're a Creep (But I Love You)," "Jerkface," and "Why Can't You Be Hit By a Bus?" would later inspire some of the era's biggest talents...
I SAID **SUFFRIN'** IS THE SUFFRIN' OF **ALL HUMANITY.** WE'RE NOT DOIN' **ENOUGH**... SO I BOUGHT A RAINFOREST.
I JUST THOUGHT SHE WAS A **HOTTIE**.
OH, BROTHER

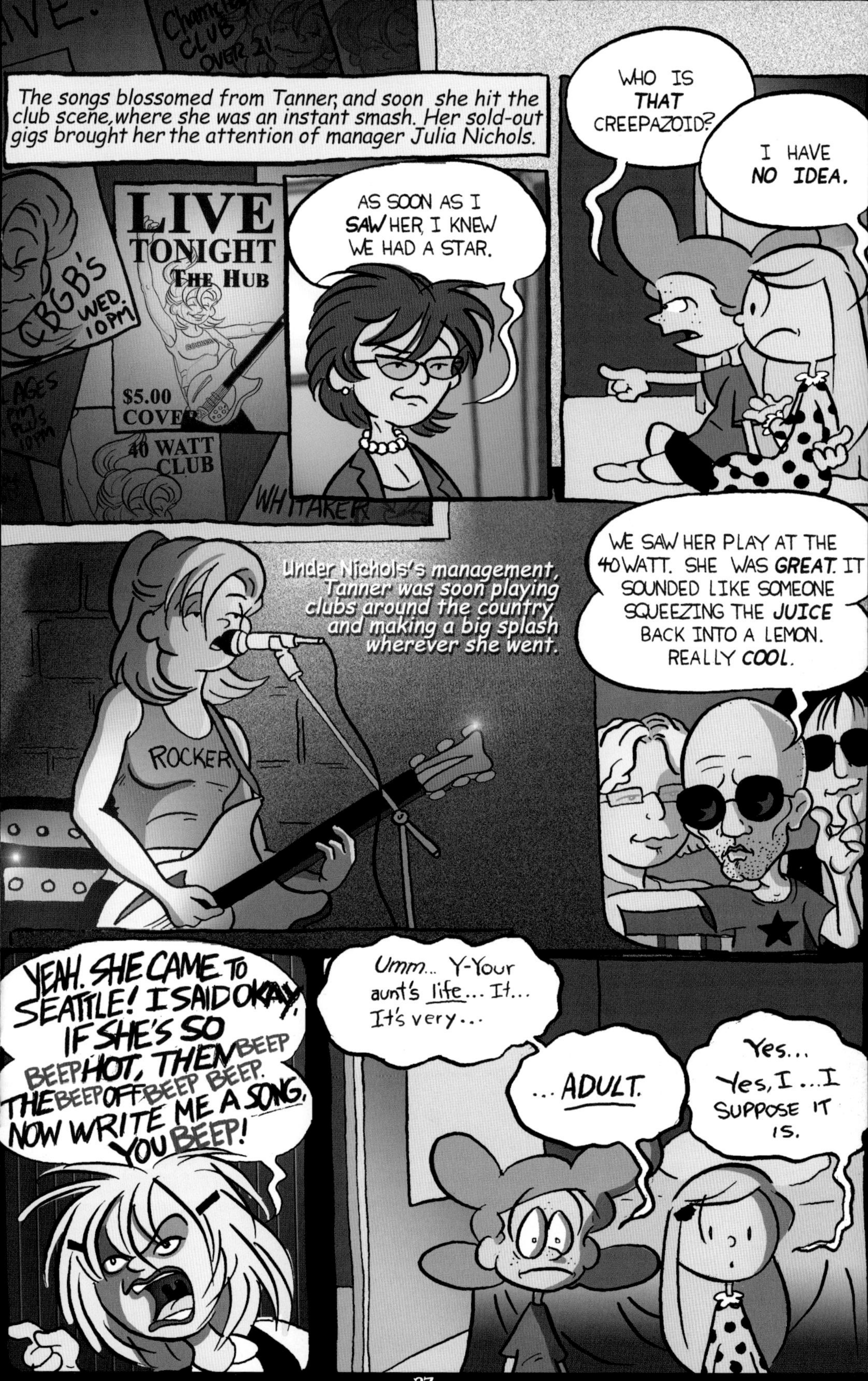

The songs blossomed from Tanner, and soon she hit the club scene, where she was an instant smash. Her sold-out gigs brought her the attention of manager Julia Nichols.
LIVE TONIGHT THE HUB
$5.00 COVER
CBGB's WED. 10PM
40 WATT CLUB
WHITAKER
AS SOON AS I SAW HER, I KNEW WE HAD A STAR.
WHO IS THAT CREEPAZOID?
I HAVE NO IDEA.
Under Nichols's management, Tanner was soon playing clubs around the country and making a big splash wherever she went.
ROCKER
WE SAW HER PLAY AT THE 40 WATT. SHE WAS GREAT. IT SOUNDED LIKE SOMEONE SQUEEZING THE JUICE BACK INTO A LEMON. REALLY COOL.
YEAH. SHE CAME TO SEATTLE! I SAID OKAY, IF SHE'S SO BEEP HOT, THEN BEEP THE BEEP OFF BEEP BEEP. NOW WRITE ME A SONG, YOU BEEP!
Umm... Y-Your aunt's life... It... It's very...
...ADULT.
Yes... Yes, I...I suppose it is.

I GUESS MOM FIGURED THE LAST EPISODE WOULD BE *TAME*, SO SHE LET ME WATCH IT AT *HOME*. NOT THAT ANY OF US GOT TO *SEE* MUCH, ANYWAY.

Nichols was a master of promotion, and Tanner's debut single Gabardine Prom Queen *was already in the top 20 when her album* Broken Record *hit the shelves. It looked like the beginning of a long pop reign, but then, just days after the release of* Broken Record*, Tanner Clark cancelled her tour, stopped further recording, and vanished from the music scene entirely.*

BROKEN RECORD

The Pick

ALT-COUNTRY WI... VICTORIA WILLIAMS

ALT-SIT COM... JERRY SEINFELD

IT WAS A REAL *SHOCK*. I DIDN'T SEE IT COMING. NO ONE KNOWS *WHY* SHE DID WHAT SHE DID, BUT I *HOPE* TO *WORK* WITH HER AGAIN.

YOU DO TOO KNOW WHY, YOU... YOU... YOU... *NERDYBUTTBRAINFACE!*

>SIGH< YA KNOW, I COULD USE BETTER *WORDS* IF *YOU* WEREN'T HERE.

SORRY.

Even though her time in the spotlight was brief, her influence was strong, and her peers remember her fondly.

THE LAST TIME I SAW HER, SHE SAID, "IN YOUR NEXT VIDEO YOU SHOULD BE *NAKED*." I REALIZE *NOW* SHE WAS *KIDDING*.

Oh, of COURSE I was kidding, you DUMB... OOOOOH!

-CLICK

I WENT UP TO BED AND LAY THERE FOR A WHILE, LISTENING TO TANNER USE WORDS LESS *CREATIVE* THAN "*NERDYBUTTBRAINFACE*."

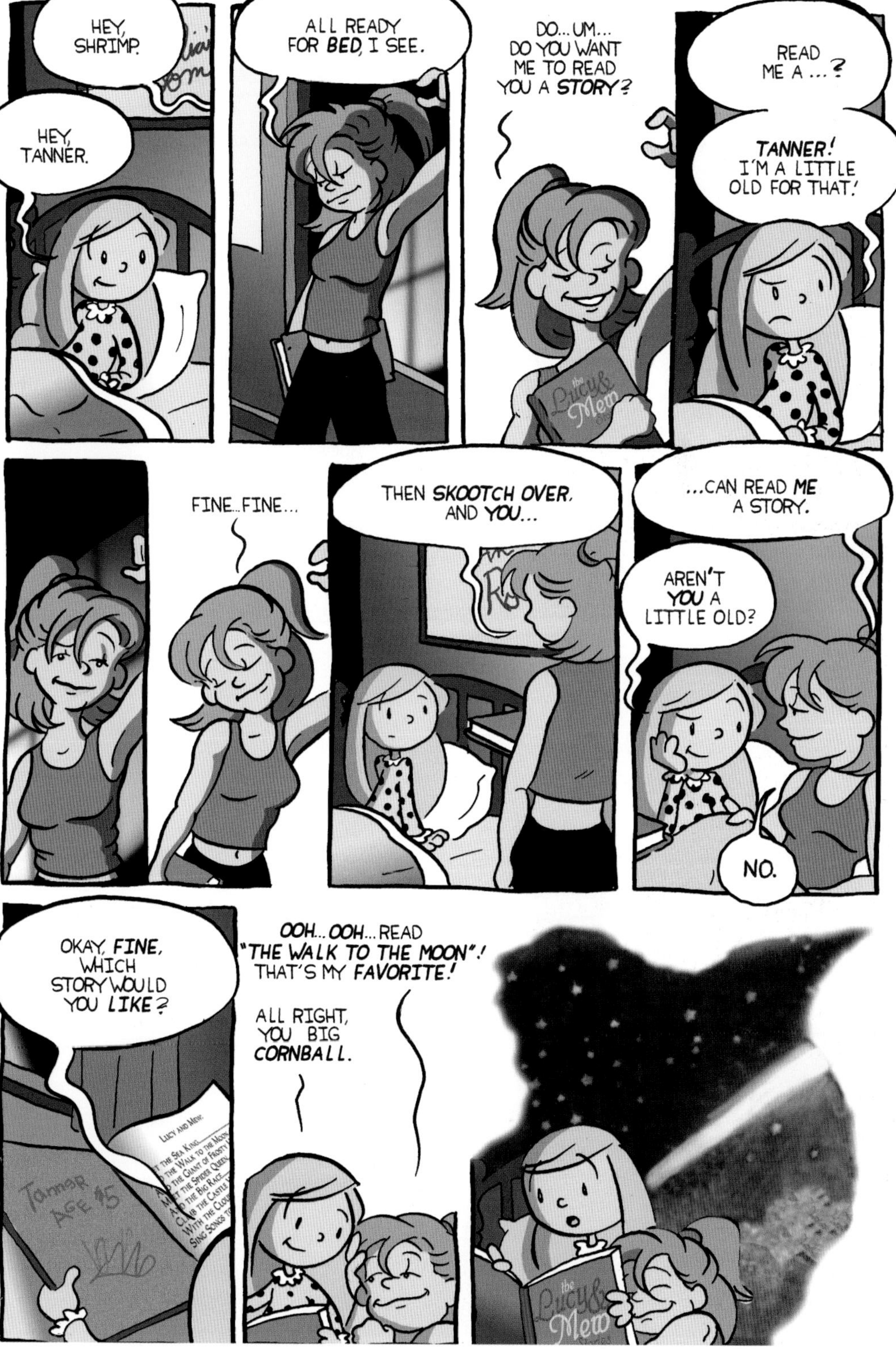
HEY, SHRIMP.
HEY, TANNER.
ALL READY FOR BED, I SEE.
DO... UM... DO YOU WANT ME TO READ YOU A STORY?
READ ME A ...?
TANNER! I'M A LITTLE OLD FOR THAT!
FINE...FINE...
THEN SKOOTCH OVER, AND YOU...
...CAN READ ME A STORY.
AREN'T YOU A LITTLE OLD?
NO.
OKAY, FINE, WHICH STORY WOULD YOU LIKE?
OOH...OOH...READ "THE WALK TO THE MOON"! THAT'S MY FAVORITE!
ALL RIGHT, YOU BIG CORNBALL.

The Walk to the Moon

by Beth Ellen Welch

Once upon a time there was a poor young girl named Lucy who lived with a cat named Mew. Lucy and Mew lived in a very small house in a very small village in an enormous country that probably never existed, but which seemed quite nice. Lucy had no parents, and so she relied on Mew to care for her. This was not a problem, for Mew was a talented cat and earned more than many of the men in the village, and even as much as a few of the more prominent sheep. In exchange for her keep, Lucy kept the house tidy, the food and water dishes full, and the litter box clean. But Lucy was bored.

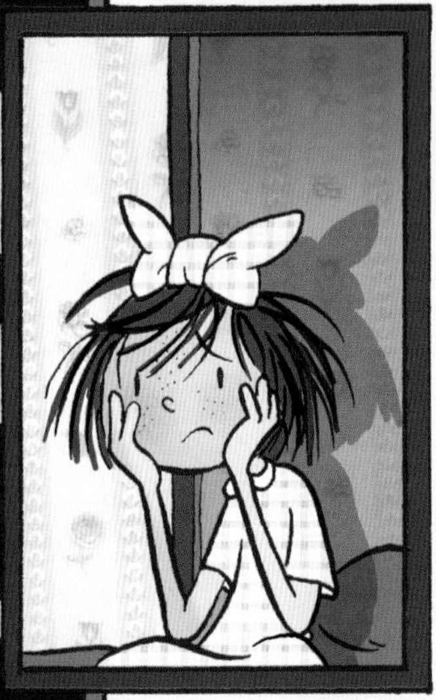

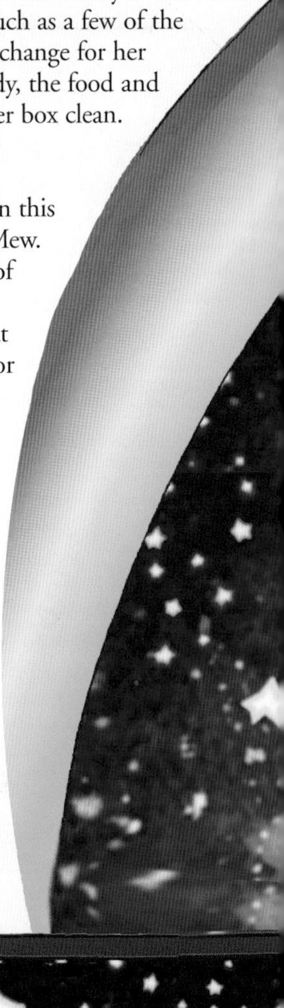

"There's nothing ever to do in this village," she complained to Mew. "I've heard other girls speak of villages with many dwellings under one roof, staircases that carry you magically from floor to floor, and merchants with goods from faraway lands; shops of all kinds selling fragrances, literature, garments, and equipment for sport, a common area where people may sample morsels and delicacies from all the world over. And outside yet another dining hall, set under glorious, illuminated golden arches."

"My business dealings have taken me to such villages," said Mew. "The people seem no happier there than they do any place else on Earth."

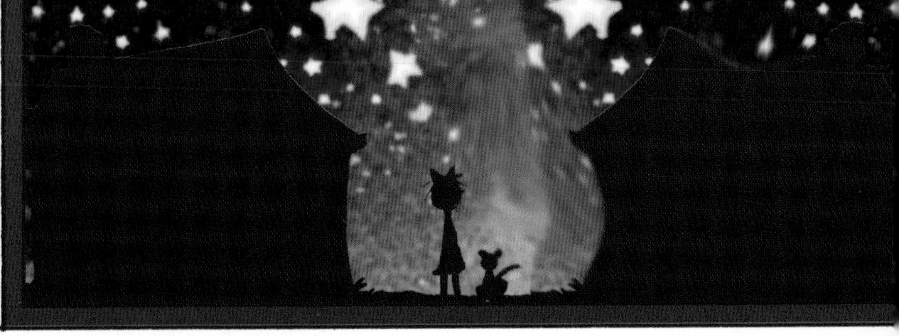

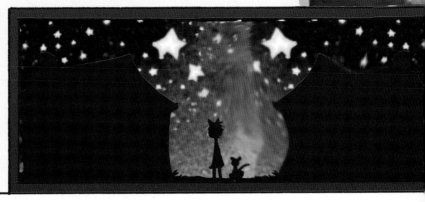

It was then that Lucy had a brilliant idea.

"But what about off the Earth?" she cried. "What about the village on the moon!" Mew had to admit that he had never heard of such villages, but still he was intrigued. "I imagine a cat with my skills in accounting could make as good a living on the moon as in this village," he said. And so Lucy and Mew decided to walk to the moon.

The plan was simple: Wait until the next rainbow appeared, walk to the top, then jump the remaining distance to the moon. "A brilliant plan," said Mew. "It's a wonder no one has thought of it before."

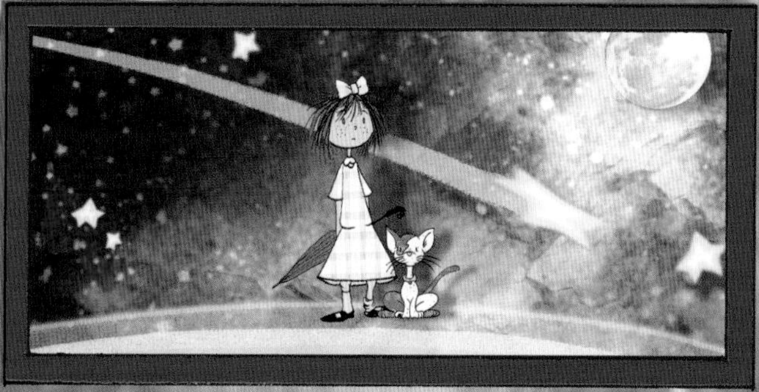

The two travelers took nothing with them save Lucy's umbrella and a large roll of cash. Everything they needed, they reasoned, they would get in the wondrous moon village.

The trip was longer than they expected, and Mew was very cross at Lucy for not having thought to bring even a small can of tuna. Lucy's legs got tired, but she sustained herself by thinking of the wonders the moon village were sure to contain.

Finally, the top of the rainbow was reached. The leap was taken, and Lucy and Mew landed on the moon. They were so happy to have arrived that they danced as only an orphan girl and her benefactor cat can dance.

Unfortunately, after celebrating, they realized

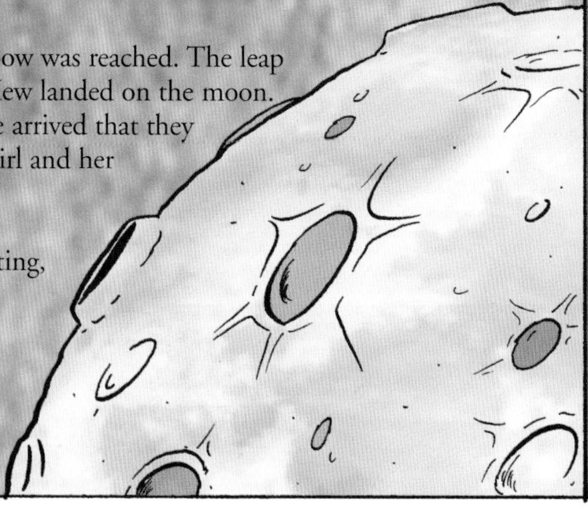

there was not a village in sight. "I'm sure they are here," said Lucy. "We just need to explore a bit."

But after hours and days and weeks of exploring, all Lucy and Mew had found were some flags, a sculpture, and a carriage (but no horse).

"This is terrible!" cried Lucy. "We're completely alone!"

"We're never alone if we have each other," said Mew.

"Oh, shut up," said Lucy.

With nothing to do but sit on the rim of a crater and stare at Earth, Lucy and Mew both became melancholy.

"I miss having a home to clean and dishes to fill, and, well . . . maybe not the litter box," said Lucy.

"I'm just glad that cheese thing turned out to be true," said Mew. "Otherwise we would have starved."

Lucy decided that enough was enough, and, grabbing Mew with one hand and her umbrella with the other, she leaped off the edge of the moon.

Lucy opened her umbrella and used it to slow their fall, so they drifted down to Earth in just a little less than four days.

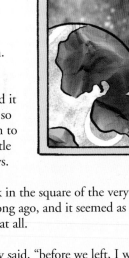

They landed back in the square of the very village they had left so long ago, and it seemed as if it had not changed at all.

"You know," Lucy said, "before we left, I wanted nothing more than to live the rest of my life on the moon, but now that we're back, I can't imagine why we ever left."

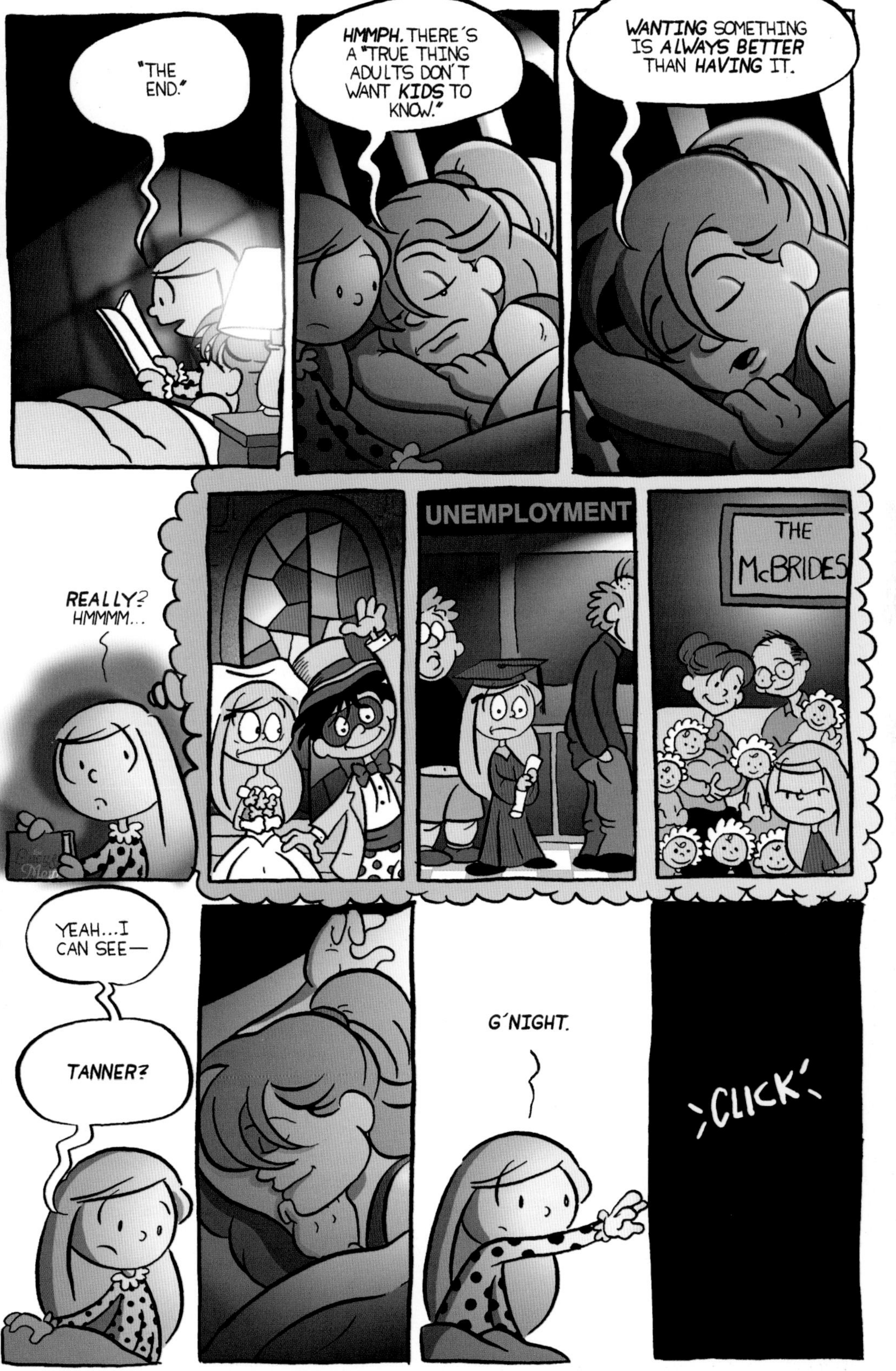

"THE END."
HMMPH. THERE´S A "TRUE THING ADULTS DON´T WANT KIDS TO KNOW."
WANTING SOMETHING IS ALWAYS BETTER THAN HAVING IT.
REALLY? HMMMM...
UNEMPLOYMENT
THE McBRIDES
YEAH...I CAN SEE—
TANNER?
G´NIGHT.
CLICK

I COULDN'T STOP THINKING ABOUT THE **SHOW** AND WHY TANNER QUIT SINGING. IT WASN'T LIKE HER TO BE A **QUITTER!** SO THE NEXT DAY AFTER SCHOOL, I DECIDED TO TRY TO WEASEL SOME INFO OUT OF **MOM**.

I WAS **SURPRISED**, CUZ MOM SEEMED KINDA **HAPPY** TO TALK ABOUT IT. SHE TOLD ME THAT WHEN TANNER WAS OUT IN CALIFORNIA AND **LATER** WHEN SHE WAS ON TOUR, THAT THEY DIDN'T REALLY **TALK MUCH**. I GUESS NO ONE THOUGHT TANNER SHOULD BE DOING WHAT SHE WAS DOING, CUZ SHE WAS SO SMART AND ALL.

(**PLUS** NO ONE **LIKED** THAT ERNIE CREEP.)

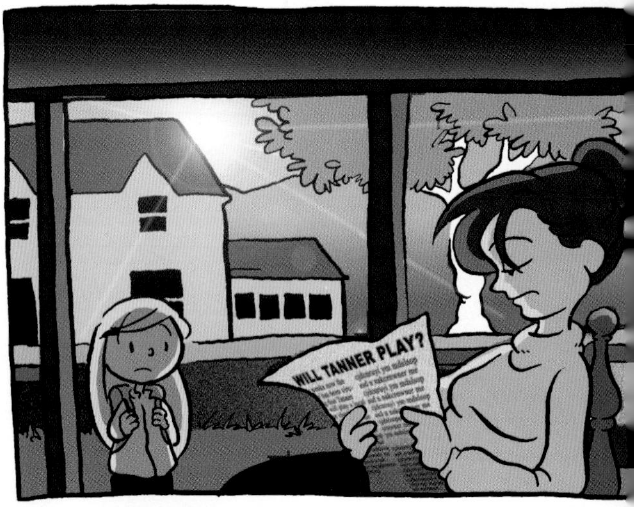
WILL TANNER PLAY?

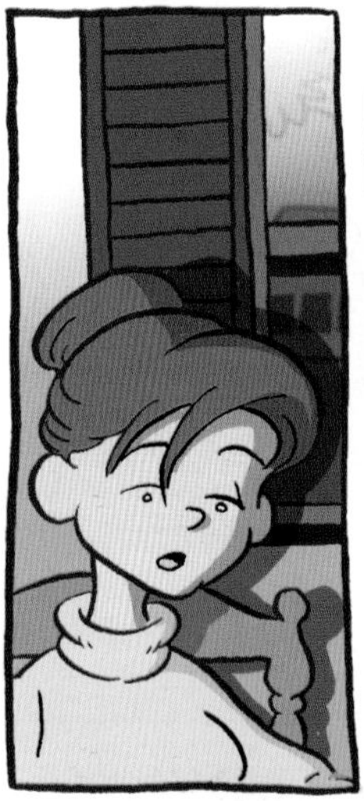

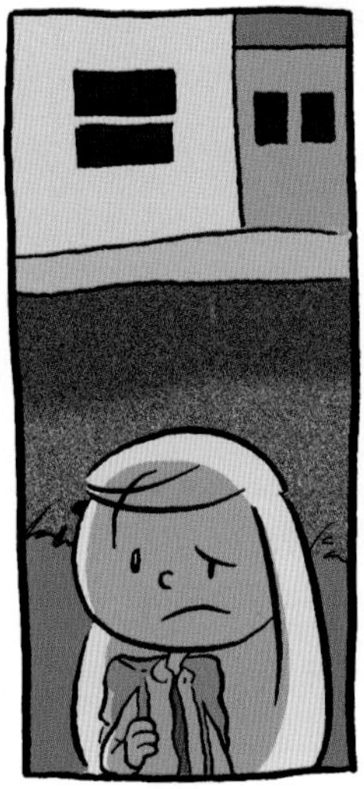

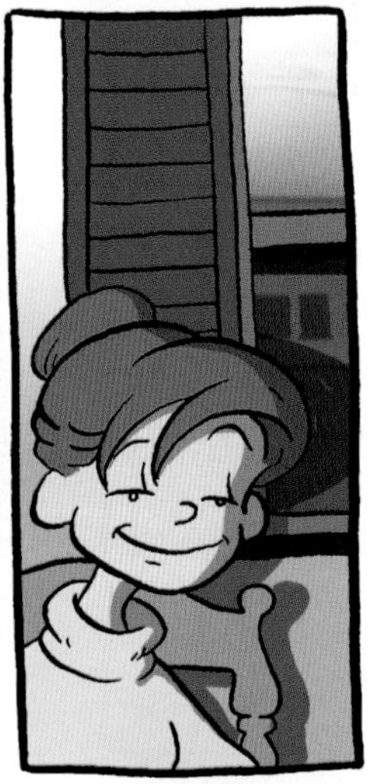

I DON'T THINK MOM HAD ANY **REAL** IDEA WHY TANNER QUIT SINGING. WHEN I **ASKED** HER ABOUT IT, ALL SHE SAID WAS THAT TANNER WAS A VERY **HONEST** PERSON AND THAT NOT ALL THE PEOPLE SHE **DEALT** WITH WERE AS HONEST AS TANNER IS.

MOM ALSO SAID THAT SHE DIDN'T THINK TANNER REALIZED HOW BIG A **FAN** MY **MOM** WAS. SHE SAID **SHE** UNDERSTOOD WHY TANNER WAS A SINGER EVEN BETTER THAN TANNER **HERSELF** DID.

I DIDN'T REALLY UNDERSTAND WHAT SHE **MEANT**, BUT I THINK I DO **NOW**.

THEN MOM LET LOOSE WITH **THIS** BOMBSHELL: SHE HAD KEPT A COLLECTION OF **SOUVENIRS** FROM TANNER'S CAREER. MAGAZINES AND VIDEOS AND TAPES AND STUFF TANNER **HERSELF** PROBABLY DIDN'T EVEN REMEMBER. SHE SAID THAT EVEN THOUGH TANNER DIDN'T WANT TO LOOK AT THAT STUFF **NOW**, SHE WOULD **SOMEDAY**. AND THEN SHE'D REALIZE HOW **BIG A FAN** MY MOM HAD BEEN.

SHE SAID SHE HAD IT ALL IN A TRUNK IN THE **ATTIC**.

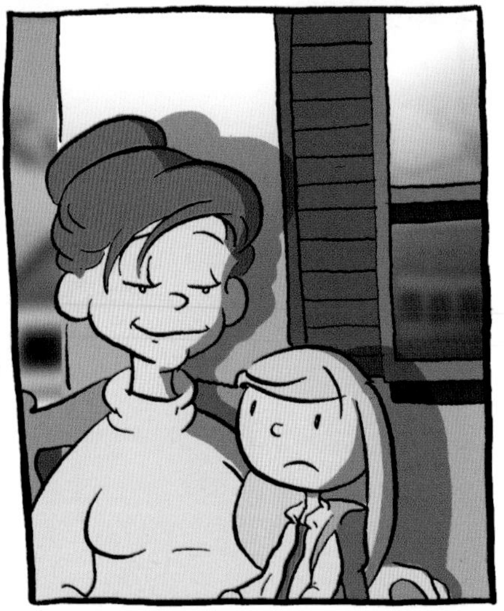

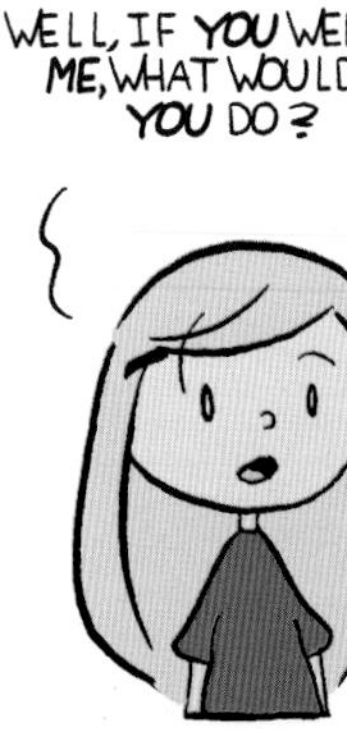
WELL, IF YOU WERE ME, WHAT WOULD YOU DO?

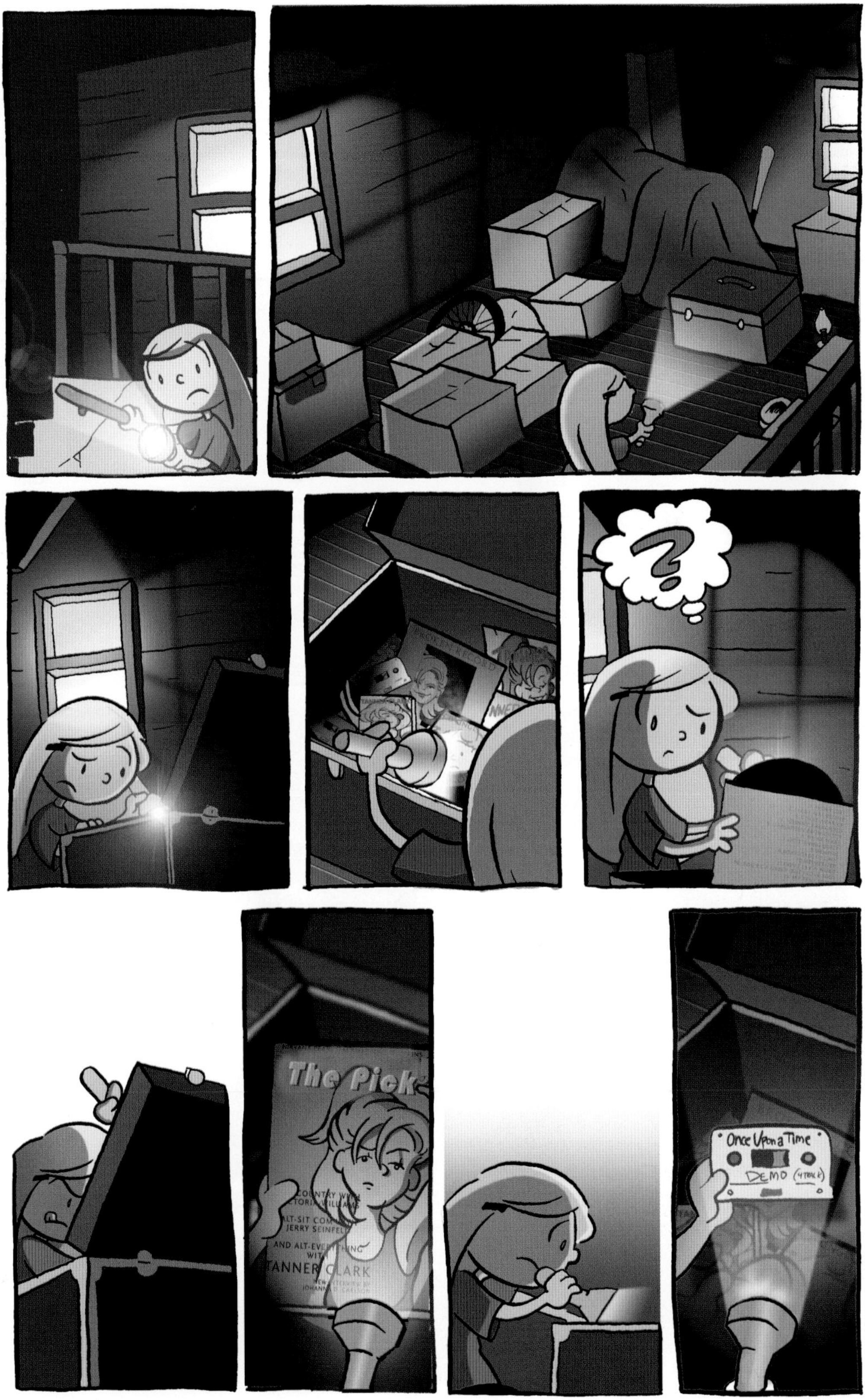
?
The Pick
TANNER CLARK
Once Upon a Time
DEMO

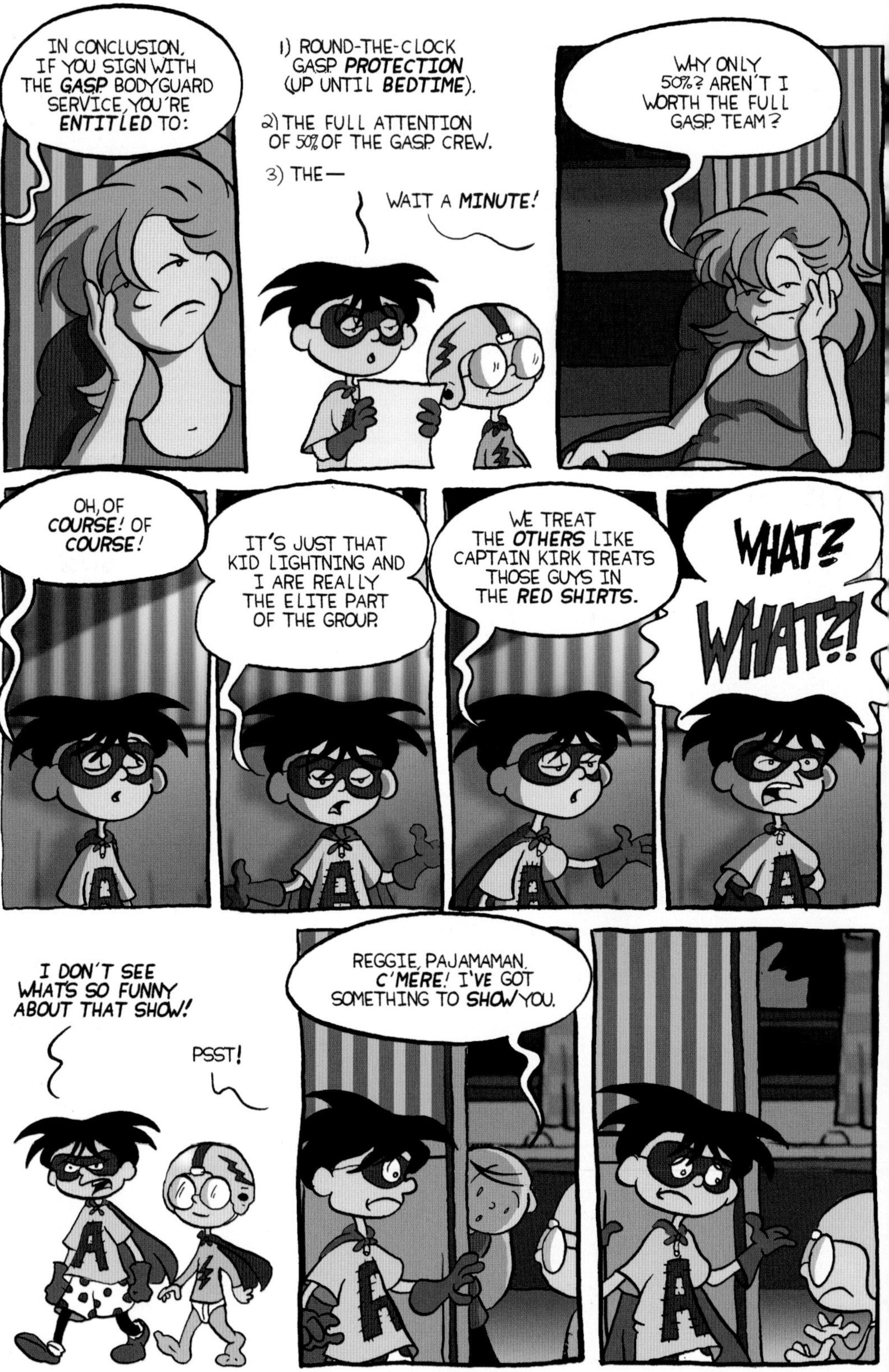
IN CONCLUSION, IF YOU SIGN WITH THE GASP BODYGUARD SERVICE, YOU'RE ENTITLED TO:
1) ROUND-THE-CLOCK GASP PROTECTION (UP UNTIL BEDTIME).
2) THE FULL ATTENTION OF 50% OF THE GASP CREW.
3) THE—
WAIT A MINUTE!
WHY ONLY 50%? AREN'T I WORTH THE FULL GASP TEAM?
OH, OF COURSE! OF COURSE!
IT'S JUST THAT KID LIGHTNING AND I ARE REALLY THE ELITE PART OF THE GROUP.
WE TREAT THE OTHERS LIKE CAPTAIN KIRK TREATS THOSE GUYS IN THE RED SHIRTS.
WHAT?
WHAT?!
I DON'T SEE WHAT'S SO FUNNY ABOUT THAT SHOW!
PSST!
REGGIE, PAJAMAMAN, C'MERE! I'VE GOT SOMETHING TO SHOW YOU.

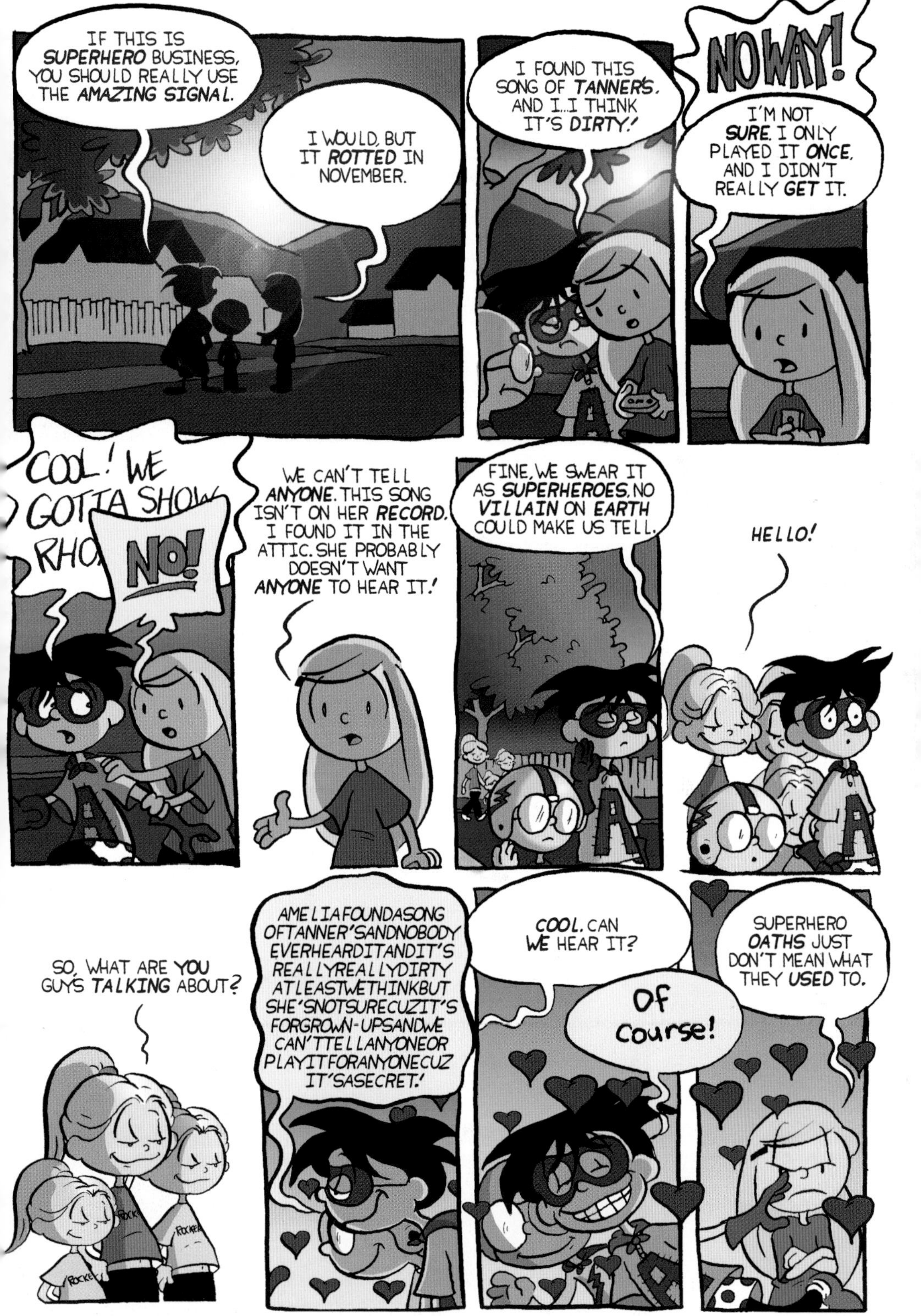

IF THIS IS SUPERHERO BUSINESS, YOU SHOULD REALLY USE THE AMAZING SIGNAL.
I WOULD, BUT IT ROTTED IN NOVEMBER.
I FOUND THIS SONG OF TANNER'S. AND I...I THINK IT'S DIRTY!
NO WAY!
I'M NOT SURE. I ONLY PLAYED IT ONCE, AND I DIDN'T REALLY GET IT.
COOL! WE GOTTA SHOW RHO
NO!
WE CAN'T TELL ANYONE. THIS SONG ISN'T ON HER RECORD. I FOUND IT IN THE ATTIC. SHE PROBABLY DOESN'T WANT ANYONE TO HEAR IT!
FINE, WE SWEAR IT AS SUPERHEROES. NO VILLAIN ON EARTH COULD MAKE US TELL.
HELLO!
SO, WHAT ARE YOU GUYS TALKING ABOUT?
AMELIAFOUNDASONG OFTANNER'SANDNOBODY EVERHEARDITANDIT'S REALLYREALLYDIRTY ATLEASTWETHINKBUT SHE'SNOTSURECUZIT'S FORGROWN-UPSANDWE CAN'TTELLANYONEOR PLAYITFORANYONECUZ IT'SASECRET!
COOL. CAN WE HEAR IT?
Of course!
SUPERHERO OATHS JUST DON'T MEAN WHAT THEY USED TO.

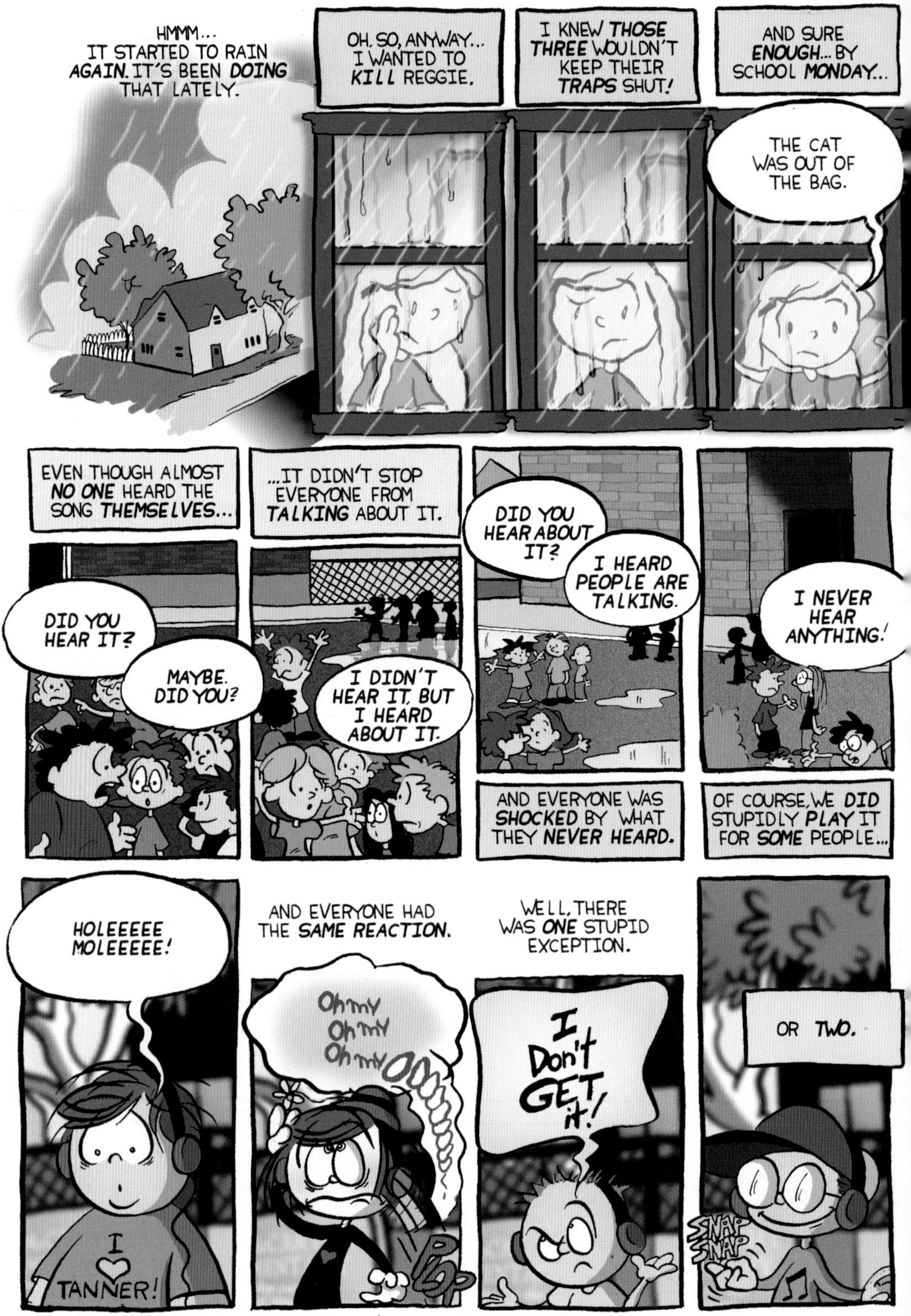
HMMM... IT STARTED TO RAIN AGAIN. IT'S BEEN DOING THAT LATELY.
OH, SO, ANYWAY... I WANTED TO KILL REGGIE.
I KNEW THOSE THREE WOULDN'T KEEP THEIR TRAPS SHUT!
AND SURE ENOUGH... BY SCHOOL MONDAY...
THE CAT WAS OUT OF THE BAG.
EVEN THOUGH ALMOST NO ONE HEARD THE SONG THEMSELVES...
DID YOU HEAR IT?
MAYBE. DID YOU?
...IT DIDN'T STOP EVERYONE FROM TALKING ABOUT IT.
I DIDN'T HEAR IT, BUT I HEARD ABOUT IT.
DID YOU HEAR ABOUT IT?
I HEARD PEOPLE ARE TALKING.
AND EVERYONE WAS SHOCKED BY WHAT THEY NEVER HEARD.
I NEVER HEAR ANYTHING!
OF COURSE, WE DID STUPIDLY PLAY IT FOR SOME PEOPLE...
HOLEEEEE MOLEEEEE!
I ♥ TANNER!
AND EVERYONE HAD THE SAME REACTION.
Oh my Oh my Oh my
WELL, THERE WAS ONE STUPID EXCEPTION.
I Don't GET it!
OR TWO.
SNAP SNAP

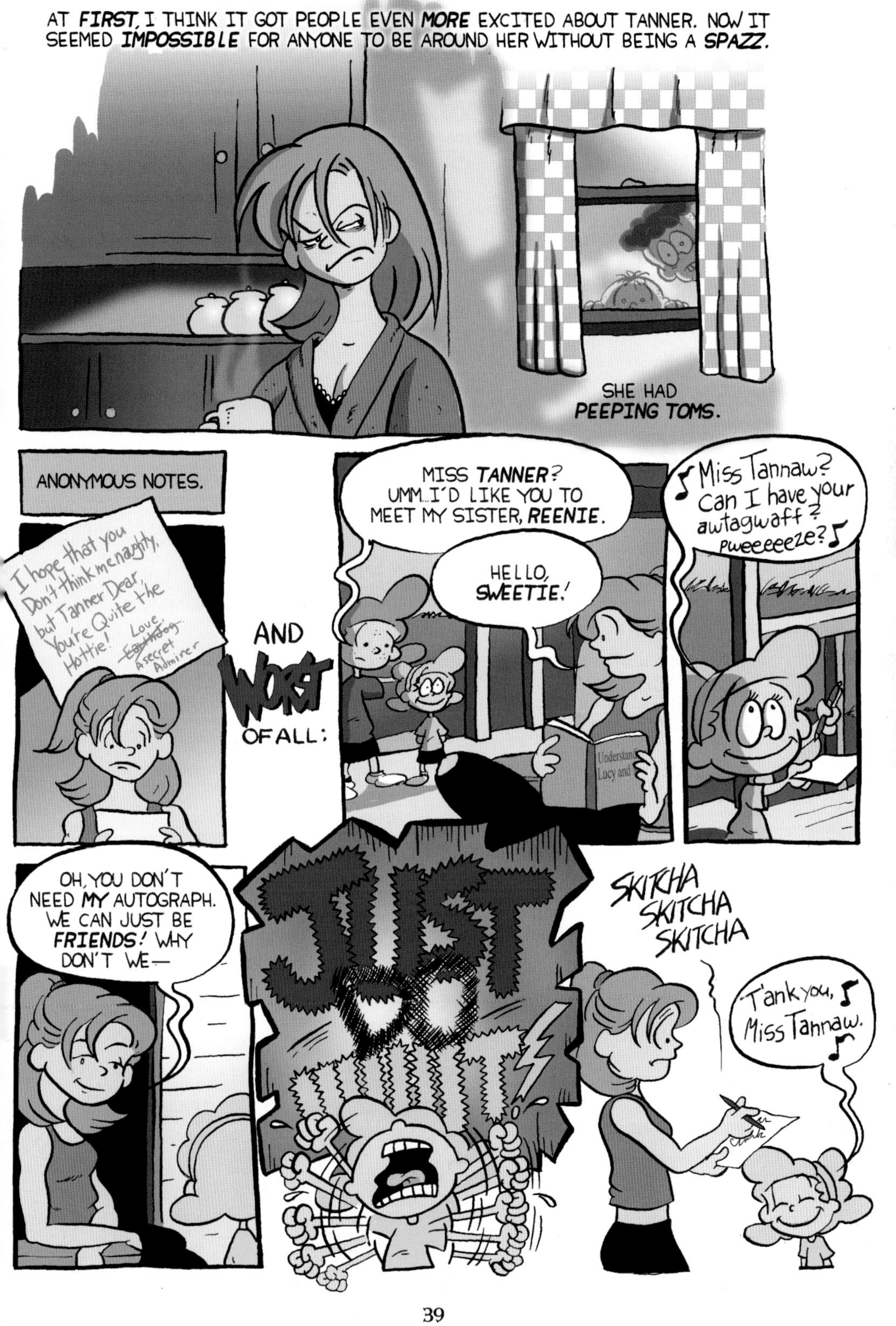
AT FIRST, I THINK IT GOT PEOPLE EVEN MORE EXCITED ABOUT TANNER. NOW IT SEEMED IMPOSSIBLE FOR ANYONE TO BE AROUND HER WITHOUT BEING A SPAZZ.
SHE HAD PEEPING TOMS.
ANONYMOUS NOTES.
I hope that you Don't think me naughty, but Tanner Dear, You're Quite the Hottie! Love, Asecret Admirer
AND WORST OF ALL:
MISS TANNER? UMM...I'D LIKE YOU TO MEET MY SISTER, REENIE.
HELLO, SWEETIE!
Miss Tannaw? Can I have your awtagwaff? Pweeeeeze?
OH, YOU DON'T NEED MY AUTOGRAPH. WE CAN JUST BE FRIENDS! WHY DON'T WE—
JUST
SKITCHA SKITCHA SKITCHA
T'ank you, Miss Tannaw.

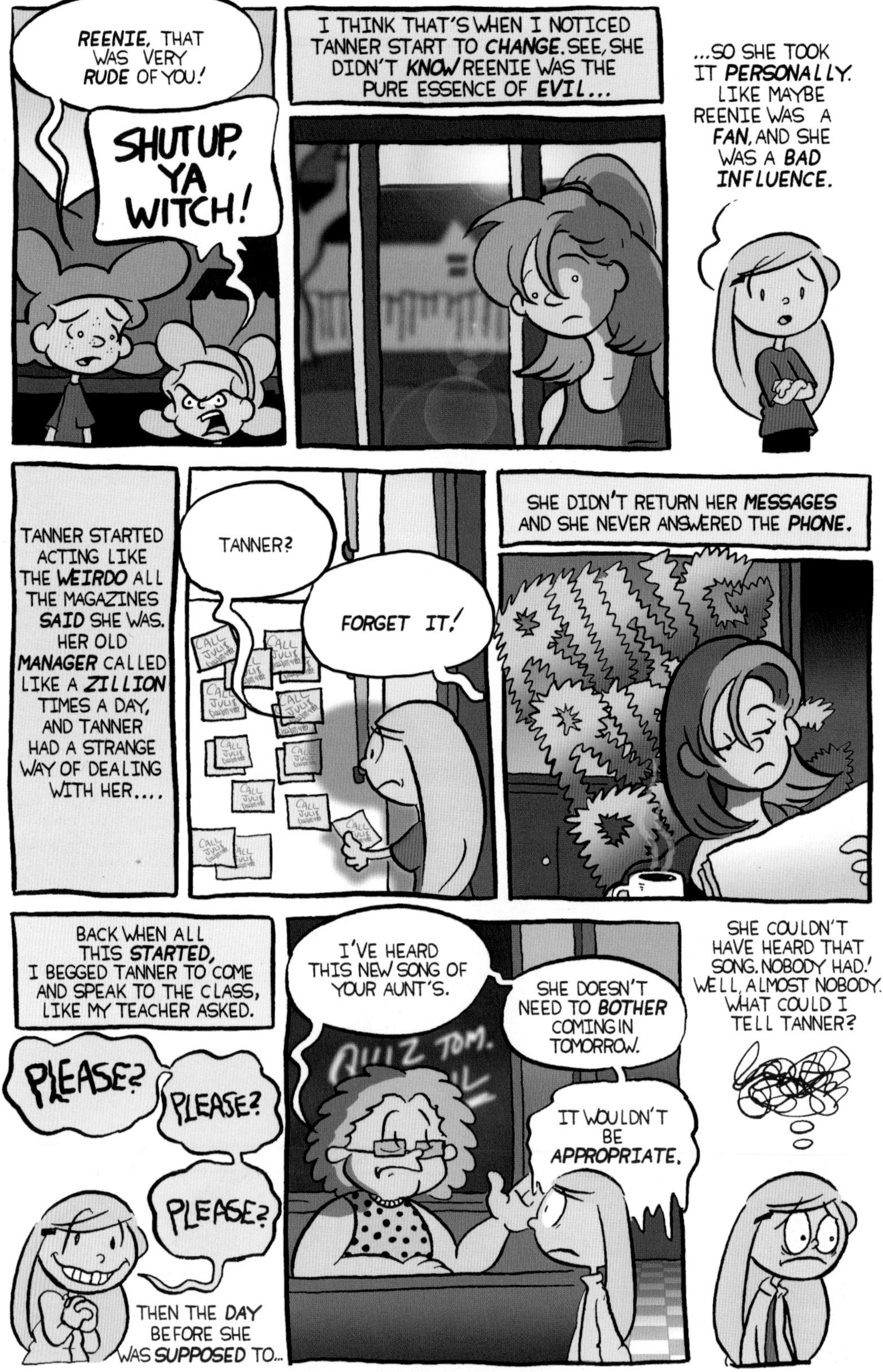
REENIE, THAT WAS VERY RUDE OF YOU!
SHUT UP, YA WITCH!
I THINK THAT'S WHEN I NOTICED TANNER START TO CHANGE. SEE, SHE DIDN'T KNOW REENIE WAS THE PURE ESSENCE OF EVIL...
...SO SHE TOOK IT PERSONALLY. LIKE MAYBE REENIE WAS A FAN, AND SHE WAS A BAD INFLUENCE.
TANNER STARTED ACTING LIKE THE WEIRDO ALL THE MAGAZINES SAID SHE WAS. HER OLD MANAGER CALLED LIKE A ZILLION TIMES A DAY, AND TANNER HAD A STRANGE WAY OF DEALING WITH HER....
TANNER?
FORGET IT!
SHE DIDN'T RETURN HER MESSAGES AND SHE NEVER ANSWERED THE PHONE.
BACK WHEN ALL THIS STARTED, I BEGGED TANNER TO COME AND SPEAK TO THE CLASS, LIKE MY TEACHER ASKED.
PLEASE?
PLEASE?
PLEASE?
THEN THE DAY BEFORE SHE WAS SUPPOSED TO...
I'VE HEARD THIS NEW SONG OF YOUR AUNT'S.
SHE DOESN'T NEED TO BOTHER COMING IN TOMORROW.
IT WOULDN'T BE APPROPRIATE.
SHE COULDN'T HAVE HEARD THAT SONG. NOBODY HAD! WELL, ALMOST NOBODY. WHAT COULD I TELL TANNER?

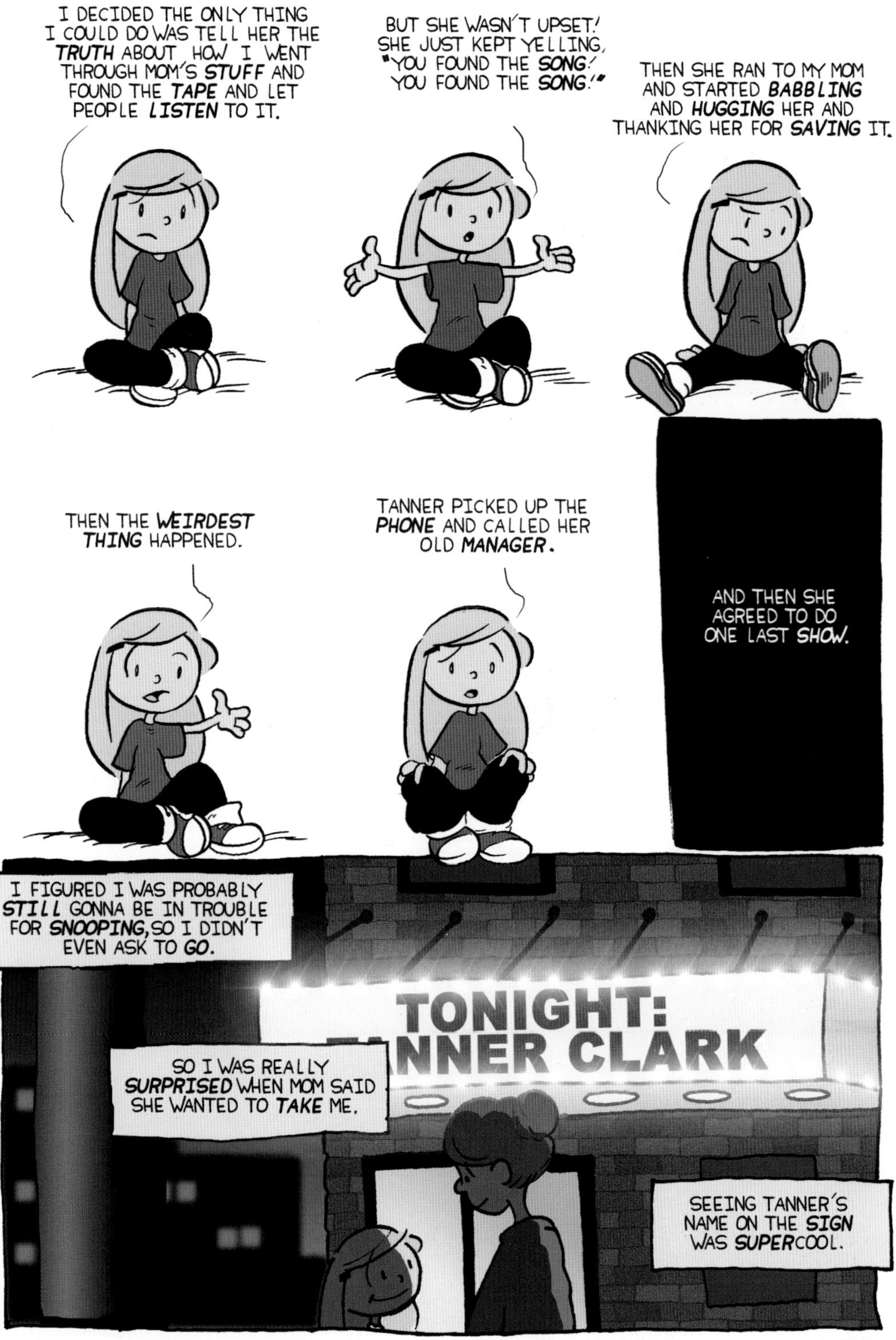
I DECIDED THE ONLY THING I COULD DO WAS TELL HER THE TRUTH ABOUT HOW I WENT THROUGH MOM'S STUFF AND FOUND THE TAPE AND LET PEOPLE LISTEN TO IT.
BUT SHE WASN'T UPSET! SHE JUST KEPT YELLING, "YOU FOUND THE SONG! YOU FOUND THE SONG!"
THEN SHE RAN TO MY MOM AND STARTED BABBLING AND HUGGING HER AND THANKING HER FOR SAVING IT.
THEN THE WEIRDEST THING HAPPENED.
TANNER PICKED UP THE PHONE AND CALLED HER OLD MANAGER.
AND THEN SHE AGREED TO DO ONE LAST SHOW.
I FIGURED I WAS PROBABLY STILL GONNA BE IN TROUBLE FOR SNOOPING, SO I DIDN'T EVEN ASK TO GO.
TONIGHT:
NNER CLARK
SO I WAS REALLY SURPRISED WHEN MOM SAID SHE WANTED TO TAKE ME.
SEEING TANNER'S NAME ON THE SIGN WAS SUPERCOOL.

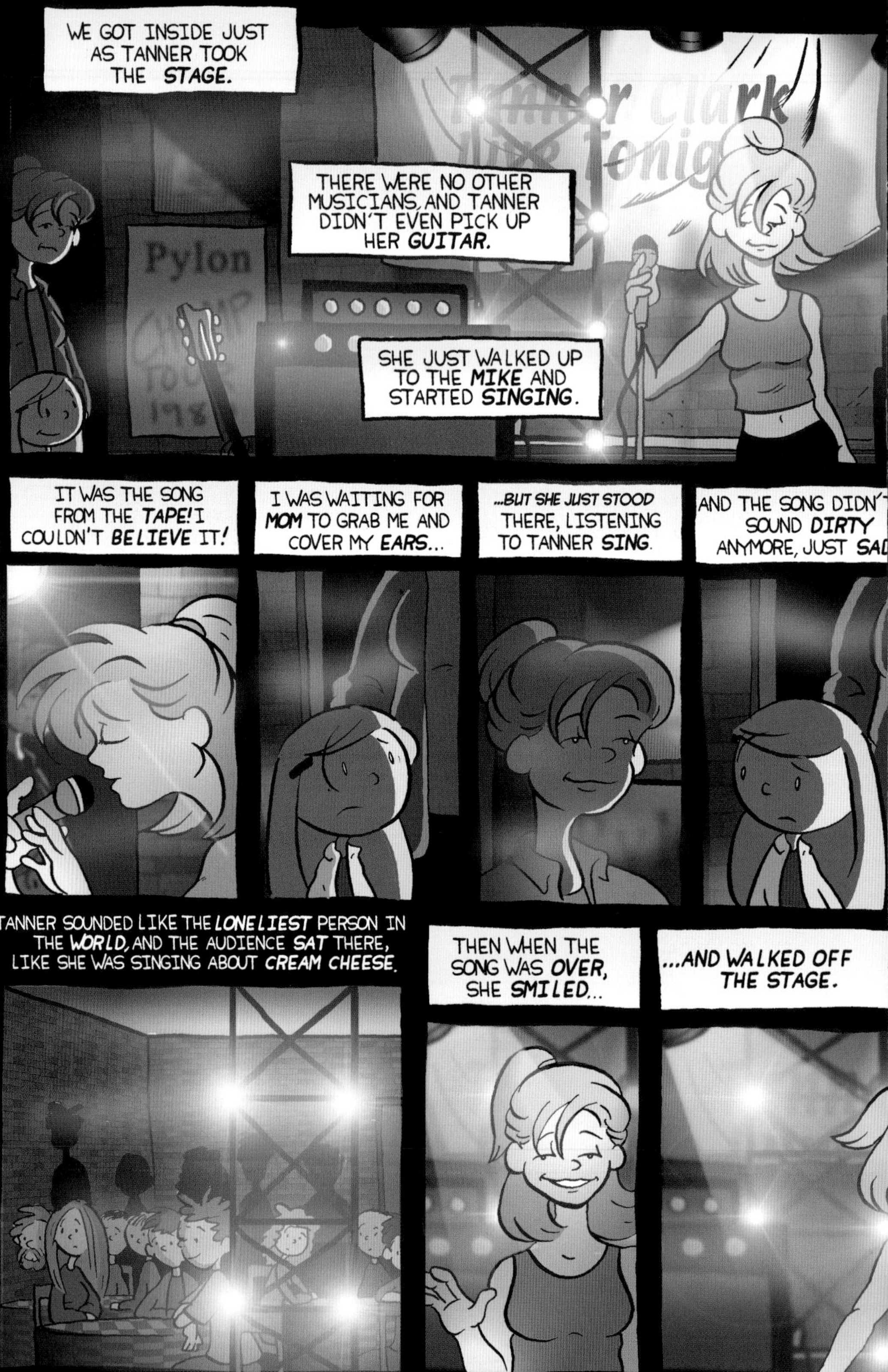
WE GOT INSIDE JUST AS TANNER TOOK THE STAGE.
Pylon
THERE WERE NO OTHER MUSICIANS, AND TANNER DIDN'T EVEN PICK UP HER GUITAR.
SHE JUST WALKED UP TO THE MIKE AND STARTED SINGING.
IT WAS THE SONG FROM THE TAPE! I COULDN'T BELIEVE IT!
I WAS WAITING FOR MOM TO GRAB ME AND COVER MY EARS...
...BUT SHE JUST STOOD THERE, LISTENING TO TANNER SING.
AND THE SONG DIDN'T SOUND DIRTY ANYMORE, JUST SAD
TANNER SOUNDED LIKE THE LONELIEST PERSON IN THE WORLD, AND THE AUDIENCE SAT THERE, LIKE SHE WAS SINGING ABOUT CREAM CHEESE.
THEN WHEN THE SONG WAS OVER, SHE SMILED...
...AND WALKED OFF THE STAGE.

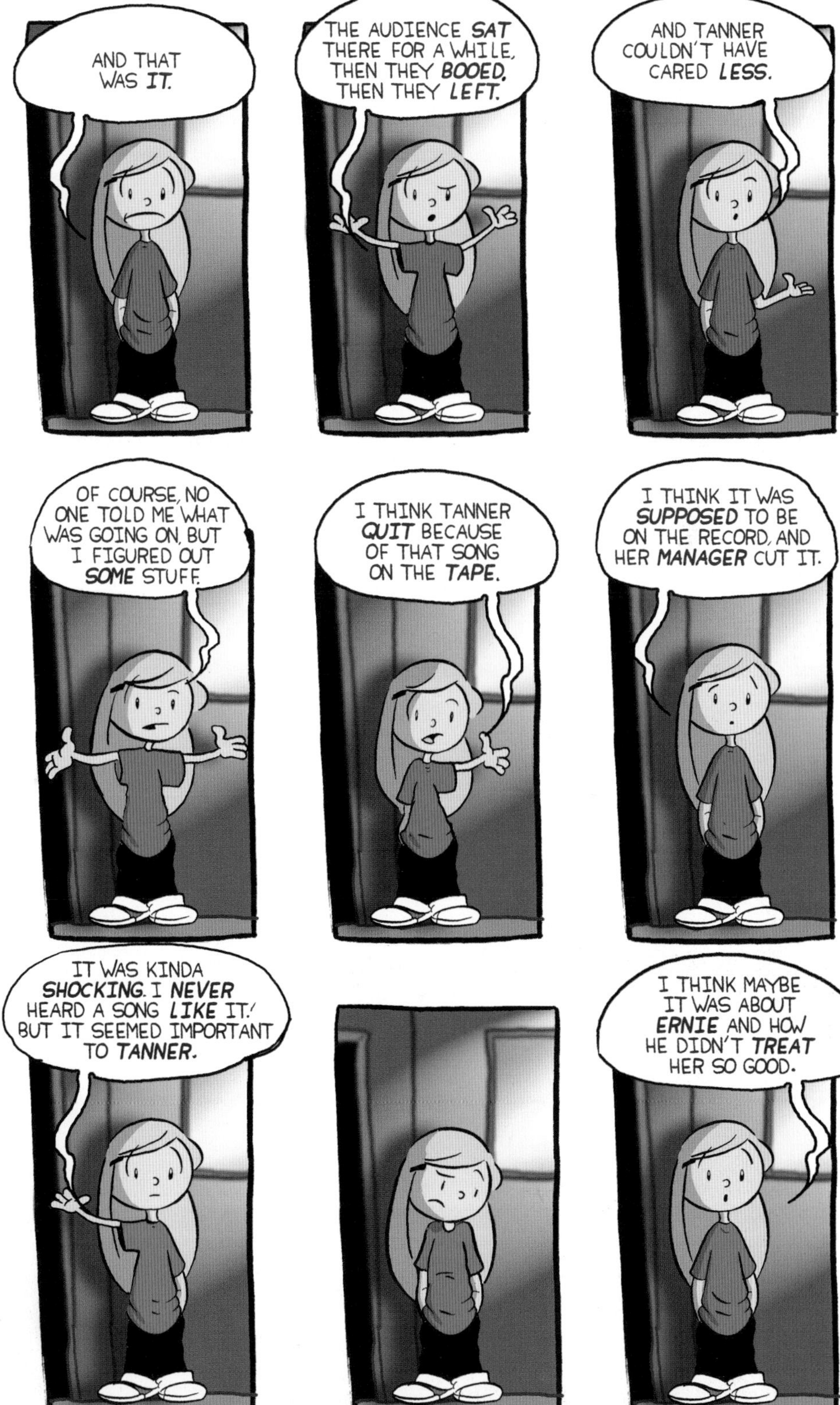
AND THAT WAS IT.
THE AUDIENCE SAT THERE FOR A WHILE, THEN THEY BOOED, THEN THEY LEFT.
AND TANNER COULDN'T HAVE CARED LESS.
OF COURSE, NO ONE TOLD ME WHAT WAS GOING ON, BUT I FIGURED OUT SOME STUFF.
I THINK TANNER QUIT BECAUSE OF THAT SONG ON THE TAPE.
I THINK IT WAS SUPPOSED TO BE ON THE RECORD, AND HER MANAGER CUT IT.
IT WAS KINDA SHOCKING. I NEVER HEARD A SONG LIKE IT! BUT IT SEEMED IMPORTANT TO TANNER.
I THINK MAYBE IT WAS ABOUT ERNIE AND HOW HE DIDN'T TREAT HER SO GOOD.

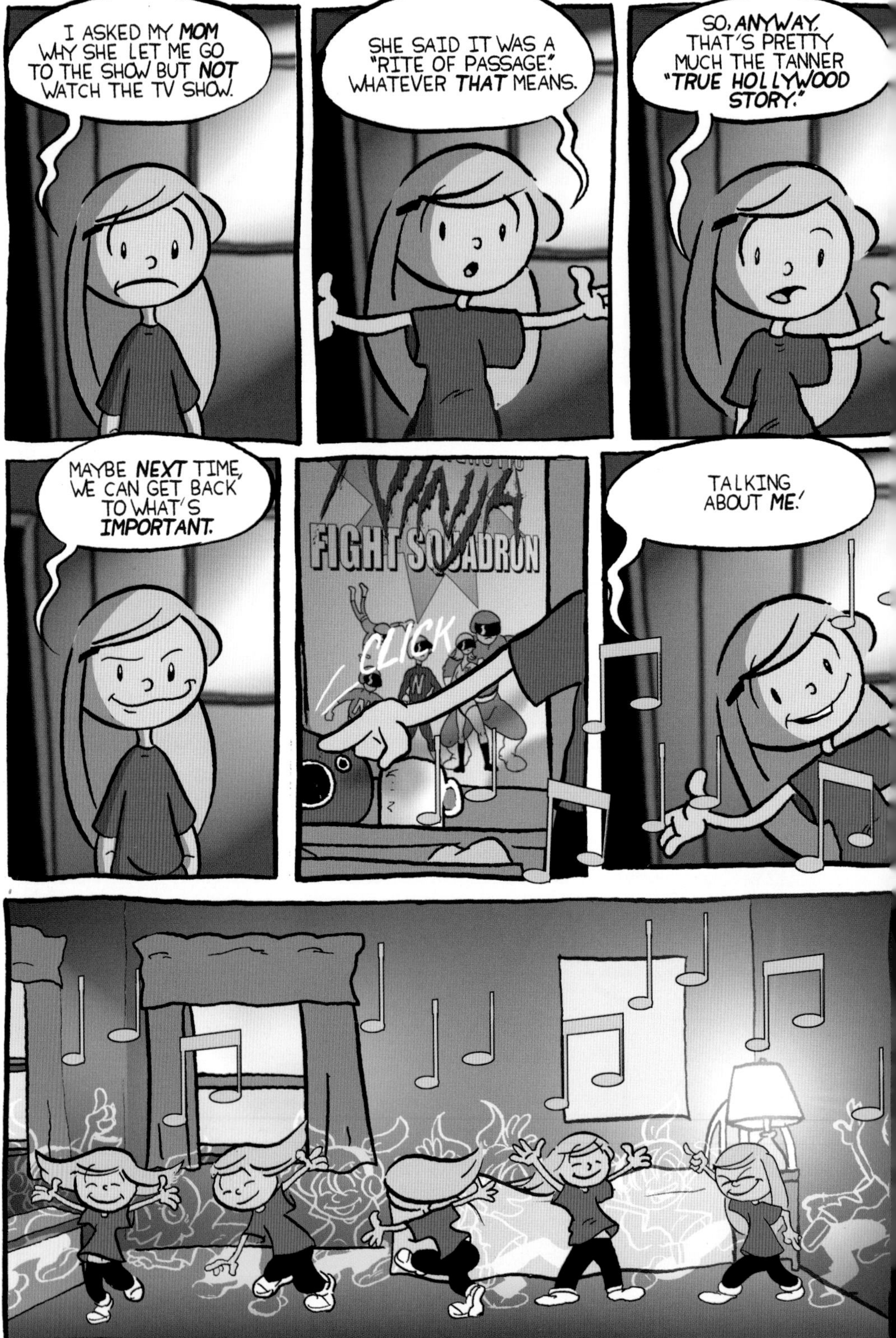
I ASKED MY MOM WHY SHE LET ME GO TO THE SHOW BUT NOT WATCH THE TV SHOW.
SHE SAID IT WAS A "RITE OF PASSAGE." WHATEVER THAT MEANS.
SO, ANYWAY, THAT'S PRETTY MUCH THE TANNER "TRUE HOLLYWOOD STORY."
MAYBE NEXT TIME, WE CAN GET BACK TO WHAT'S IMPORTANT.
FIGHT SQUADRON
CLICK
TALKING ABOUT ME!

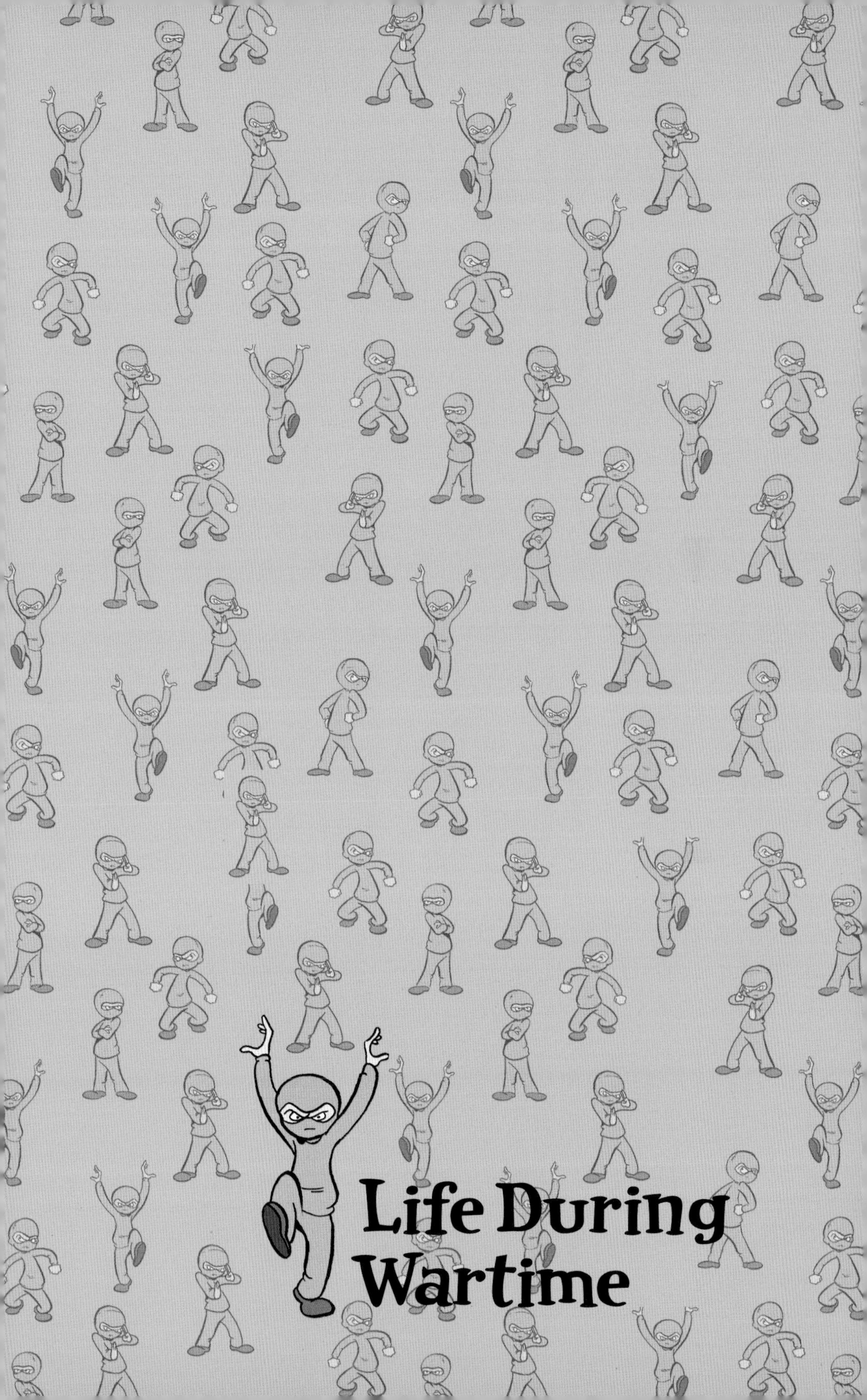

Life During Wartime

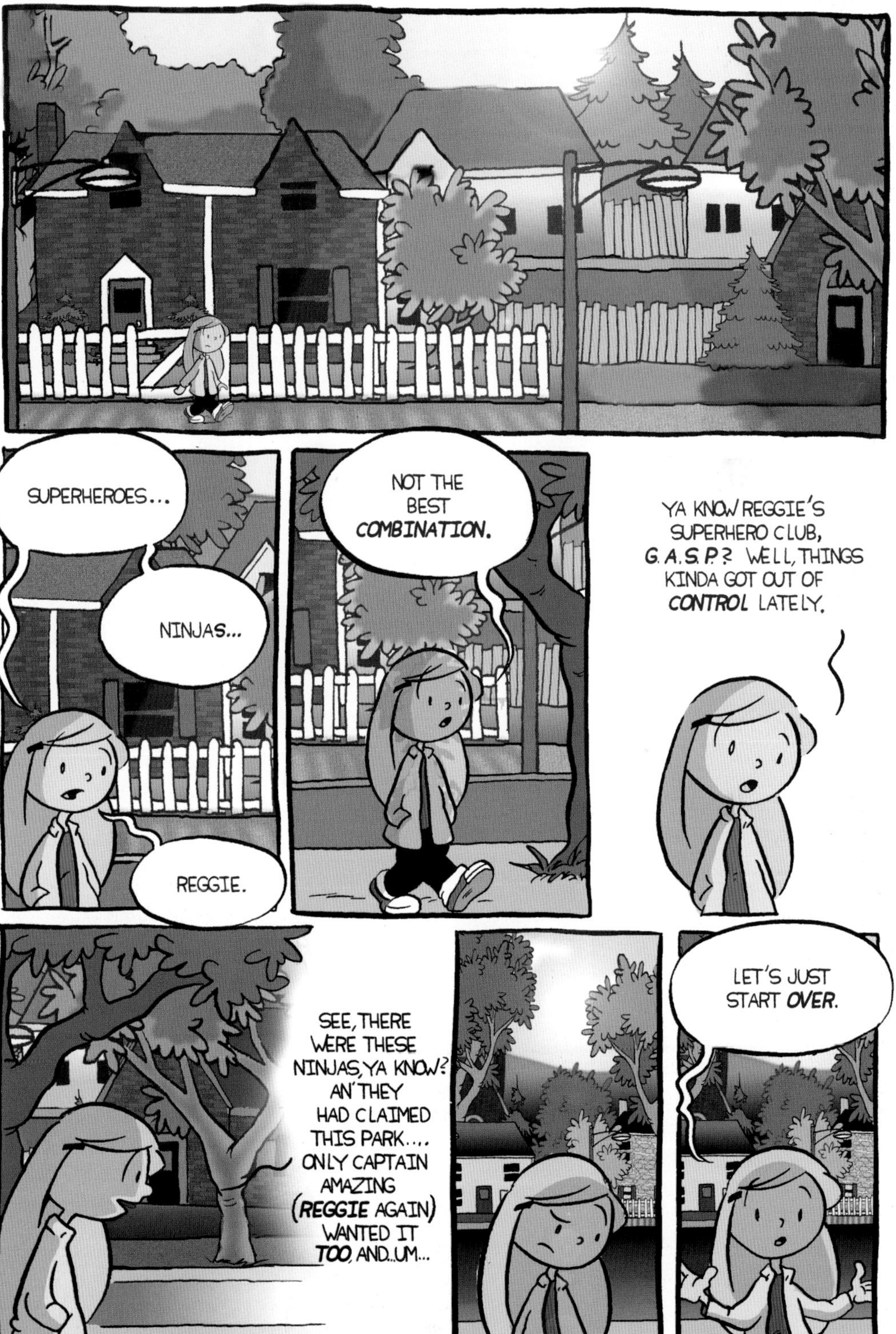
SUPERHEROES...
NINJAS...
REGGIE.
NOT THE BEST **COMBINATION.**
YA KNOW REGGIE'S SUPERHERO CLUB, G.A.S.P.? WELL, THINGS KINDA GOT OUT OF **CONTROL** LATELY.
SEE, THERE WERE THESE NINJAS, YA KNOW? AN' THEY HAD CLAIMED THIS PARK.... ONLY CAPTAIN AMAZING (**REGGIE** AGAIN) WANTED IT **TOO**, AND...UM...
LET'S JUST START **OVER.**

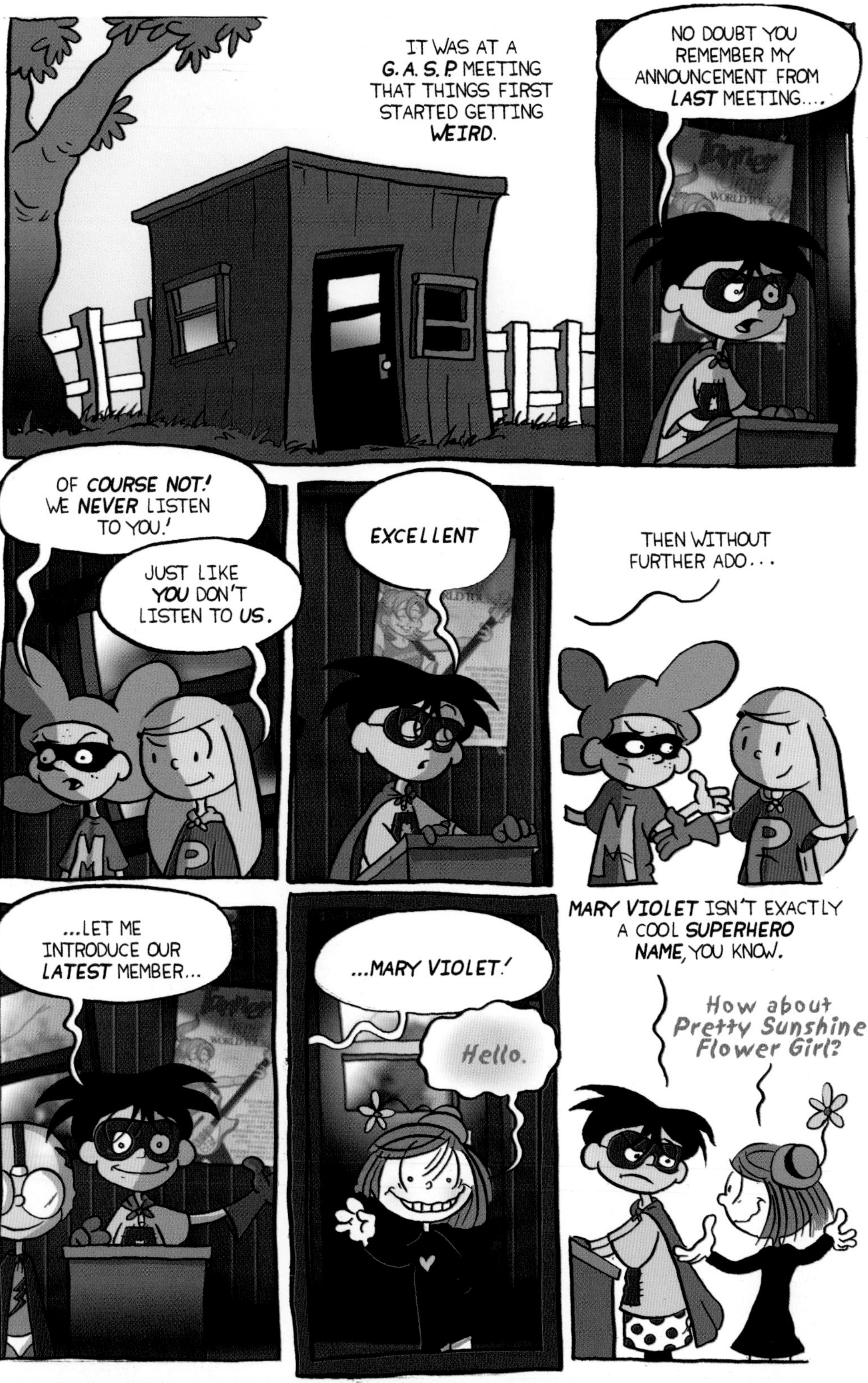
IT WAS AT A G. A. S. P. MEETING THAT THINGS FIRST STARTED GETTING WEIRD.
NO DOUBT YOU REMEMBER MY ANNOUNCEMENT FROM LAST MEETING....
OF COURSE NOT! WE NEVER LISTEN TO YOU!
JUST LIKE YOU DON'T LISTEN TO US.
EXCELLENT
THEN WITHOUT FURTHER ADO...
...LET ME INTRODUCE OUR LATEST MEMBER...
...MARY VIOLET!
Hello.
MARY VIOLET ISN'T EXACTLY A COOL SUPERHERO NAME, YOU KNOW.
How about Pretty Sunshine Flower Girl?

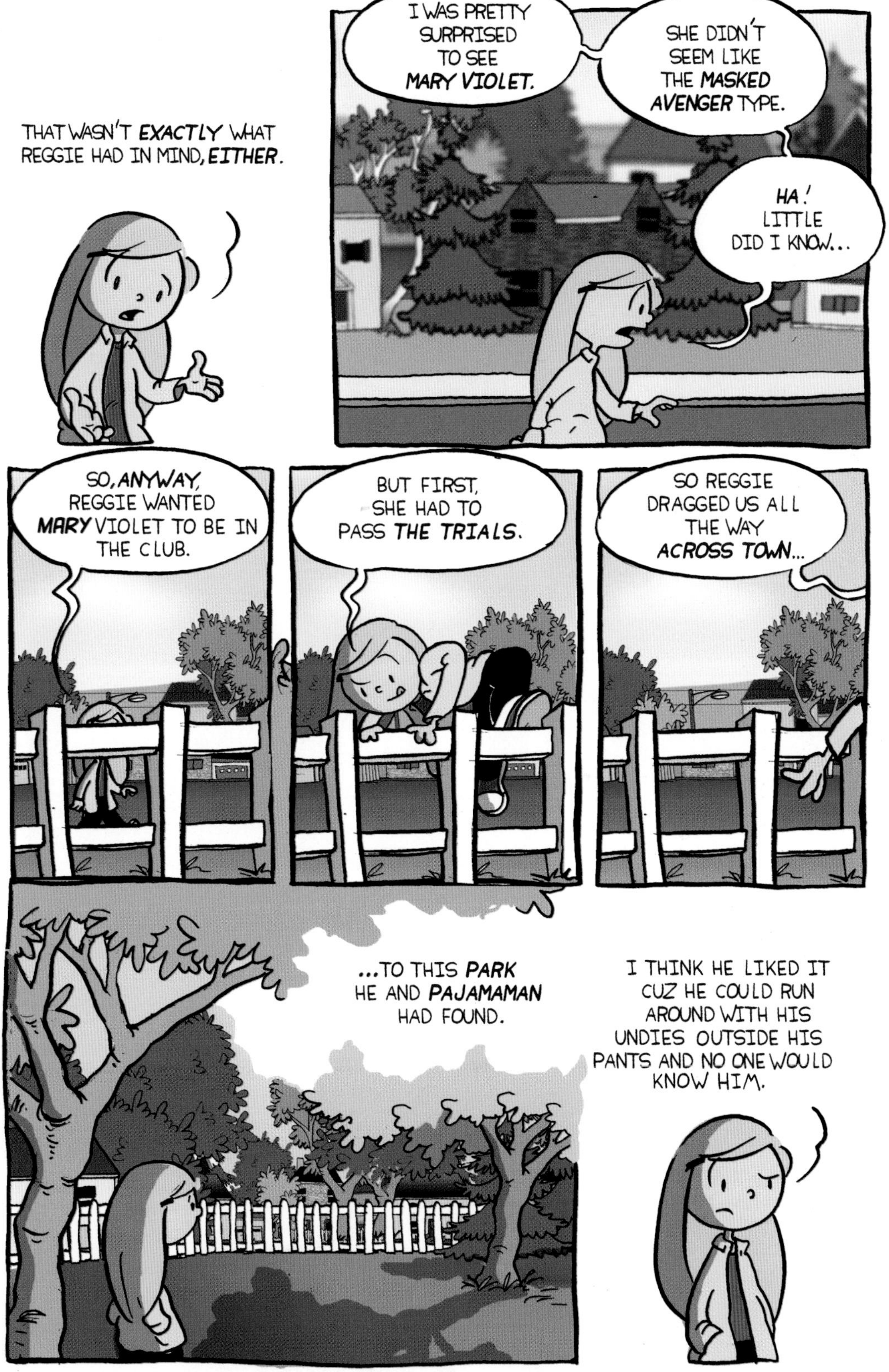
THAT WASN'T EXACTLY WHAT REGGIE HAD IN MIND, EITHER.
I WAS PRETTY SURPRISED TO SEE MARY VIOLET.
SHE DIDN'T SEEM LIKE THE MASKED AVENGER TYPE.
HA! LITTLE DID I KNOW...
SO, ANYWAY, REGGIE WANTED MARY VIOLET TO BE IN THE CLUB.
BUT FIRST, SHE HAD TO PASS THE TRIALS.
SO REGGIE DRAGGED US ALL THE WAY ACROSS TOWN...
...TO THIS PARK HE AND PAJAMAMAN HAD FOUND.
I THINK HE LIKED IT CUZ HE COULD RUN AROUND WITH HIS UNDIES OUTSIDE HIS PANTS AND NO ONE WOULD KNOW HIM.

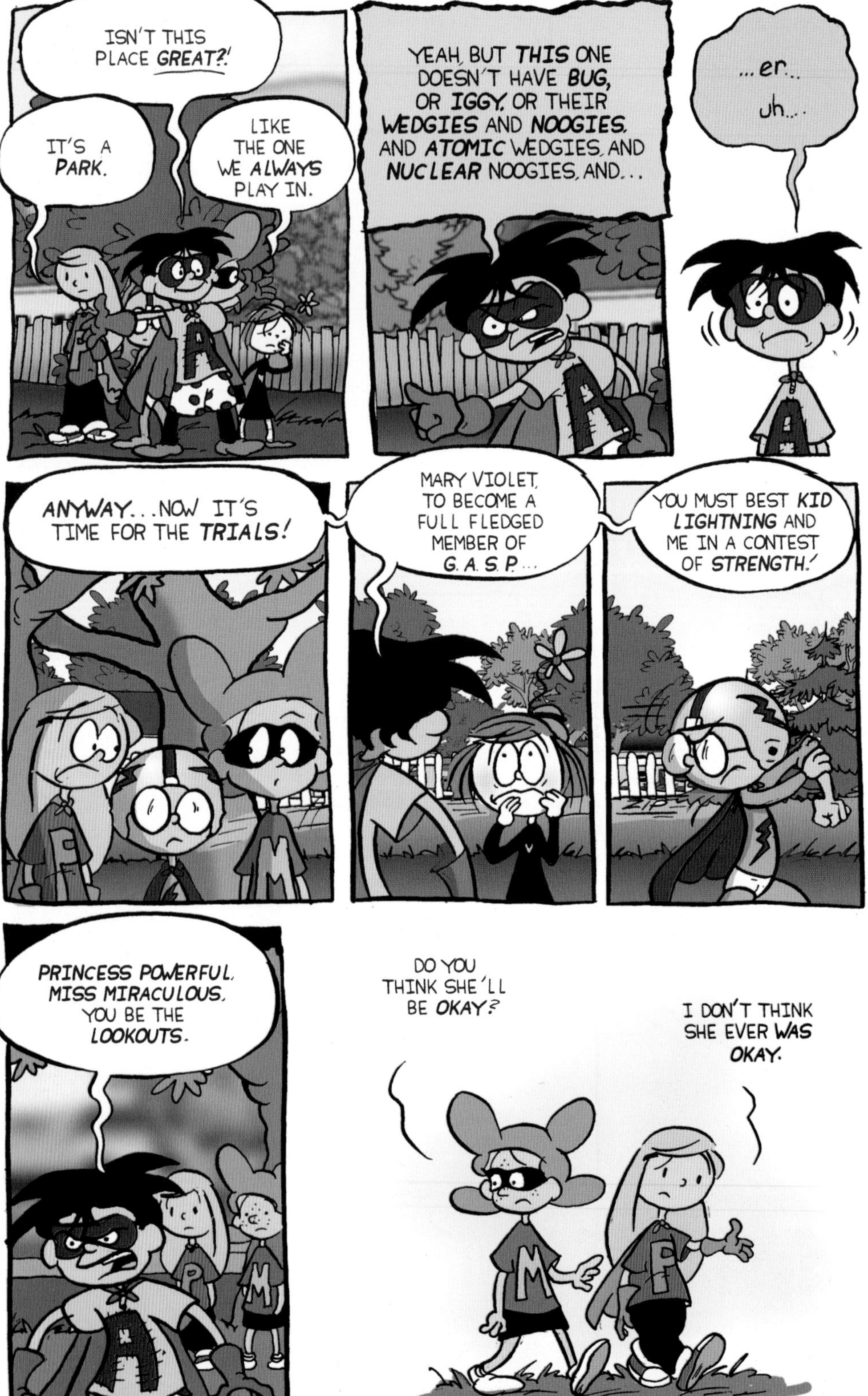
ISN'T THIS PLACE GREAT?!
IT'S A PARK.
LIKE THE ONE WE ALWAYS PLAY IN.
YEAH, BUT THIS ONE DOESN'T HAVE BUG, OR IGGY, OR THEIR WEDGIES AND NOOGIES, AND ATOMIC WEDGIES, AND NUCLEAR NOOGIES, AND...
...er... uh...
ANYWAY...NOW IT'S TIME FOR THE TRIALS!
MARY VIOLET, TO BECOME A FULL FLEDGED MEMBER OF G.A.S.P....
YOU MUST BEST KID LIGHTNING AND ME IN A CONTEST OF STRENGTH!
PRINCESS POWERFUL, MISS MIRACULOUS, YOU BE THE LOOKOUTS.
DO YOU THINK SHE'LL BE OKAY?
I DON'T THINK SHE EVER WAS OKAY.

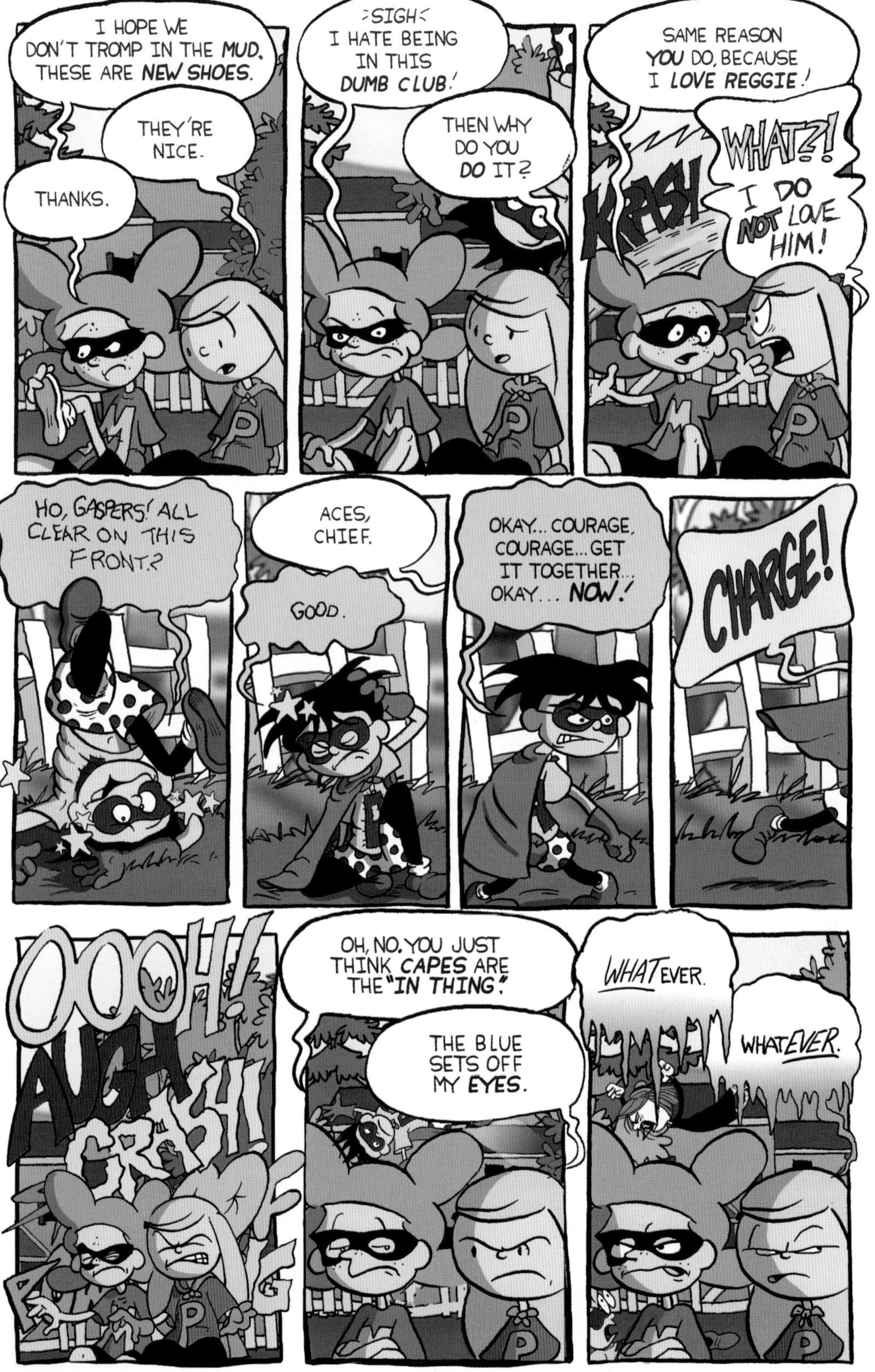
I HOPE WE DON'T TROMP IN THE MUD. THESE ARE NEW SHOES.
THEY'RE NICE.
THANKS.
>SIGH< I HATE BEING IN THIS DUMB CLUB!
THEN WHY DO YOU DO IT?
SAME REASON YOU DO, BECAUSE I LOVE REGGIE!
KRASH
WHAT?! I DO NOT LOVE HIM!
HO, GASPERS! ALL CLEAR ON THIS FRONT?
ACES, CHIEF.
GOOD.
OKAY... COURAGE, COURAGE... GET IT TOGETHER... OKAY... NOW!
CHARGE!
OOOH!
AUGH
CRASH!
OH, NO. YOU JUST THINK CAPES ARE THE "IN THING."
THE BLUE SETS OFF MY EYES.
WHATEVER.
WHATEVER.

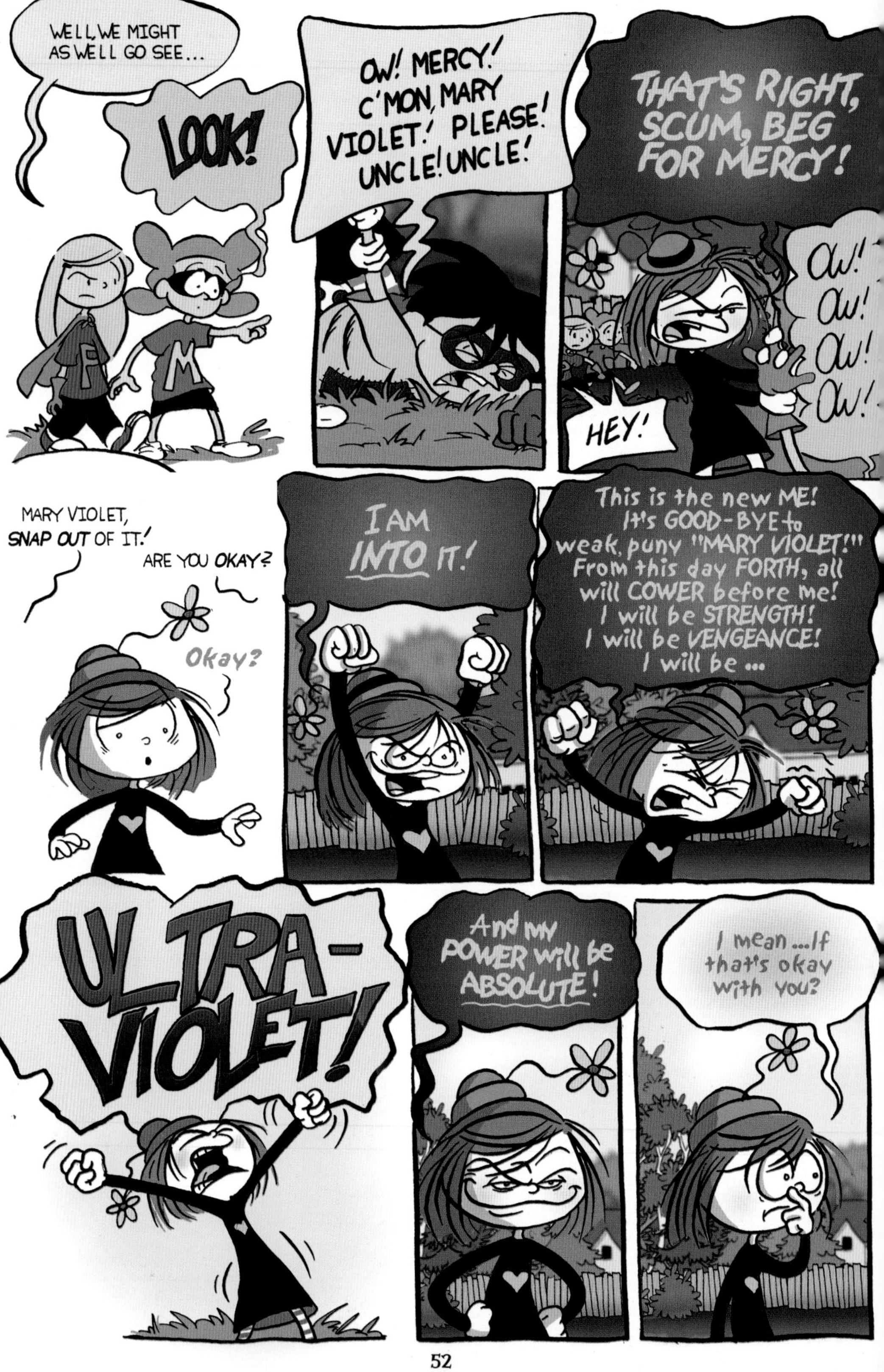

WELL, WE MIGHT AS WELL GO SEE...
LOOK!
OW! MERCY! C'MON, MARY VIOLET! PLEASE! UNCLE! UNCLE!
THAT'S RIGHT, SCUM, BEG FOR MERCY!
Ow! Ow! Ow! Ow!
HEY!
MARY VIOLET, SNAP OUT OF IT!
ARE YOU OKAY?
Okay?
I AM INTO IT!
This is the new ME! It's GOOD-BYE to weak, puny "MARY VIOLET!" From this day FORTH, all will COWER before me! I will be STRENGTH! I will be VENGEANCE! I will be...
ULTRA-VIOLET!
And my POWER will be ABSOLUTE!
I mean...If that's okay with you?

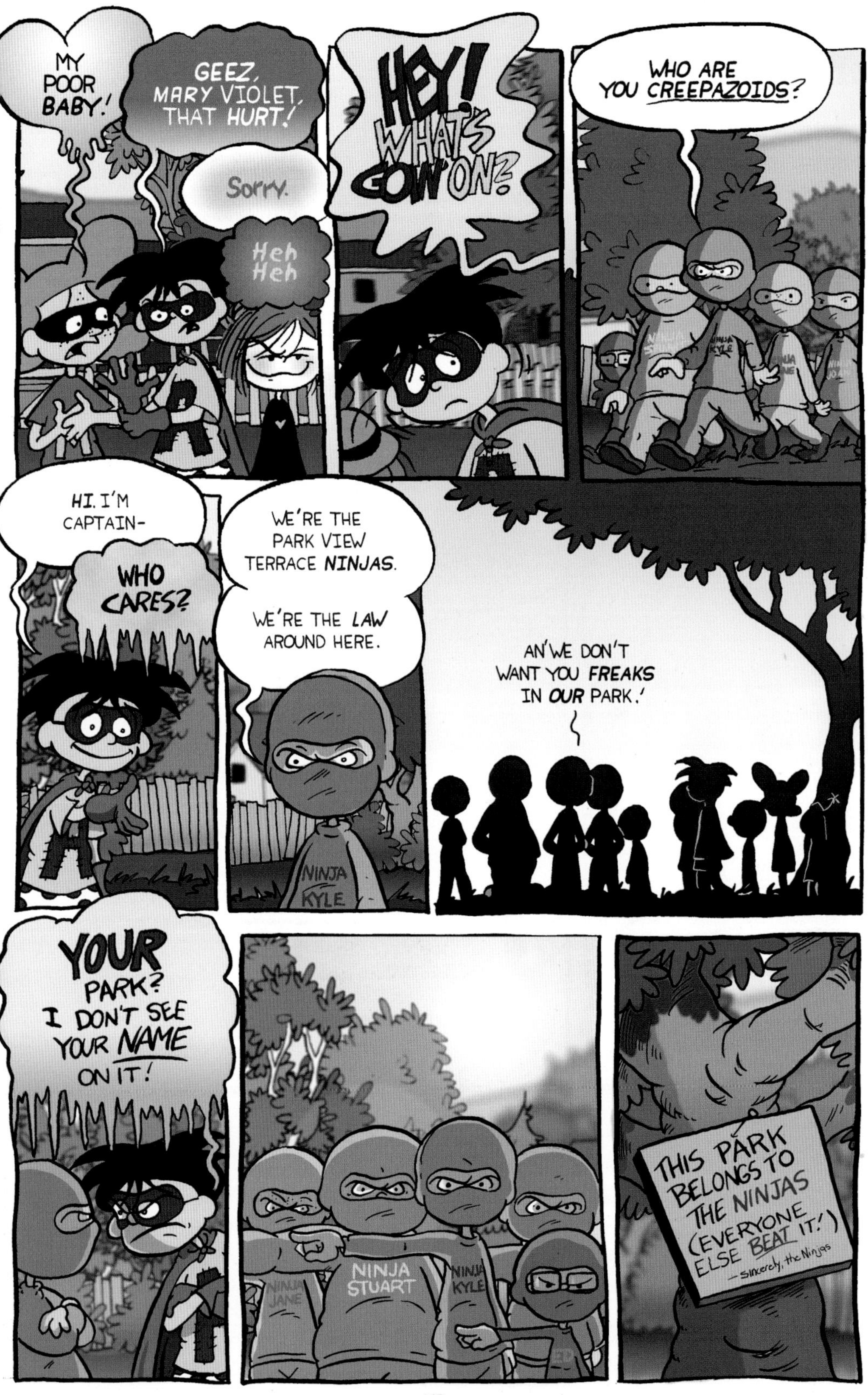
MY POOR BABY!
GEEZ, MARY VIOLET, THAT HURT!
Sorry.
Heh Heh
HEY! WHAT'S GOIN' ON?
WHO ARE YOU CREEPAZOIDS?
HI. I'M CAPTAIN-
WHO CARES?
WE'RE THE PARK VIEW TERRACE NINJAS.
WE'RE THE LAW AROUND HERE.
NINJA KYLE
AN' WE DON'T WANT YOU FREAKS IN OUR PARK.'
YOUR PARK? I DON'T SEE YOUR NAME ON IT!
NINJA JANE
NINJA STUART
NINJA KYLE
THIS PARK BELONGS TO THE NINJAS (EVERYONE ELSE BEAT IT!)
—sincerely, the Ninjas

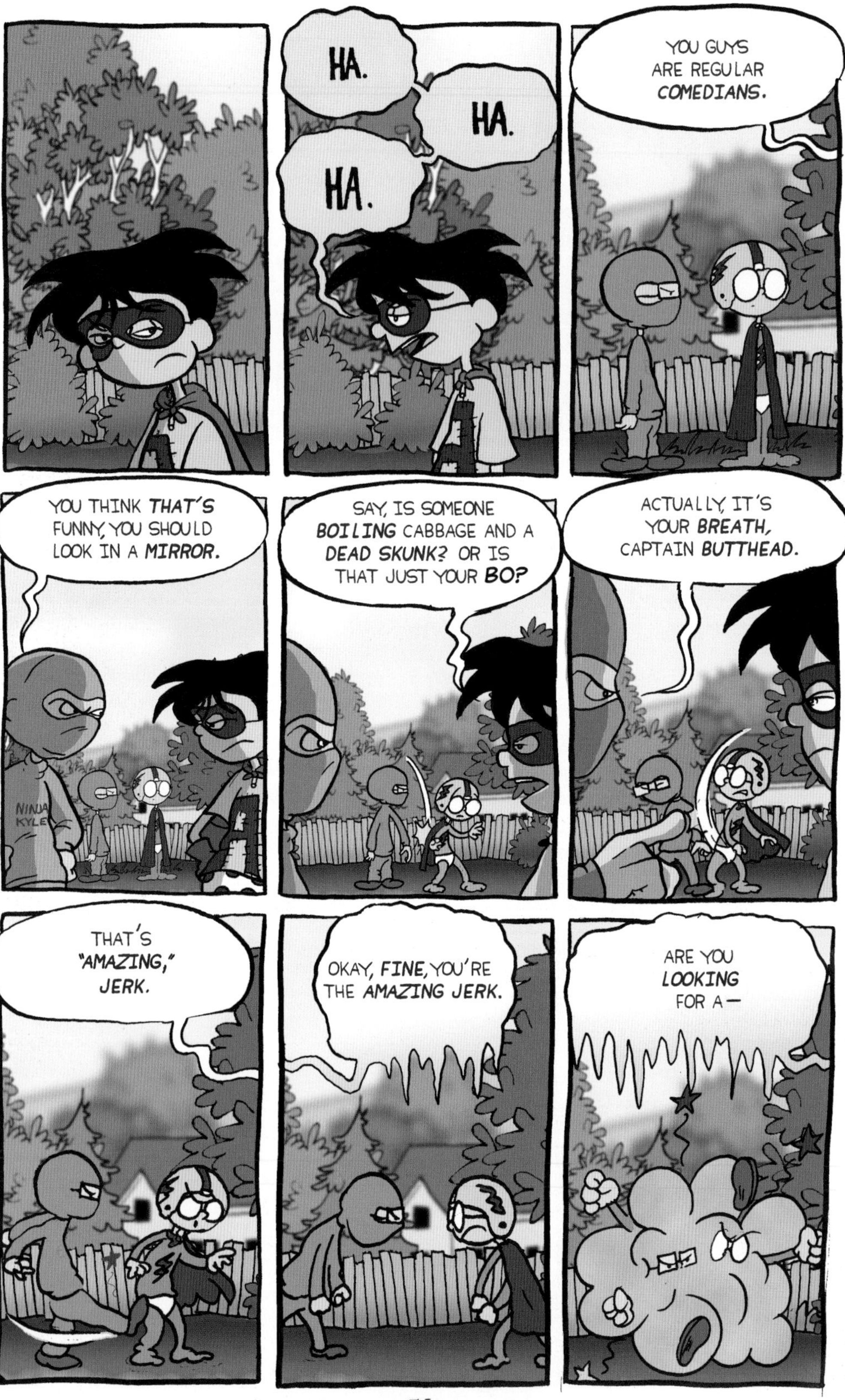
HA.
HA.
HA.
YOU GUYS ARE REGULAR COMEDIANS.
YOU THINK THAT'S FUNNY, YOU SHOULD LOOK IN A MIRROR.
NINJA KYLE
SAY, IS SOMEONE BOILING CABBAGE AND A DEAD SKUNK? OR IS THAT JUST YOUR BO?
ACTUALLY, IT'S YOUR BREATH, CAPTAIN BUTTHEAD.
THAT'S "AMAZING," JERK.
OKAY, FINE, YOU'RE THE AMAZING JERK.
ARE YOU LOOKING FOR A—

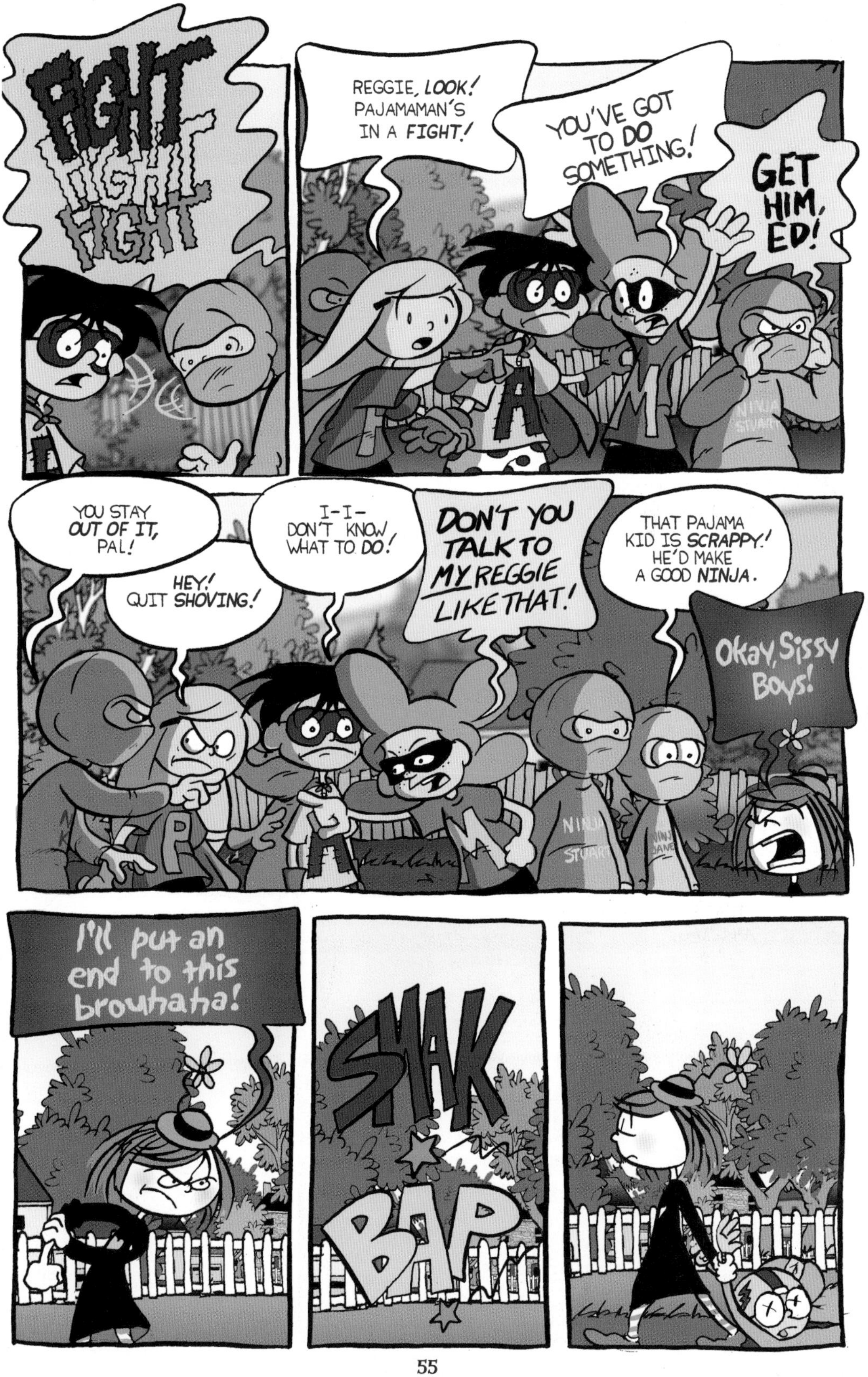
FIGHT FIGHT FIGHT
REGGIE, LOOK! PAJAMAMAN'S IN A FIGHT!
YOU'VE GOT TO DO SOMETHING!
GET HIM, ED!
NINJA STUART
YOU STAY OUT OF IT, PAL!
HEY! QUIT SHOVING!
I-I- DON'T KNOW WHAT TO DO!
DON'T YOU TALK TO MY REGGIE LIKE THAT!
THAT PAJAMA KID IS SCRAPPY! HE'D MAKE A GOOD NINJA.
Okay, Sissy Boys!
I'll put an end to this brouhaha!
SHAK
BAP

56

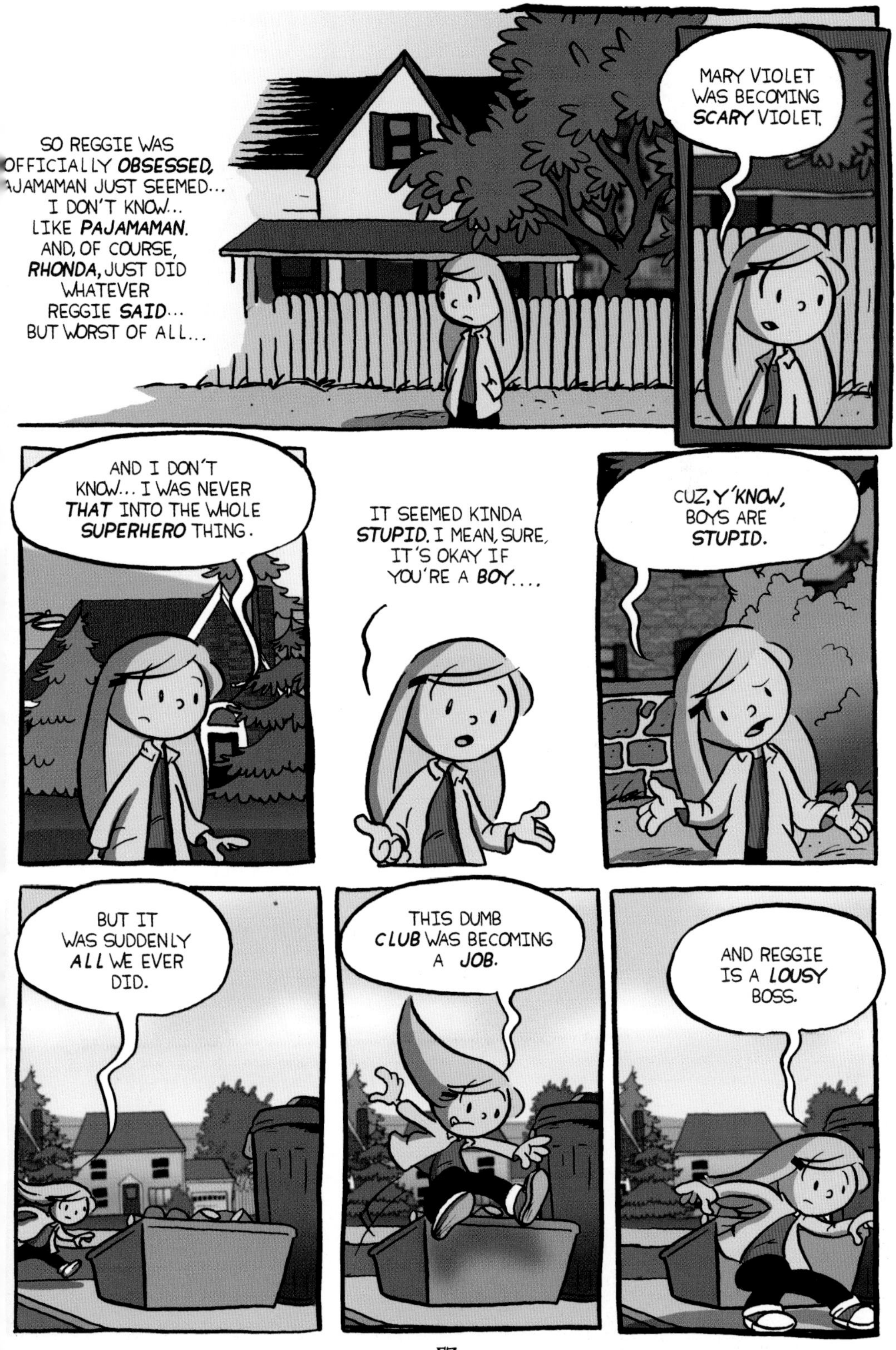
SO REGGIE WAS OFFICIALLY OBSESSED, PAJAMAMAN JUST SEEMED... I DON'T KNOW... LIKE PAJAMAMAN. AND, OF COURSE, RHONDA, JUST DID WHATEVER REGGIE SAID... BUT WORST OF ALL...
MARY VIOLET WAS BECOMING SCARY VIOLET.
AND I DON'T KNOW... I WAS NEVER THAT INTO THE WHOLE SUPERHERO THING.
IT SEEMED KINDA STUPID. I MEAN, SURE, IT'S OKAY IF YOU'RE A BOY....
CUZ, Y'KNOW, BOYS ARE STUPID.
BUT IT WAS SUDDENLY ALL WE EVER DID.
THIS DUMB CLUB WAS BECOMING A JOB.
AND REGGIE IS A LOUSY BOSS.

59

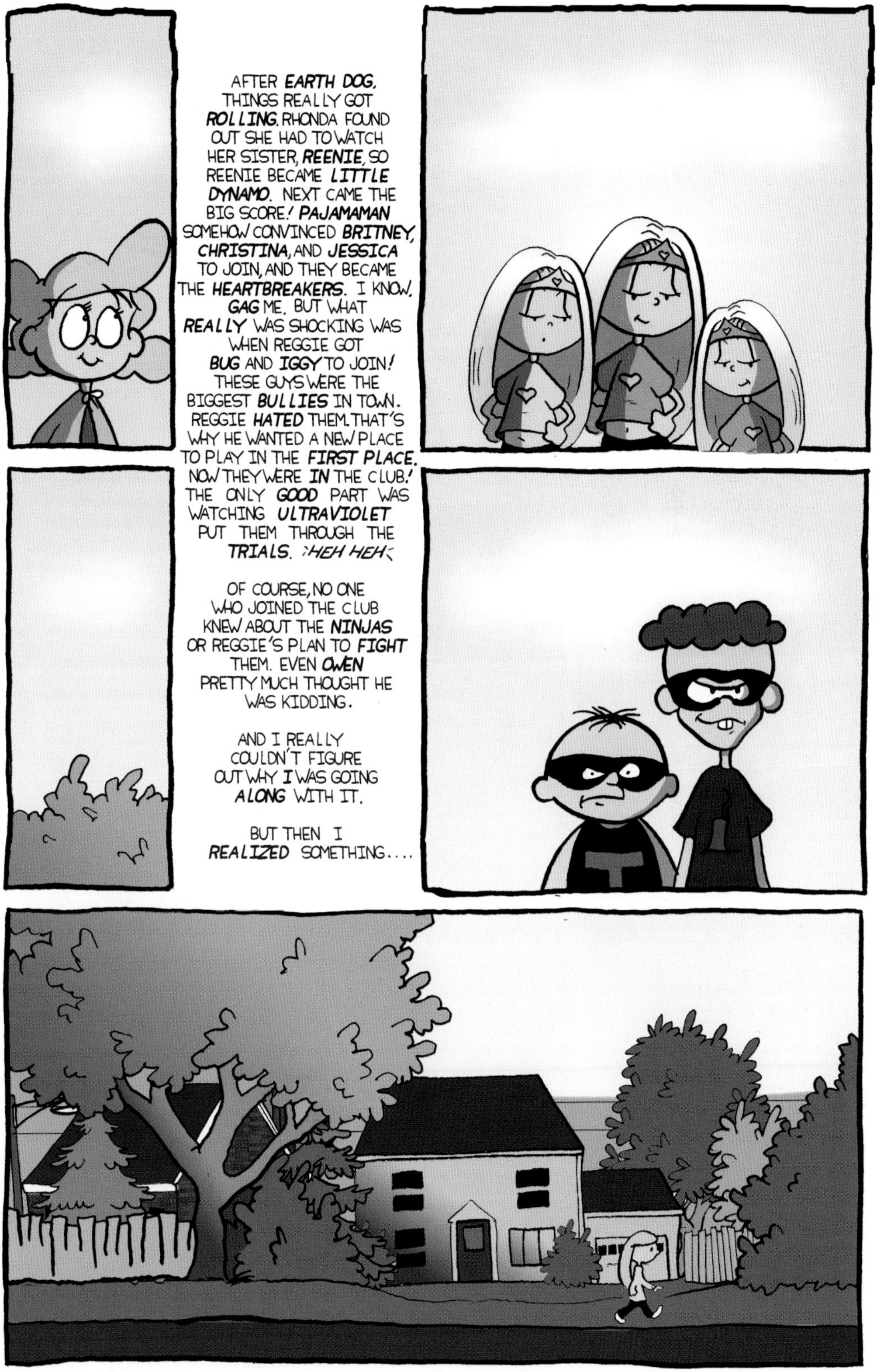
AFTER EARTH DOG, THINGS REALLY GOT ROLLING. RHONDA FOUND OUT SHE HAD TO WATCH HER SISTER, REENIE, SO REENIE BECAME LITTLE DYNAMO. NEXT CAME THE BIG SCORE! PAJAMAMAN SOMEHOW CONVINCED BRITNEY, CHRISTINA, AND JESSICA TO JOIN, AND THEY BECAME THE HEARTBREAKERS. I KNOW, GAG ME. BUT WHAT REALLY WAS SHOCKING WAS WHEN REGGIE GOT BUG AND IGGY TO JOIN! THESE GUYS WERE THE BIGGEST BULLIES IN TOWN. REGGIE HATED THEM. THAT'S WHY HE WANTED A NEW PLACE TO PLAY IN THE FIRST PLACE. NOW THEY WERE IN THE CLUB! THE ONLY GOOD PART WAS WATCHING ULTRAVIOLET PUT THEM THROUGH THE TRIALS. >HEH HEH<
OF COURSE, NO ONE WHO JOINED THE CLUB KNEW ABOUT THE NINJAS OR REGGIE'S PLAN TO FIGHT THEM. EVEN OWEN PRETTY MUCH THOUGHT HE WAS KIDDING.
AND I REALLY COULDN'T FIGURE OUT WHY I WAS GOING ALONG WITH IT.
BUT THEN I REALIZED SOMETHING....

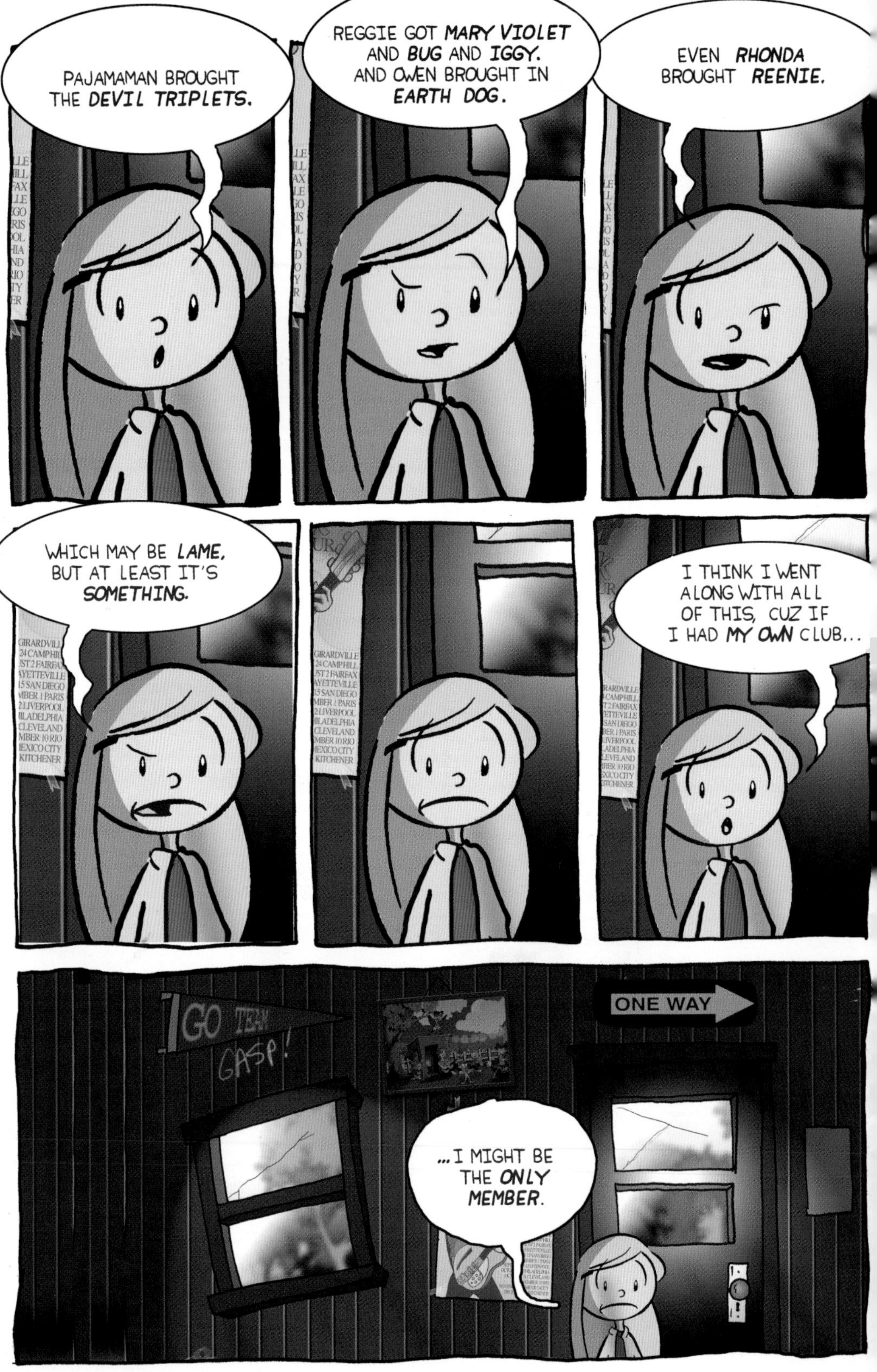
PAJAMAMAN BROUGHT THE DEVIL TRIPLETS.
REGGIE GOT MARY VIOLET AND BUG AND IGGY. AND OWEN BROUGHT IN EARTH DOG.
EVEN RHONDA BROUGHT REENIE.
WHICH MAY BE LAME, BUT AT LEAST IT'S SOMETHING.
I THINK I WENT ALONG WITH ALL OF THIS, CUZ IF I HAD MY OWN CLUB...
GO TEAM
GASP!
ONE WAY
...I MIGHT BE THE ONLY MEMBER.

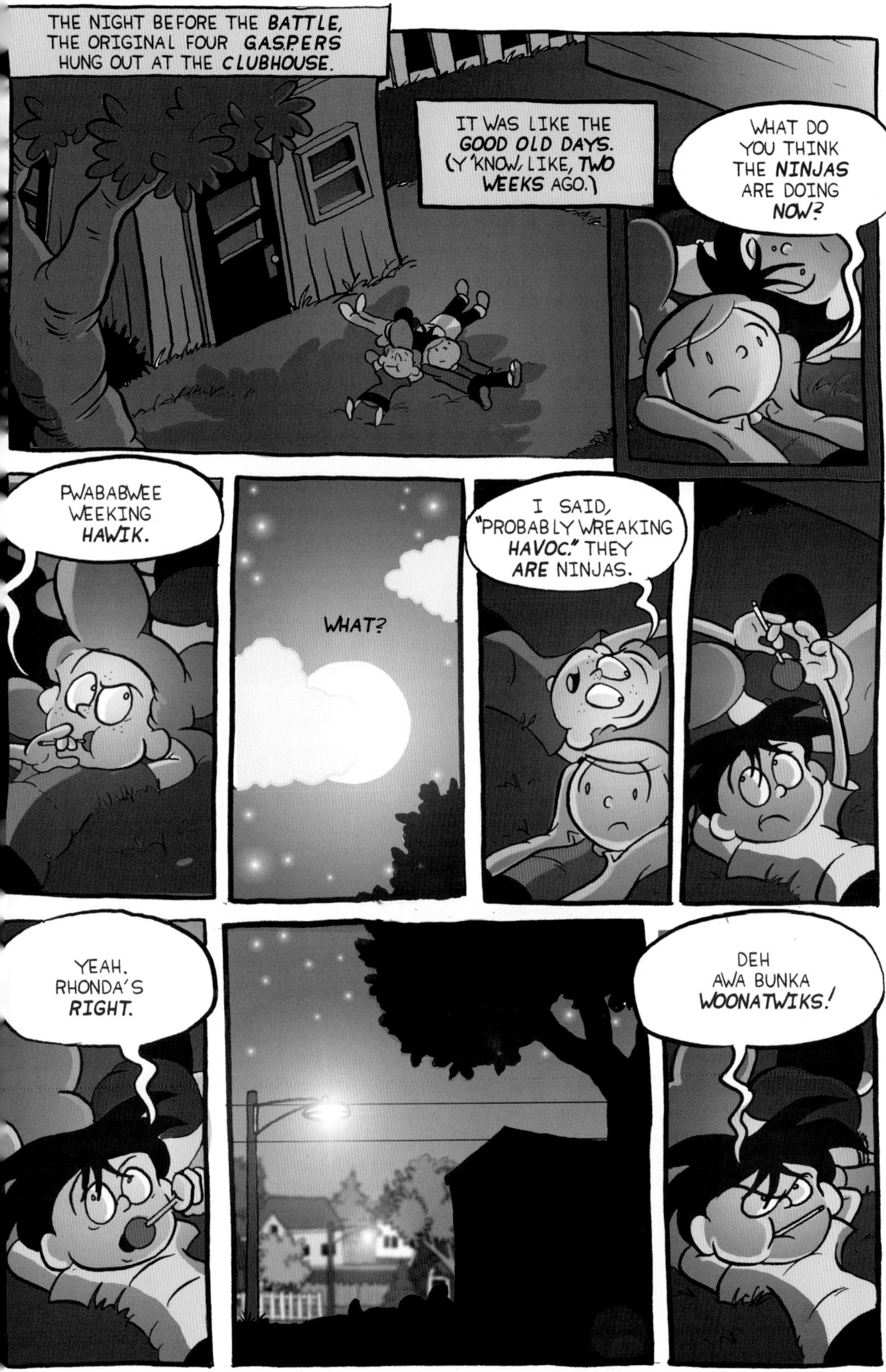
THE NIGHT BEFORE THE BATTLE, THE ORIGINAL FOUR GAS.P.ERS HUNG OUT AT THE CLUBHOUSE.
IT WAS LIKE THE GOOD OLD DAYS. (Y'KNOW, LIKE, TWO WEEKS AGO.)
WHAT DO YOU THINK THE NINJAS ARE DOING NOW?
PWABABWEE WEEKING HAWIK.
WHAT?
I SAID, "PROBABLY WREAKING HAVOC." THEY ARE NINJAS.
YEAH. RHONDA'S RIGHT.
DEH AWA BUNKA WOONATWIKS!

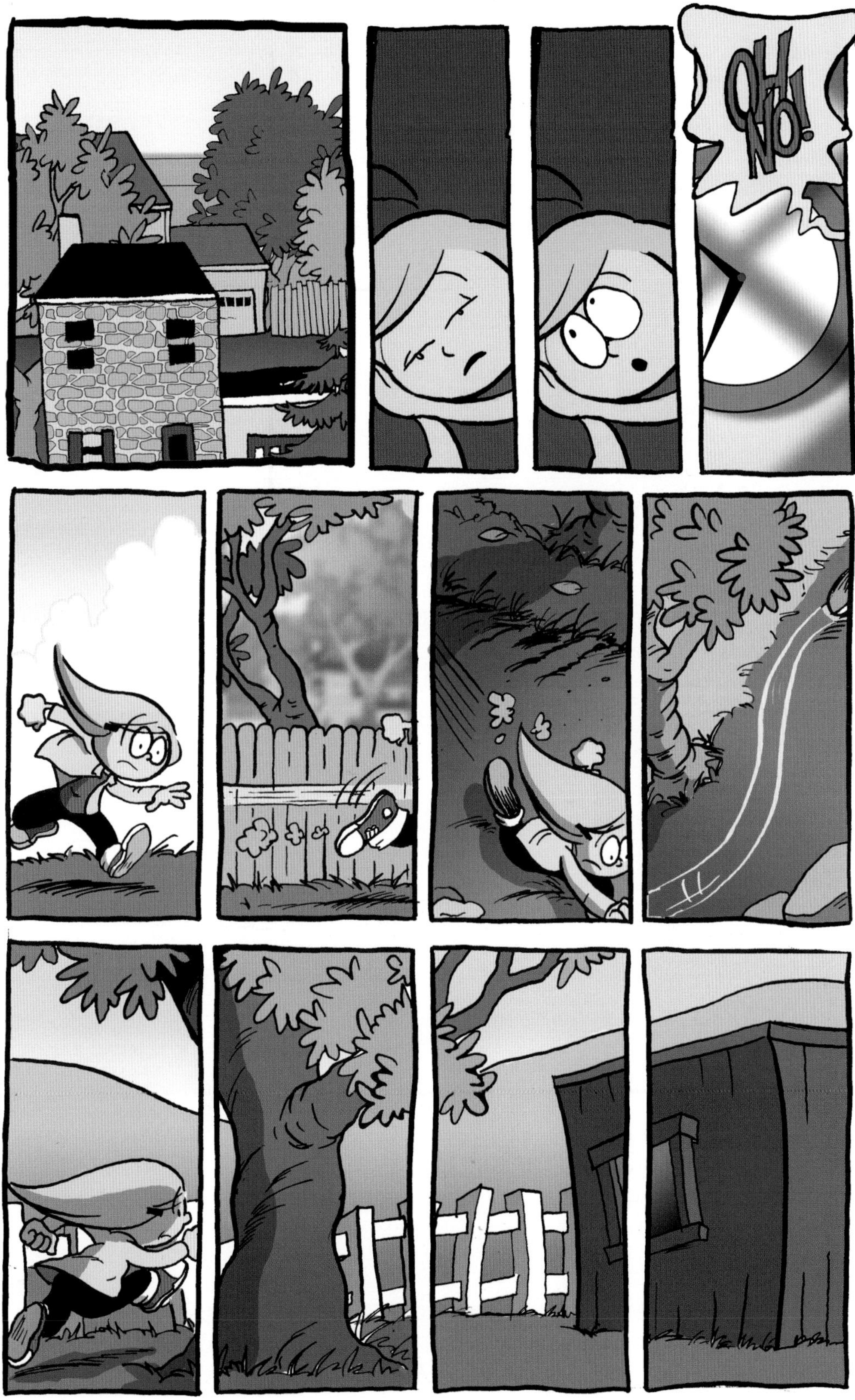
OH NO!

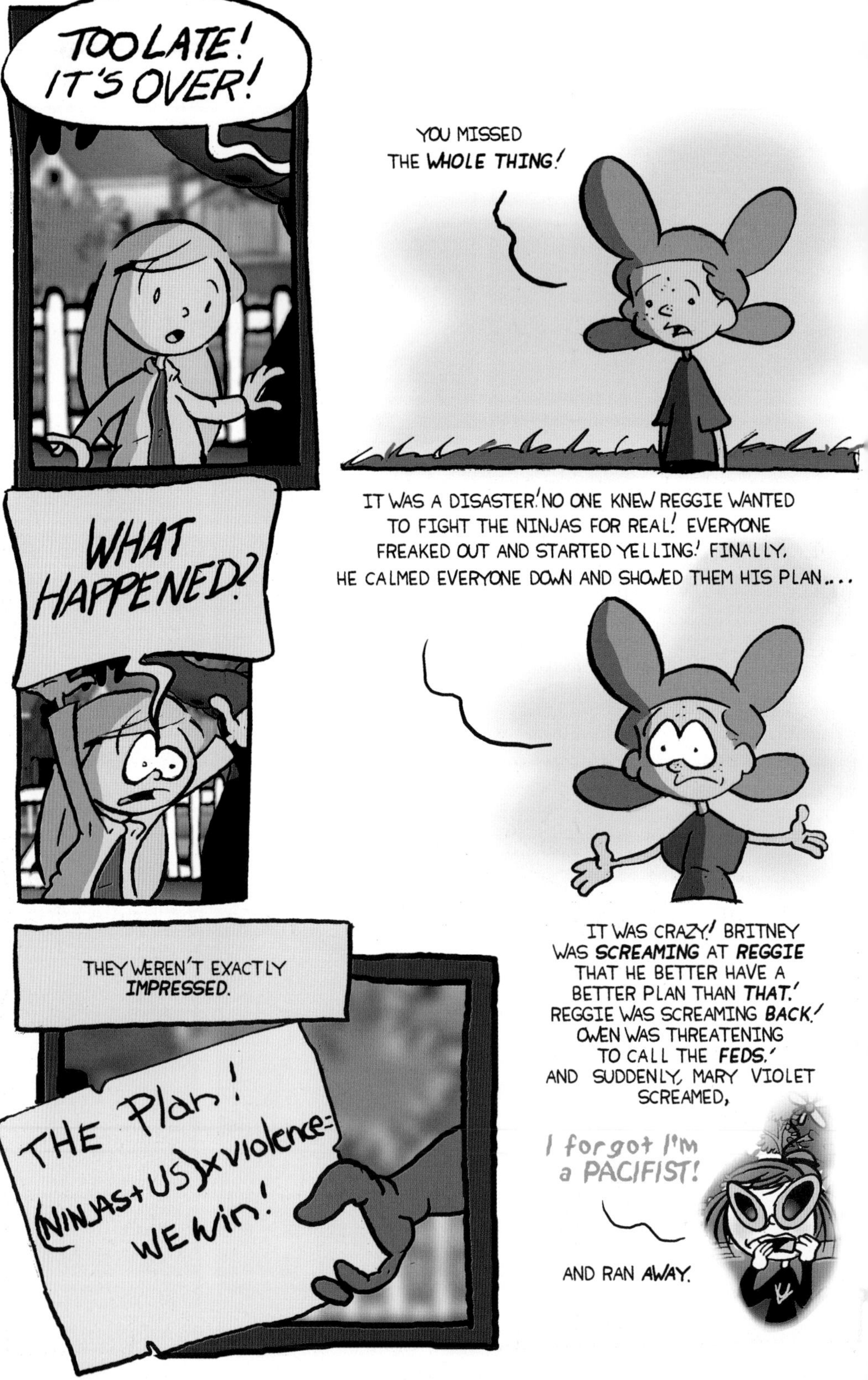
TOO LATE! IT'S OVER!
YOU MISSED THE WHOLE THING!
WHAT HAPPENED?
IT WAS A DISASTER! NO ONE KNEW REGGIE WANTED TO FIGHT THE NINJAS FOR REAL! EVERYONE FREAKED OUT AND STARTED YELLING! FINALLY, HE CALMED EVERYONE DOWN AND SHOWED THEM HIS PLAN....
THEY WEREN'T EXACTLY IMPRESSED.
THE Plan!
(NINJAS+US)x violence=
WE win!
IT WAS CRAZY! BRITNEY WAS SCREAMING AT REGGIE THAT HE BETTER HAVE A BETTER PLAN THAN THAT! REGGIE WAS SCREAMING BACK! OWEN WAS THREATENING TO CALL THE FEDS! AND SUDDENLY, MARY VIOLET SCREAMED,
I forgot I'm a PACIFIST!
AND RAN AWAY.

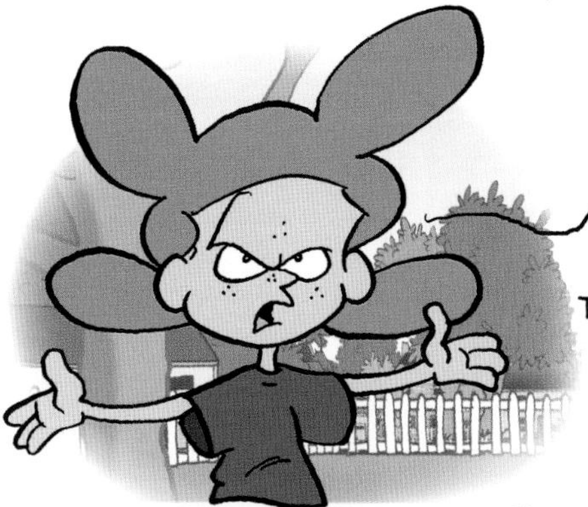

NO ONE KNEW WHAT WAS GOING ON, ***EVERYONE*** WAS FIGHTING!

THE WHOLE CLUB WAS FALLING ***APART***!

THEN REGGIE CLIMBED UP TO THE ***ROOF*** OF THE CLUBHOUSE AND STARTED TO GIVE THIS ***SPEECH***....

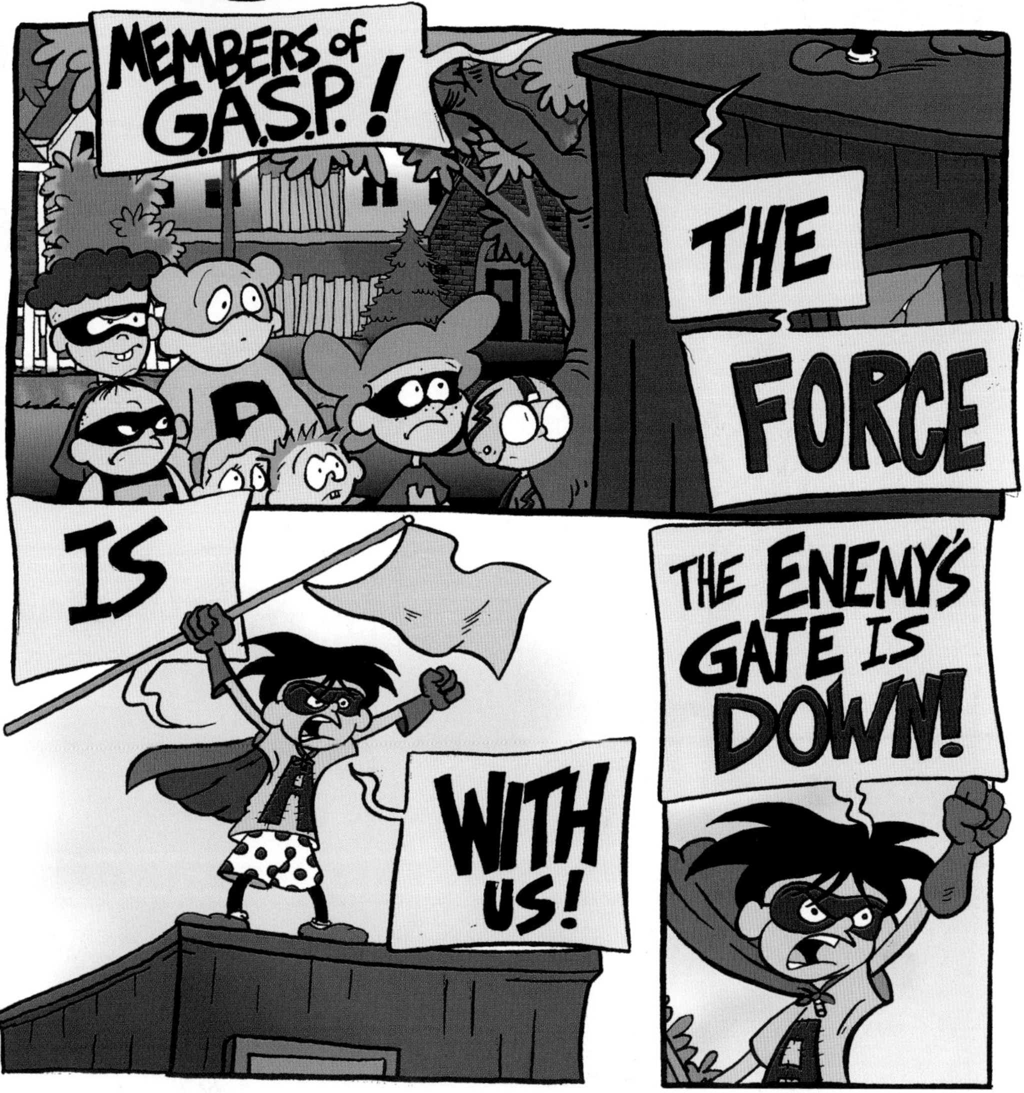

MEMBERS of G.A.S.P.!
THE
FORCE
IS
WITH US!
THE ENEMY'S GATE IS DOWN!

BUT A SHADOW RISES IN THE **EAST!**

WHICH SEEKS TO BE THE ULTIMATE POWER IN THE UNIVERSE!

BUT BY THE **POWER** OF G.A.S.P., WE HAVE THE **POWER!**

YET WITH **GREAT POWER** COMES **GREAT RESPONSIBILITY!** AND THOUGH NINJAS ARE A **SUPERSTITIOUS** AND **COWARDLY LOT**, WE MUST BE **DAREDEVILS**, THE MEN WITHOUT **FEAR!** WHO **BOLDLY GO** WHERE **NO ONE** HAS GONE **BEFORE!** AND WHEN WE GO, WE GO IN SEARCH OF **TRUTH, JUSTICE**, AND THE **AMERICAN WAY!** FOR THE NINJAS MUST <u>KNOW THE TRUTH!</u> FOR THE **TRUTH** IS <u>**OUT THERE!**</u>

MEMBERS OF G.A.S.P, *TODAY* IS *OUR* DAY.

VICTORY IS OUR DESTINY.

AND SO I SAY TO YOU...

WIZZ

THOK!

CHILDREN!

G.A.S.P.

70

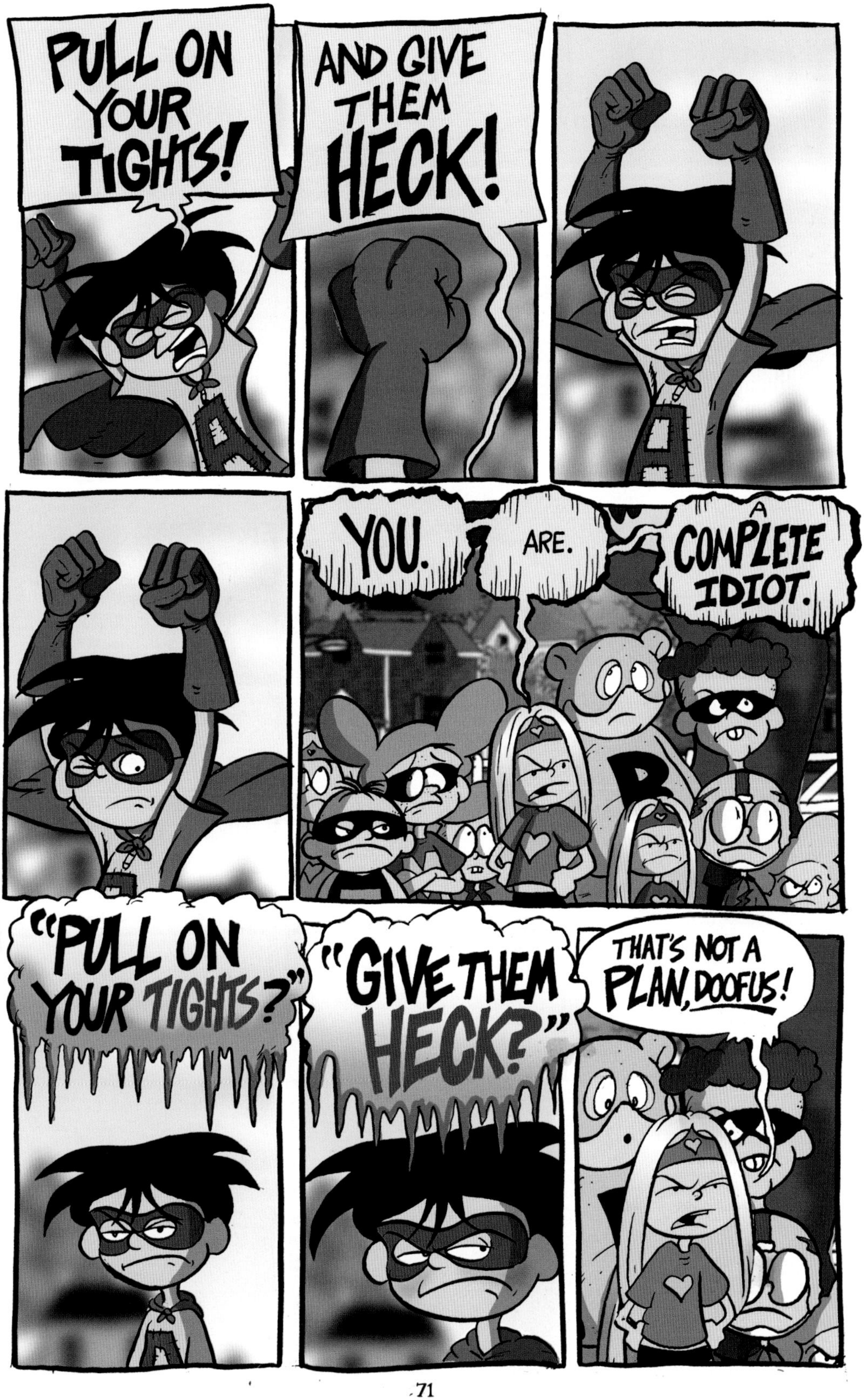
PULL ON YOUR TIGHTS!
AND GIVE THEM HECK!
YOU.
ARE.
A COMPLETE IDIOT.
"PULL ON YOUR TIGHTS?"
"GIVE THEM HECK?"
THAT'S NOT A PLAN, DOOFUS!

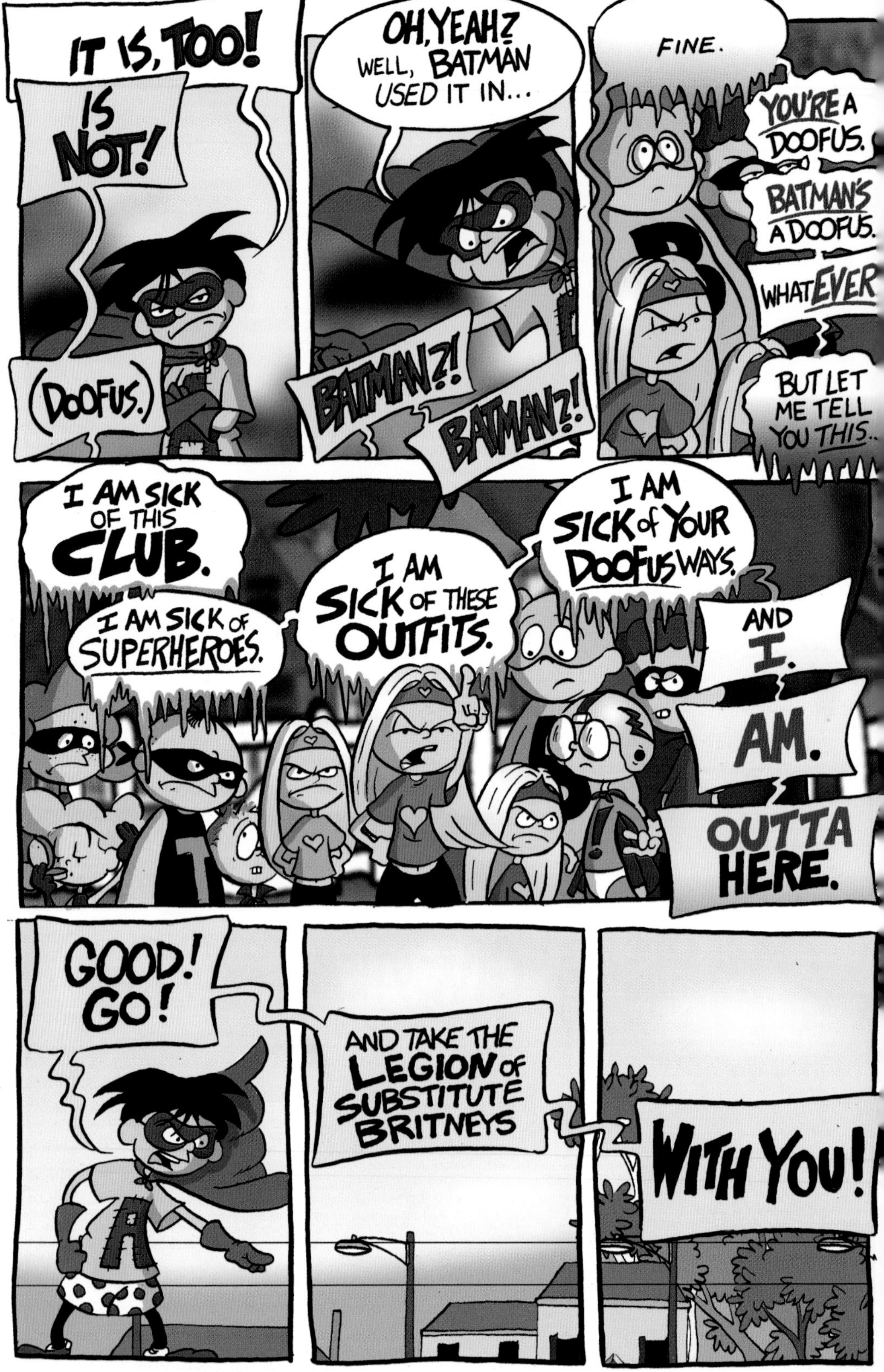
IT IS, TOO!
IS NOT!
(DOOFUS.)
OH, YEAH? WELL, BATMAN USED IT IN...
BATMAN?!
BATMAN?!
FINE.
YOU'RE A DOOFUS.
BATMAN'S A DOOFUS.
WHATEVER
BUT LET ME TELL YOU THIS...
I AM SICK OF THIS CLUB.
I AM SICK OF SUPERHEROES.
I AM SICK OF THESE OUTFITS.
I AM SICK OF YOUR DOOFUS WAYS.
AND I.
AM.
OUTTA HERE.
GOOD! GO!
AND TAKE THE LEGION OF SUBSTITUTE BRITNEYS
WITH YOU!

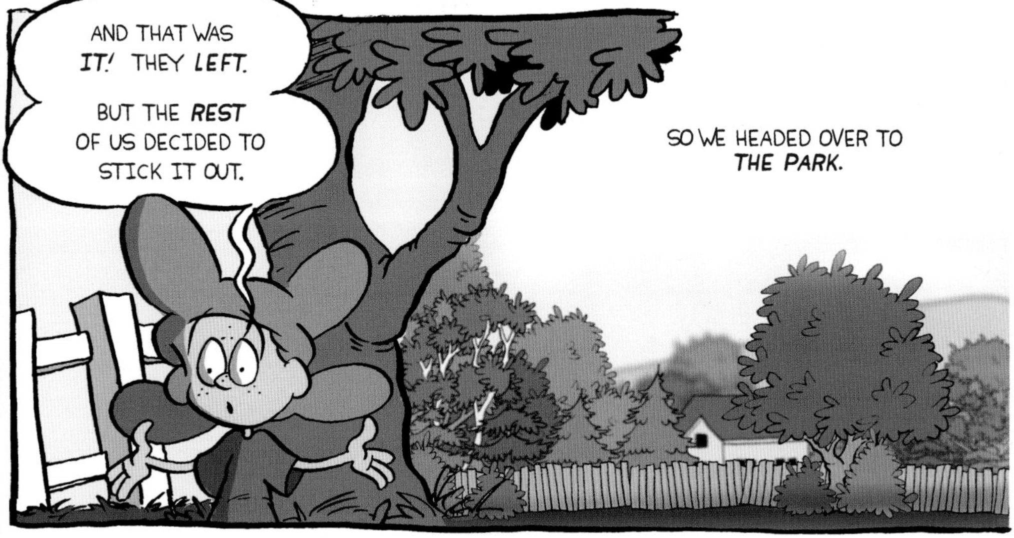
AND THAT WAS IT! THEY LEFT.
BUT THE REST OF US DECIDED TO STICK IT OUT.
SO WE HEADED OVER TO THE PARK.

THERE WAS **NO SIGN** OF THE NINJAS WHEN WE GOT THERE, SO WE DECIDED TO TRY AN **AMBUSH.**

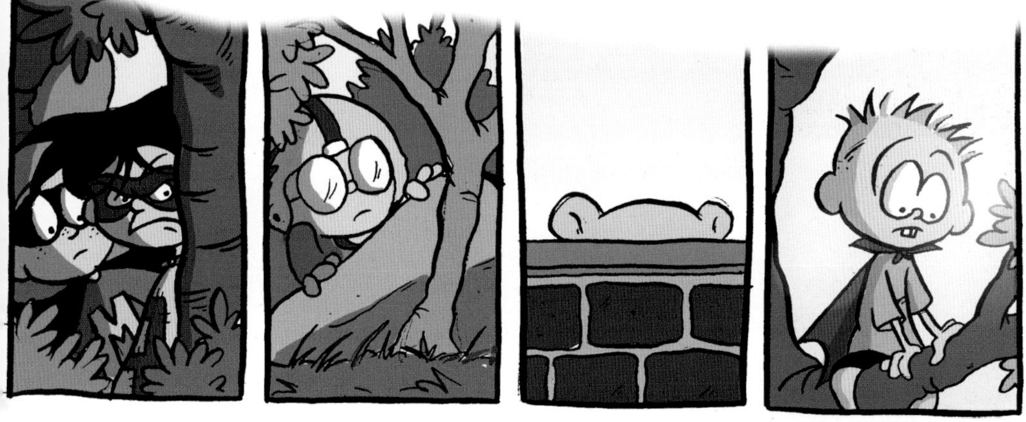

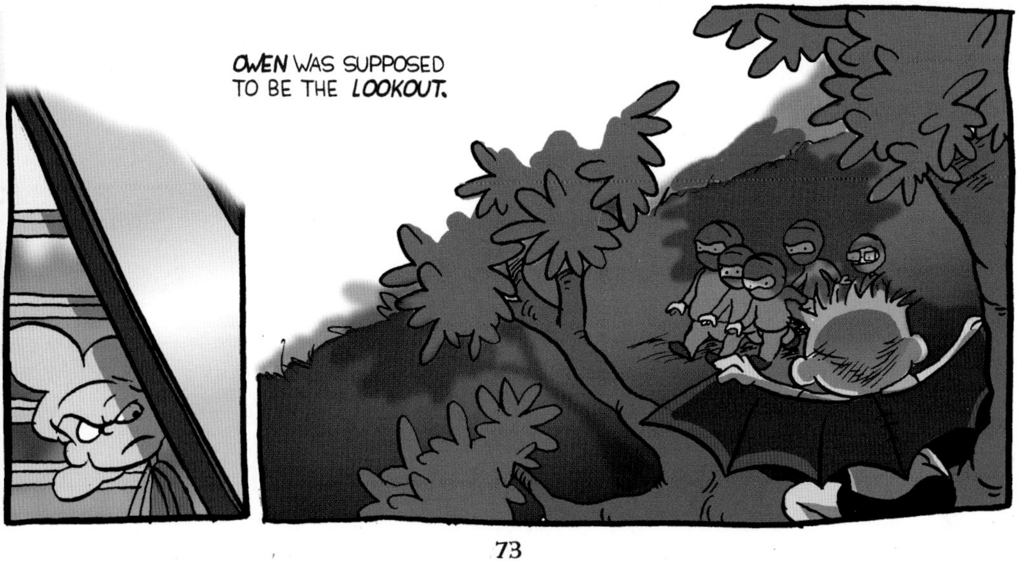
OWEN WAS SUPPOSED TO BE THE LOOKOUT.

NO ONE'S REALLY SURE WHAT **HAPPENED.**

MAYBE OWEN DECIDED TO **JUMP.**

MAYBE HE **REALLY THOUGHT** HE COULD **FLY.**

OR MAYBE HE JUST **FELL.**

ALL WE KNOW IS...

...ONE MINUTE HE WAS **IN** THE TREE...

...AND THE **NEXT**...

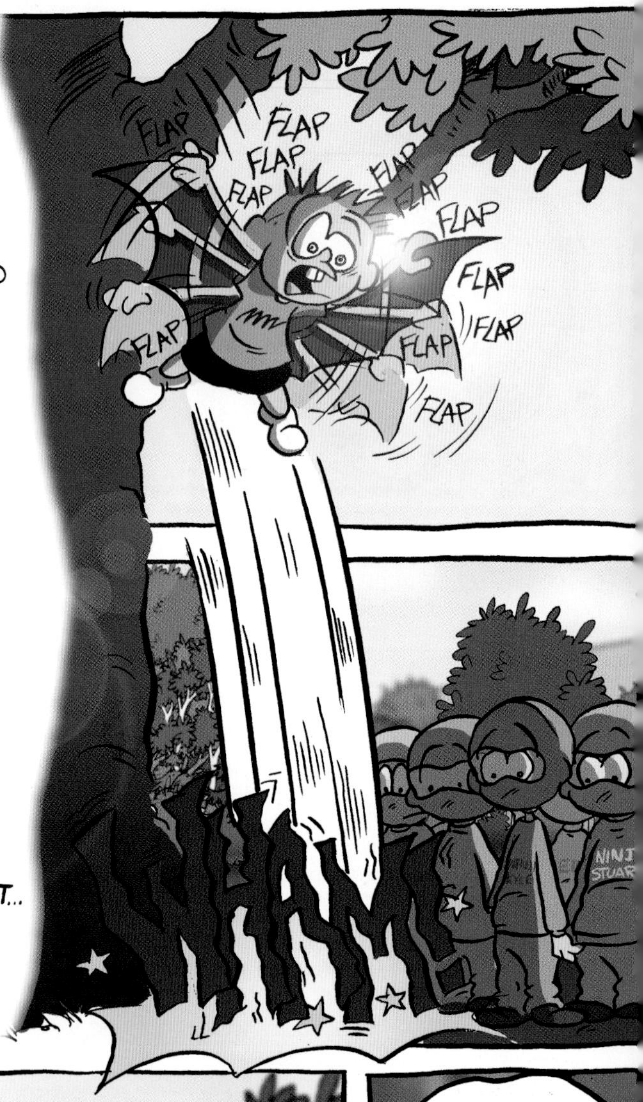
FLAP
FLAP
FLAP
FLAP
FLAP
FLAP
FLAP
FLAP
FLAP
FLAP
FLAP
FLAP
WHAM

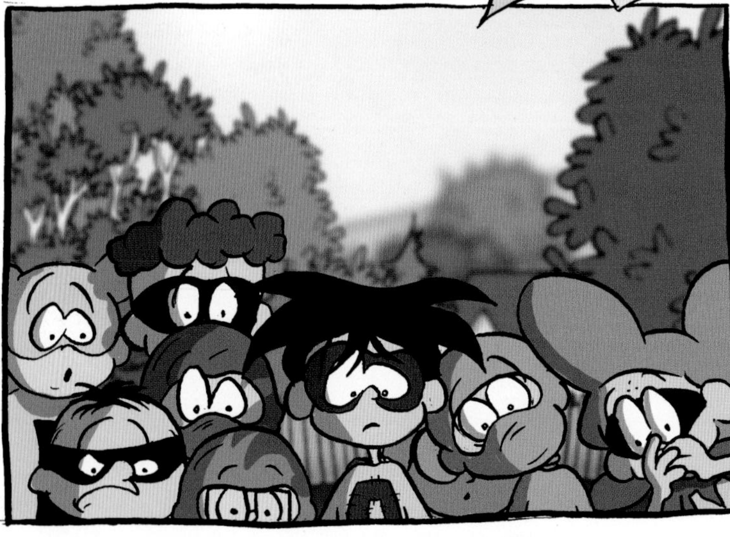

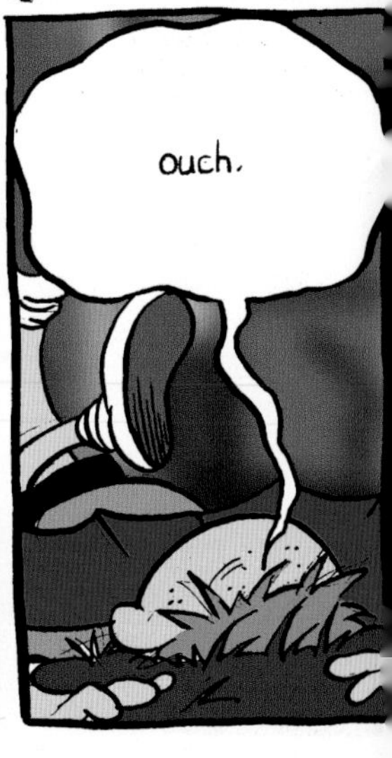
ouch.

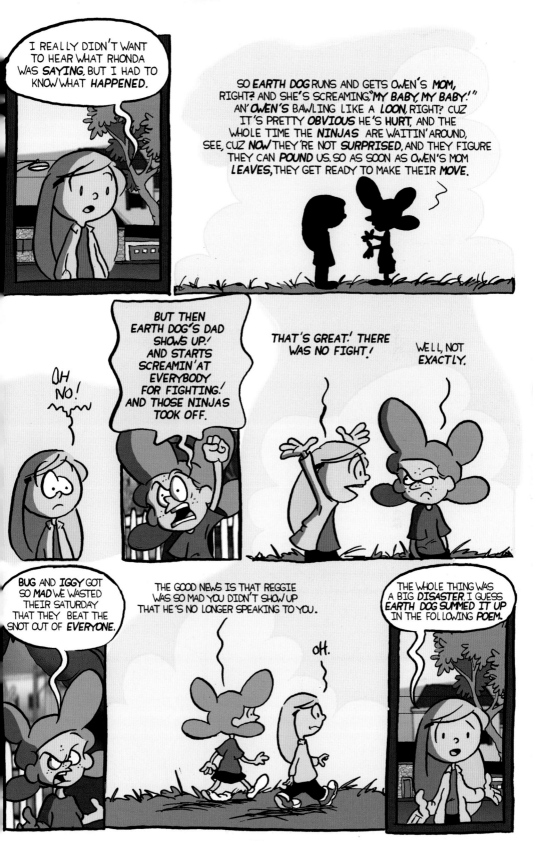

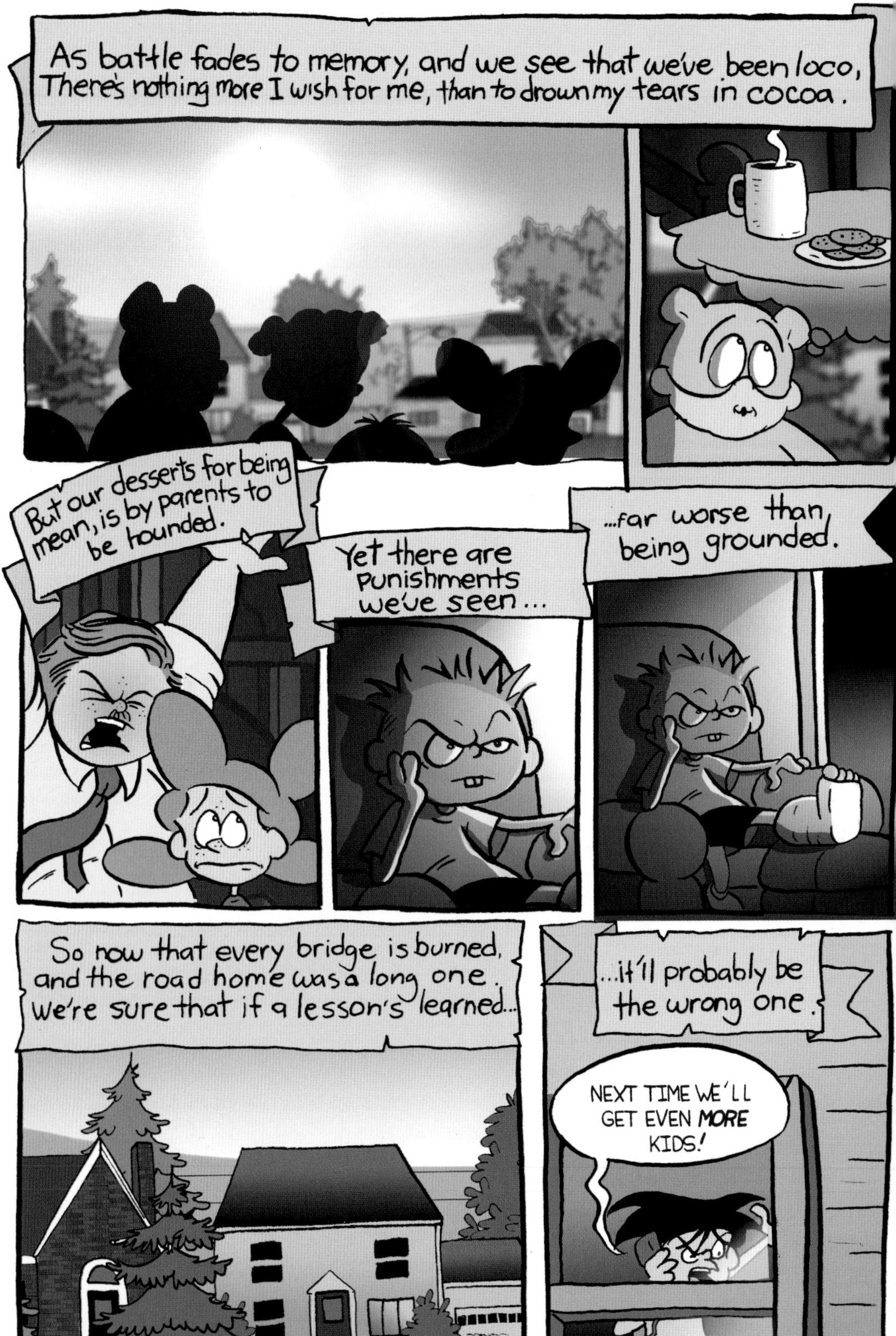
As battle fades to memory, and we see that we've been loco,
There's nothing more I wish for me, than to drown my tears in cocoa.
But our desserts for being mean, is by parents to be hounded.
Yet there are punishments we've seen...
...far worse than being grounded.
So now that every bridge is burned, and the road home was a long one.
We're sure that if a lesson's learned...
...it'll probably be the wrong one.
NEXT TIME WE'LL GET EVEN MORE KIDS!

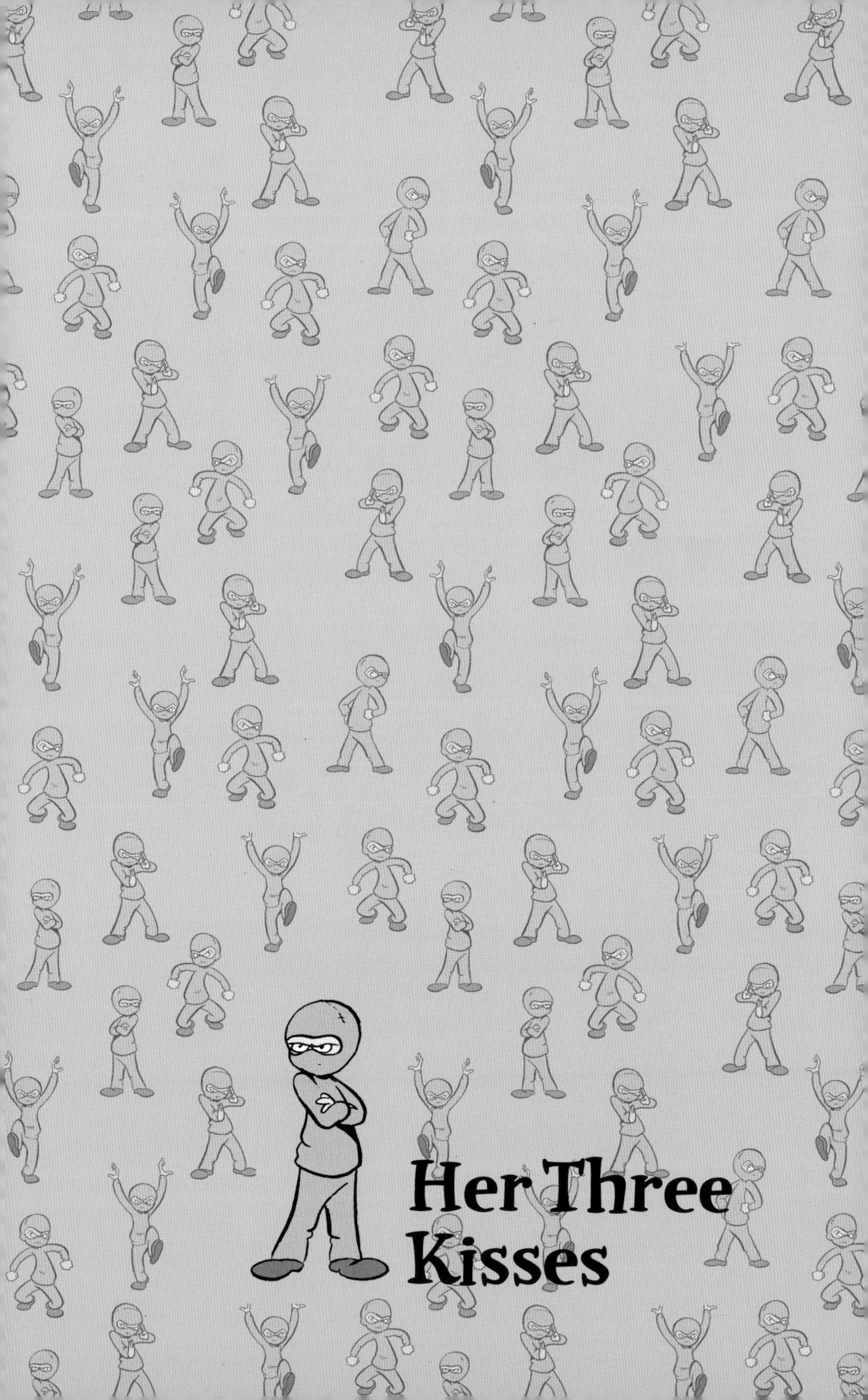

Her Three Kisses

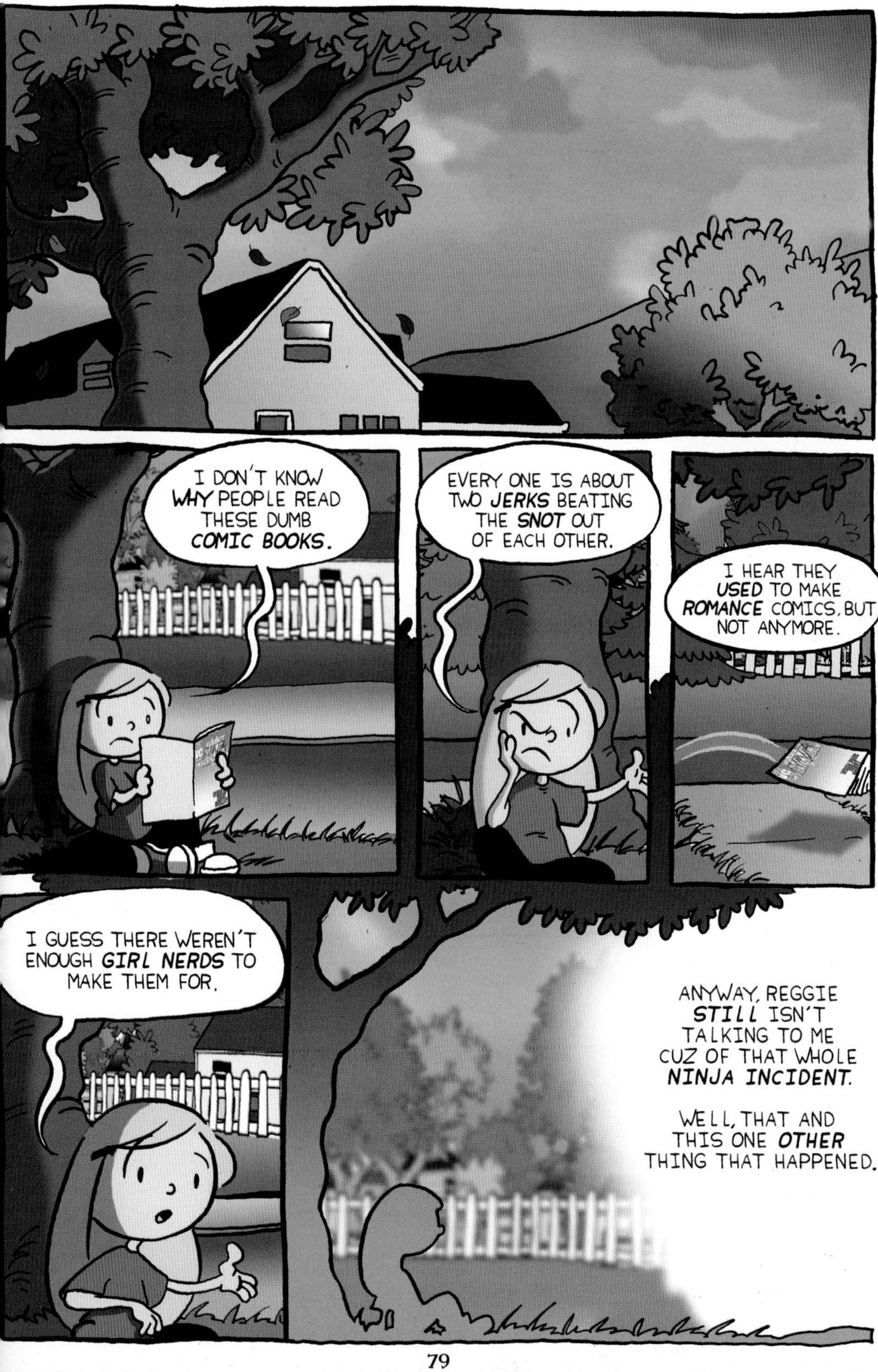
I DON'T KNOW WHY PEOPLE READ THESE DUMB COMIC BOOKS.
EVERY ONE IS ABOUT TWO JERKS BEATING THE SNOT OUT OF EACH OTHER.
I HEAR THEY USED TO MAKE ROMANCE COMICS, BUT NOT ANYMORE.
I GUESS THERE WEREN'T ENOUGH GIRL NERDS TO MAKE THEM FOR.
ANYWAY, REGGIE STILL ISN'T TALKING TO ME CUZ OF THAT WHOLE NINJA INCIDENT.
WELL, THAT AND THIS ONE OTHER THING THAT HAPPENED.

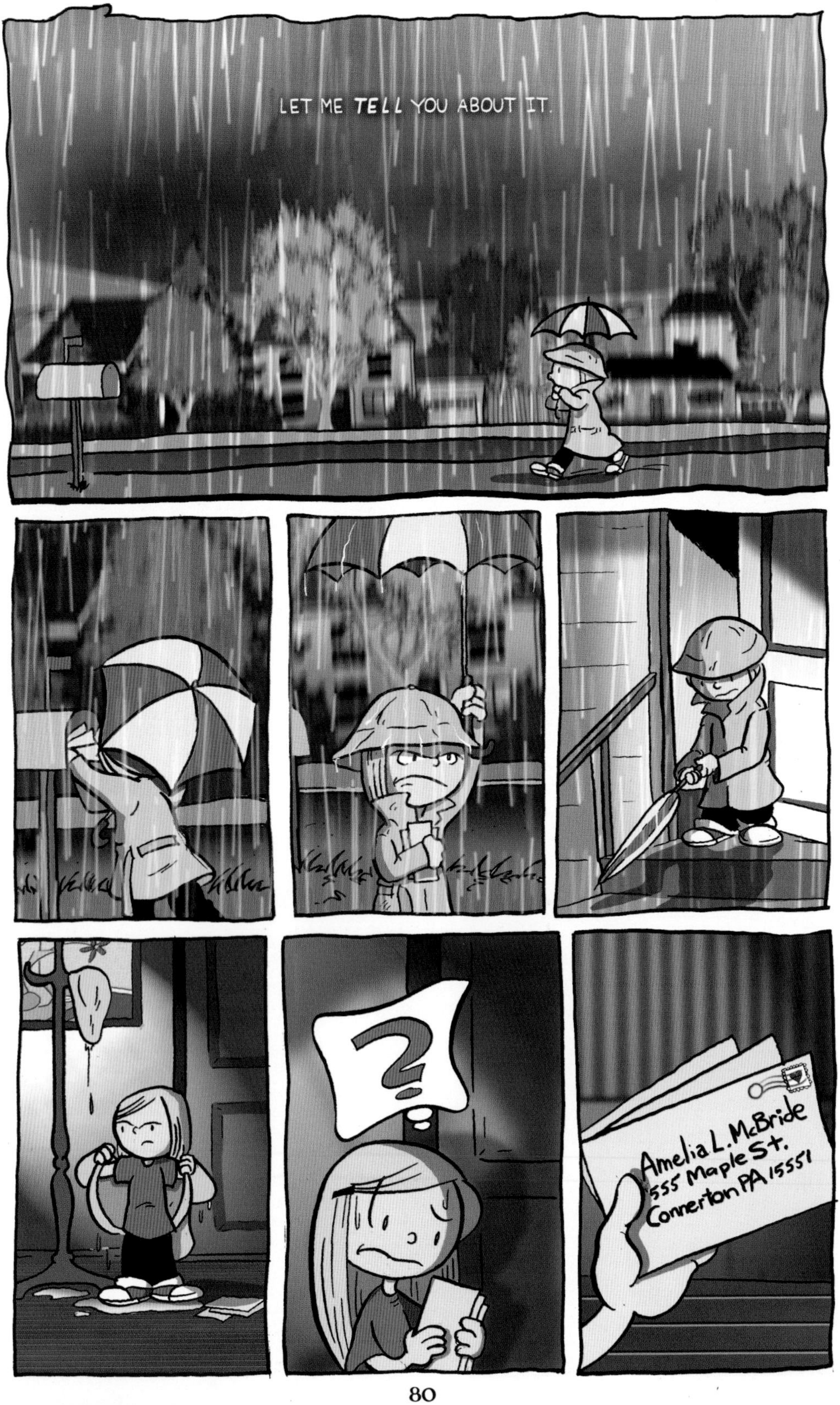
LET ME TELL YOU ABOUT IT.
?
Amelia L. McBride
555 Maple St.
Connerton PA 15551

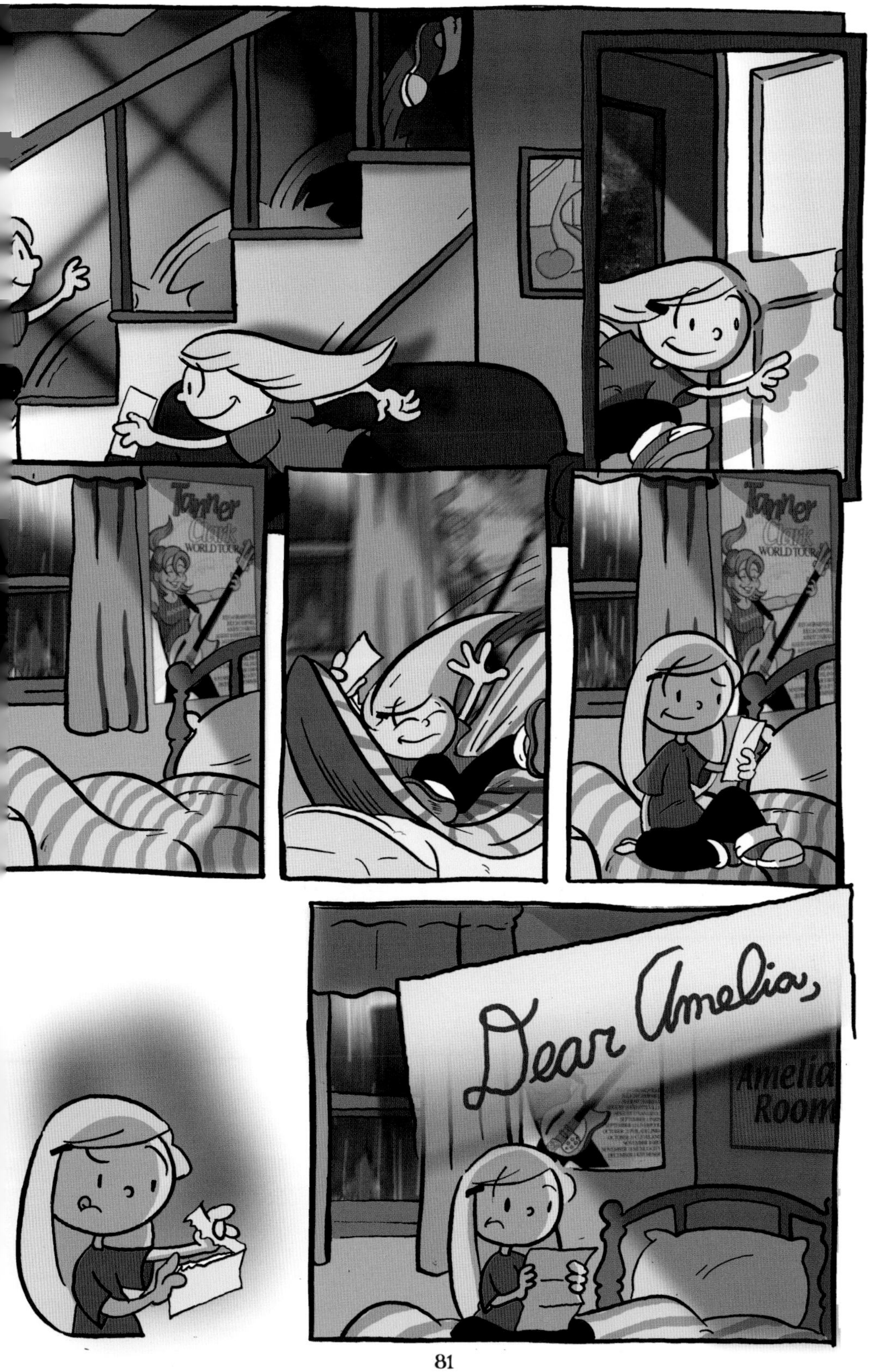
Tanner
Clark
WORLD TOUR
Tanner
Clark
WORLD TOUR
Dear Amelia,
Amelia
Room

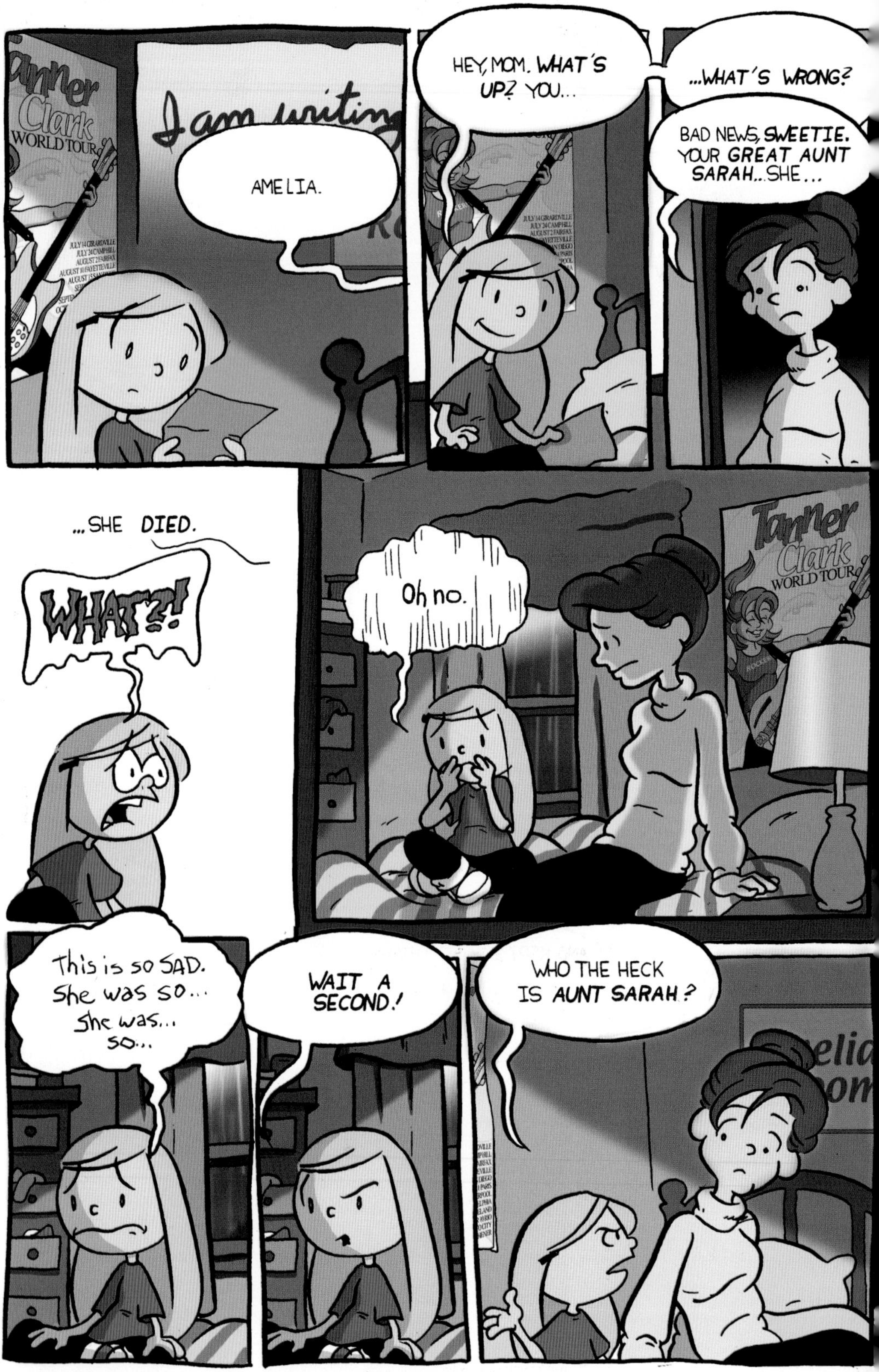
Tanner Clark WORLD TOUR
I am writing
AMELIA.
HEY, MOM. WHAT'S UP? YOU...
...WHAT'S WRONG?
BAD NEWS, SWEETIE. YOUR GREAT AUNT SARAH...SHE...
...SHE DIED.
WHAT?!
Oh no.
Tanner Clark WORLD TOUR
This is so SAD. She was so... She was... so...
WAIT A SECOND!
WHO THE HECK IS AUNT SARAH?

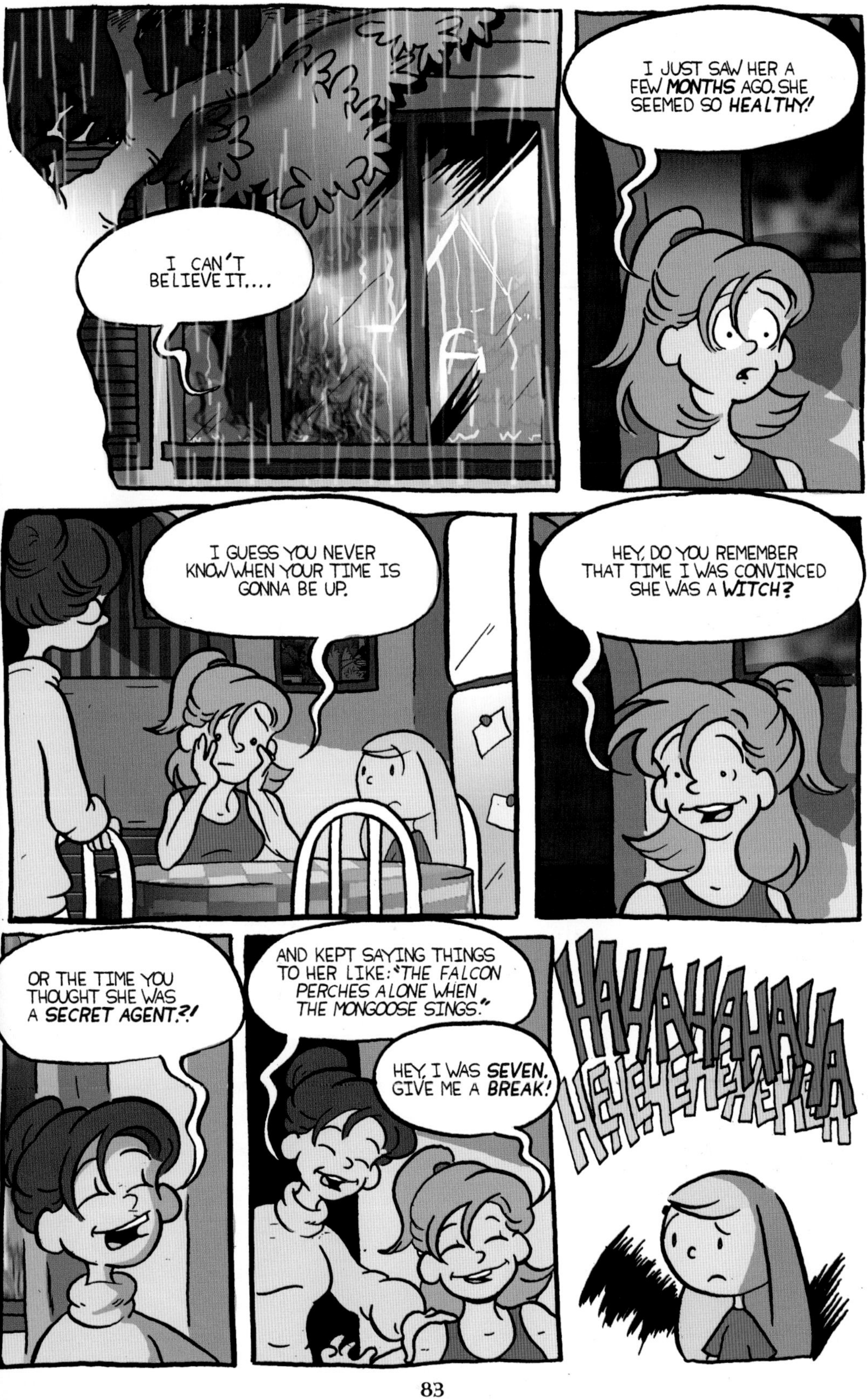
I CAN'T BELIEVE IT....
I JUST SAW HER A FEW **MONTHS** AGO. SHE SEEMED SO **HEALTHY!**
I GUESS YOU NEVER KNOW WHEN YOUR TIME IS GONNA BE UP.
HEY, DO YOU REMEMBER THAT TIME I WAS CONVINCED SHE WAS A **WITCH?**
OR THE TIME YOU THOUGHT SHE WAS A **SECRET AGENT?!**
AND KEPT SAYING THINGS TO HER LIKE: "*THE FALCON PERCHES ALONE WHEN THE MONGOOSE SINGS.*"
HEY, I WAS **SEVEN.** GIVE ME A **BREAK!**
HAHAHAHAHAHA
HEHEHEHEHEHEHEHA

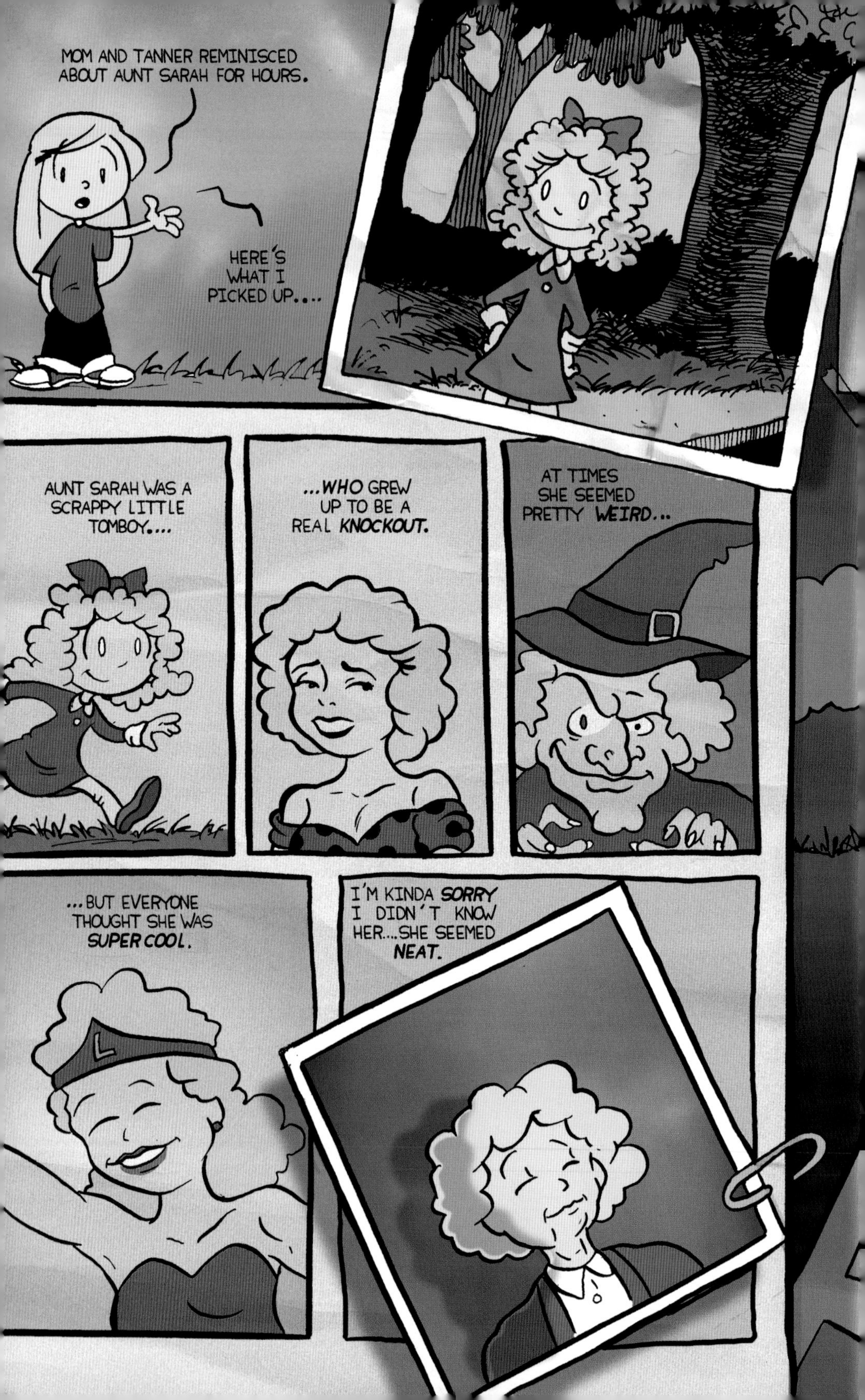
MOM AND TANNER REMINISCED ABOUT AUNT SARAH FOR HOURS.
HERE'S WHAT I PICKED UP....
AUNT SARAH WAS A SCRAPPY LITTLE TOMBOY....
...WHO GREW UP TO BE A REAL KNOCKOUT.
AT TIMES SHE SEEMED PRETTY WEIRD...
...BUT EVERYONE THOUGHT SHE WAS SUPER COOL.
I'M KINDA SORRY I DIDN'T KNOW HER....SHE SEEMED NEAT.

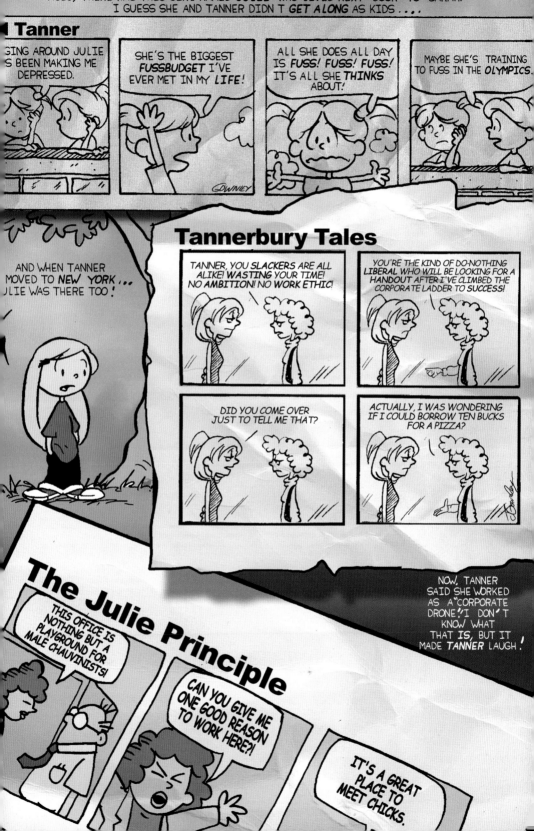

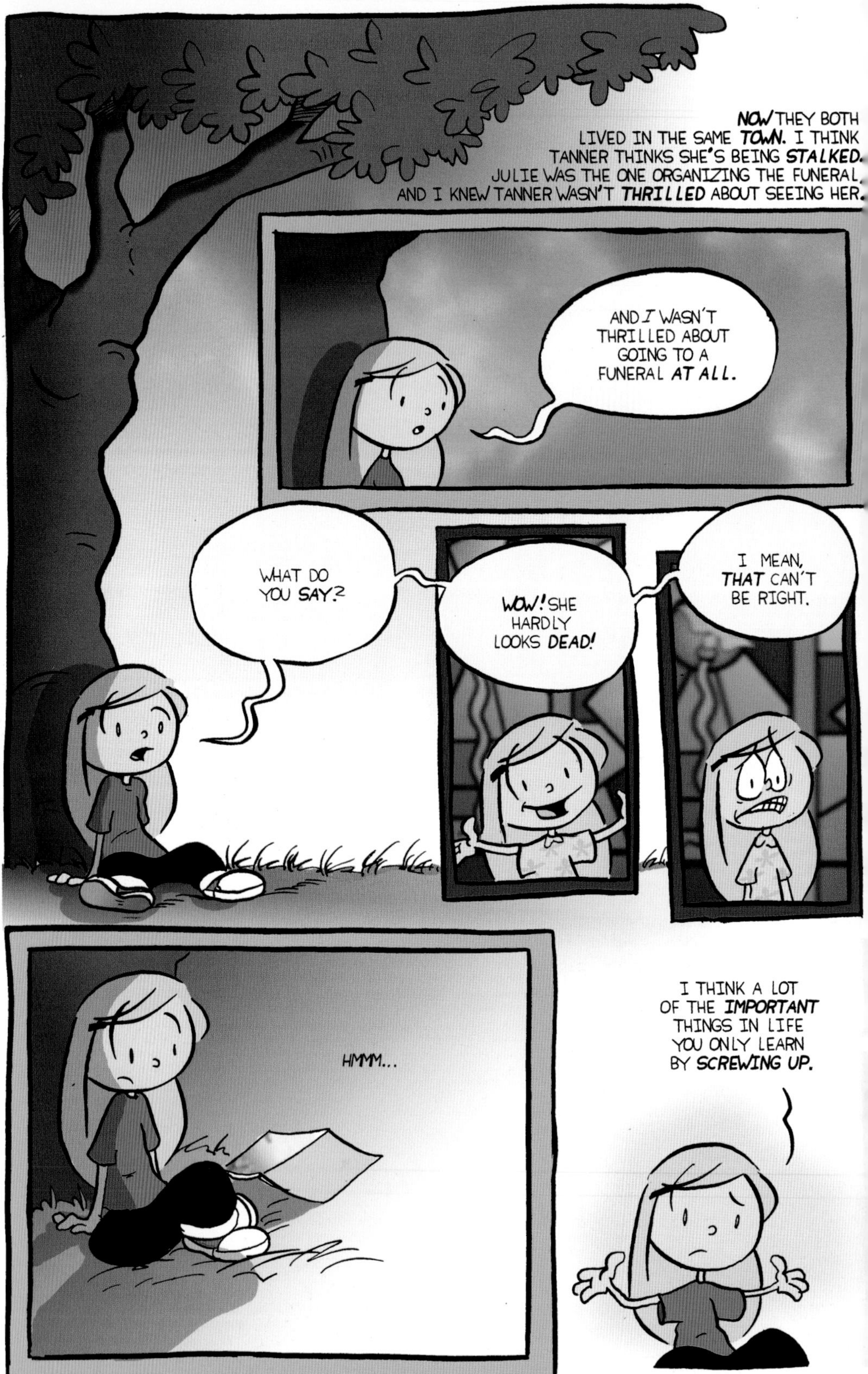
NOW THEY BOTH LIVED IN THE SAME TOWN. I THINK TANNER THINKS SHE'S BEING STALKED. JULIE WAS THE ONE ORGANIZING THE FUNERAL. AND I KNEW TANNER WASN'T THRILLED ABOUT SEEING HER.
AND I WASN'T THRILLED ABOUT GOING TO A FUNERAL AT ALL.
WHAT DO YOU SAY?
WOW! SHE HARDLY LOOKS DEAD!
I MEAN, THAT CAN'T BE RIGHT.
HMMM...
I THINK A LOT OF THE IMPORTANT THINGS IN LIFE YOU ONLY LEARN BY SCREWING UP.

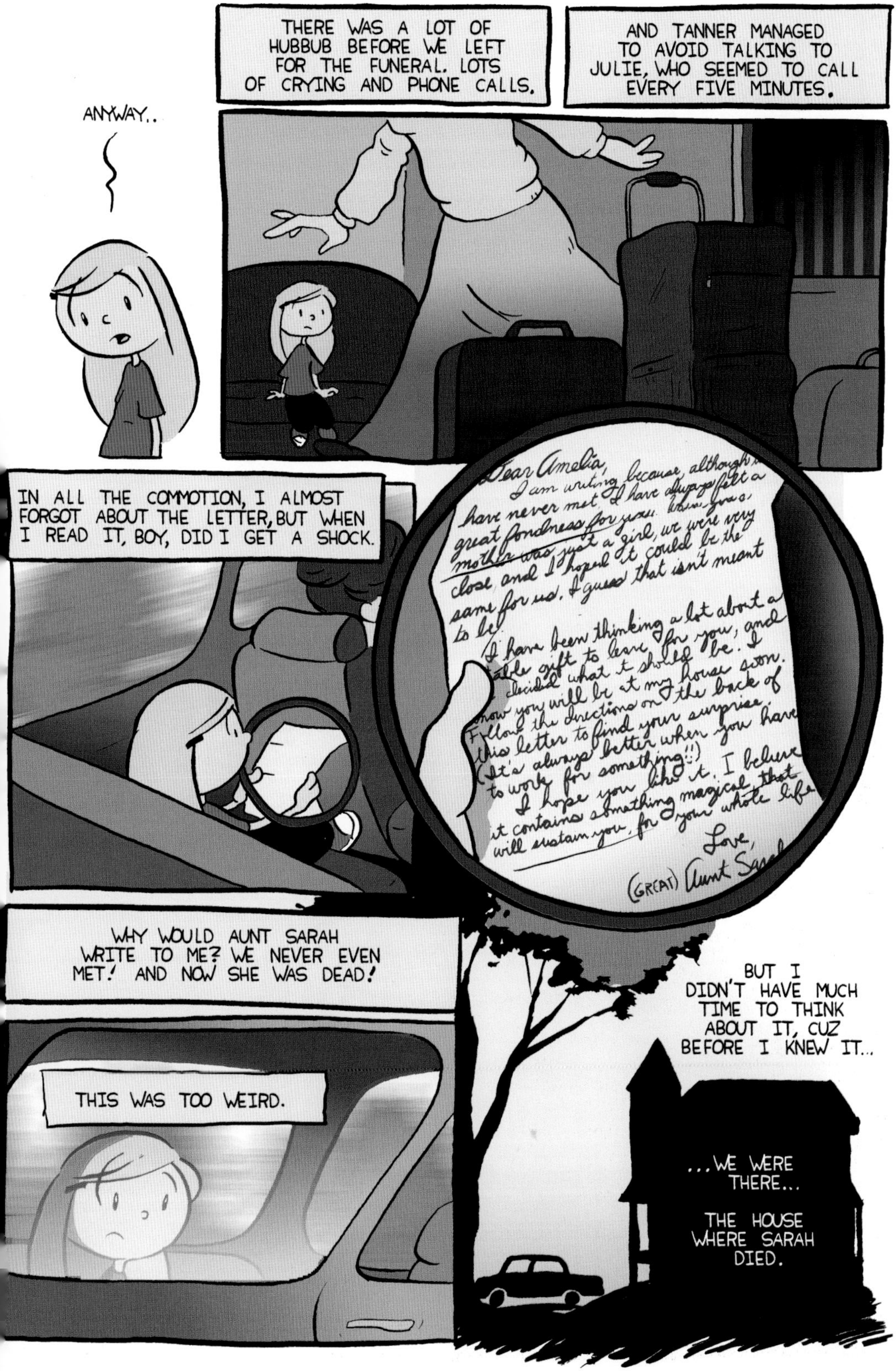

THERE WAS A LOT OF HUBBUB BEFORE WE LEFT FOR THE FUNERAL. LOTS OF CRYING AND PHONE CALLS.
AND TANNER MANAGED TO AVOID TALKING TO JULIE, WHO SEEMED TO CALL EVERY FIVE MINUTES.
ANYWAY..
IN ALL THE COMMOTION, I ALMOST FORGOT ABOUT THE LETTER, BUT WHEN I READ IT, BOY, DID I GET A SHOCK.
Dear Amelia,
I am writing because, although
have never met I have always felt a
great fondness for you. When your
mother was just a girl, we were very
close and I hoped it could be the
same for us. I guess that isn't meant
to be.
I have been thinking a lot about a
gift to leave for you, and
decided what it should be. I
know you will be at my house soon.
Follow the directions on the back of
this letter to find your surprise.
(It's always better when you have
to work for something!!)
I hope you like it. I believe
it contains something magical that
will sustain you for your whole life.
Love,
(GREAT) Aunt
WHY WOULD AUNT SARAH WRITE TO ME? WE NEVER EVEN MET! AND NOW SHE WAS DEAD!
THIS WAS TOO WEIRD.
BUT I DIDN'T HAVE MUCH TIME TO THINK ABOUT IT, CUZ BEFORE I KNEW IT...
...WE WERE THERE...
THE HOUSE WHERE SARAH DIED.

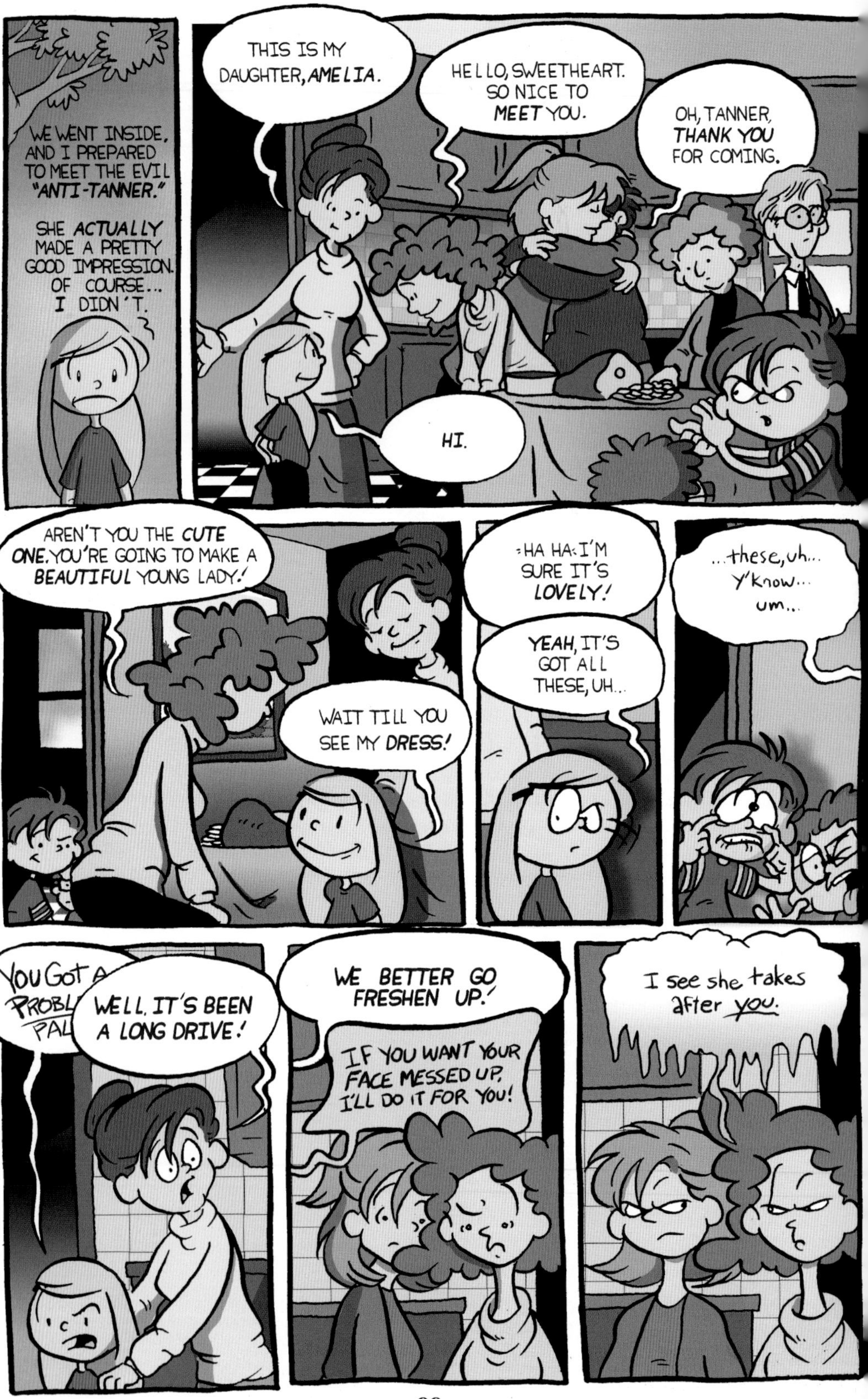
WE WENT INSIDE, AND I PREPARED TO MEET THE EVIL "ANTI-TANNER."
SHE ACTUALLY MADE A PRETTY GOOD IMPRESSION. OF COURSE... I DIDN'T.
THIS IS MY DAUGHTER, AMELIA.
HELLO, SWEETHEART. SO NICE TO MEET YOU.
OH, TANNER, THANK YOU FOR COMING.
HI.
AREN'T YOU THE CUTE ONE. YOU'RE GOING TO MAKE A BEAUTIFUL YOUNG LADY!
WAIT TILL YOU SEE MY DRESS!
HA HA I'M SURE IT'S LOVELY!
YEAH, IT'S GOT ALL THESE, UH...
...these, uh... y'know... um...
YOU GOT A PROBL PAL
WELL, IT'S BEEN A LONG DRIVE!
WE BETTER GO FRESHEN UP!
IF YOU WANT YOUR FACE MESSED UP, I'LL DO IT FOR YOU!
I see she takes after you.

I DON'T KNOW, I WAS ACTUALLY KINDA LOOKING FORWARD TO WEARING A **DRESS**. IT FELT KINDA **GROWN UP**, AND I THOUGHT I'D LOOK... DIFFERENT OR SOMETHING. IT TURNS OUT I JUST LOOK LIKE **ME**, ONLY **PINKER** AND WITH A BOW ON MY **BUTT**.

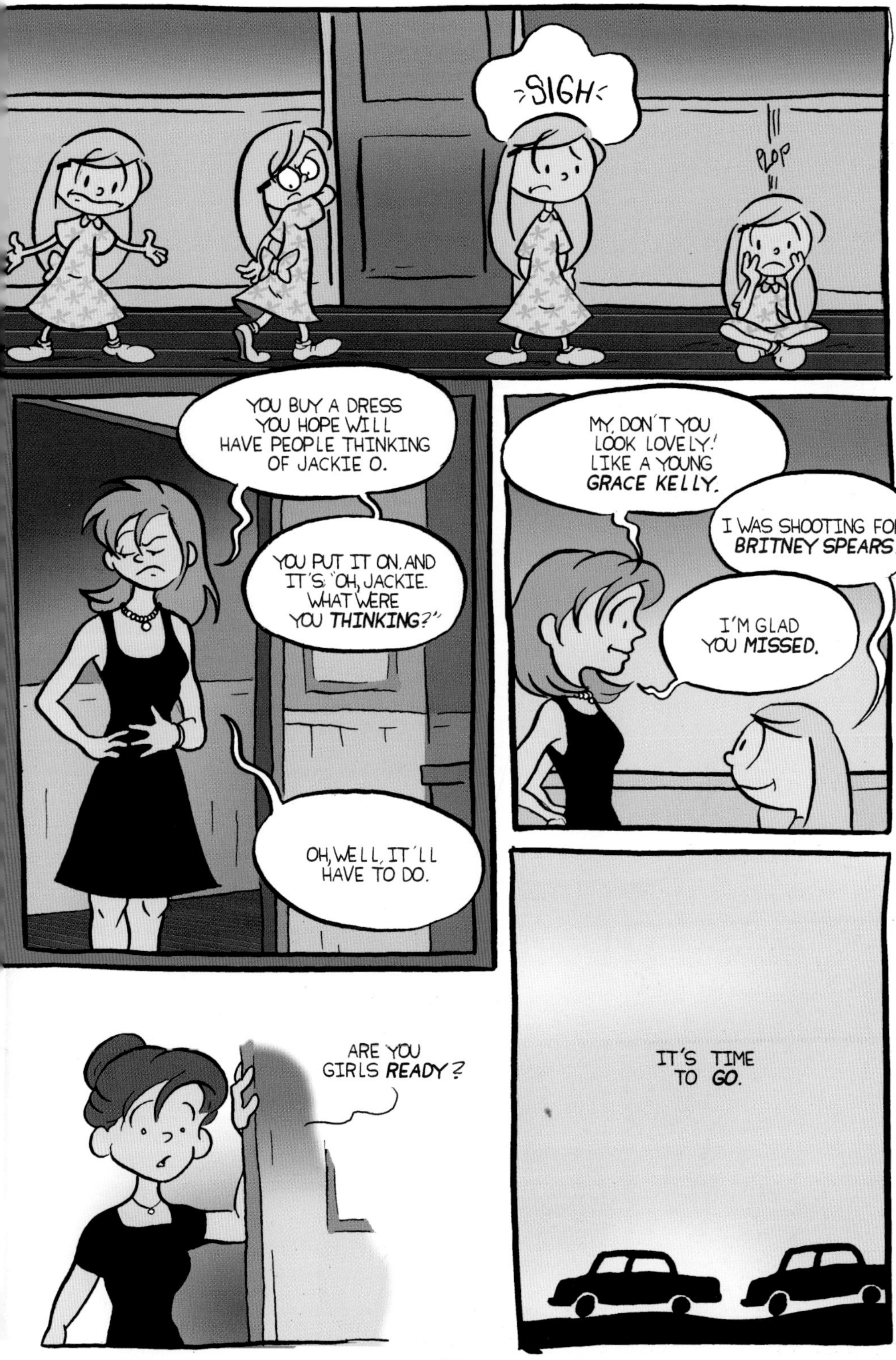

SIGH
PLOP
YOU BUY A DRESS YOU HOPE WILL HAVE PEOPLE THINKING OF JACKIE O.
YOU PUT IT ON, AND IT'S: "OH, JACKIE. WHAT WERE YOU THINKING?"
OH, WELL, IT'LL HAVE TO DO.
MY, DON'T YOU LOOK LOVELY! LIKE A YOUNG GRACE KELLY.
I WAS SHOOTING FOR BRITNEY SPEARS.
I'M GLAD YOU MISSED.
ARE YOU GIRLS READY?
IT'S TIME TO GO.

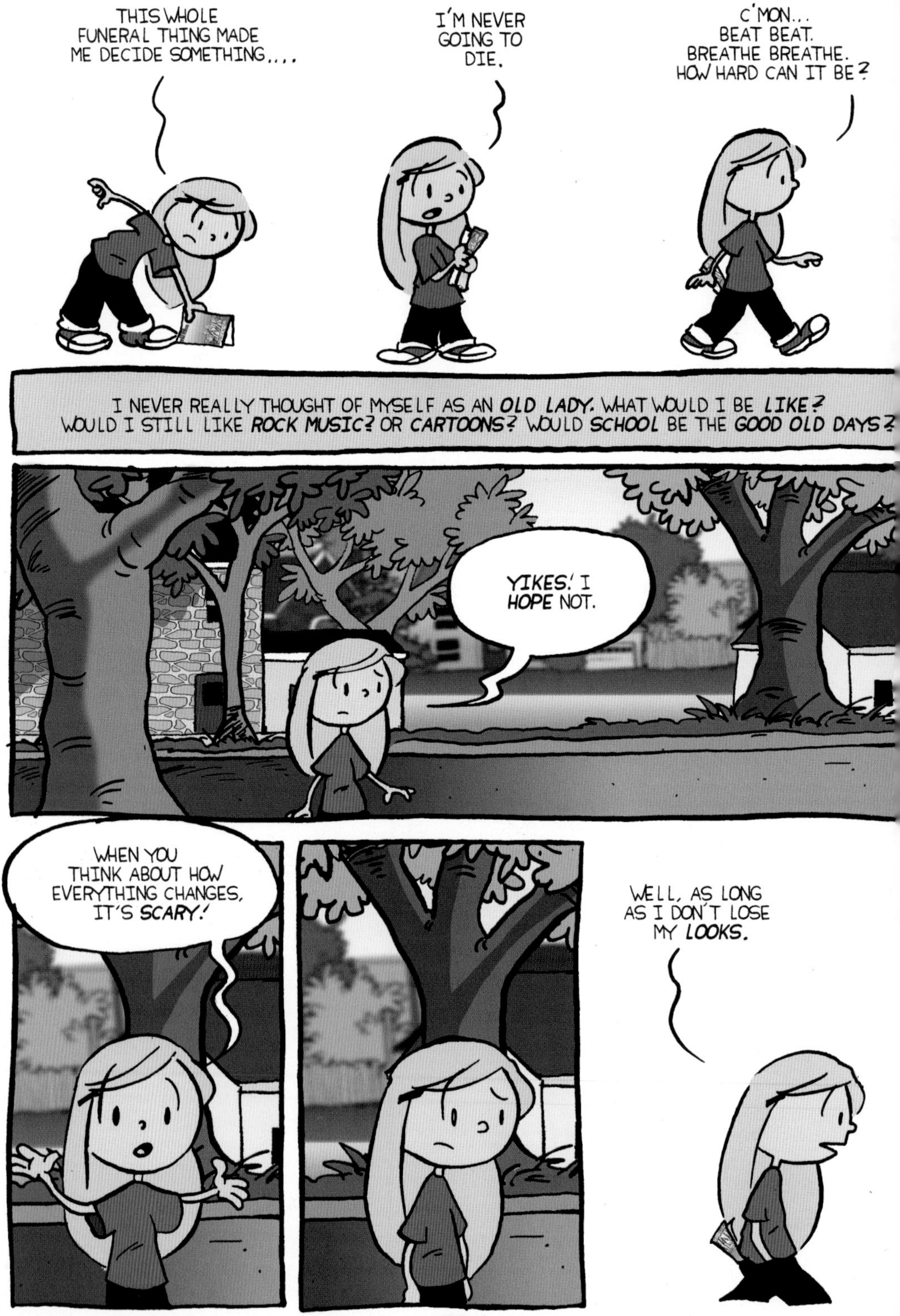
THIS WHOLE FUNERAL THING MADE ME DECIDE SOMETHING....
I'M NEVER GOING TO DIE.
C'MON... BEAT BEAT. BREATHE BREATHE. HOW HARD CAN IT BE?
I NEVER REALLY THOUGHT OF MYSELF AS AN OLD LADY. WHAT WOULD I BE LIKE? WOULD I STILL LIKE ROCK MUSIC? OR CARTOONS? WOULD SCHOOL BE THE GOOD OLD DAYS?
YIKES! I HOPE NOT.
WHEN YOU THINK ABOUT HOW EVERYTHING CHANGES, IT'S SCARY!
WELL, AS LONG AS I DON'T LOSE MY LOOKS.

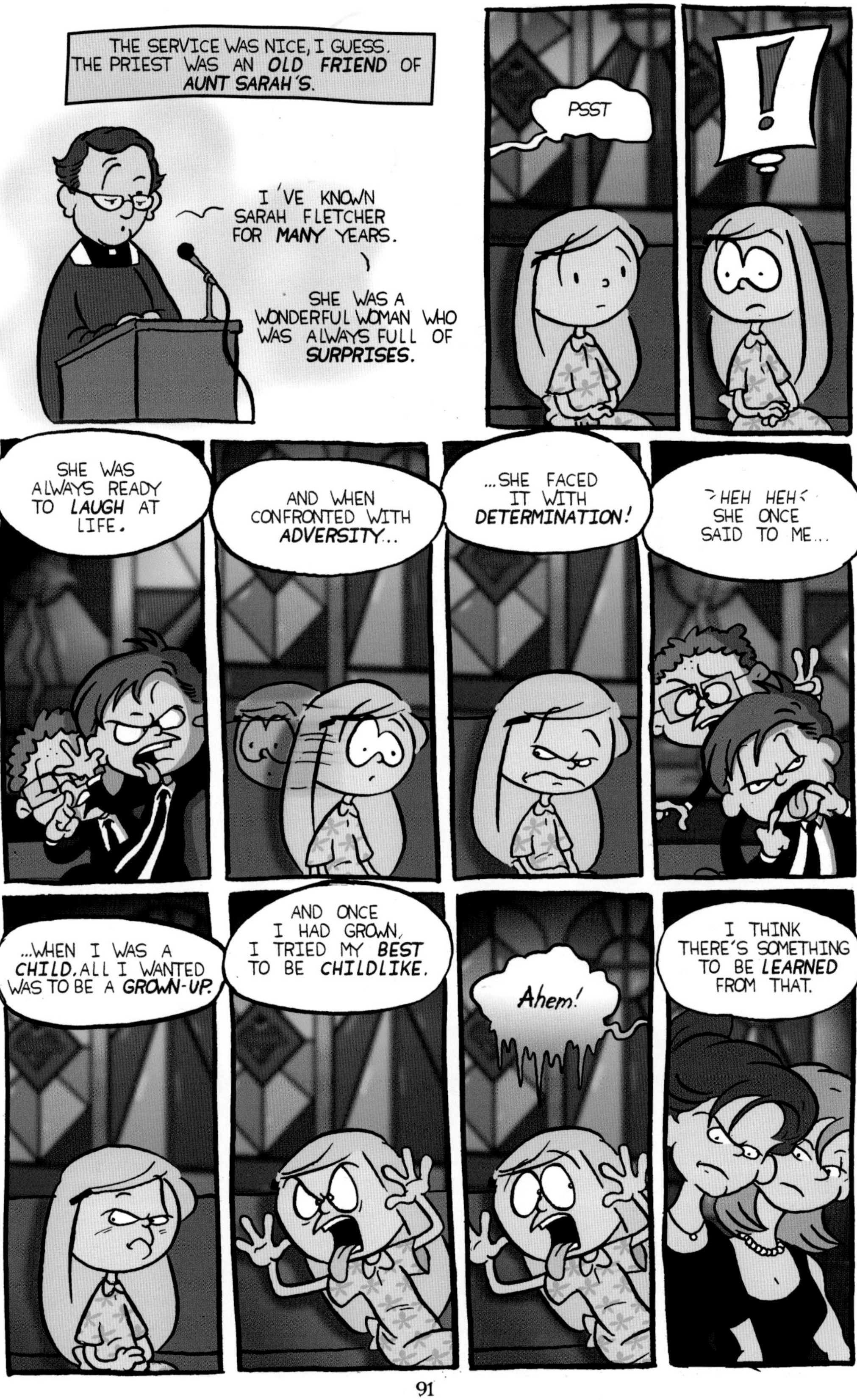
THE SERVICE WAS NICE, I GUESS. THE PRIEST WAS AN OLD FRIEND OF AUNT SARAH'S.
I'VE KNOWN SARAH FLETCHER FOR MANY YEARS.
SHE WAS A WONDERFUL WOMAN WHO WAS ALWAYS FULL OF SURPRISES.
PSST
!
SHE WAS ALWAYS READY TO LAUGH AT LIFE.
AND WHEN CONFRONTED WITH ADVERSITY...
...SHE FACED IT WITH DETERMINATION!
HEH HEH SHE ONCE SAID TO ME...
...WHEN I WAS A CHILD, ALL I WANTED WAS TO BE A GROWN-UP.
AND ONCE I HAD GROWN, I TRIED MY BEST TO BE CHILDLIKE.
Ahem!
I THINK THERE'S SOMETHING TO BE LEARNED FROM THAT.

AFTERWARD THERE WAS A RECEPTION AT THE HOUSE, BUT ALL *I* WANTED TO DO WAS GET ***CHANGED*** AND ***GET AWAY.***

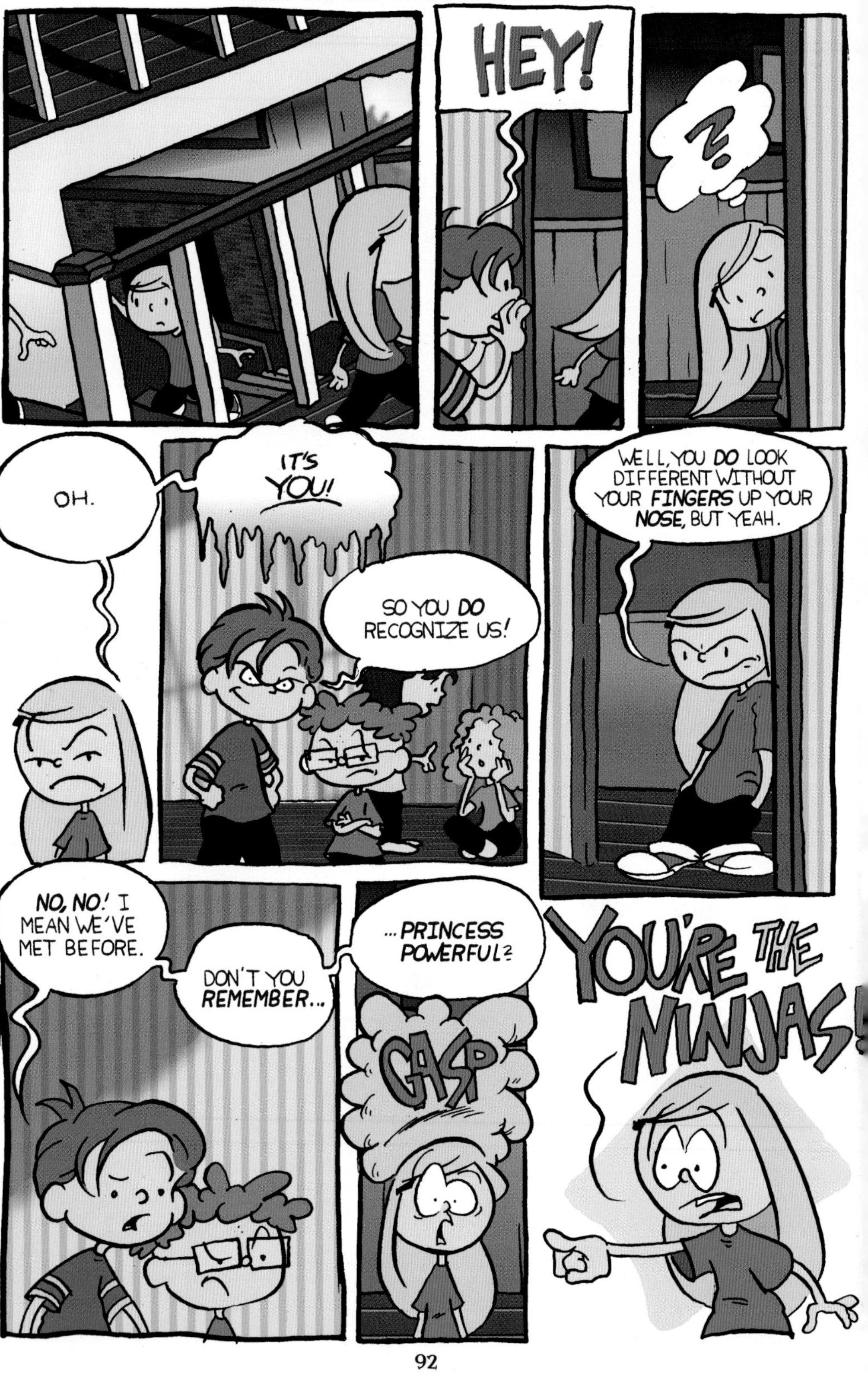
HEY!
?
OH.
IT'S YOU!
SO YOU DO RECOGNIZE US!
WELL, YOU DO LOOK DIFFERENT WITHOUT YOUR FINGERS UP YOUR NOSE, BUT YEAH.
NO, NO! I MEAN WE'VE MET BEFORE.
DON'T YOU REMEMBER...
...PRINCESS POWERFUL?
GASP
YOU'RE THE NINJAS!

NINJA *KYLE* AND *ED!* I NEVER IN A MILLION YEARS THOUGHT I'D RUN INTO THEM *HERE!*

IF REGGIE WAS MAD *BEFORE*, HE'D *FREAK* IF HE KNEW I WAS SHAKING HANDS WITH THE *ENEMY*.

THERE WERE OTHER KIDS, TOO, LIKE THIS ONE *WEIRDO* WHO JUST STOOD IN THE *CORNER*...

...AND THESE TWO GIRLS, TRISH AND JOANNE (NONE OF THEM *WERE* NINJAS).

THE *WEIRDEST* THING ABOUT ED AND KYLE IS THAT THEIR MOM IS *JULIE*, THE EVIL *ANTI-TANNER*. I MEAN, WHO *KNEW?*

IT TURNED OUT *THEIR* PARENTS WERE DIVORCED *TOO*.

ALL OF THEM WERE AT THE FUNERAL.

BUT WE STARTED TALKING, AND THEY SEEMED *OKAY*.

DID THEY BUY YOU ANY OF THOSE *CORNY* *BOOKS* TO "HELP YOU THROUGH IT"?

LIKE, *EVEN PENGUINS SOMETIMES PART?*

OR *WHEN KOALAS CAN'T COMMUNICATE?*

OR *YOUR PARENTS LOVE YOU: THEY JUST HATE EACH OTHER?*

OR *MOMMY'S NEW FRIEND THE MAILMAN?*

THIS IS *BORING!*

YIKES! I'M *GLAD* I DIDN'T HAVE TO READ *THAT* ONE!

HAHAHAHAHAHAHA

CAN'T WE PLAY A GAME OR SOMETHING?

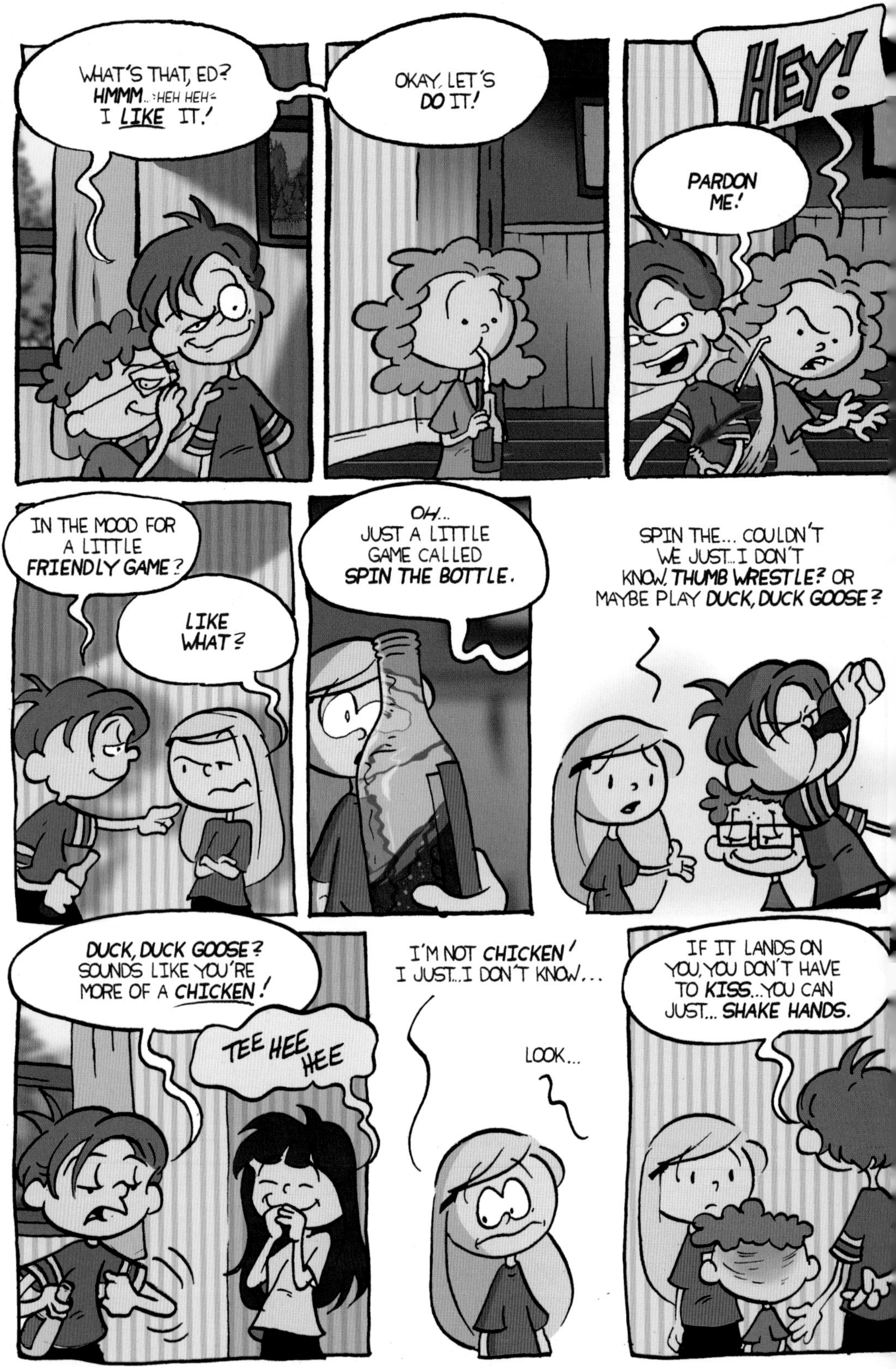
WHAT'S THAT, ED? HMMM... HEH HEH... I LIKE IT!
OKAY, LET'S DO IT!
HEY!
PARDON ME!
IN THE MOOD FOR A LITTLE FRIENDLY GAME?
LIKE WHAT?
OH... JUST A LITTLE GAME CALLED SPIN THE BOTTLE.
SPIN THE... COULDN'T WE JUST...I DON'T KNOW, THUMB WRESTLE? OR MAYBE PLAY DUCK, DUCK GOOSE?
DUCK, DUCK GOOSE? SOUNDS LIKE YOU'RE MORE OF A CHICKEN!
TEE HEE HEE
I'M NOT CHICKEN! I JUST...I DON'T KNOW...
LOOK...
IF IT LANDS ON YOU, YOU DON'T HAVE TO KISS...YOU CAN JUST... SHAKE HANDS.

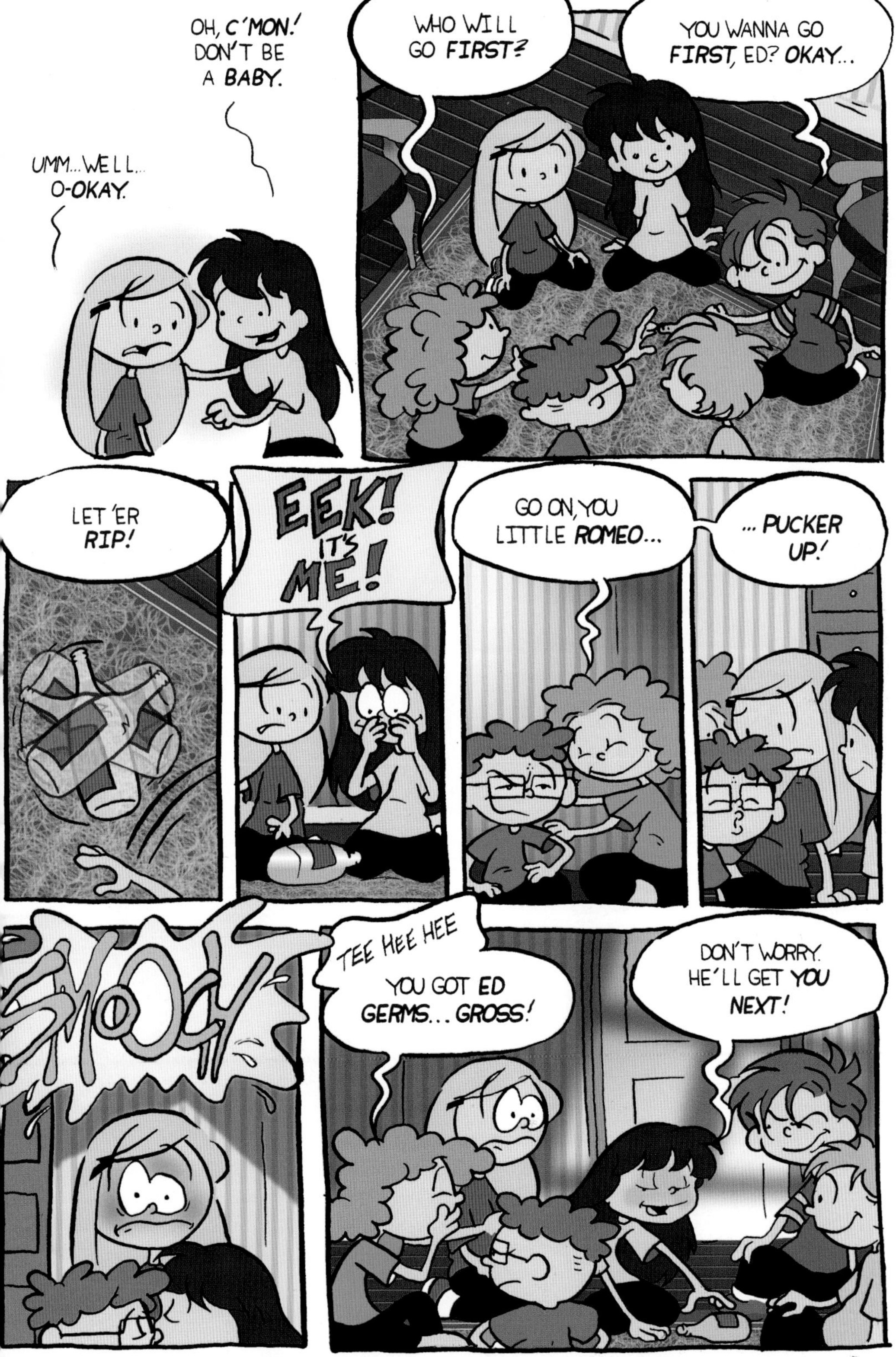

UMM...WELL... O-OKAY.
OH, C'MON! DON'T BE A BABY.
WHO WILL GO FIRST?
YOU WANNA GO FIRST, ED? OKAY...
LET 'ER RIP!
EEK! IT'S ME!
GO ON, YOU LITTLE ROMEO...
... PUCKER UP!
SMOOCH
TEE HEE HEE
YOU GOT ED GERMS... GROSS!
DON'T WORRY. HE'LL GET YOU NEXT!

97

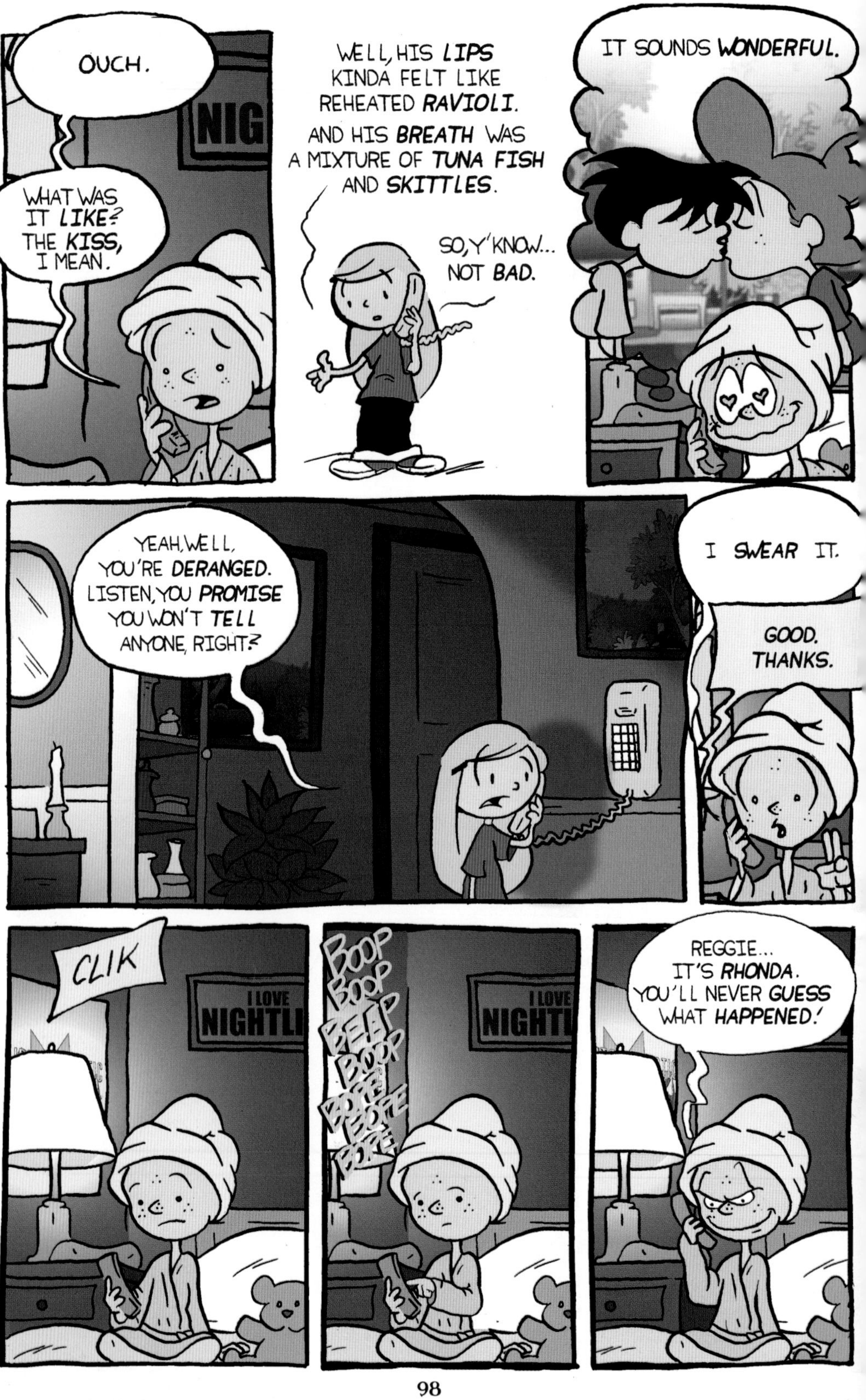
OUCH.
NIG
WHAT WAS IT LIKE? THE KISS, I MEAN.
WELL, HIS LIPS KINDA FELT LIKE REHEATED RAVIOLI.
AND HIS BREATH WAS A MIXTURE OF TUNA FISH AND SKITTLES.
SO, Y'KNOW... NOT BAD.
IT SOUNDS WONDERFUL.
YEAH, WELL, YOU'RE DERANGED. LISTEN, YOU PROMISE YOU WON'T TELL ANYONE, RIGHT?
I SWEAR IT.
GOOD. THANKS.
CLIK
I LOVE NIGHTLI
BOOP BOOP BEEP BOOP
I LOVE NIGHTL
REGGIE... IT'S RHONDA. YOU'LL NEVER GUESS WHAT HAPPENED!

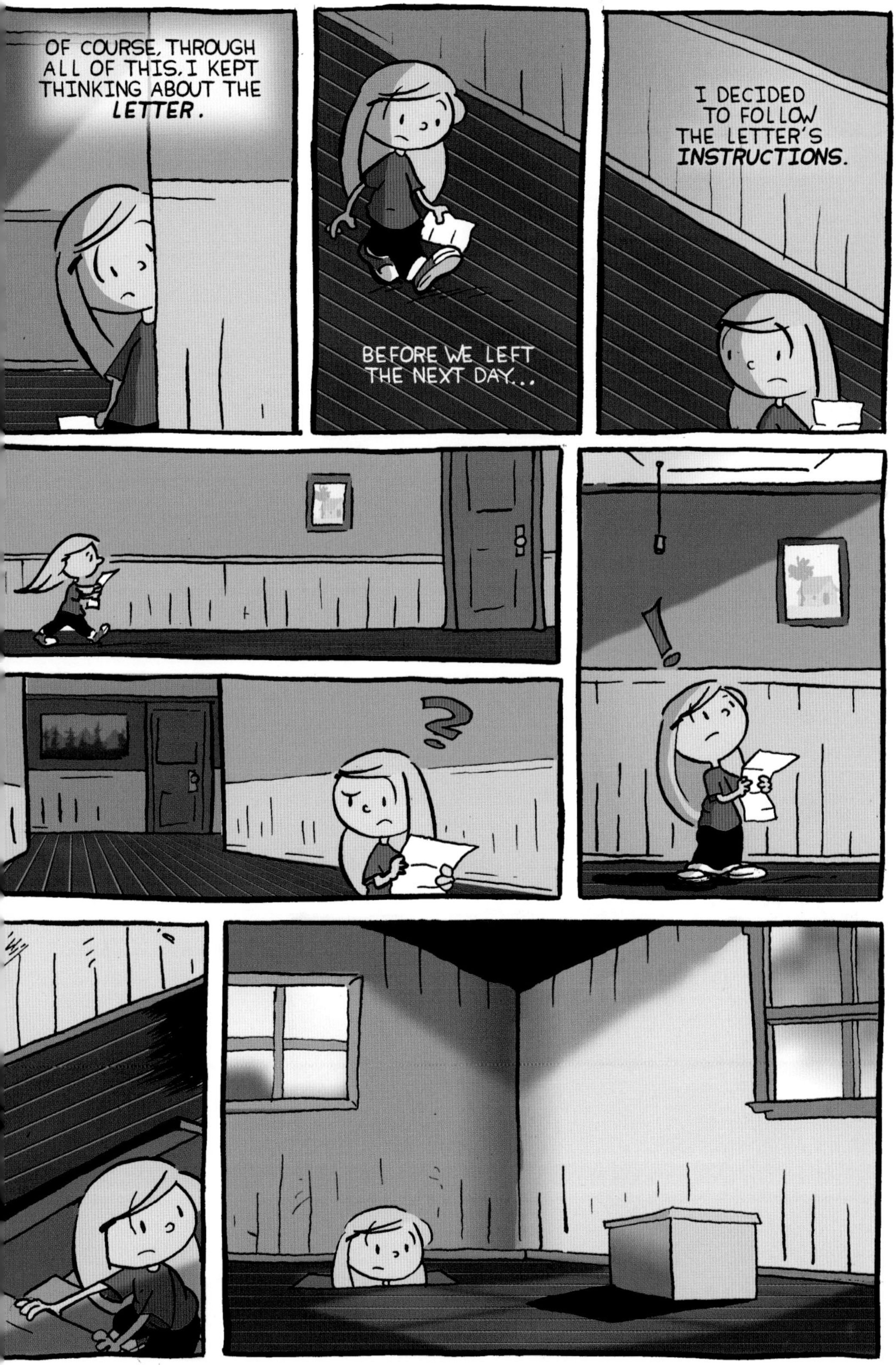
OF COURSE, THROUGH ALL OF THIS, I KEPT THINKING ABOUT THE LETTER.
BEFORE WE LEFT THE NEXT DAY...
I DECIDED TO FOLLOW THE LETTER'S INSTRUCTIONS.

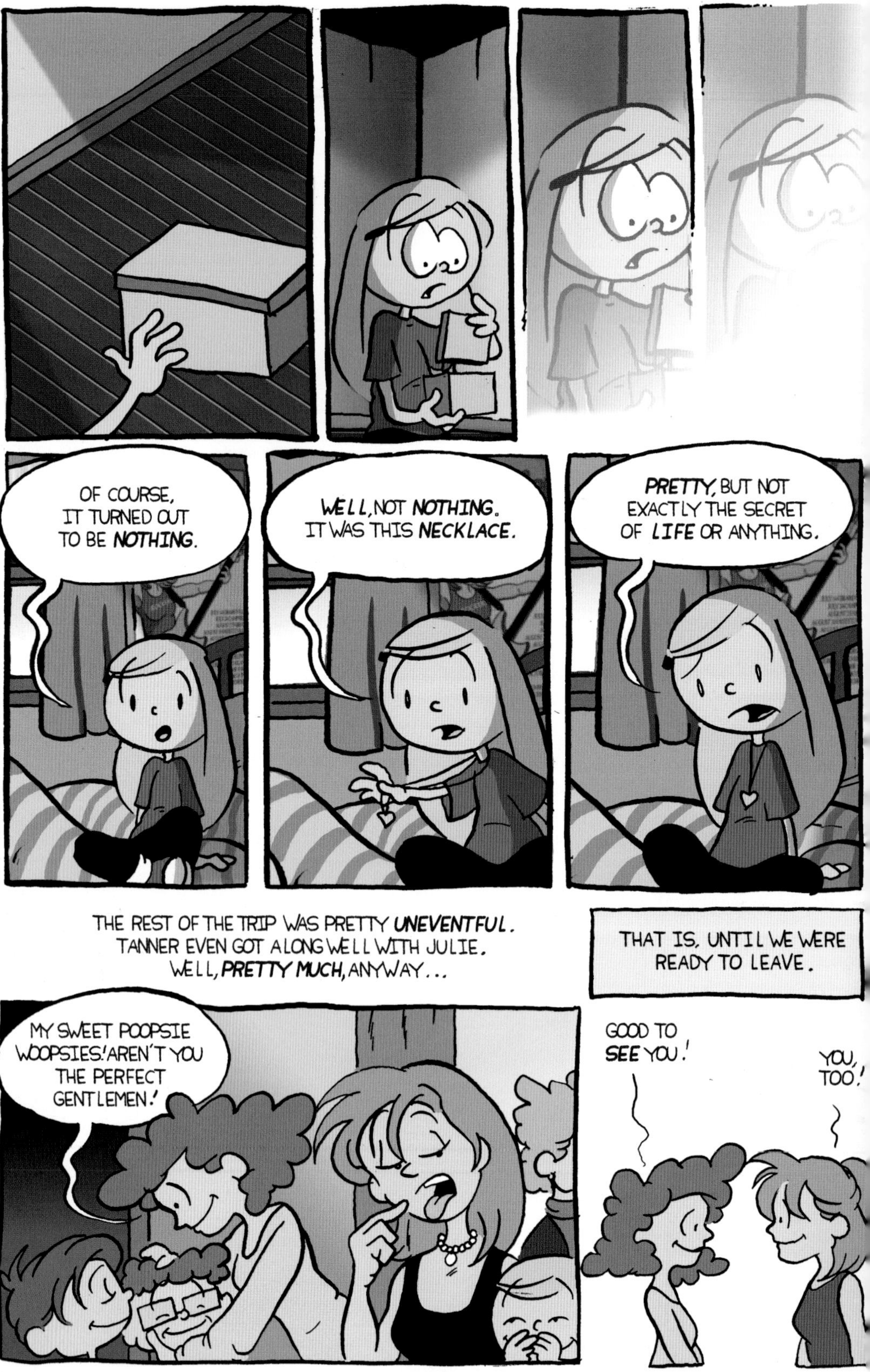
OF COURSE, IT TURNED OUT TO BE NOTHING.
WELL, NOT NOTHING. IT WAS THIS NECKLACE.
PRETTY, BUT NOT EXACTLY THE SECRET OF LIFE OR ANYTHING.
THE REST OF THE TRIP WAS PRETTY UNEVENTFUL. TANNER EVEN GOT ALONG WELL WITH JULIE. WELL, PRETTY MUCH, ANYWAY...
THAT IS, UNTIL WE WERE READY TO LEAVE.
MY SWEET POOPSIE WOOPSIES! AREN'T YOU THE PERFECT GENTLEMEN!
GOOD TO SEE YOU!
YOU, TOO!

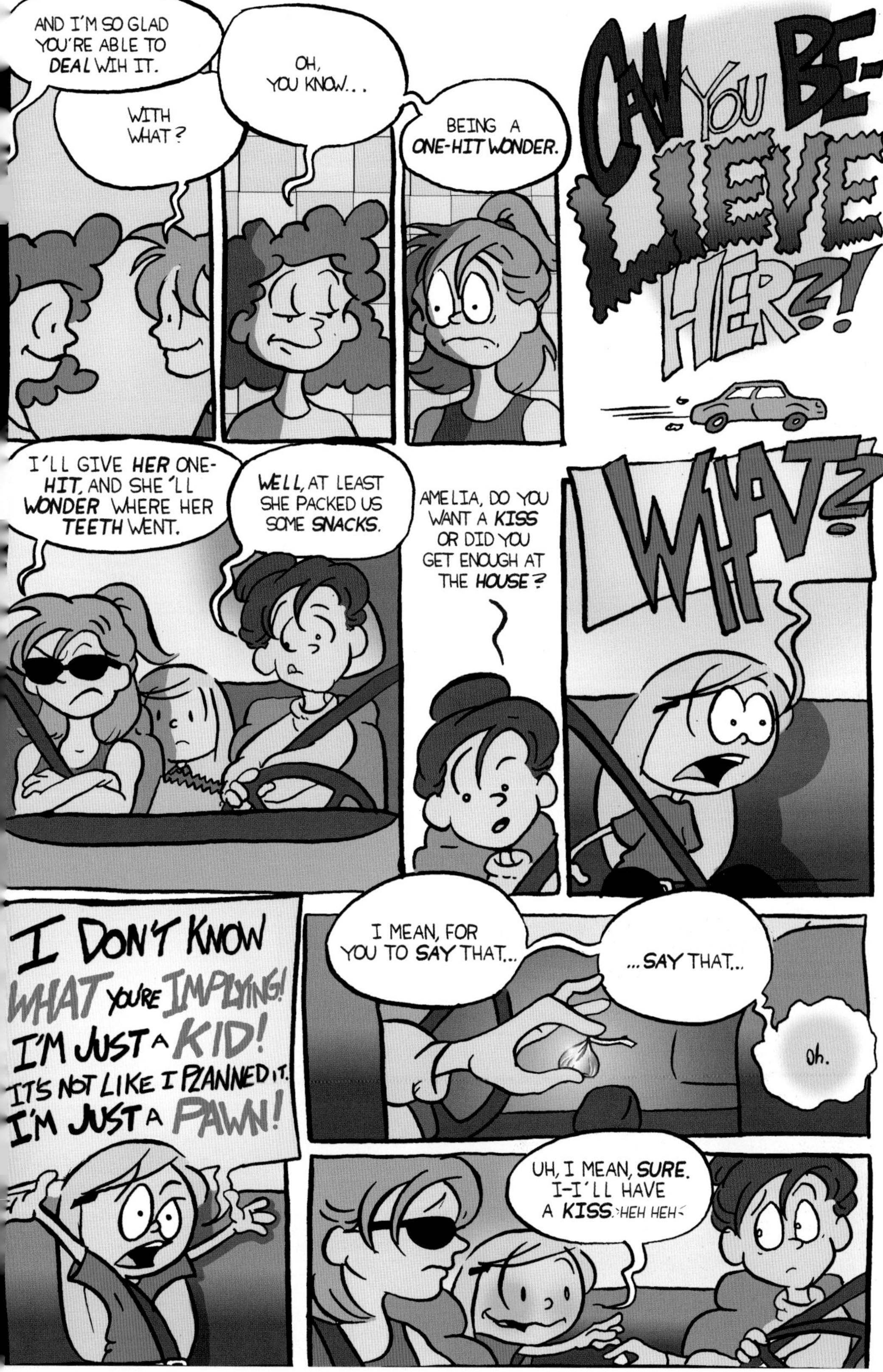

AND I'M SO GLAD YOU'RE ABLE TO DEAL WIH IT.
WITH WHAT?
OH, YOU KNOW...
BEING A ONE-HIT WONDER.
CAN YOU BE-LIEVE HER?!
I'LL GIVE HER ONE-HIT, AND SHE'LL WONDER WHERE HER TEETH WENT.
WELL, AT LEAST SHE PACKED US SOME SNACKS.
AMELIA, DO YOU WANT A KISS OR DID YOU GET ENOUGH AT THE HOUSE?
WHAT?!
I DON'T KNOW WHAT YOU'RE IMPLYING! I'M JUST A KID! IT'S NOT LIKE I PLANNED IT. I'M JUST A PAWN!
I MEAN, FOR YOU TO SAY THAT...
...SAY THAT...
Oh.
UH, I MEAN, SURE. I-I'LL HAVE A KISS. >HEH HEH<

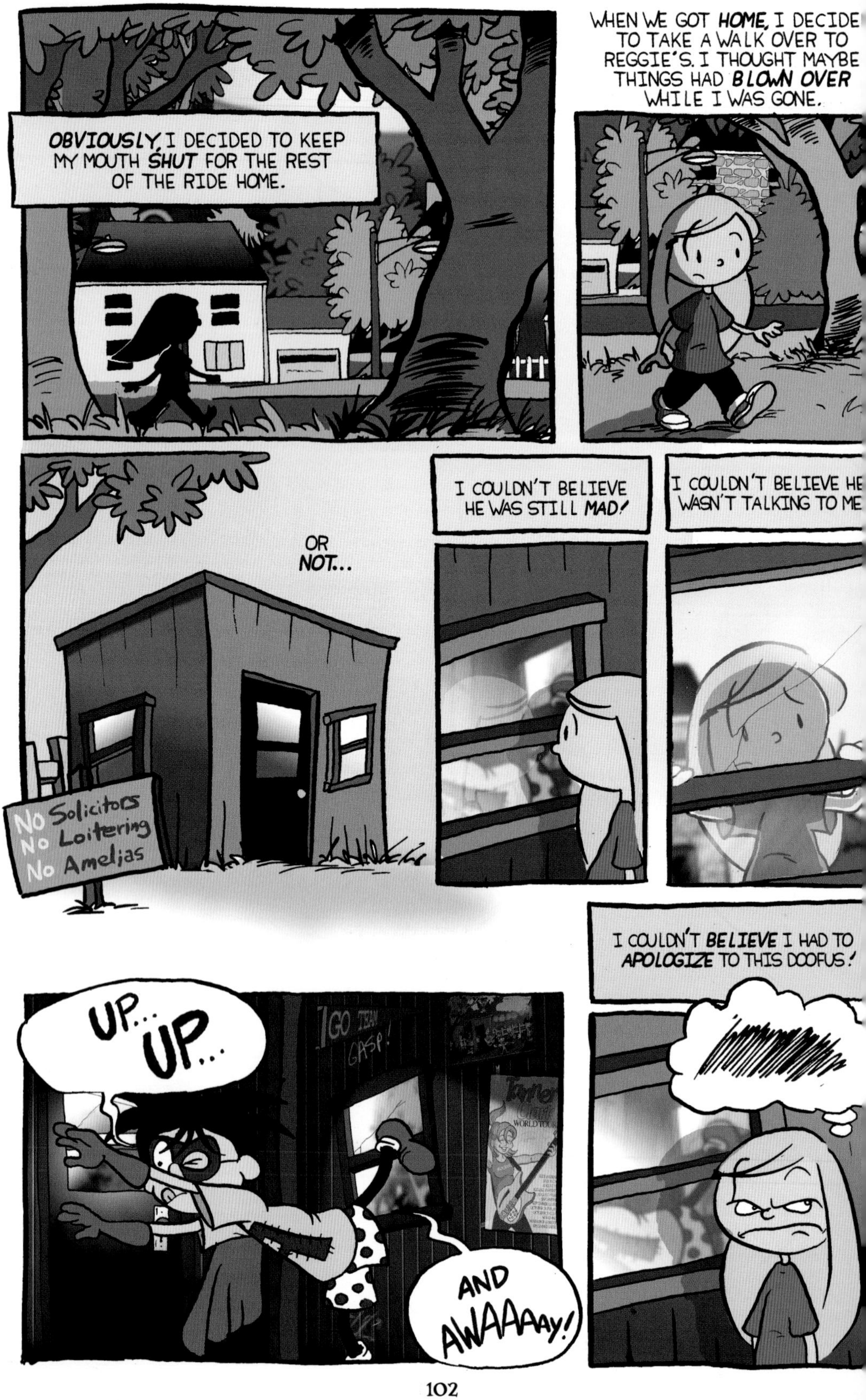
OBVIOUSLY, I DECIDED TO KEEP MY MOUTH SHUT FOR THE REST OF THE RIDE HOME.
WHEN WE GOT HOME, I DECIDED TO TAKE A WALK OVER TO REGGIE'S. I THOUGHT MAYBE THINGS HAD BLOWN OVER WHILE I WAS GONE.
OR NOT...
No Solicitors
No Loitering
No Amelias
I COULDN'T BELIEVE HE WAS STILL MAD!
I COULDN'T BELIEVE HE WASN'T TALKING TO ME
I COULDN'T BELIEVE I HAD TO APOLOGIZE TO THIS DOOFUS!
UP... UP...
AND AWAAAAAY!
GO TEAM GASP!
WORLD TOUR

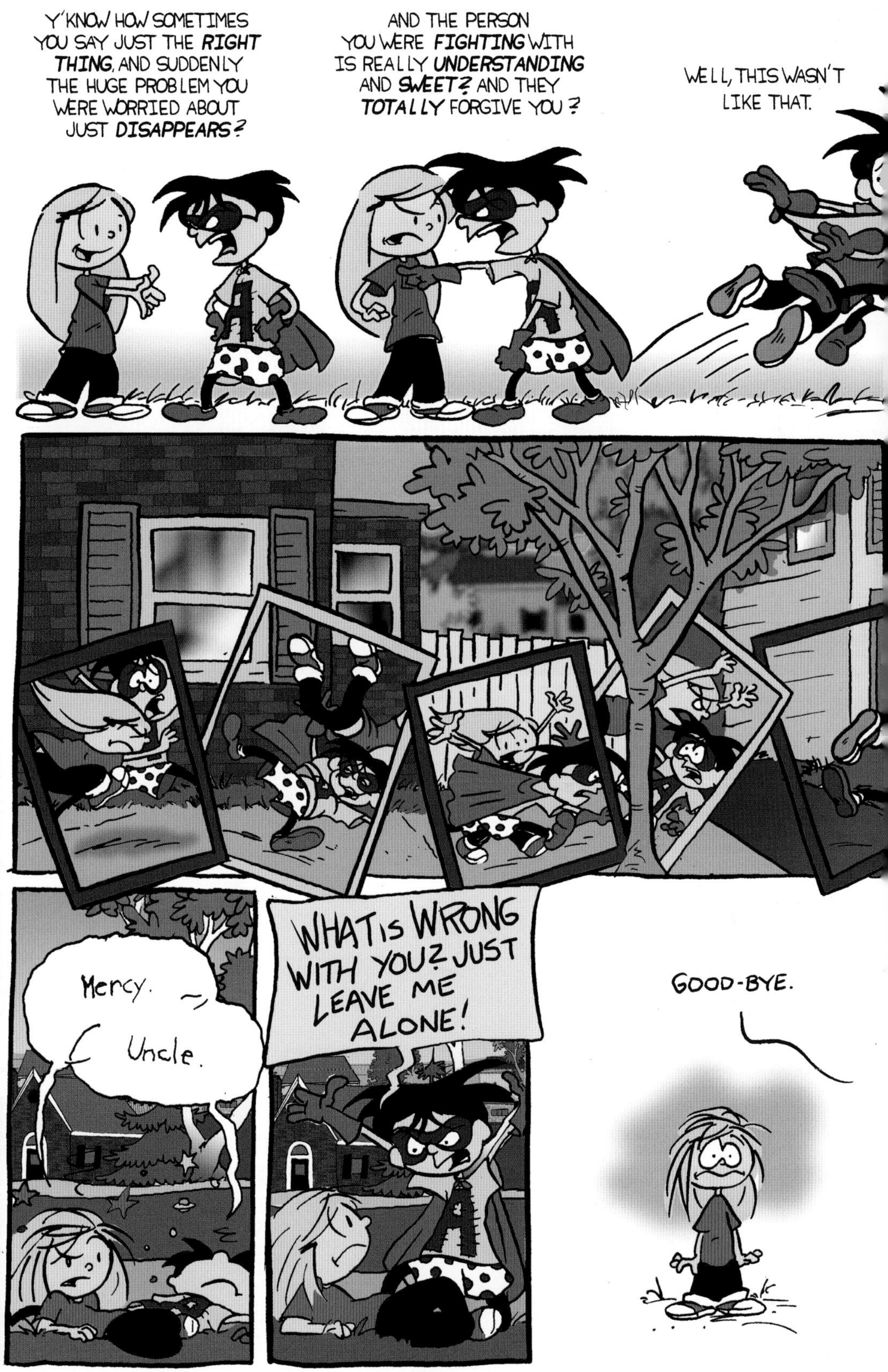
Y'KNOW HOW SOMETIMES YOU SAY JUST THE **RIGHT THING**, AND SUDDENLY THE HUGE PROBLEM YOU WERE WORRIED ABOUT JUST **DISAPPEARS**?
AND THE PERSON YOU WERE **FIGHTING** WITH IS REALLY **UNDERSTANDING** AND **SWEET**? AND THEY **TOTALLY** FORGIVE YOU?
WELL, THIS WASN'T LIKE THAT.
Mercy.
Uncle.
WHAT IS WRONG WITH YOU? JUST LEAVE ME ALONE!
GOOD-BYE.

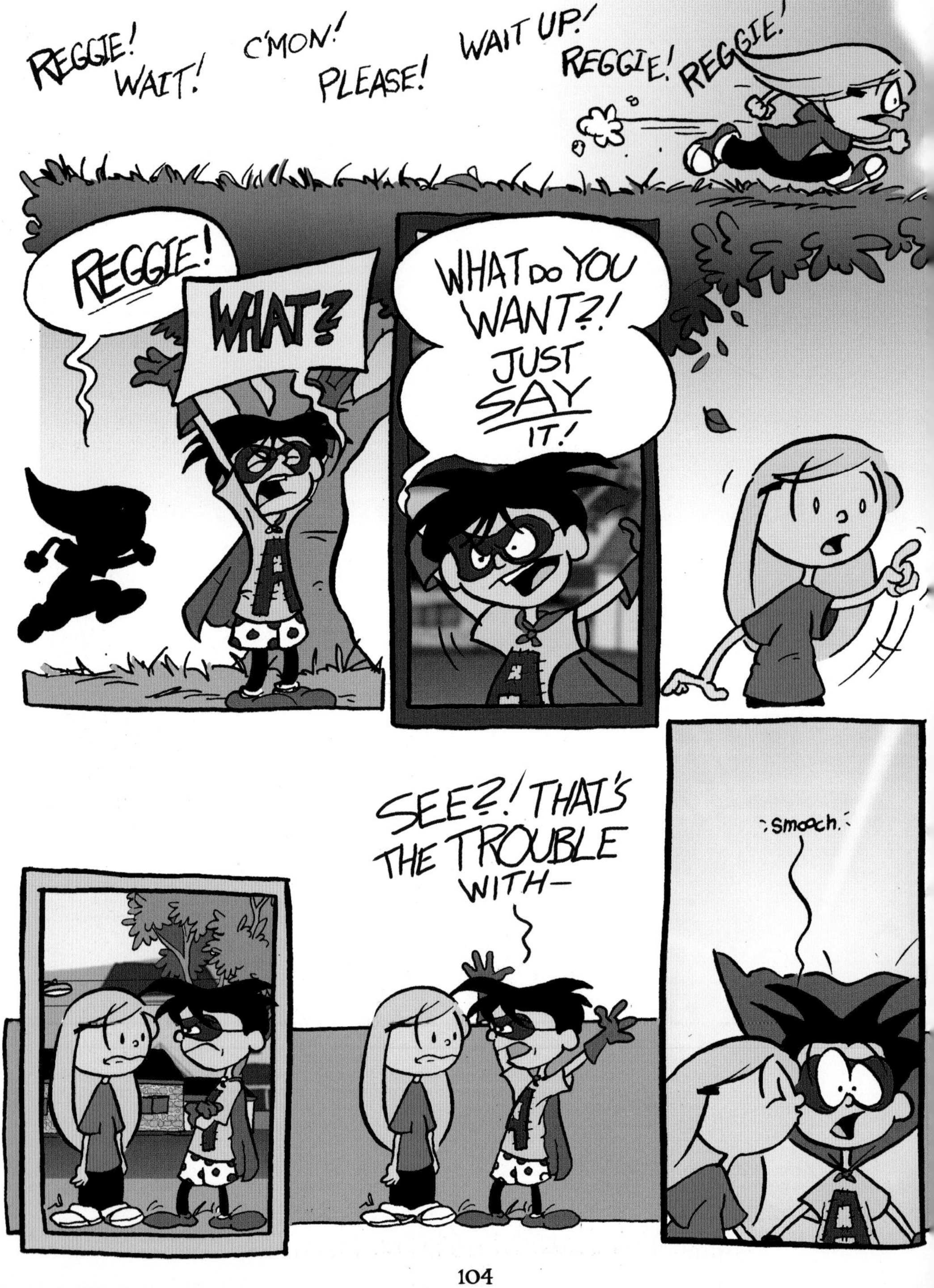
REGGIE! WAIT!
C'MON! PLEASE!
WAIT UP!
REGGIE!
REGGIE!
REGGIE!
WHAT?
WHAT DO YOU WANT?! JUST SAY IT!
SEE?! THAT'S THE TROUBLE WITH—
:smooch.:

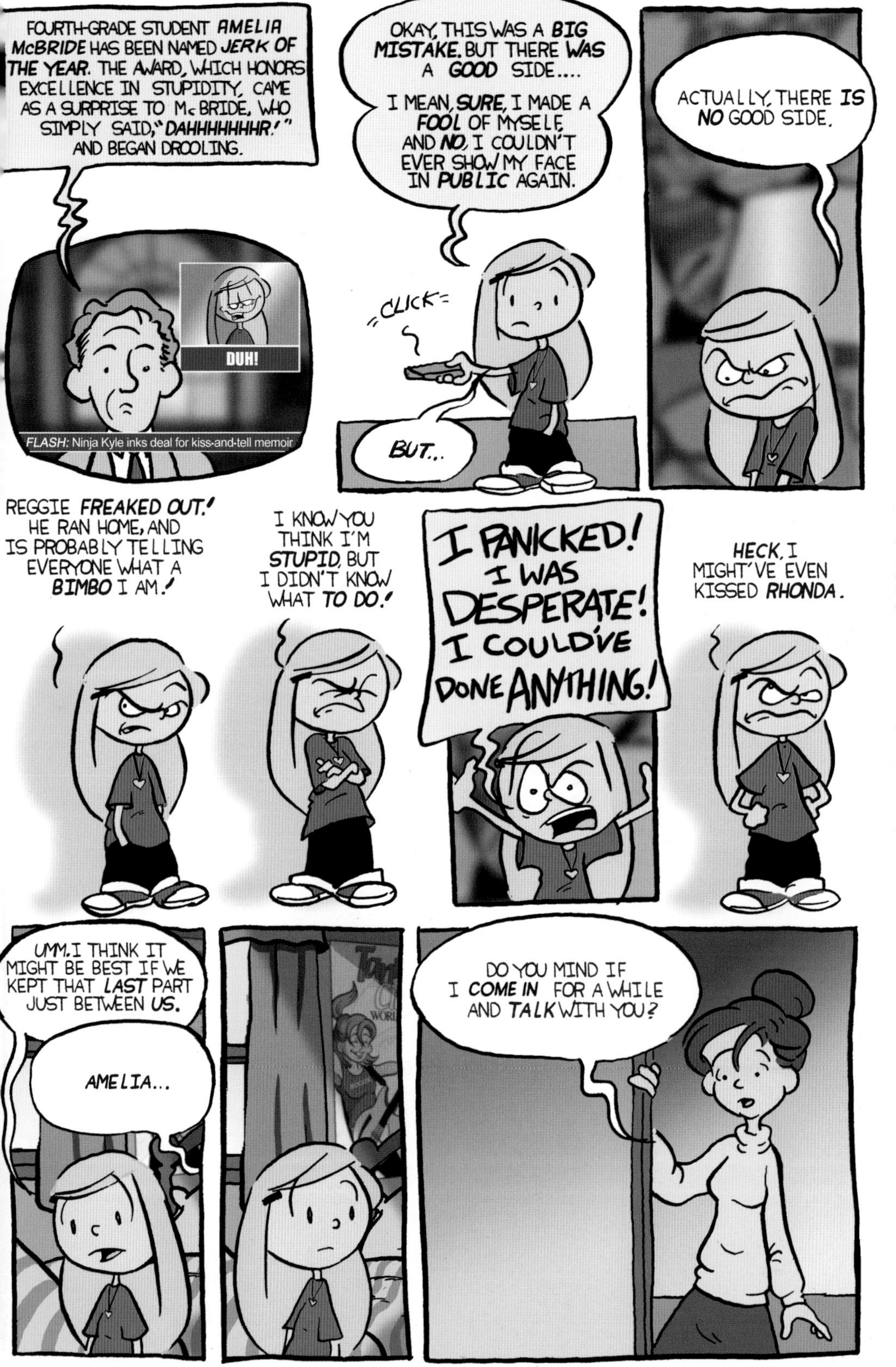
FOURTH-GRADE STUDENT AMELIA McBRIDE HAS BEEN NAMED JERK OF THE YEAR. THE AWARD, WHICH HONORS EXCELLENCE IN STUPIDITY, CAME AS A SURPRISE TO McBRIDE, WHO SIMPLY SAID, "DAHHHHHHHR!" AND BEGAN DROOLING.
DUH!
FLASH: Ninja Kyle inks deal for kiss-and-tell memoir
OKAY, THIS WAS A BIG MISTAKE. BUT THERE WAS A GOOD SIDE....
I MEAN, SURE, I MADE A FOOL OF MYSELF, AND NO, I COULDN'T EVER SHOW MY FACE IN PUBLIC AGAIN.
CLICK
BUT...
ACTUALLY, THERE IS NO GOOD SIDE.
REGGIE FREAKED OUT! HE RAN HOME, AND IS PROBABLY TELLING EVERYONE WHAT A BIMBO I AM!
I KNOW YOU THINK I'M STUPID, BUT I DIDN'T KNOW WHAT TO DO!
I PANICKED! I WAS DESPERATE! I COULD'VE DONE ANYTHING!
HECK, I MIGHT'VE EVEN KISSED RHONDA.
UMM. I THINK IT MIGHT BE BEST IF WE KEPT THAT LAST PART JUST BETWEEN US.
AMELIA...
DO YOU MIND IF I COME IN FOR A WHILE AND TALK WITH YOU?

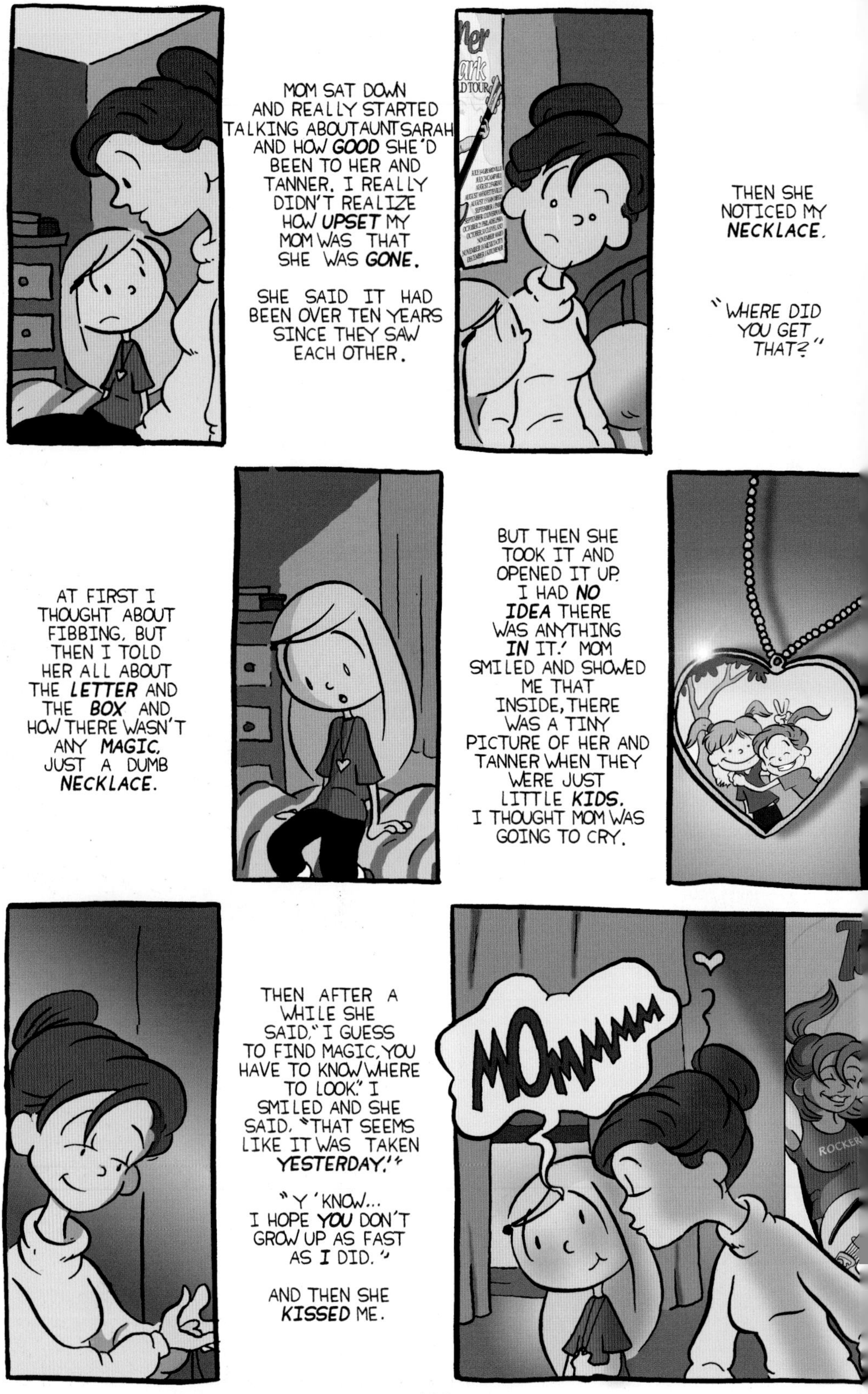
MOM SAT DOWN AND REALLY STARTED TALKING ABOUT AUNT SARAH AND HOW **GOOD** SHE'D BEEN TO HER AND TANNER. I REALLY DIDN'T REALIZE HOW **UPSET** MY MOM WAS THAT SHE WAS **GONE**.
SHE SAID IT HAD BEEN OVER TEN YEARS SINCE THEY SAW EACH OTHER.
THEN SHE NOTICED MY **NECKLACE**.
"WHERE DID YOU GET THAT?"
AT FIRST I THOUGHT ABOUT FIBBING, BUT THEN I TOLD HER ALL ABOUT THE **LETTER** AND THE **BOX** AND HOW THERE WASN'T ANY **MAGIC**, JUST A DUMB **NECKLACE**.
BUT THEN SHE TOOK IT AND OPENED IT UP. I HAD **NO IDEA** THERE WAS ANYTHING **IN** IT! MOM SMILED AND SHOWED ME THAT INSIDE, THERE WAS A TINY PICTURE OF HER AND TANNER WHEN THEY WERE JUST LITTLE **KIDS**. I THOUGHT MOM WAS GOING TO CRY.
THEN AFTER A WHILE SHE SAID, "I GUESS TO FIND MAGIC, YOU HAVE TO KNOW WHERE TO LOOK." I SMILED AND SHE SAID, "THAT SEEMS LIKE IT WAS TAKEN **YESTERDAY**!"
"Y'KNOW... I HOPE **YOU** DON'T GROW UP AS FAST AS **I** DID."
AND THEN SHE **KISSED** ME.
MOMMMMMM
ROCKER

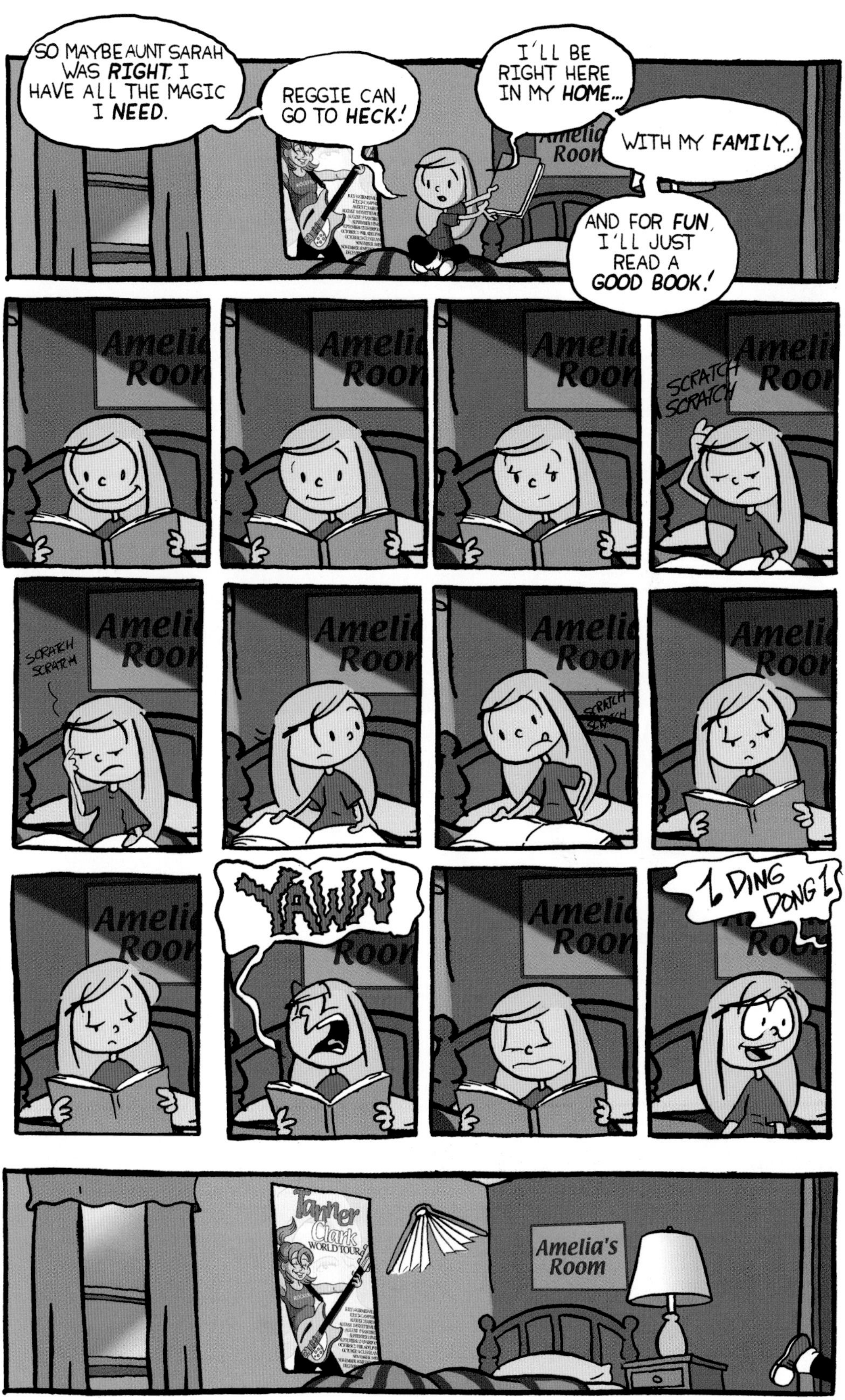
SO MAYBE AUNT SARAH WAS RIGHT. I HAVE ALL THE MAGIC I NEED.
REGGIE CAN GO TO HECK!
I'LL BE RIGHT HERE IN MY HOME...
WITH MY FAMILY...
AND FOR FUN, I'LL JUST READ A GOOD BOOK!
Amelia's Room
SCRATCH SCRATCH
SCRATCH SCRATCH
SCRATCH SCRATCH
YAWN
DING DONG
Tanner Clark WORLD TOUR
Amelia's Room

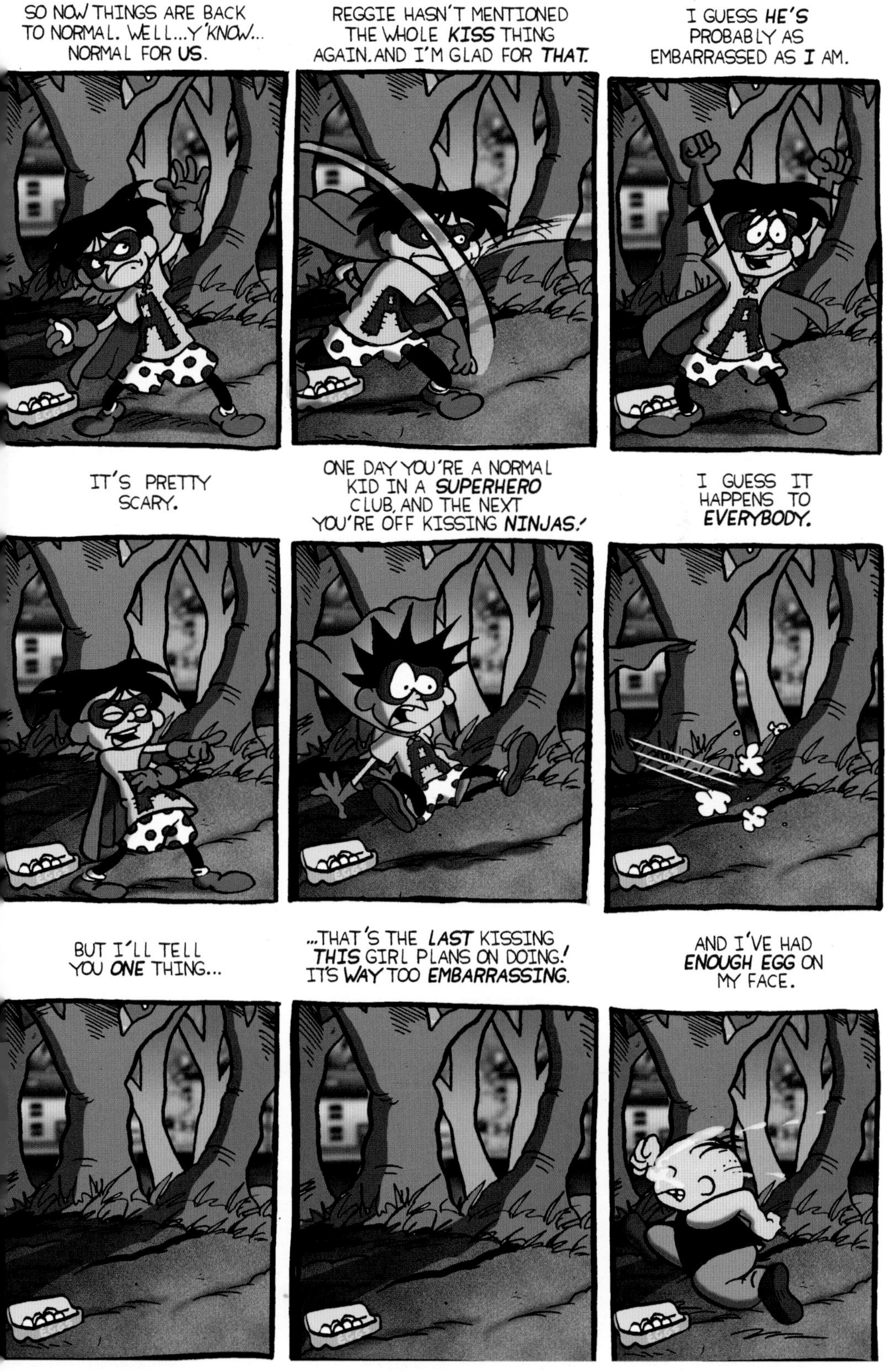
SO NOW THINGS ARE BACK TO NORMAL. WELL...Y'KNOW... NORMAL FOR US.
REGGIE HASN'T MENTIONED THE WHOLE KISS THING AGAIN. AND I'M GLAD FOR THAT.
I GUESS HE'S PROBABLY AS EMBARRASSED AS I AM.
IT'S PRETTY SCARY.
ONE DAY YOU'RE A NORMAL KID IN A SUPERHERO CLUB, AND THE NEXT YOU'RE OFF KISSING NINJAS!
I GUESS IT HAPPENS TO EVERYBODY.
BUT I'LL TELL YOU ONE THING...
...THAT'S THE LAST KISSING THIS GIRL PLANS ON DOING! IT'S WAY TOO EMBARRASSING.
AND I'VE HAD ENOUGH EGG ON MY FACE.

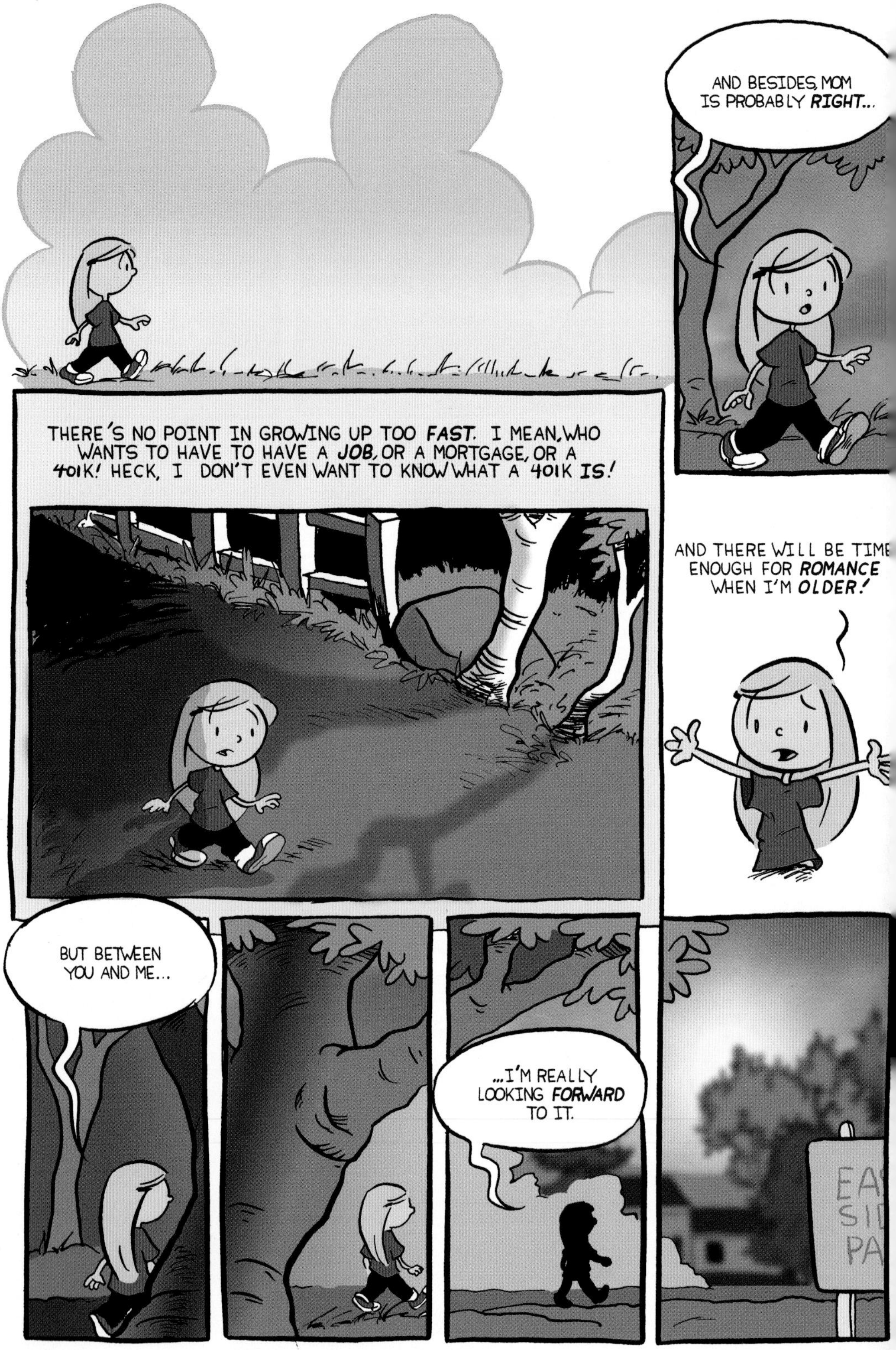
AND BESIDES, MOM IS PROBABLY RIGHT...
THERE'S NO POINT IN GROWING UP TOO FAST. I MEAN, WHO WANTS TO HAVE TO HAVE A JOB, OR A MORTGAGE, OR A 401K! HECK, I DON'T EVEN WANT TO KNOW WHAT A 401K IS!
AND THERE WILL BE TIME ENOUGH FOR ROMANCE WHEN I'M OLDER!
BUT BETWEEN YOU AND ME...
...I'M REALLY LOOKING FORWARD TO IT.

Joy and Wonder

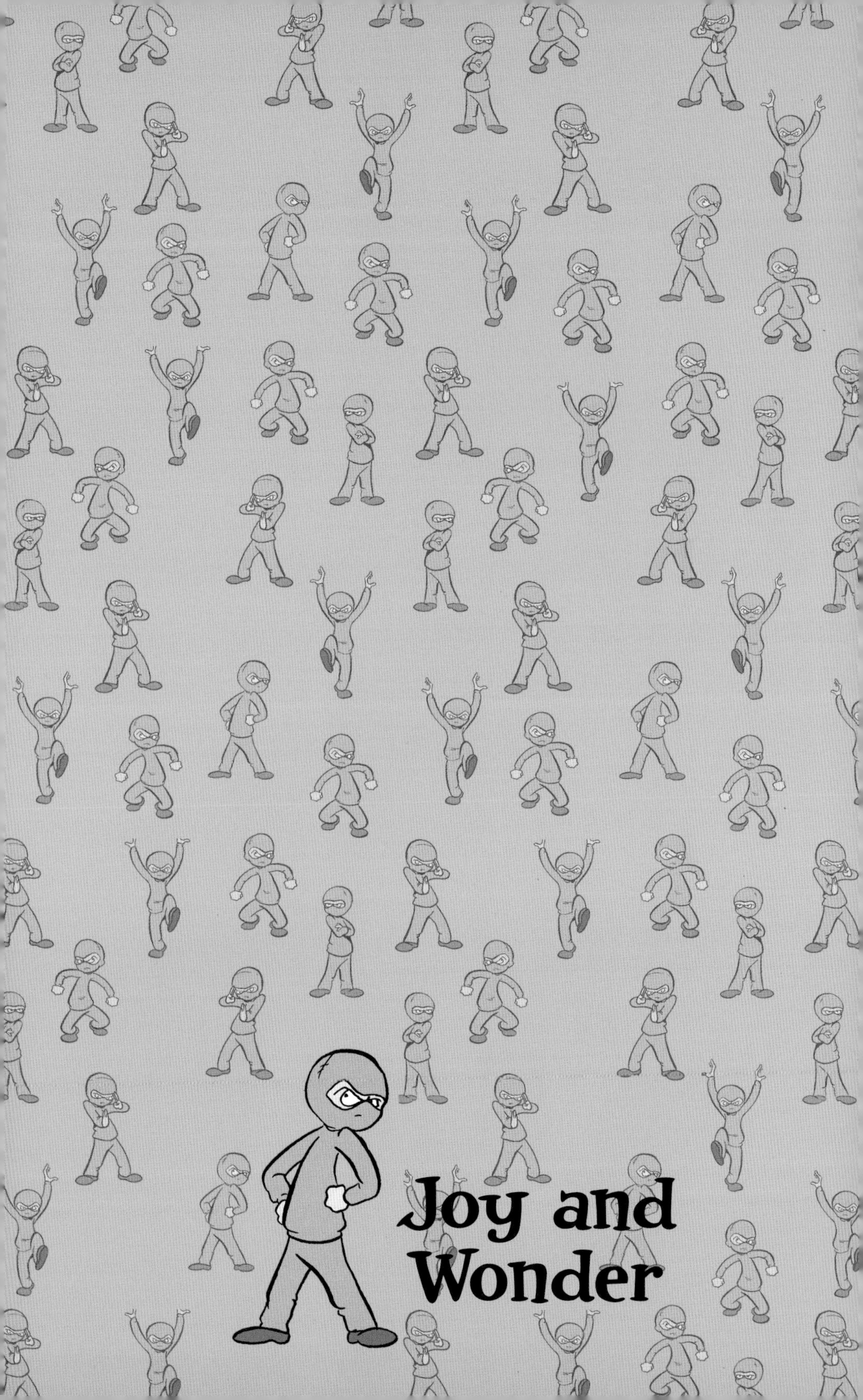

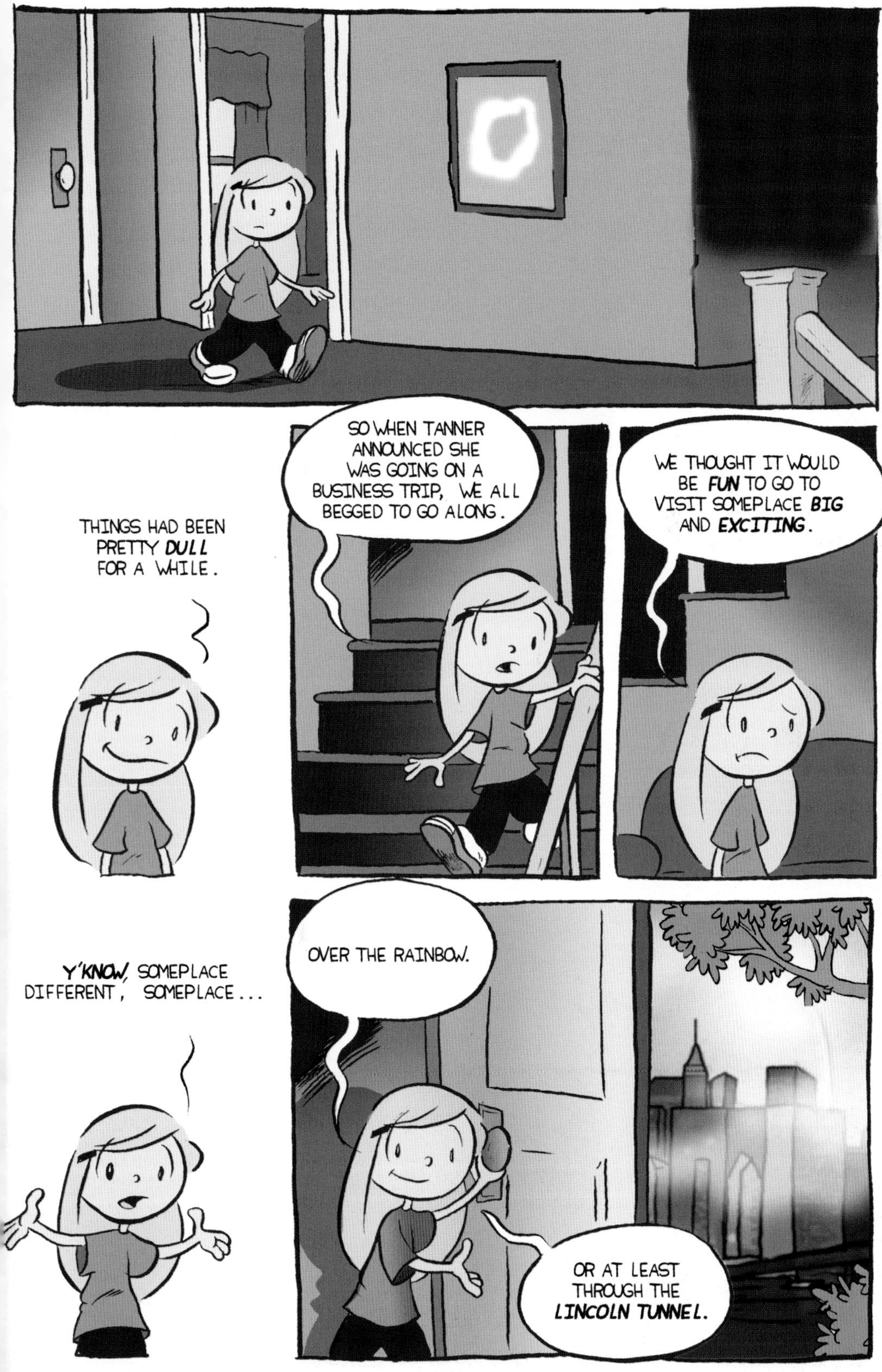

THINGS HAD BEEN PRETTY DULL FOR A WHILE.
SO WHEN TANNER ANNOUNCED SHE WAS GOING ON A BUSINESS TRIP, WE ALL BEGGED TO GO ALONG.
WE THOUGHT IT WOULD BE FUN TO GO TO VISIT SOMEPLACE BIG AND EXCITING.
Y'KNOW, SOMEPLACE DIFFERENT, SOMEPLACE...
OVER THE RAINBOW.
OR AT LEAST THROUGH THE LINCOLN TUNNEL.

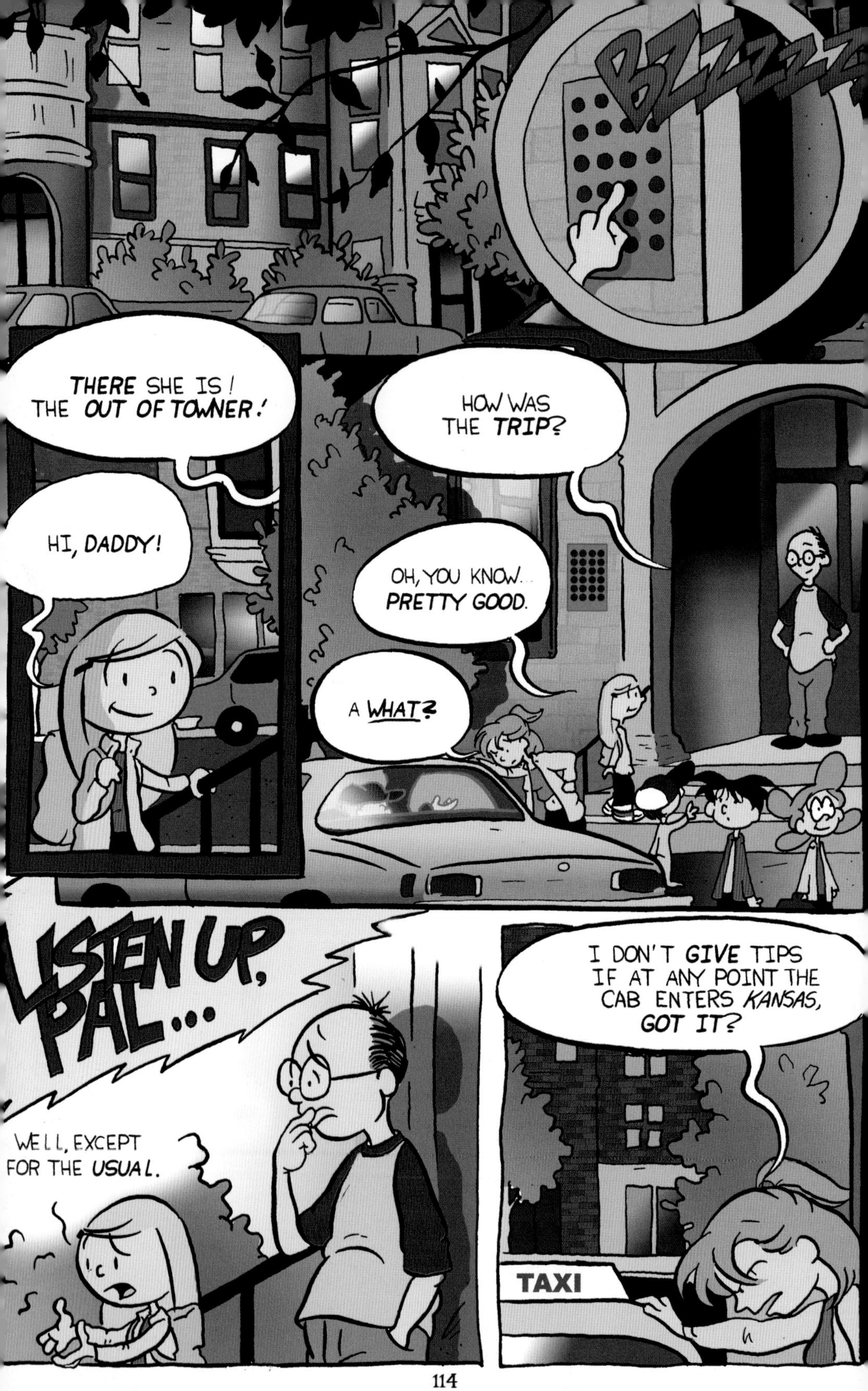

BZZZZZ
THERE SHE IS! THE OUT OF TOWNER!
HI, DADDY!
HOW WAS THE TRIP?
OH, YOU KNOW... PRETTY GOOD.
A WHAT?
LISTEN UP, PAL...
WELL, EXCEPT FOR THE USUAL.
I DON'T GIVE TIPS IF AT ANY POINT THE CAB ENTERS KANSAS, GOT IT?
TAXI

115

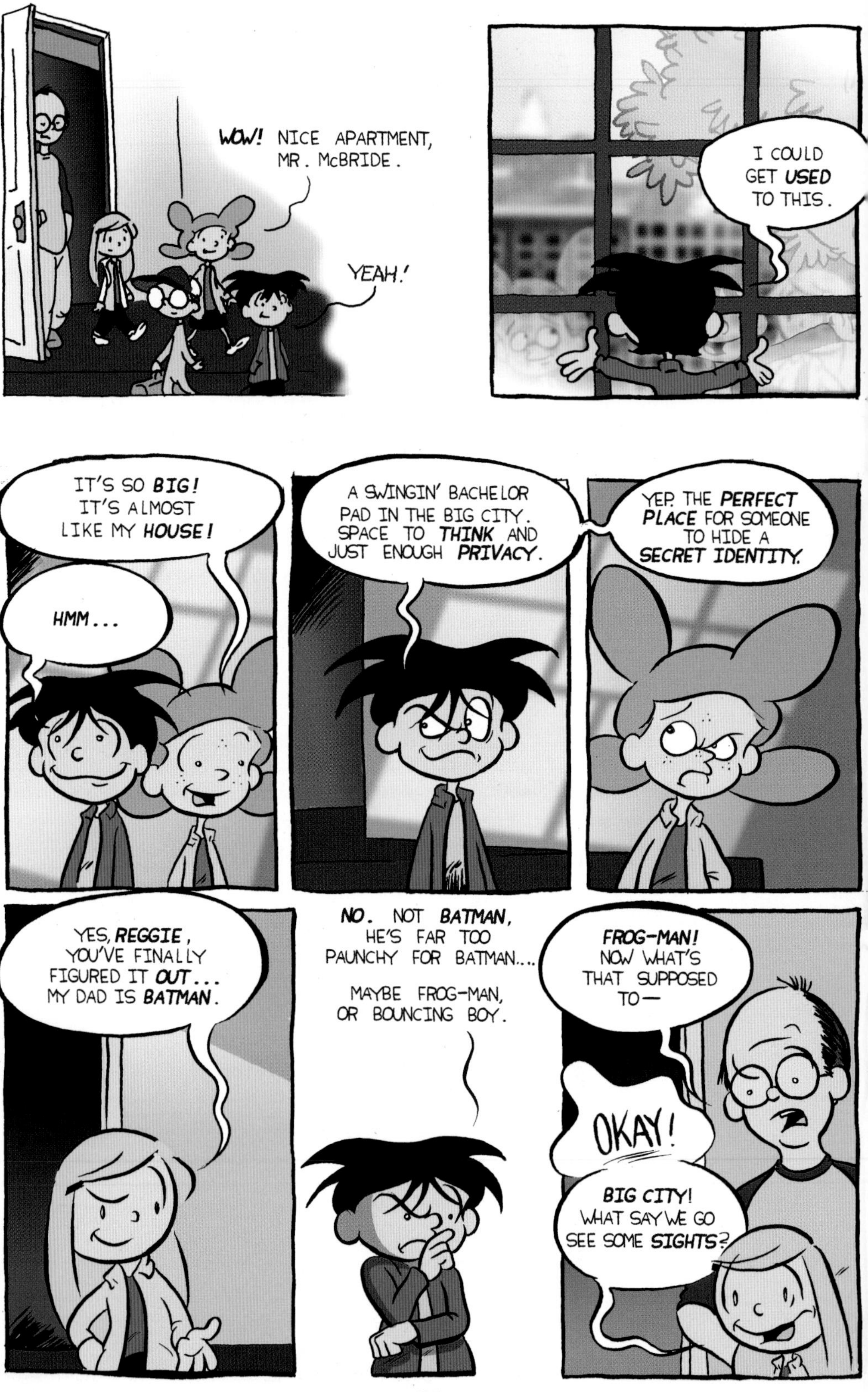
WOW! NICE APARTMENT, MR. McBRIDE.
YEAH!
I COULD GET USED TO THIS.
IT'S SO BIG! IT'S ALMOST LIKE MY HOUSE!
HMM...
A SWINGIN' BACHELOR PAD IN THE BIG CITY. SPACE TO THINK AND JUST ENOUGH PRIVACY.
YEP. THE PERFECT PLACE FOR SOMEONE TO HIDE A SECRET IDENTITY.
YES, REGGIE, YOU'VE FINALLY FIGURED IT OUT... MY DAD IS BATMAN.
NO. NOT BATMAN, HE'S FAR TOO PAUNCHY FOR BATMAN....
MAYBE FROG-MAN, OR BOUNCING BOY.
FROG-MAN! NOW WHAT'S THAT SUPPOSED TO—
OKAY!
BIG CITY! WHAT SAY WE GO SEE SOME SIGHTS?

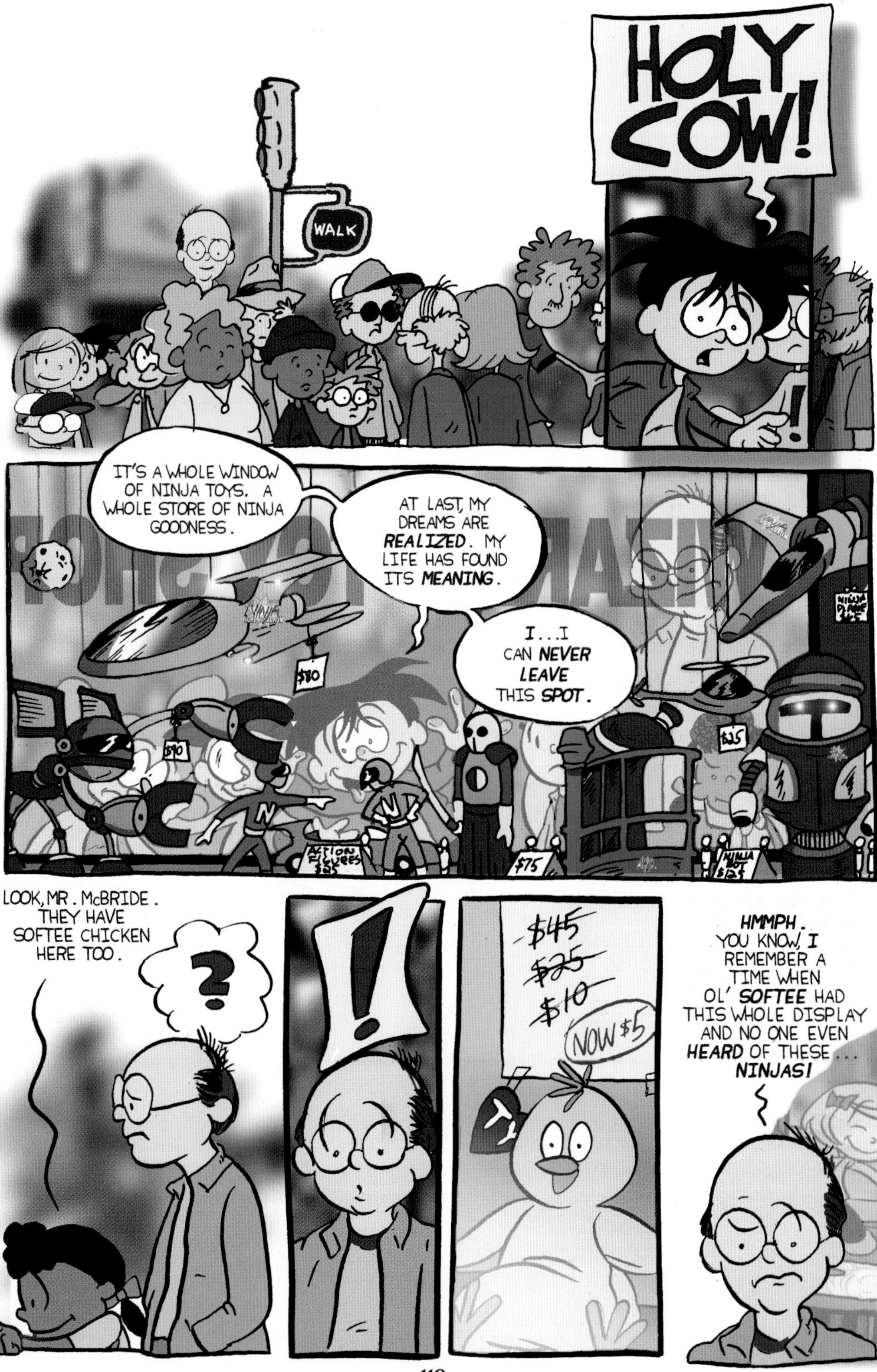
WALK
HOLY COW!
IT'S A WHOLE WINDOW OF NINJA TOYS. A WHOLE STORE OF NINJA GOODNESS.
AT LAST, MY DREAMS ARE **REALIZED**. MY LIFE HAS FOUND ITS **MEANING**.
I...I CAN **NEVER LEAVE** THIS **SPOT**.
$80
$90
$75
LOOK, MR. McBRIDE. THEY HAVE SOFTEE CHICKEN HERE TOO.
?
!
$45
$25
$10
NOW $5
HMMPH. YOU KNOW, **I** REMEMBER A TIME WHEN OL' **SOFTEE** HAD THIS WHOLE DISPLAY AND NO ONE EVEN **HEARD** OF THESE... **NINJAS!**

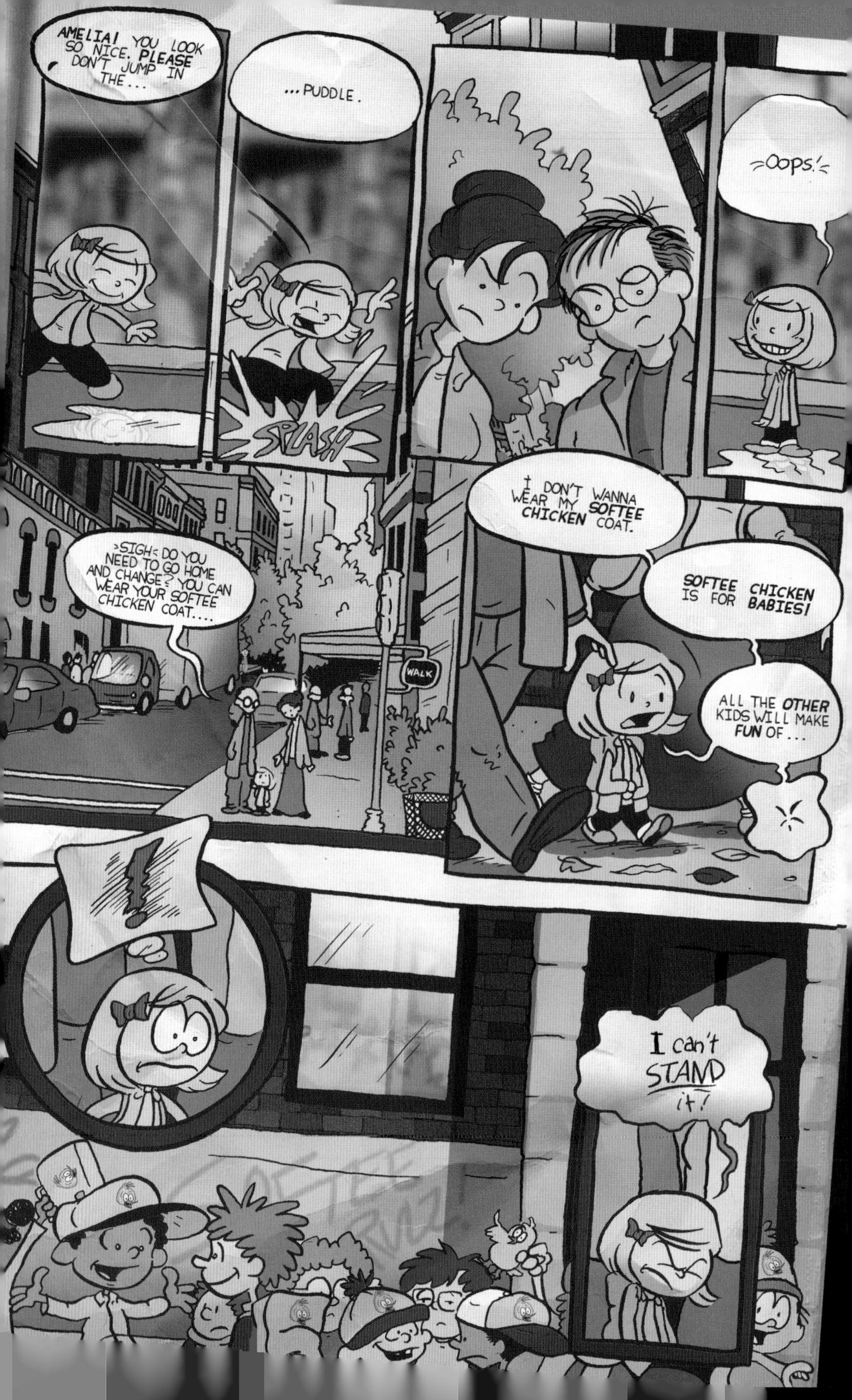
AMELIA! YOU LOOK SO NICE. PLEASE DON'T JUMP IN THE...
...PUDDLE.
SPLASH
=OOPS!=
>SIGH< DO YOU NEED TO GO HOME AND CHANGE? YOU CAN WEAR YOUR SOFTEE CHICKEN COAT....
WALK
I DON'T WANNA WEAR MY SOFTEE CHICKEN COAT.
SOFTEE CHICKEN IS FOR BABIES!
ALL THE OTHER KIDS WILL MAKE FUN OF...
I can't STAND it!

It was back in first grade. See, by the time McB came to town, school had already been rolling for a while. And let's just say I had already made my rep. What I hadn't made was, y'know, any friends. And on top of that, we had this teacher, Miss Hamilton. She was a real witch, and she had it in for me BIG TIME.

And, really, it was for no reason. I mean, sure, there were one or two little things, but the fire department was barely involved. And besides, they couldn't prove anyth–

Uh...anyway...

So when Amelia joined the class, I barely even noticed. She was just this quiet, shy girl who kept to herself, and...

Rhonda?
Rhonda? What's so funny? Are you okay? Breathe, girl! ***BREATHE!***

So like I said, I pretty much ignored her. Then one day I noticed something.

If there was one person Miss Hamilton liked less than me, it was Amelia Louise McBride.

See, that's even what she called her... Amelia Louise... Never just Amelia, she always stuck on Louise. Only it sounded like this...

Leweeeeeeeeeeez.

Like she just stepped in something nasty.

Rhonda, if you can't control the laughing, we'll have to ask you to leave.

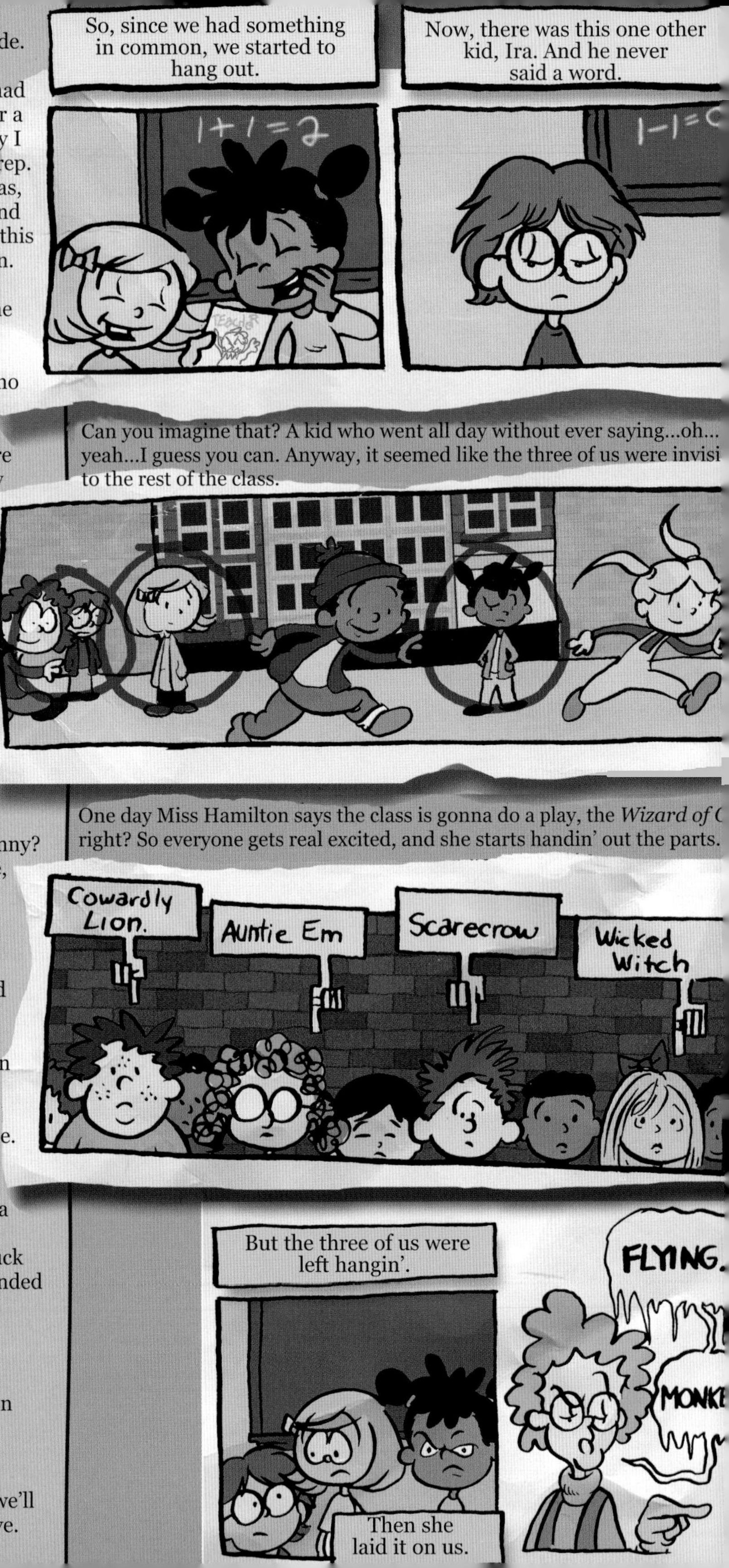

So, since we had something in common, we started to hang out.
1+1=2
Now, there was this one other kid, Ira. And he never said a word.
Can you imagine that? A kid who went all day without ever saying...oh... yeah...I guess you can. Anyway, it seemed like the three of us were invisi
to the rest of the class.
One day Miss Hamilton says the class is gonna do a play, the *Wizard of*
right? So everyone gets real excited, and she starts handin' out the parts.
Cowardly Lion.
Auntie Em
Scarecrow
Wicked Witch
But the three of us were left hangin'.
FLYING.
MONKE
Then she laid it on us.

Not exactly a compliment, y'know? I mean, it's not like she picked her favorite students and said, "Ah, yes...You shall be my monkeys." It was more like, "Let's put these numbskulls where they can do the least amount of damage."

I think Mr. and Mrs. McBride felt bad for us. They invited us over a bunch of times so we could "rehearse" with Amelia. Not that there was much to rehearse. We pretty much just ran around the apartment going, "Eek! Eek!" But, y'know, it was fun.

The best part was when Amelia's mom made us these way cool monkey costumes. They had wings and ears and big ol' monkey tails. We were stylin'! I think that's when we started getting into it. I came up with this name, "The Flying Monkey Society," and we ran around calling ourselves that. Whenever someone would ask what time it was, we'd yell, "IT'S MONKEY TIME!" (Well, me and McB would. Ira still wasn't talking) and then we'd jump around like rejects.

It must've looked like fun, cuz pretty soon everyone wanted to be a Flying Monkey. Of course, we wouldn't let them. Heh, heh...It was pretty cool.

So, anyway, the day of the big show finally comes, and everyone is freaking out. Even Miss Hamilton is kinda goin' wonky. And the more wonky she got, the more freaked out we got. It was a scene.

Then things really went downhill. First, the girl who was playing Dorothy forgot the words to "Somewhere Over the Rainbow." Then the Tin Man got the hiccups, which wouldn't have been so bad if it didn't make Carlos, the kid playing the Scarecrow, laugh. He laughed so hard he fell off the stage. By the time we came on, it was a massacre. People were leaving. I'm pretty sure I even heard another teacher boo us.

So when we went out there, we froze. We didn't "Eek!" or flap our arms or nothing. It was gonna be the most disastrous part of the big disaster.

And then...

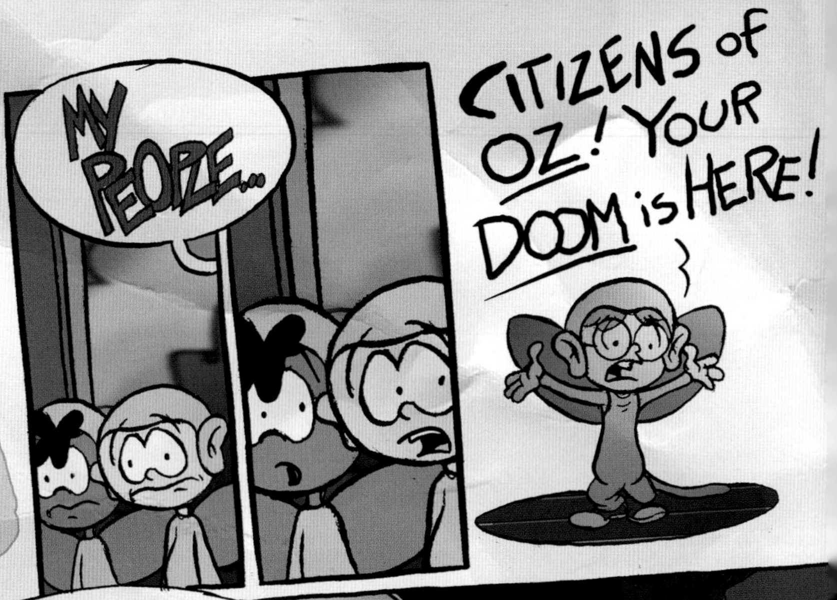

MY PEOPLE...
CITIZENS of OZ! YOUR DOOM is HERE!

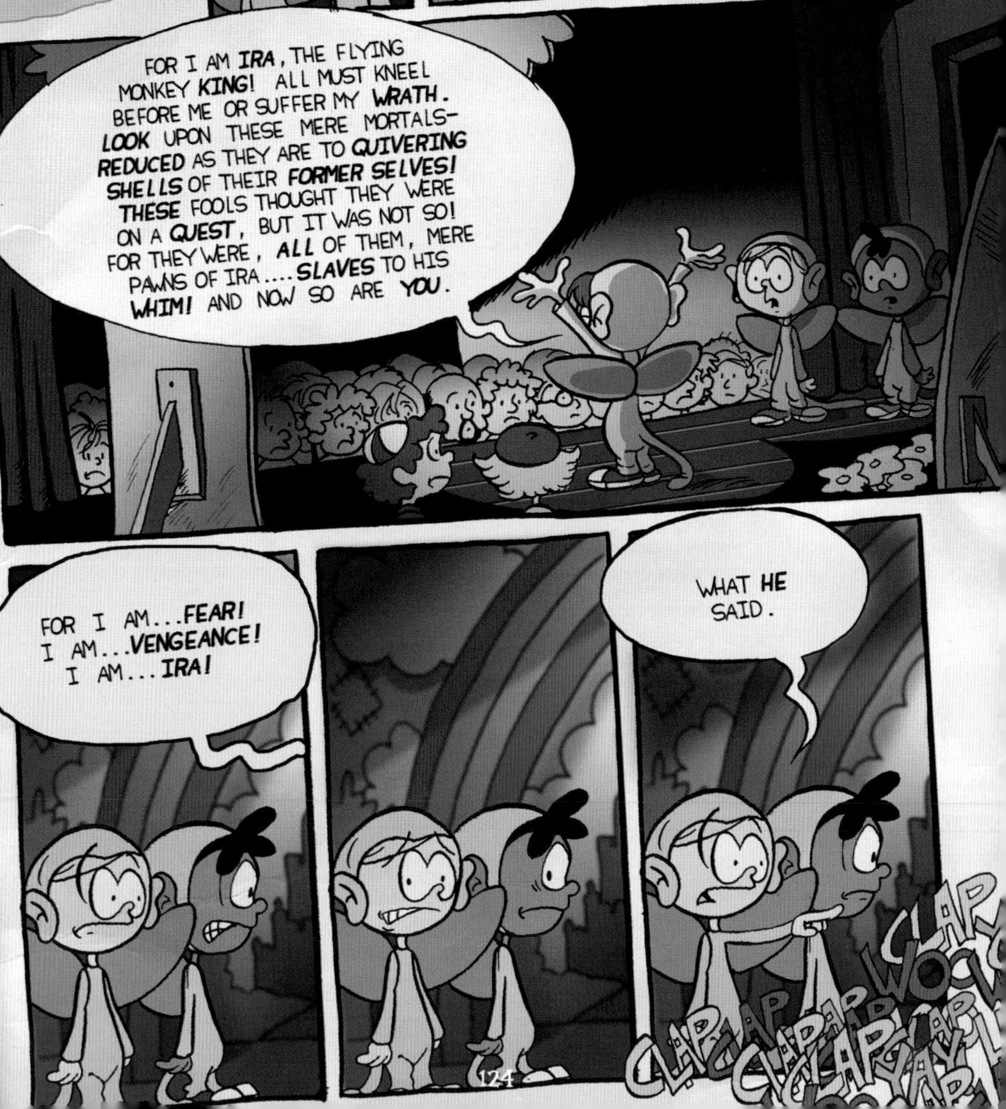

FOR I AM IRA, THE FLYING MONKEY KING! ALL MUST KNEEL BEFORE ME OR SUFFER MY WRATH. LOOK UPON THESE MERE MORTALS- REDUCED AS THEY ARE TO QUIVERING SHELLS OF THEIR FORMER SELVES! THESE FOOLS THOUGHT THEY WERE ON A QUEST, BUT IT WAS NOT SO! FOR THEY WERE, ALL OF THEM, MERE PAWNS OF IRA.... SLAVES TO HIS WHIM! AND NOW SO ARE YOU.
FOR I AM...FEAR! I AM...VENGEANCE! I AM...IRA!
WHAT HE SAID.
CLAP

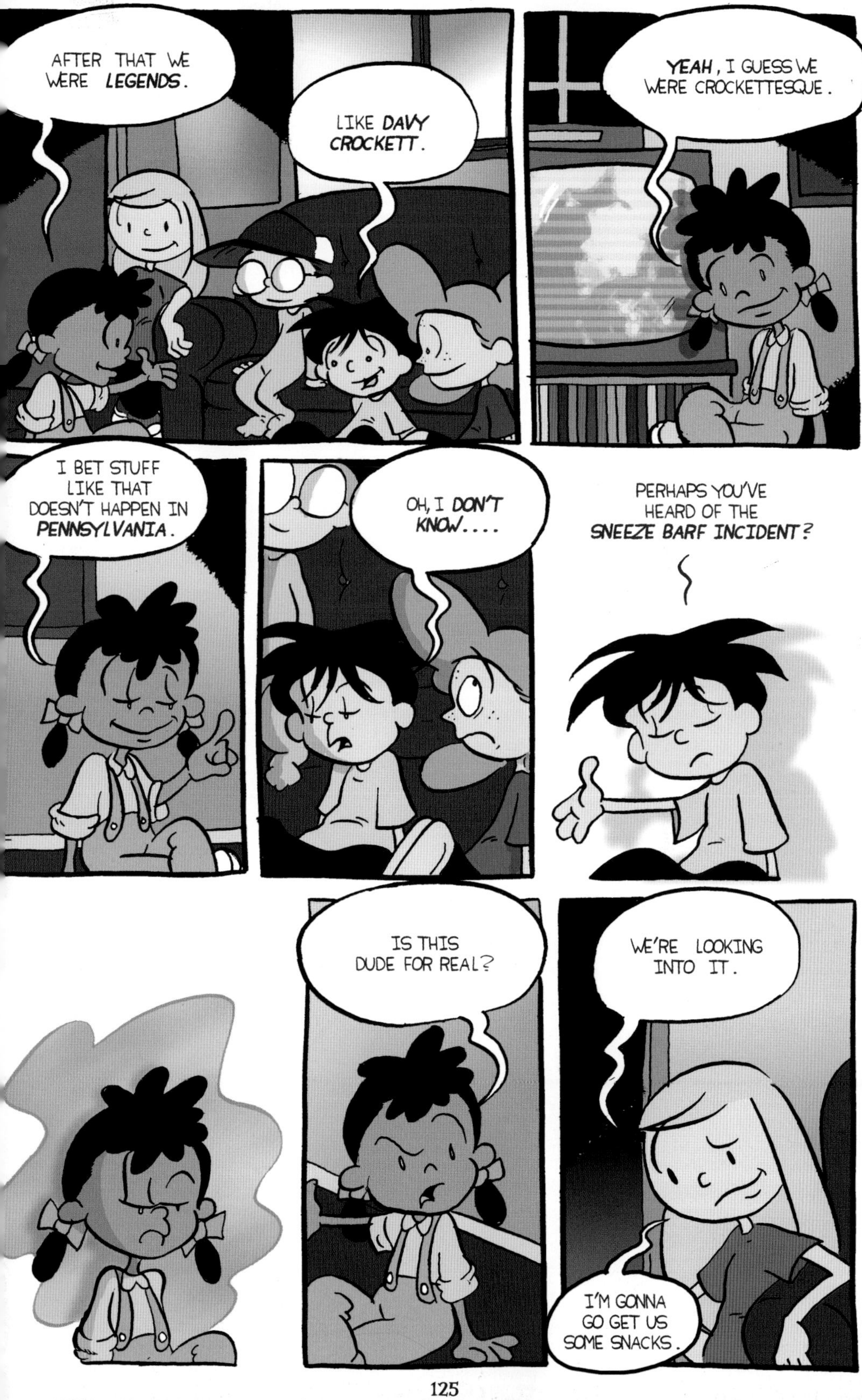
AFTER THAT WE WERE LEGENDS.
LIKE DAVY CROCKETT.
YEAH, I GUESS WE WERE CROCKETTESQUE.
I BET STUFF LIKE THAT DOESN'T HAPPEN IN PENNSYLVANIA.
OH, I DON'T KNOW....
PERHAPS YOU'VE HEARD OF THE SNEEZE BARF INCIDENT?
IS THIS DUDE FOR REAL?
WE'RE LOOKING INTO IT.
I'M GONNA GO GET US SOME SNACKS.

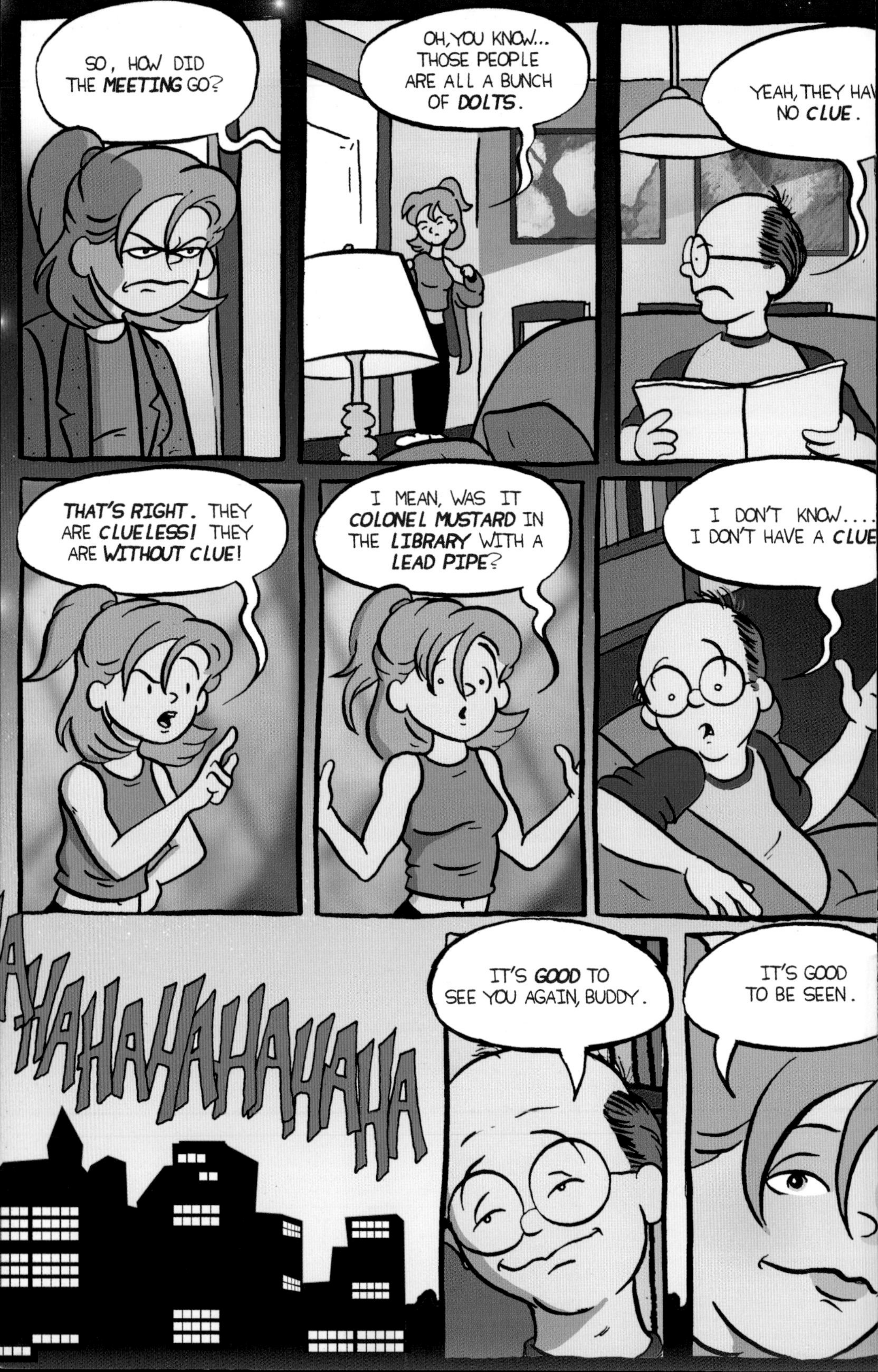
SO, HOW DID THE MEETING GO?
OH, YOU KNOW... THOSE PEOPLE ARE ALL A BUNCH OF DOLTS.
YEAH, THEY HAV NO CLUE.
THAT'S RIGHT. THEY ARE CLUELESS! THEY ARE WITHOUT CLUE!
I MEAN, WAS IT COLONEL MUSTARD IN THE LIBRARY WITH A LEAD PIPE?
I DON'T KNOW.... I DON'T HAVE A CLUE
HAHAHAHAHAHAHA
IT'S GOOD TO SEE YOU AGAIN, BUDDY.
IT'S GOOD TO BE SEEN.

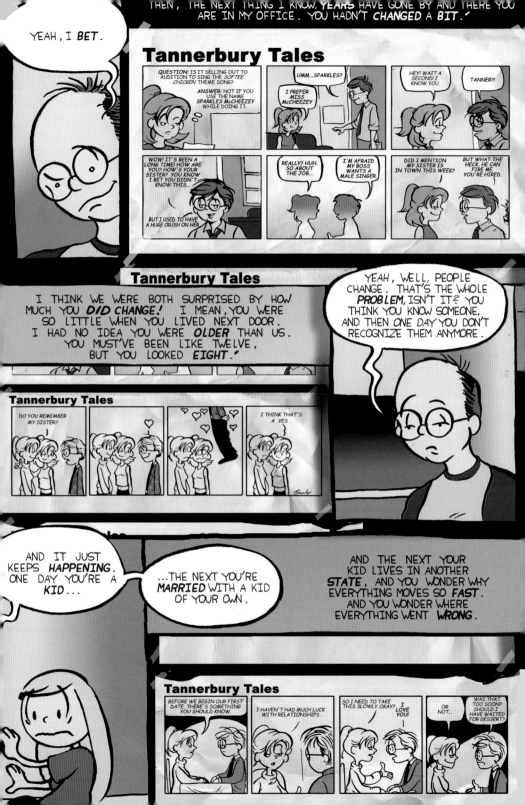

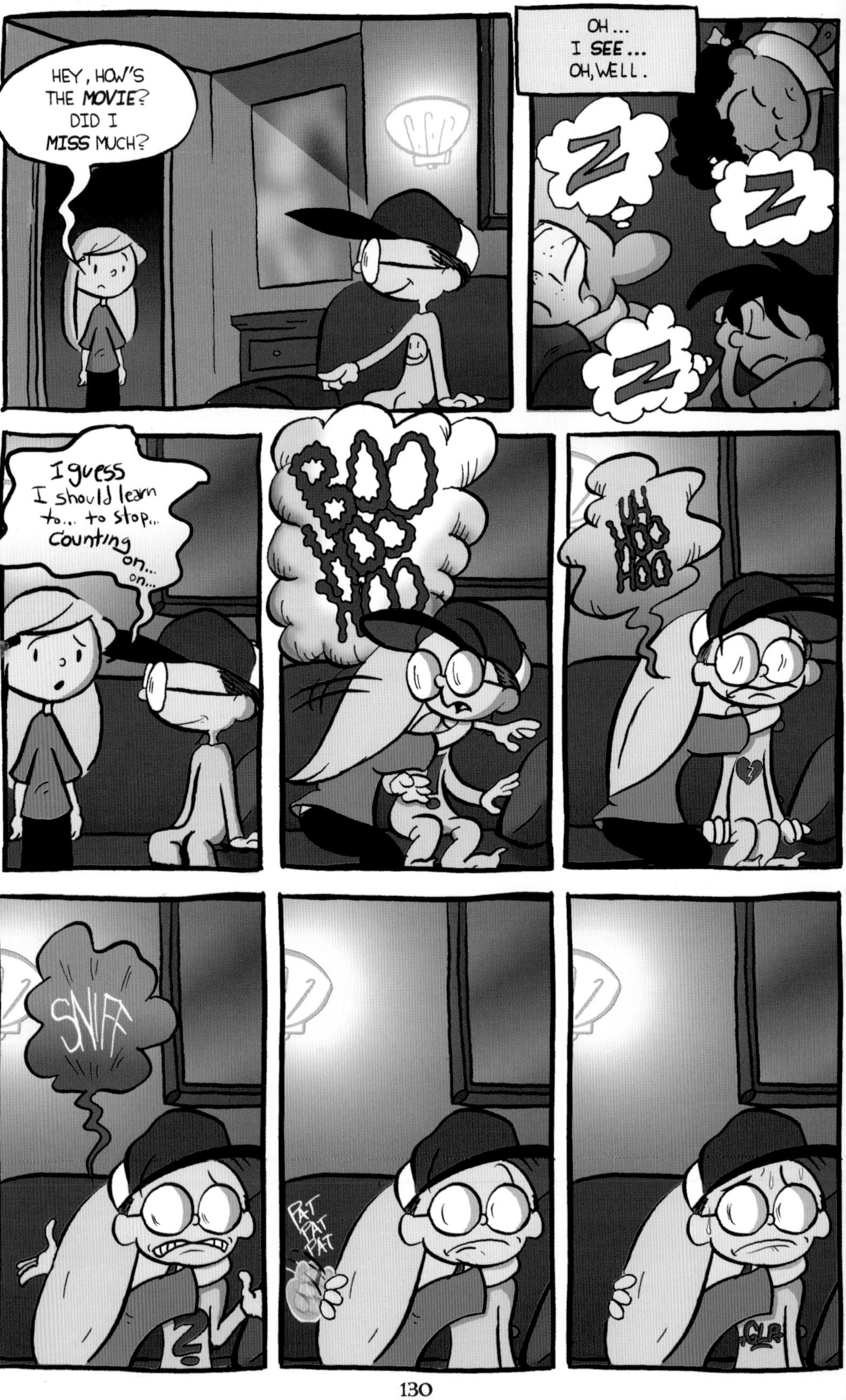
HEY, HOW'S THE MOVIE? DID I MISS MUCH?
OH... I SEE... OH, WELL.
Z
Z
Z
I guess I should learn to... to stop... counting on... on...
BOO HOO HOO
UH HOO HOO HOO
SNIFF
PAT PAT PAT

THE NEXT DAY WAS **GREAT**. DAD TOOK US TO THE **PARK** AND THE **MUSEUM**. AND WE RAN AROUND THE OLD NEIGHBORHOOD PLAYING. BUT OF COURSE...

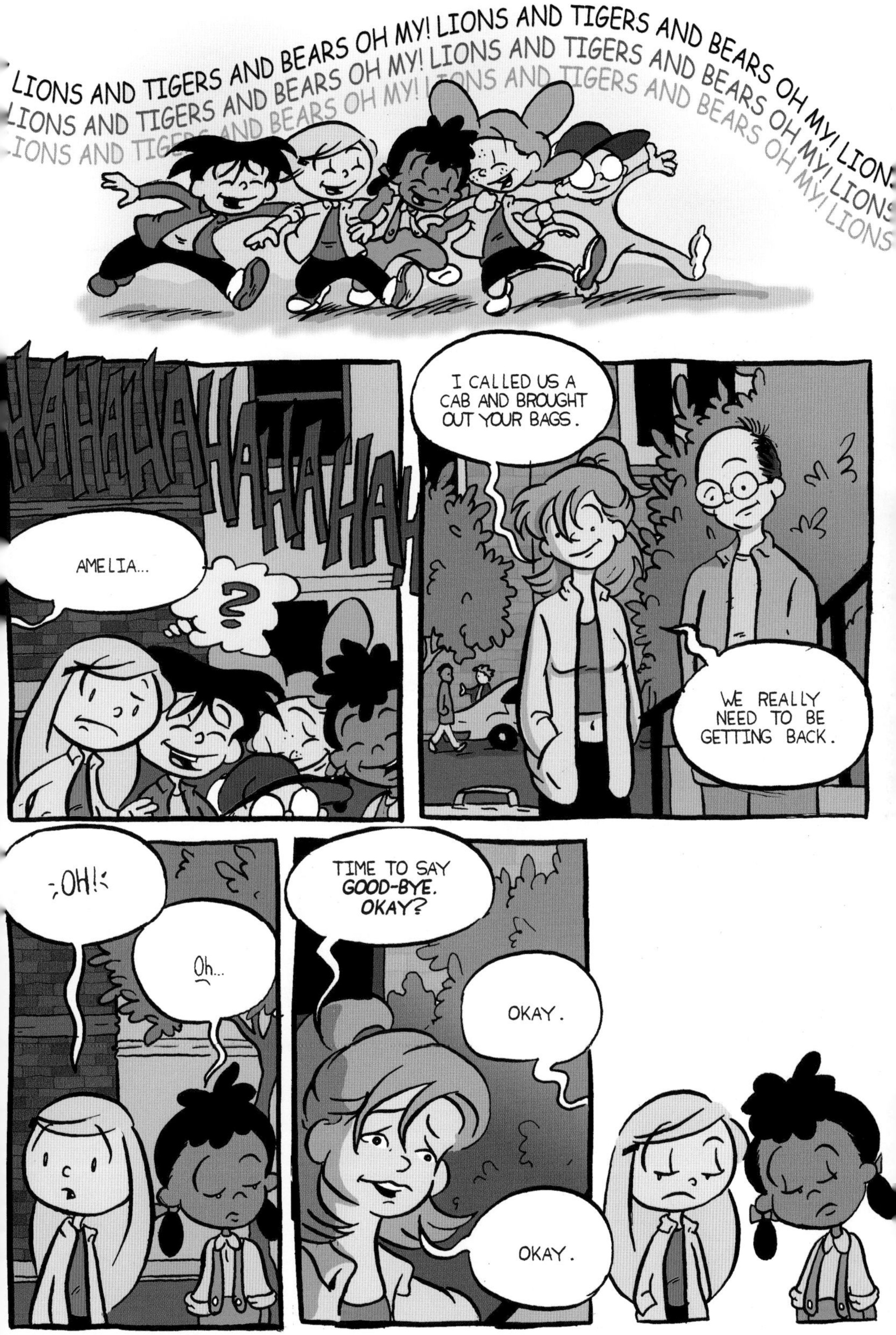

LIONS AND TIGERS AND BEARS OH MY! LIONS AND TIGERS AND BEARS OH MY! LION
LIONS AND TIGERS AND BEARS OH MY! LIONS AND TIGERS AND BEARS OH MY! LIONS
LIONS AND TIGERS AND BEARS OH MY! LIONS AND TIGERS AND BEARS OH MY! LIONS
HAHAHAHAHAHAHAH
AMELIA...
?
I CALLED US A CAB AND BROUGHT OUT YOUR BAGS.
WE REALLY NEED TO BE GETTING BACK.
OH!
Oh...
TIME TO SAY **GOOD-BYE. OKAY?**
OKAY.
OKAY.

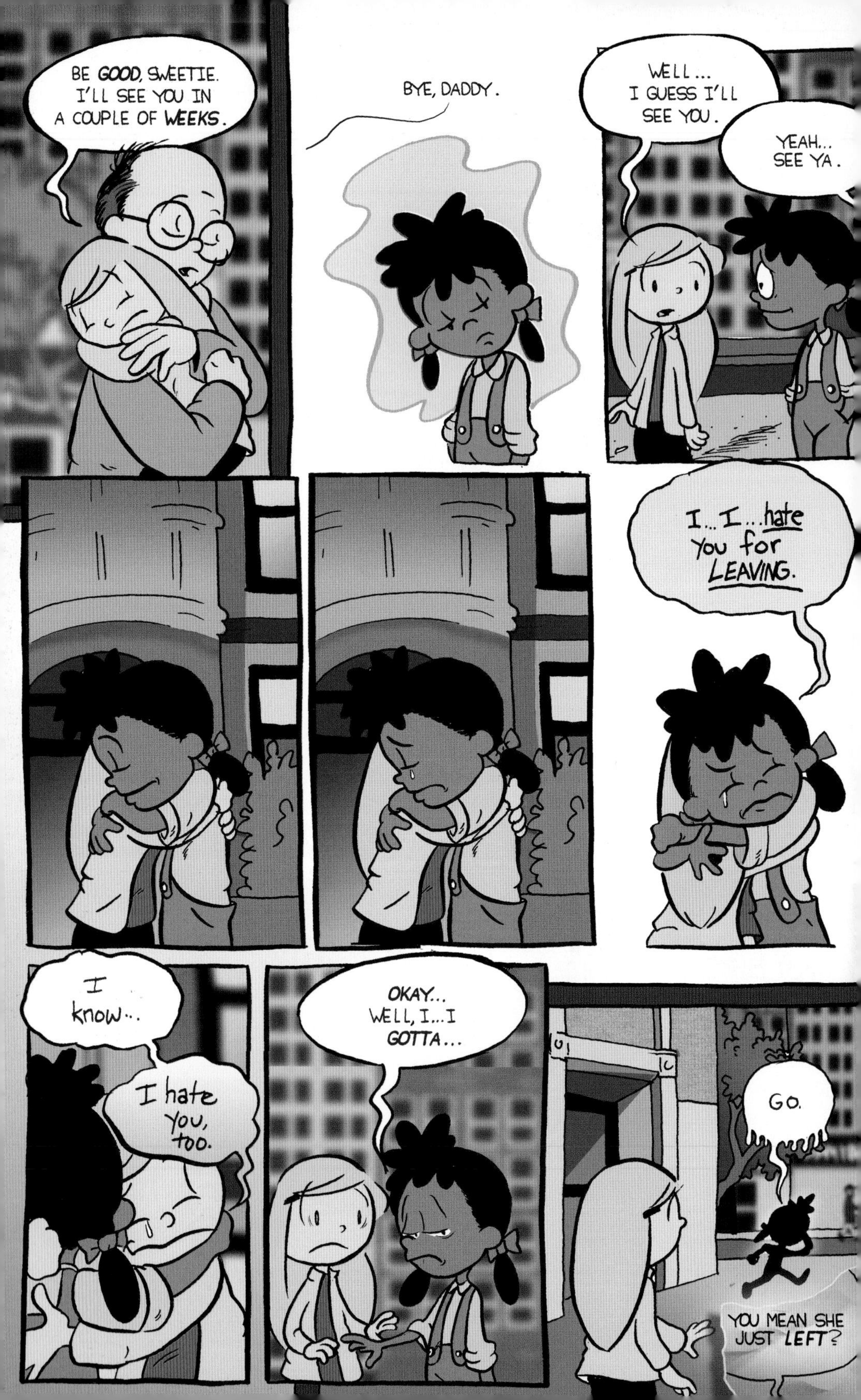
BE GOOD, SWEETIE. I'LL SEE YOU IN A COUPLE OF WEEKS.
BYE, DADDY.
WELL... I GUESS I'LL SEE YOU.
YEAH... SEE YA.
I... I... hate you for LEAVING.
I know...
I hate you, too.
OKAY... WELL, I... I GOTTA...
GO.
YOU MEAN SHE JUST LEFT?

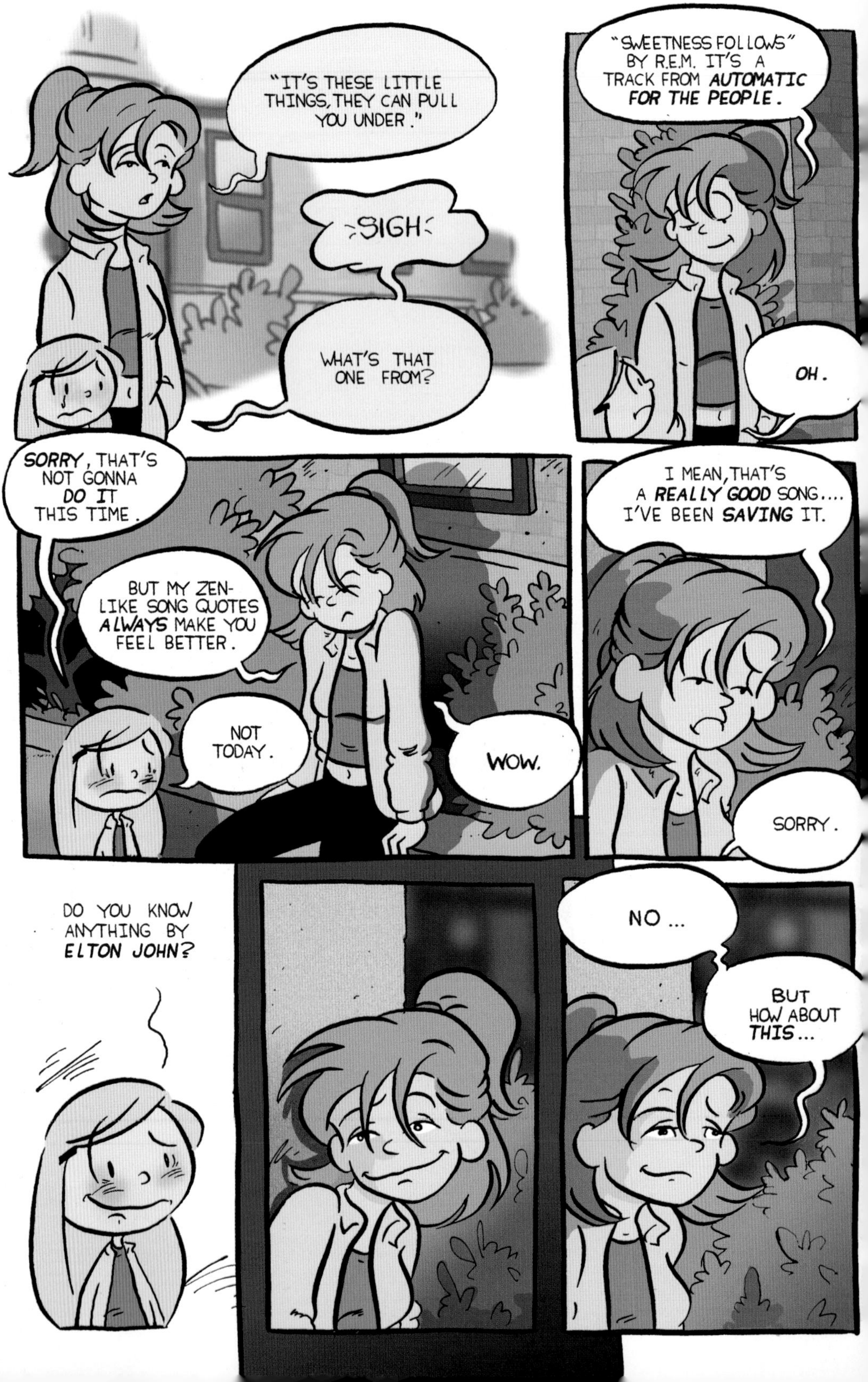
"IT'S THESE LITTLE THINGS, THEY CAN PULL YOU UNDER."
SIGH
WHAT'S THAT ONE FROM?
"SWEETNESS FOLLOWS" BY R.E.M. IT'S A TRACK FROM AUTOMATIC FOR THE PEOPLE.
OH.
SORRY, THAT'S NOT GONNA DO IT THIS TIME.
BUT MY ZEN-LIKE SONG QUOTES ALWAYS MAKE YOU FEEL BETTER.
NOT TODAY.
WOW.
I MEAN, THAT'S A REALLY GOOD SONG.... I'VE BEEN SAVING IT.
SORRY.
DO YOU KNOW ANYTHING BY ELTON JOHN?
NO ...
BUT HOW ABOUT THIS...

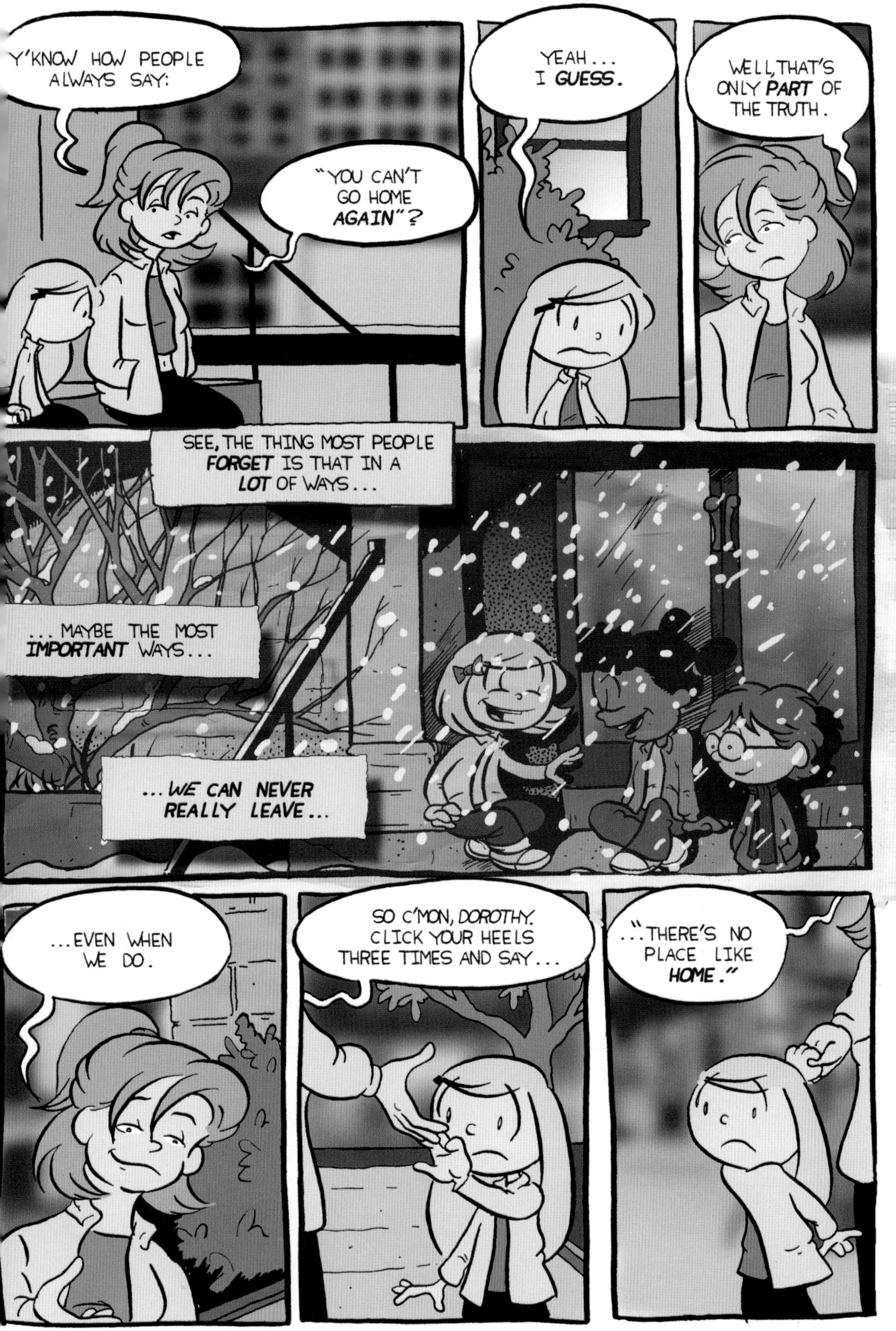
Y'KNOW HOW PEOPLE ALWAYS SAY:
"YOU CAN'T GO HOME AGAIN"?
YEAH... I GUESS.
WELL, THAT'S ONLY PART OF THE TRUTH.
SEE, THE THING MOST PEOPLE FORGET IS THAT IN A LOT OF WAYS...
...MAYBE THE MOST IMPORTANT WAYS...
...WE CAN NEVER REALLY LEAVE...
...EVEN WHEN WE DO.
SO C'MON, DOROTHY. CLICK YOUR HEELS THREE TIMES AND SAY...
..."THERE'S NO PLACE LIKE HOME."

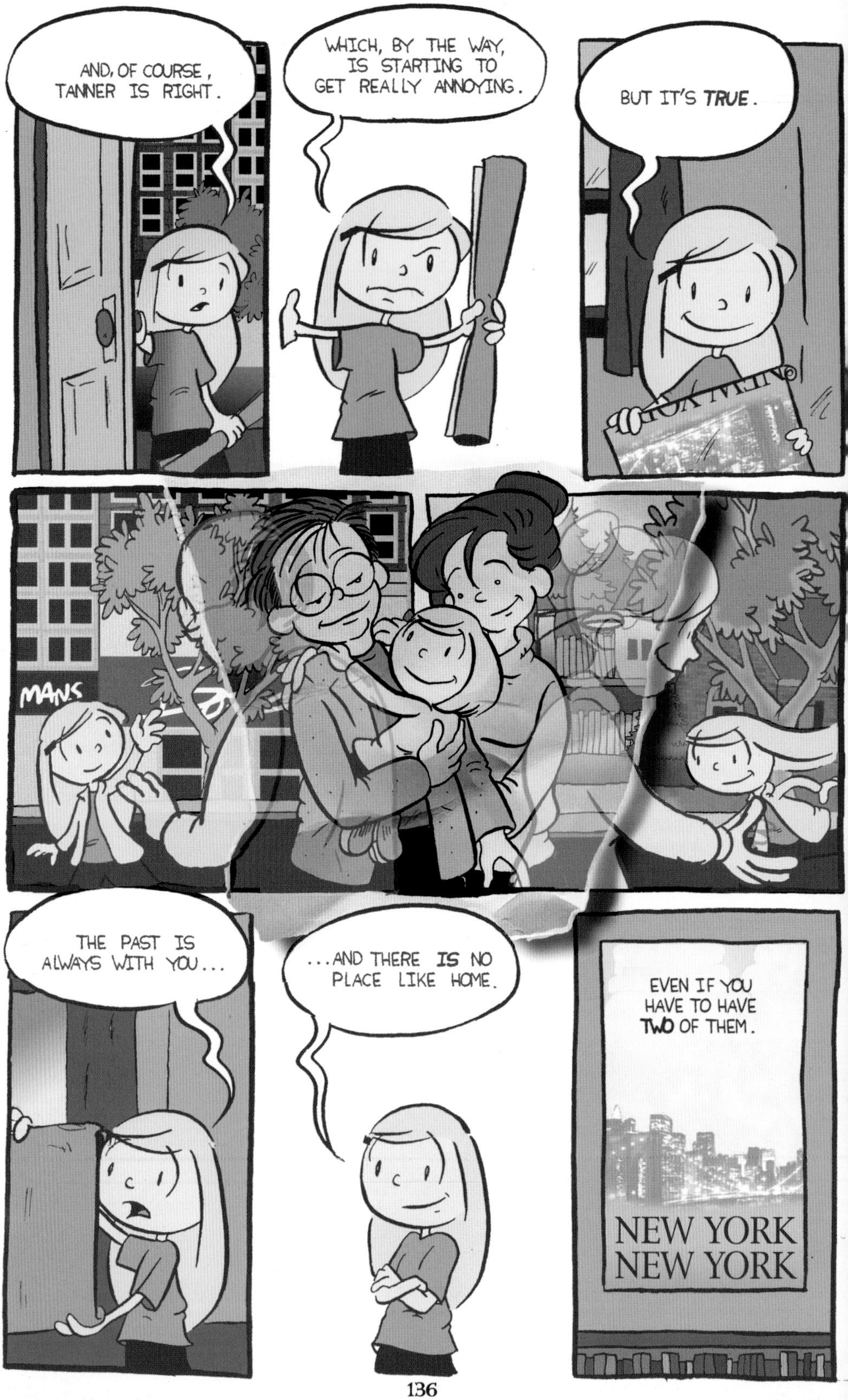
AND, OF COURSE, TANNER IS RIGHT.
WHICH, BY THE WAY, IS STARTING TO GET REALLY ANNOYING.
BUT IT'S **TRUE**.
MANS
THE PAST IS ALWAYS WITH YOU...
...AND THERE **IS** NO PLACE LIKE HOME.
EVEN IF YOU HAVE TO HAVE **TWO** OF THEM.
NEW YORK NEW YORK

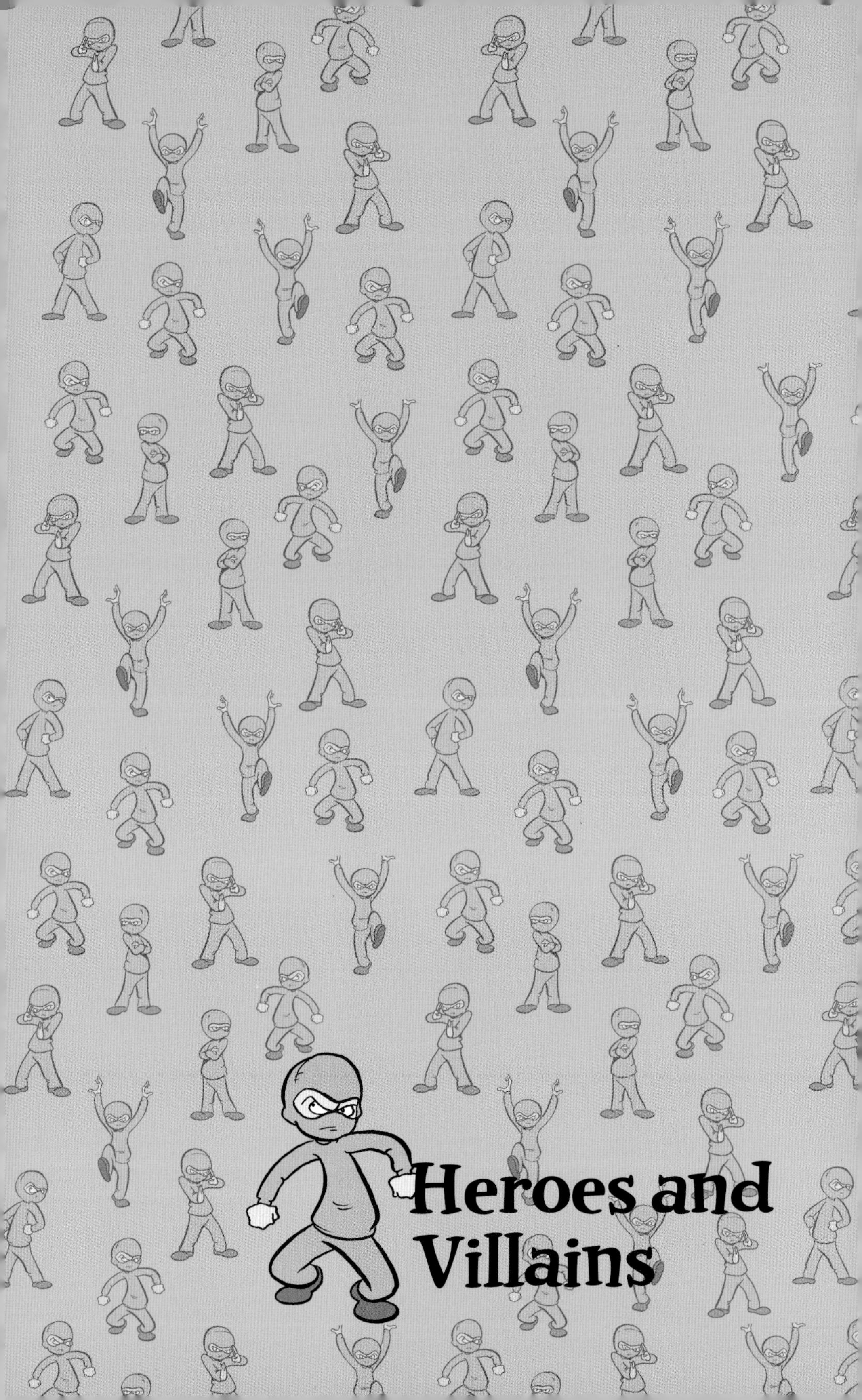

Heroes and Villains

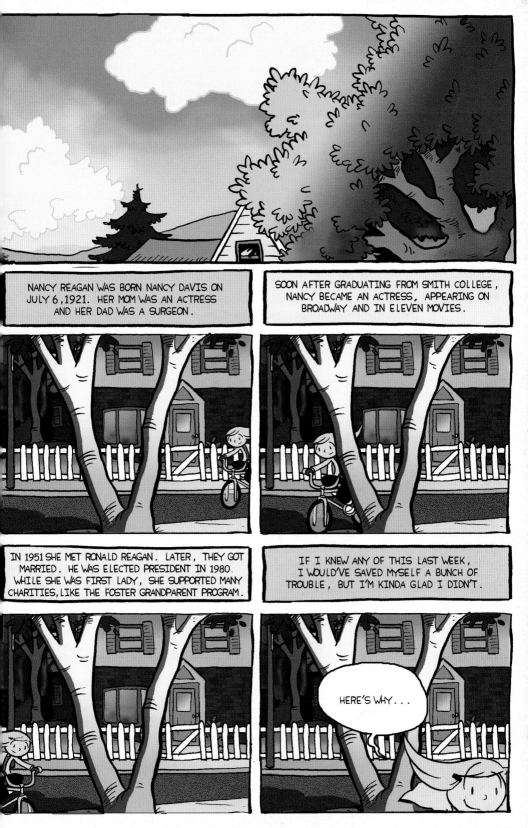

NANCY REAGAN WAS BORN NANCY DAVIS ON JULY 6, 1921. HER MOM WAS AN ACTRESS AND HER DAD WAS A SURGEON.

SOON AFTER GRADUATING FROM SMITH COLLEGE, NANCY BECAME AN ACTRESS, APPEARING ON BROADWAY AND IN ELEVEN MOVIES.

IN 1951 SHE MET RONALD REAGAN. LATER, THEY GOT MARRIED. HE WAS ELECTED PRESIDENT IN 1980. WHILE SHE WAS FIRST LADY, SHE SUPPORTED MANY CHARITIES, LIKE THE FOSTER GRANDPARENT PROGRAM.

IF I KNEW ANY OF THIS LAST WEEK, I WOULD'VE SAVED MYSELF A BUNCH OF TROUBLE, BUT I'M KINDA GLAD I DIDN'T.

HERE'S WHY...

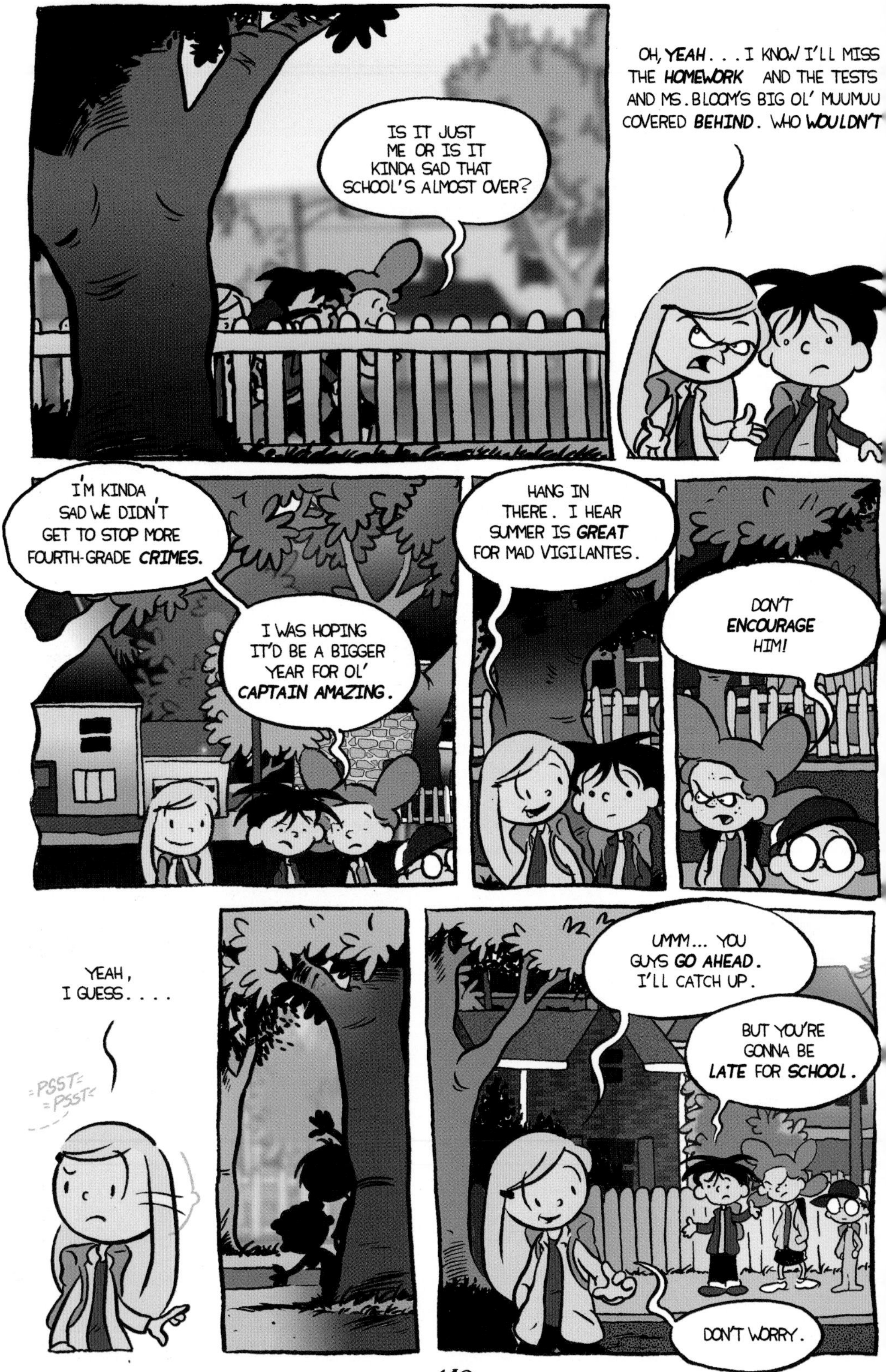
IS IT JUST ME OR IS IT KINDA SAD THAT SCHOOL'S ALMOST OVER?
OH, **YEAH** . . . I KNOW I'LL MISS THE **HOMEWORK** AND THE TESTS AND MS. BLOOM'S BIG OL' MUUMUU COVERED **BEHIND**. WHO **WOULDN'T**
I'M KINDA SAD WE DIDN'T GET TO STOP MORE FOURTH-GRADE **CRIMES.**
I WAS HOPING IT'D BE A BIGGER YEAR FOR OL' **CAPTAIN AMAZING**.
HANG IN THERE. I HEAR SUMMER IS **GREAT** FOR MAD VIGILANTES.
DON'T **ENCOURAGE** HIM!
YEAH, I GUESS. . . .
PSST PSST
UMMM... YOU GUYS **GO AHEAD**. I'LL CATCH UP.
BUT YOU'RE GONNA BE **LATE** FOR **SCHOOL**.
DON'T WORRY.

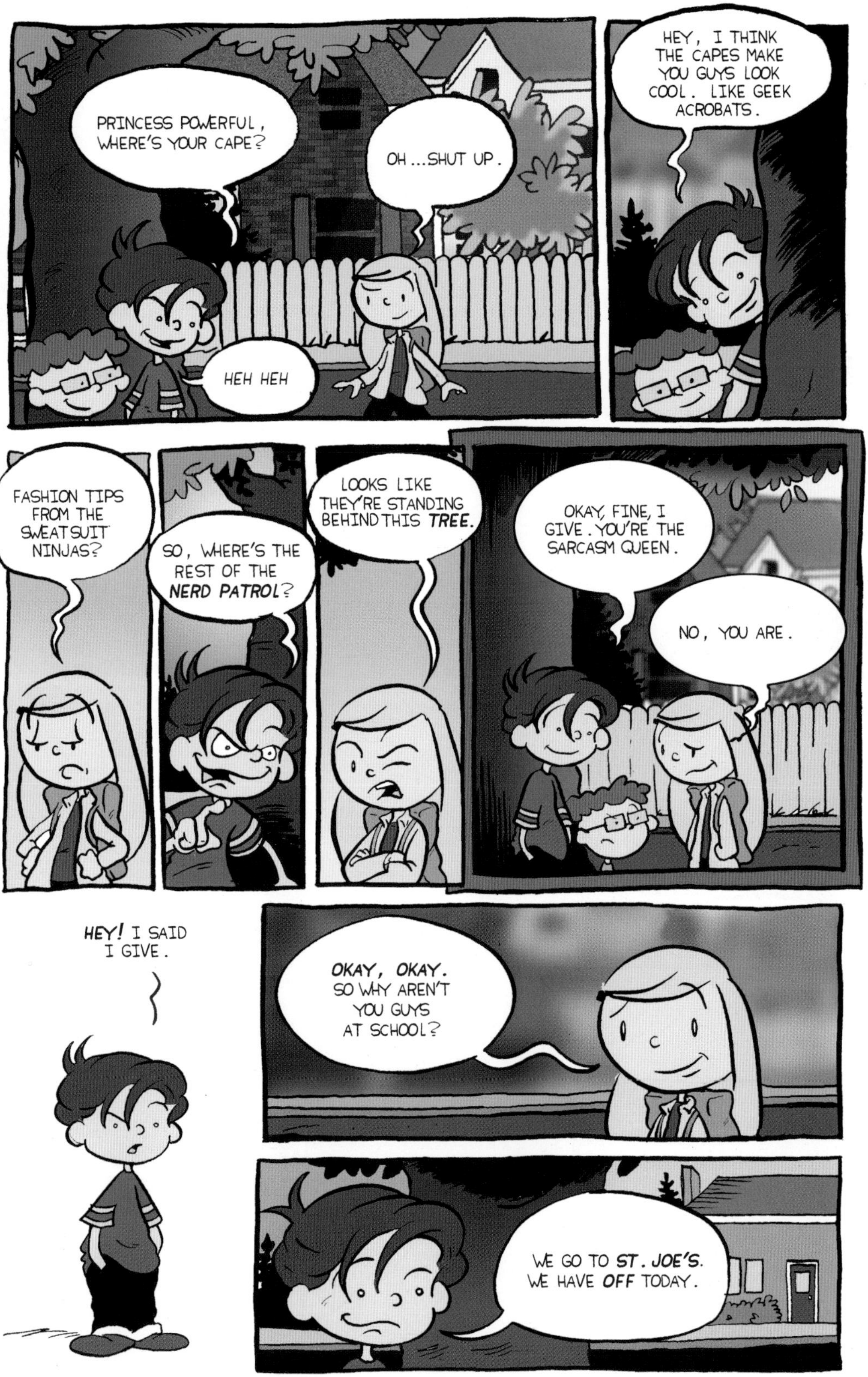
PRINCESS POWERFUL, WHERE'S YOUR CAPE?
OH ...SHUT UP.
HEH HEH
HEY, I THINK THE CAPES MAKE YOU GUYS LOOK COOL. LIKE GEEK ACROBATS.
FASHION TIPS FROM THE SWEATSUIT NINJAS?
SO, WHERE'S THE REST OF THE **NERD PATROL**?
LOOKS LIKE THEY'RE STANDING BEHIND THIS **TREE**.
OKAY, FINE, I GIVE. YOU'RE THE SARCASM QUEEN.
NO, YOU ARE.
HEY! I SAID I GIVE.
OKAY, OKAY. SO WHY AREN'T YOU GUYS AT SCHOOL?
WE GO TO **ST. JOE'S**. WE HAVE **OFF** TODAY.

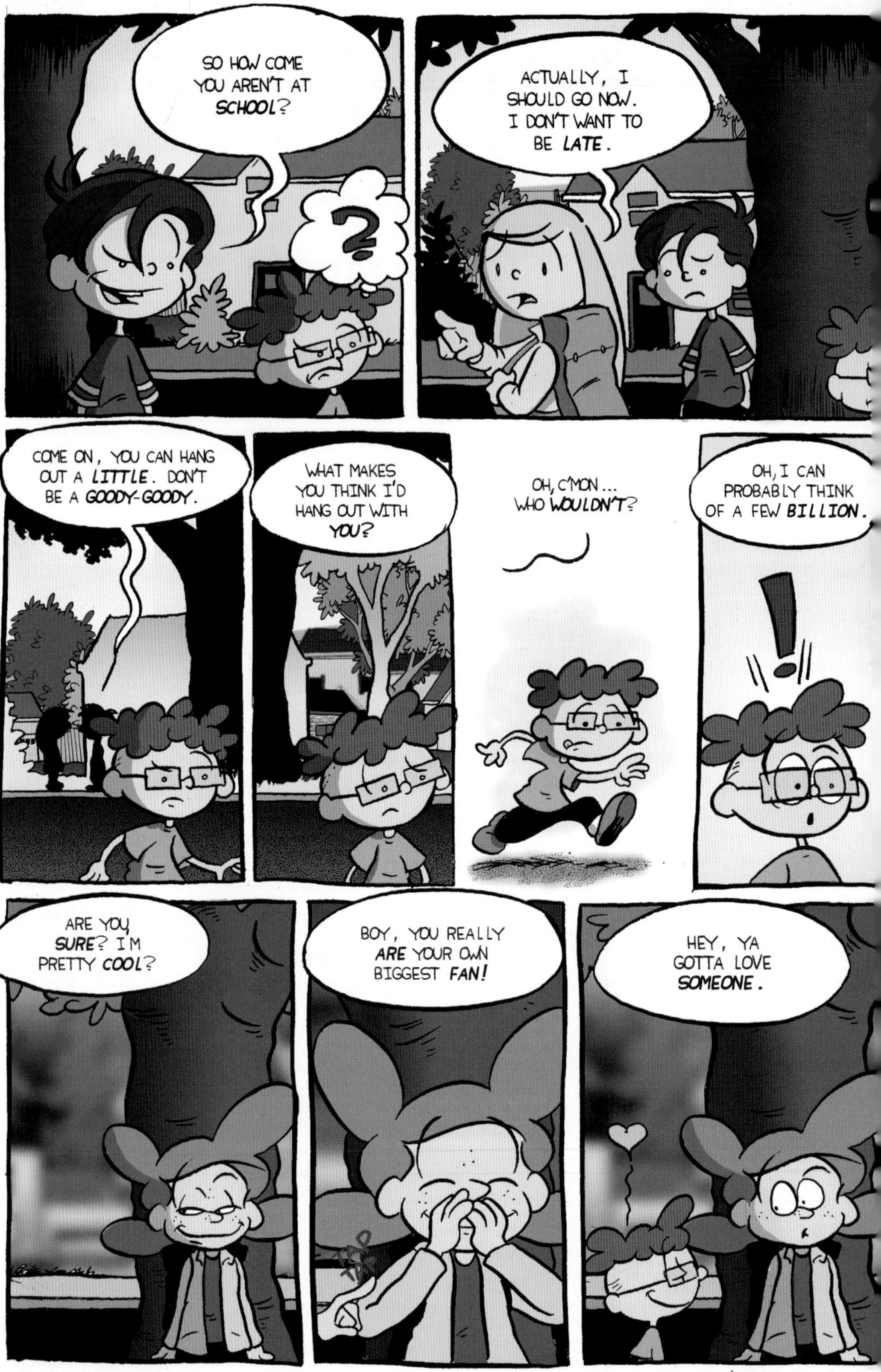

SO HOW COME YOU AREN'T AT SCHOOL?
?
ACTUALLY, I SHOULD GO NOW. I DON'T WANT TO BE LATE.
COME ON, YOU CAN HANG OUT A LITTLE. DON'T BE A GOODY-GOODY.
WHAT MAKES YOU THINK I'D HANG OUT WITH YOU?
OH, C'MON... WHO WOULDN'T?
OH, I CAN PROBABLY THINK OF A FEW BILLION.
!
ARE YOU SURE? I'M PRETTY COOL?
BOY, YOU REALLY ARE YOUR OWN BIGGEST FAN!
HEY, YA GOTTA LOVE SOMEONE.

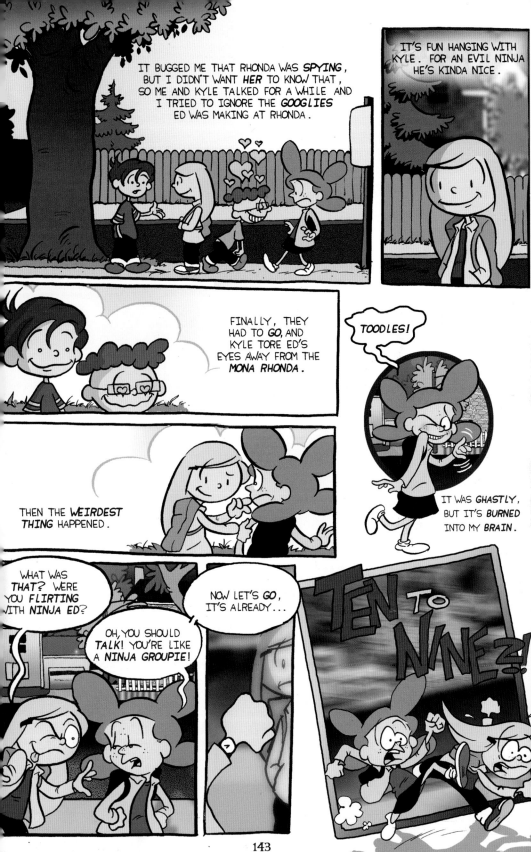

IT BUGGED ME THAT RHONDA WAS **SPYING**, BUT I DIDN'T WANT **HER** TO KNOW THAT, SO ME AND KYLE TALKED FOR A WHILE AND I TRIED TO IGNORE THE **GOOGLIES** ED WAS MAKING AT RHONDA.

IT'S FUN HANGING WITH KYLE. FOR AN EVIL NINJA HE'S KINDA NICE.

FINALLY, THEY HAD TO **GO**, AND KYLE TORE ED'S EYES AWAY FROM THE **MONA RHONDA**.

TOODLES!

THEN THE **WEIRDEST THING** HAPPENED.

IT WAS **GHASTLY**, BUT IT'S **BURNED** INTO MY **BRAIN**.

WHAT WAS **THAT**? WERE YOU **FLIRTING** WITH **NINJA ED**?

NOW LET'S **GO**, IT'S ALREADY...

OH, YOU SHOULD **TALK**! YOU'RE LIKE A NINJA **GROUPIE**!

TEN TO NINE?!

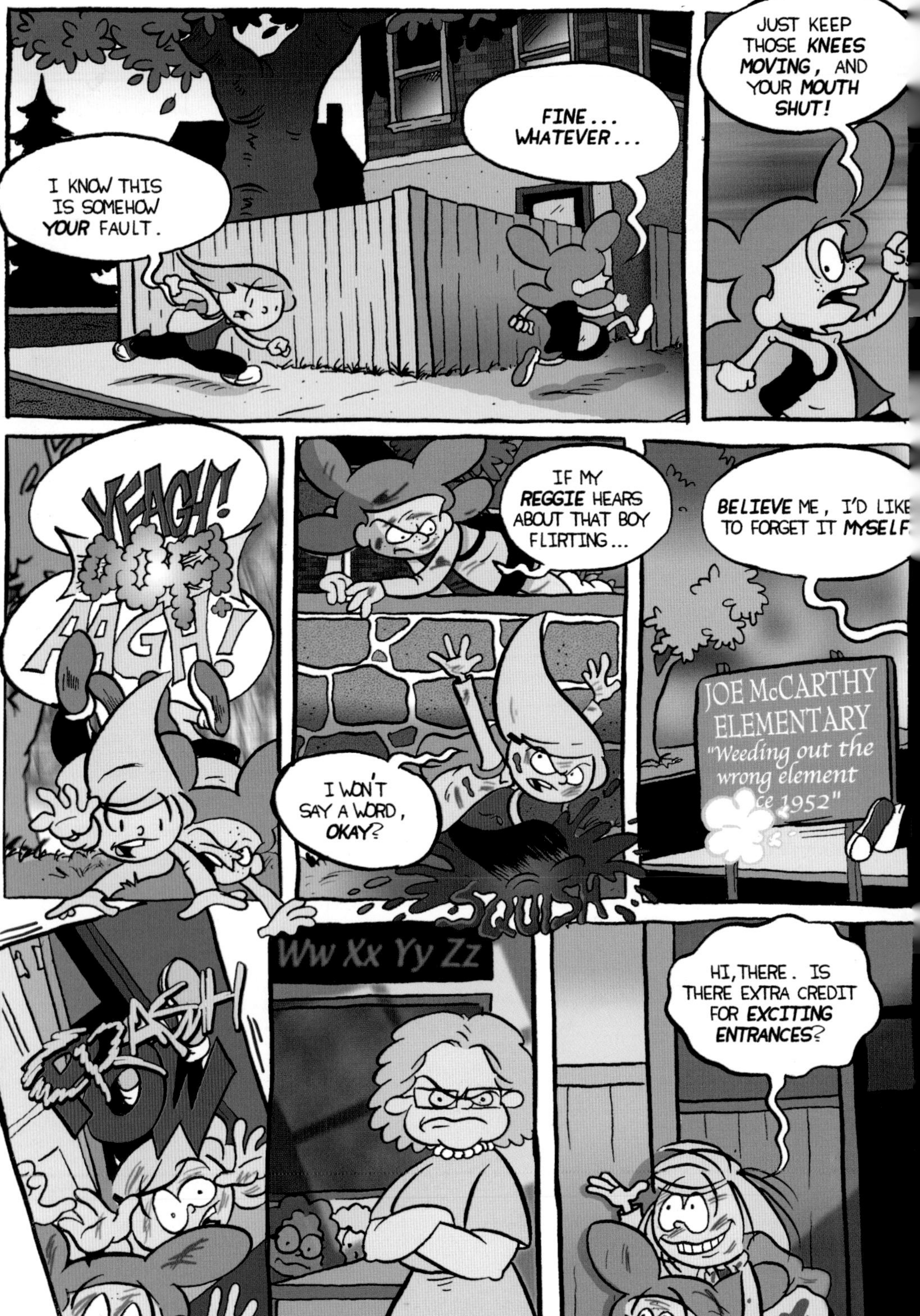
I KNOW THIS IS SOMEHOW YOUR FAULT.
FINE... WHATEVER...
JUST KEEP THOSE KNEES MOVING, AND YOUR MOUTH SHUT!
YEAGH!
OOF
AAGH!
IF MY REGGIE HEARS ABOUT THAT BOY FLIRTING...
I WON'T SAY A WORD, OKAY?
BELIEVE ME, I'D LIKE TO FORGET IT MYSELF.
JOE McCARTHY ELEMENTARY
"Weeding out the wrong element
ce 1952"
SQUISH
Ww Xx Yy Zz
HI, THERE. IS THERE EXTRA CREDIT FOR EXCITING ENTRANCES?

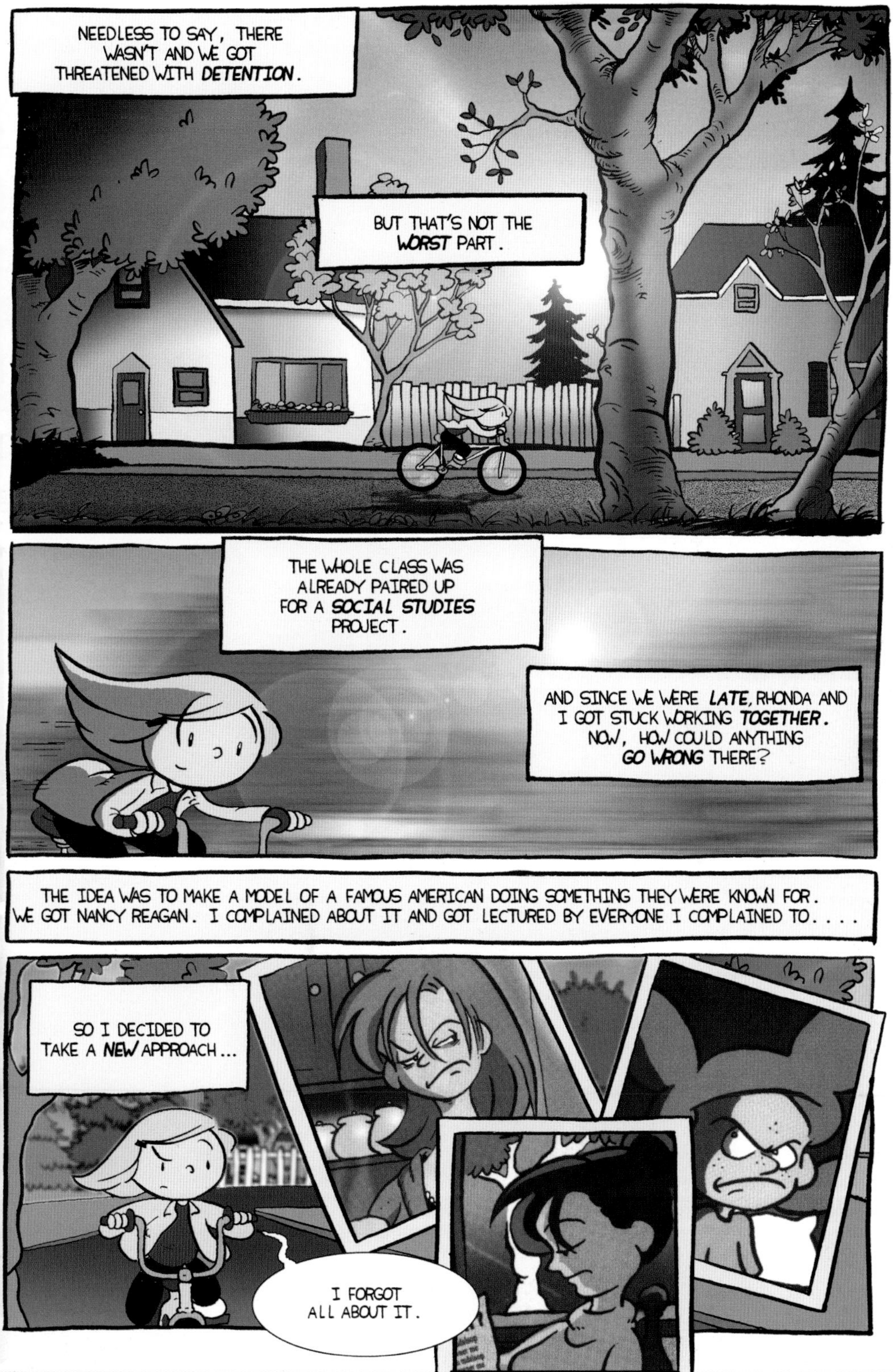
NEEDLESS TO SAY, THERE WASN'T AND WE GOT THREATENED WITH DETENTION.
BUT THAT'S NOT THE WORST PART.
THE WHOLE CLASS WAS ALREADY PAIRED UP FOR A SOCIAL STUDIES PROJECT.
AND SINCE WE WERE LATE, RHONDA AND I GOT STUCK WORKING TOGETHER. NOW, HOW COULD ANYTHING GO WRONG THERE?
THE IDEA WAS TO MAKE A MODEL OF A FAMOUS AMERICAN DOING SOMETHING THEY WERE KNOWN FOR. WE GOT NANCY REAGAN. I COMPLAINED ABOUT IT AND GOT LECTURED BY EVERYONE I COMPLAINED TO. . . .
SO I DECIDED TO TAKE A NEW APPROACH...
I FORGOT ALL ABOUT IT.

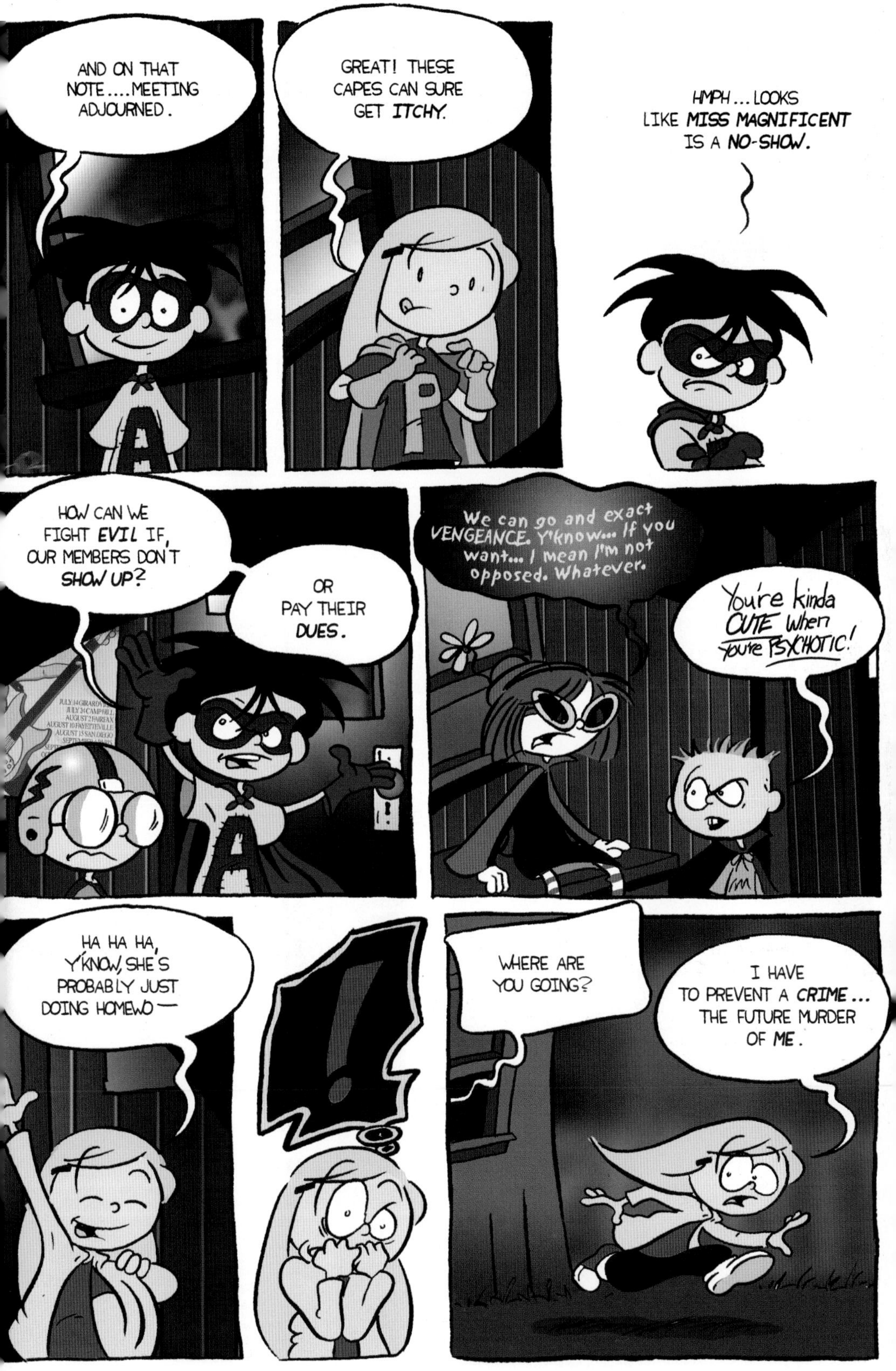
AND ON THAT NOTE....MEETING ADJOURNED.
GREAT! THESE CAPES CAN SURE GET ITCHY.
HMPH... LOOKS LIKE MISS MAGNIFICENT IS A NO-SHOW.
HOW CAN WE FIGHT EVIL IF, OUR MEMBERS DON'T SHOW UP?
OR PAY THEIR DUES.
We can go and exact VENGEANCE. Y'know... If you want... I mean I'm not opposed. Whatever.
You're kinda CUTE when you're PSYCHOTIC!
HA HA HA, Y'KNOW, SHE'S PROBABLY JUST DOING HOMEWO—
!
WHERE ARE YOU GOING?
I HAVE TO PREVENT A CRIME... THE FUTURE MURDER OF ME.

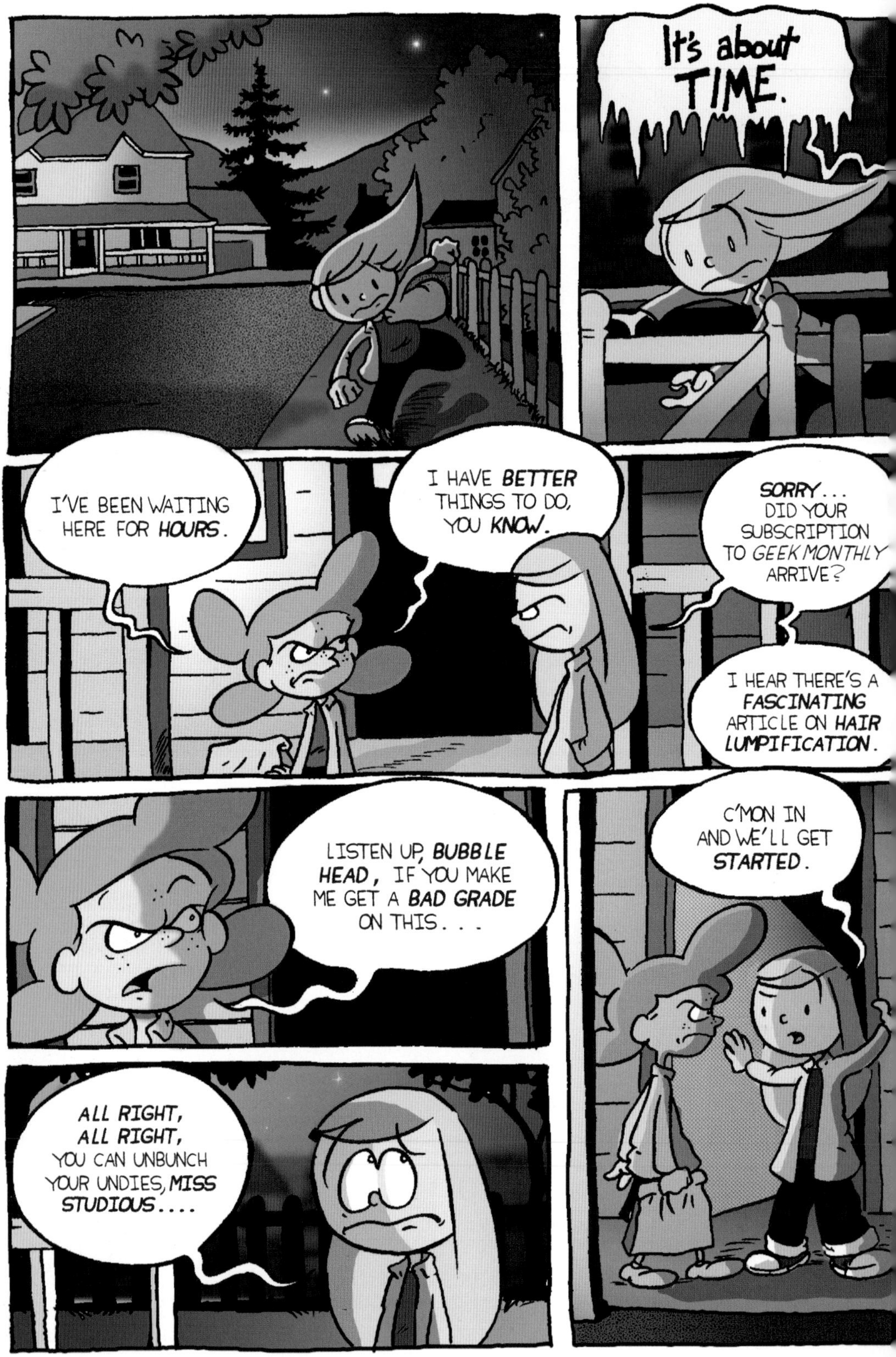
It's about TIME.
I'VE BEEN WAITING HERE FOR HOURS.
I HAVE BETTER THINGS TO DO, YOU KNOW.
SORRY... DID YOUR SUBSCRIPTION TO GEEK MONTHLY ARRIVE?
I HEAR THERE'S A FASCINATING ARTICLE ON HAIR LUMPIFICATION.
LISTEN UP, BUBBLE HEAD, IF YOU MAKE ME GET A BAD GRADE ON THIS. . .
ALL RIGHT, ALL RIGHT, YOU CAN UNBUNCH YOUR UNDIES, MISS STUDIOUS....
C'MON IN AND WE'LL GET STARTED.

149

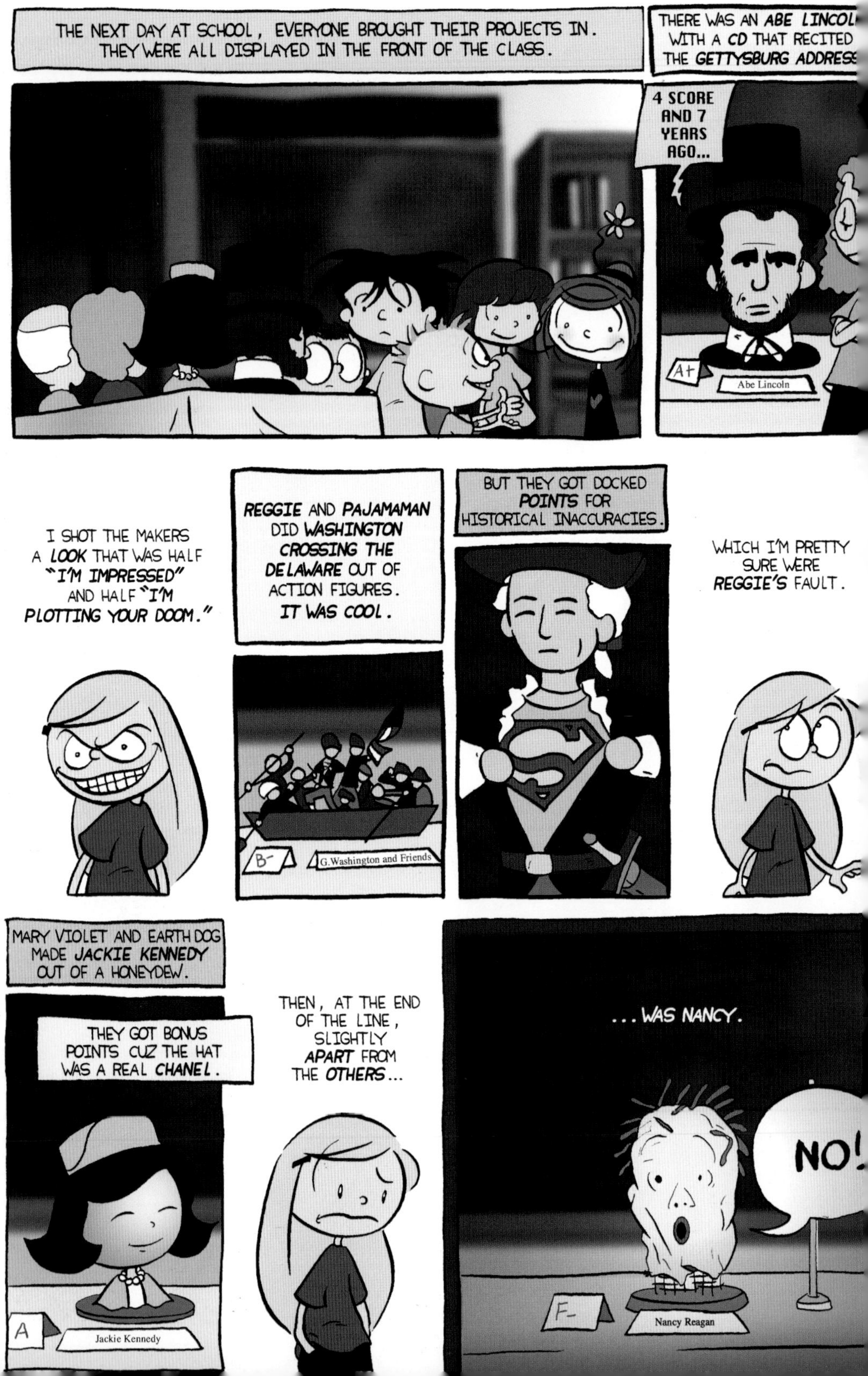
THE NEXT DAY AT SCHOOL, EVERYONE BROUGHT THEIR PROJECTS IN. THEY WERE ALL DISPLAYED IN THE FRONT OF THE CLASS.
THERE WAS AN ABE LINCOL WITH A CD THAT RECITED THE GETTYSBURG ADDRES
4 SCORE AND 7 YEARS AGO...
A+
Abe Lincoln
I SHOT THE MAKERS A LOOK THAT WAS HALF "I'M IMPRESSED" AND HALF "I'M PLOTTING YOUR DOOM."
REGGIE AND PAJAMAMAN DID WASHINGTON CROSSING THE DELAWARE OUT OF ACTION FIGURES. IT WAS COOL.
B-
G.Washington and Friends
BUT THEY GOT DOCKED POINTS FOR HISTORICAL INACCURACIES.
WHICH I'M PRETTY SURE WERE REGGIE'S FAULT.
MARY VIOLET AND EARTH DOG MADE JACKIE KENNEDY OUT OF A HONEYDEW.
THEY GOT BONUS POINTS CUZ THE HAT WAS A REAL CHANEL.
A
Jackie Kennedy
THEN, AT THE END OF THE LINE, SLIGHTLY APART FROM THE OTHERS...
...WAS NANCY.
NO!
F-
Nancy Reagan

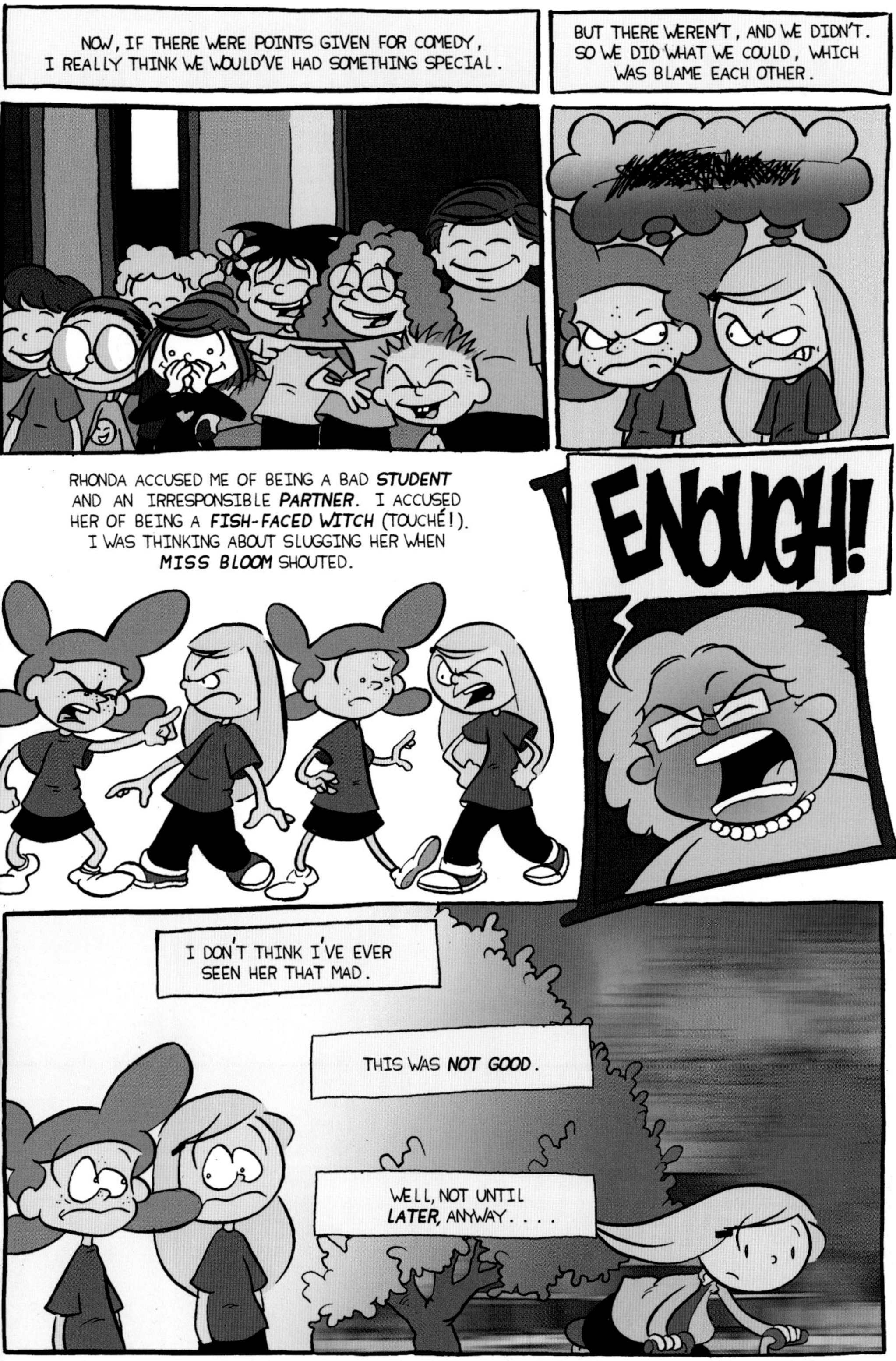
NOW, IF THERE WERE POINTS GIVEN FOR COMEDY, I REALLY THINK WE WOULD'VE HAD SOMETHING SPECIAL.
BUT THERE WEREN'T, AND WE DIDN'T. SO WE DID WHAT WE COULD, WHICH WAS BLAME EACH OTHER.
RHONDA ACCUSED ME OF BEING A BAD STUDENT AND AN IRRESPONSIBLE PARTNER. I ACCUSED HER OF BEING A FISH-FACED WITCH (TOUCHÉ!). I WAS THINKING ABOUT SLUGGING HER WHEN MISS BLOOM SHOUTED.
ENOUGH!
I DON'T THINK I'VE EVER SEEN HER THAT MAD.
THIS WAS NOT GOOD.
WELL, NOT UNTIL LATER, ANYWAY. . . .

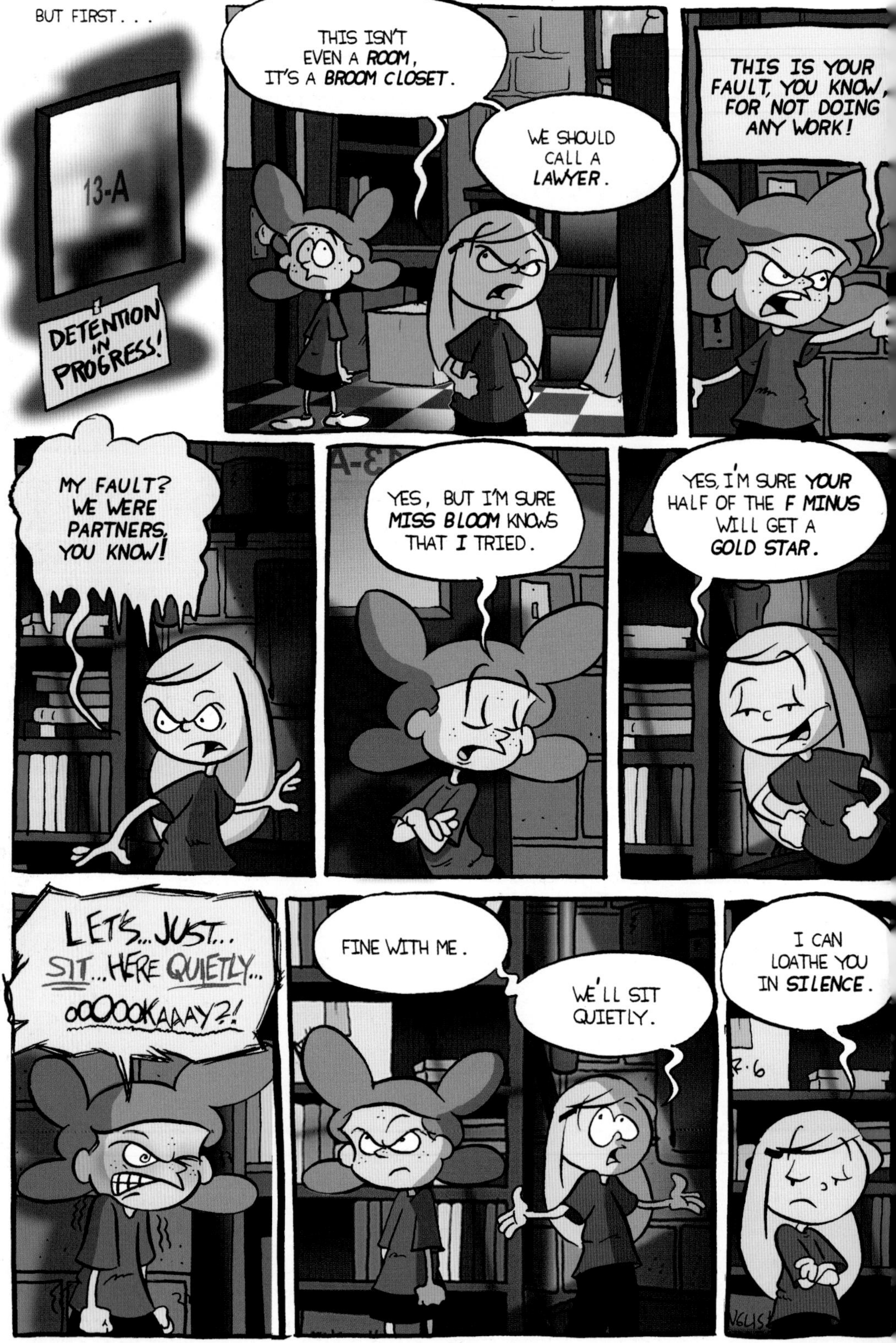
BUT FIRST . . .
13-A
DETENTION IN PROGRESS!
THIS ISN'T EVEN A ROOM, IT'S A BROOM CLOSET.
WE SHOULD CALL A LAWYER.
THIS IS YOUR FAULT, YOU KNOW, FOR NOT DOING ANY WORK!
MY FAULT? WE WERE PARTNERS, YOU KNOW!
YES, BUT I'M SURE MISS BLOOM KNOWS THAT I TRIED.
YES, I'M SURE YOUR HALF OF THE F MINUS WILL GET A GOLD STAR.
LET'S...JUST... SIT...HERE QUIETLY... OOOOOKAAAY?!
FINE WITH ME.
WE'LL SIT QUIETLY.
I CAN LOATHE YOU IN SILENCE.

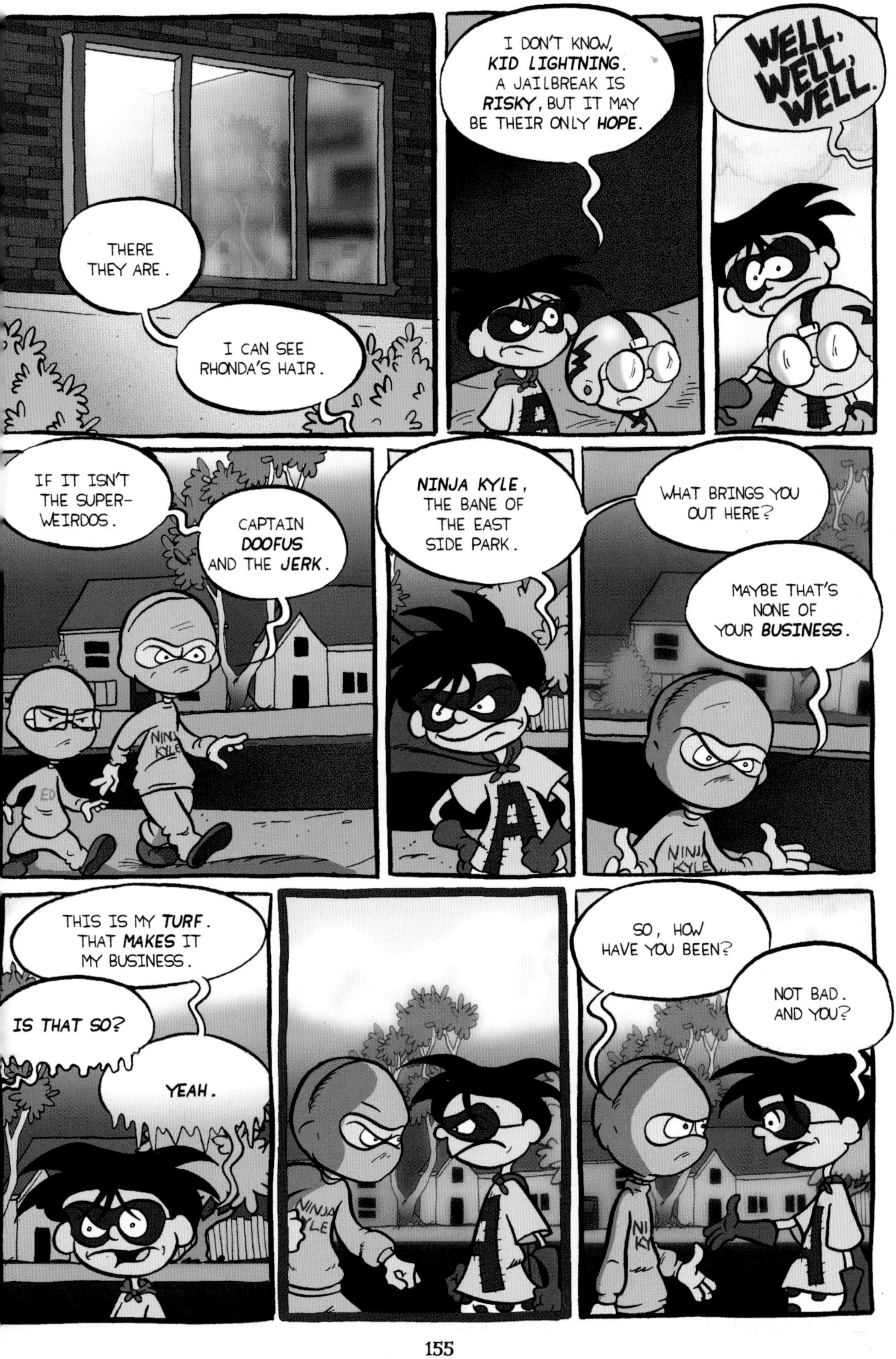
THERE THEY ARE.
I CAN SEE RHONDA'S HAIR.
I DON'T KNOW, KID LIGHTNING. A JAILBREAK IS RISKY, BUT IT MAY BE THEIR ONLY HOPE.
WELL, WELL, WELL.
IF IT ISN'T THE SUPER-WEIRDOS.
CAPTAIN DOOFUS AND THE JERK.
NINJA KYLE
ED
NINJA KYLE, THE BANE OF THE EAST SIDE PARK.
WHAT BRINGS YOU OUT HERE?
MAYBE THAT'S NONE OF YOUR BUSINESS.
THIS IS MY TURF. THAT MAKES IT MY BUSINESS.
IS THAT SO?
YEAH.
SO, HOW HAVE YOU BEEN?
NOT BAD. AND YOU?

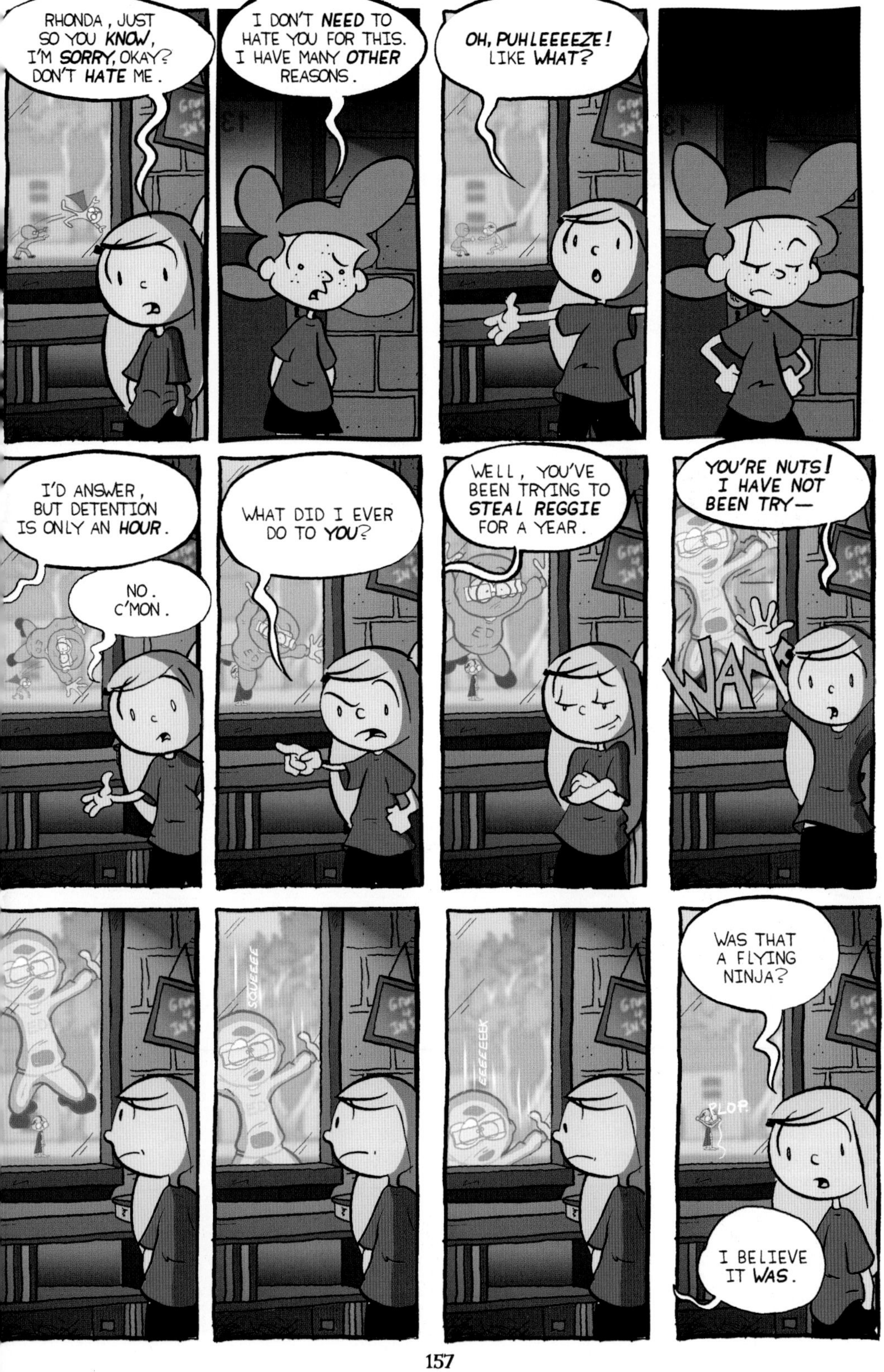
RHONDA, JUST SO YOU **KNOW**, I'M **SORRY**, OKAY? DON'T **HATE** ME.
I DON'T **NEED** TO HATE YOU FOR THIS. I HAVE MANY **OTHER** REASONS.
OH, PUHLEEEEZE! LIKE **WHAT**?
I'D ANSWER, BUT DETENTION IS ONLY AN **HOUR**.
NO. C'MON.
WHAT DID I EVER DO TO **YOU**?
WELL, YOU'VE BEEN TRYING TO **STEAL REGGIE** FOR A YEAR.
YOU'RE NUTS! I HAVE NOT BEEN TRY—
WA
SQUEEEEE
EEEEEEEK
WAS THAT A FLYING NINJA?
PLOP.
I BELIEVE IT **WAS**.

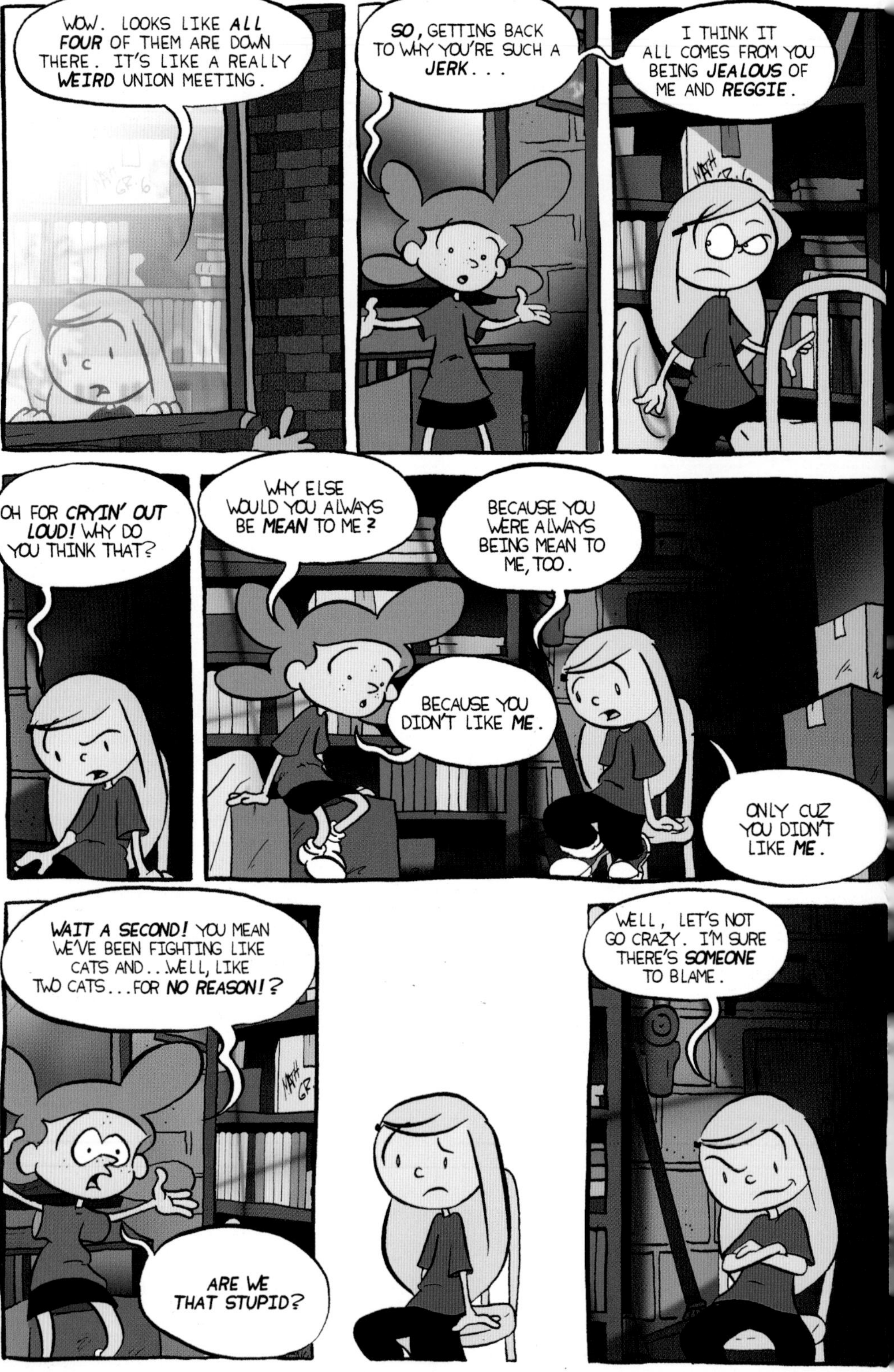
WOW. LOOKS LIKE ALL FOUR OF THEM ARE DOWN THERE. IT'S LIKE A REALLY WEIRD UNION MEETING.
MATH GR. 6
SO, GETTING BACK TO WHY YOU'RE SUCH A JERK...
I THINK IT ALL COMES FROM YOU BEING JEALOUS OF ME AND REGGIE.
OH FOR CRYIN' OUT LOUD! WHY DO YOU THINK THAT?
WHY ELSE WOULD YOU ALWAYS BE MEAN TO ME?
BECAUSE YOU WERE ALWAYS BEING MEAN TO ME, TOO.
BECAUSE YOU DIDN'T LIKE ME.
ONLY CUZ YOU DIDN'T LIKE ME.
WAIT A SECOND! YOU MEAN WE'VE BEEN FIGHTING LIKE CATS AND...WELL, LIKE TWO CATS...FOR NO REASON!?
ARE WE THAT STUPID?
WELL, LET'S NOT GO CRAZY. I'M SURE THERE'S SOMEONE TO BLAME.

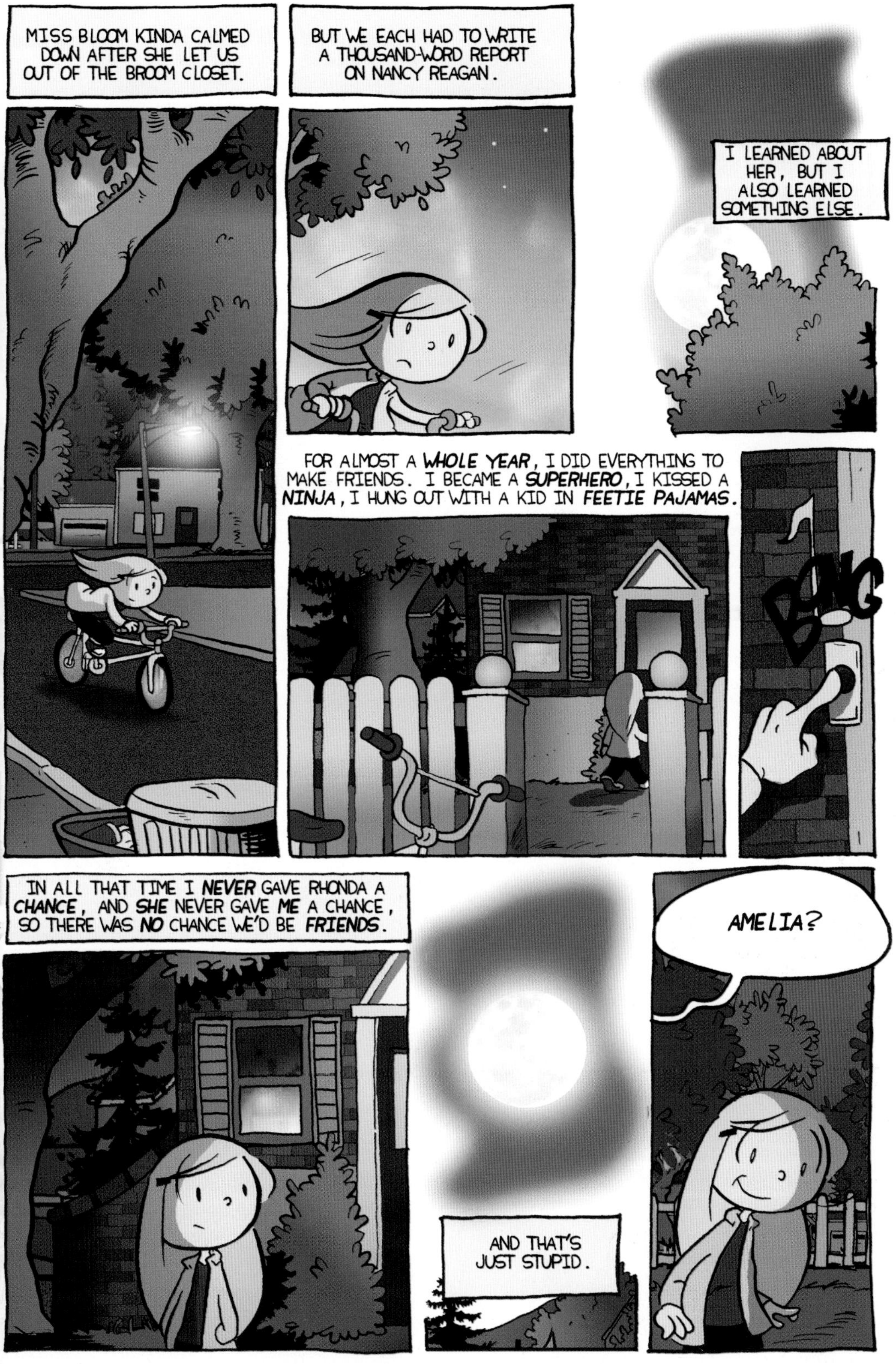
MISS BLOOM KINDA CALMED DOWN AFTER SHE LET US OUT OF THE BROOM CLOSET.
BUT WE EACH HAD TO WRITE A THOUSAND-WORD REPORT ON NANCY REAGAN.
I LEARNED ABOUT HER, BUT I ALSO LEARNED SOMETHING ELSE.
FOR ALMOST A WHOLE YEAR, I DID EVERYTHING TO MAKE FRIENDS. I BECAME A SUPERHERO, I KISSED A NINJA, I HUNG OUT WITH A KID IN FEETIE PAJAMAS.
BONG
IN ALL THAT TIME I NEVER GAVE RHONDA A CHANCE, AND SHE NEVER GAVE ME A CHANCE, SO THERE WAS NO CHANCE WE'D BE FRIENDS.
AND THAT'S JUST STUPID.
AMELIA?

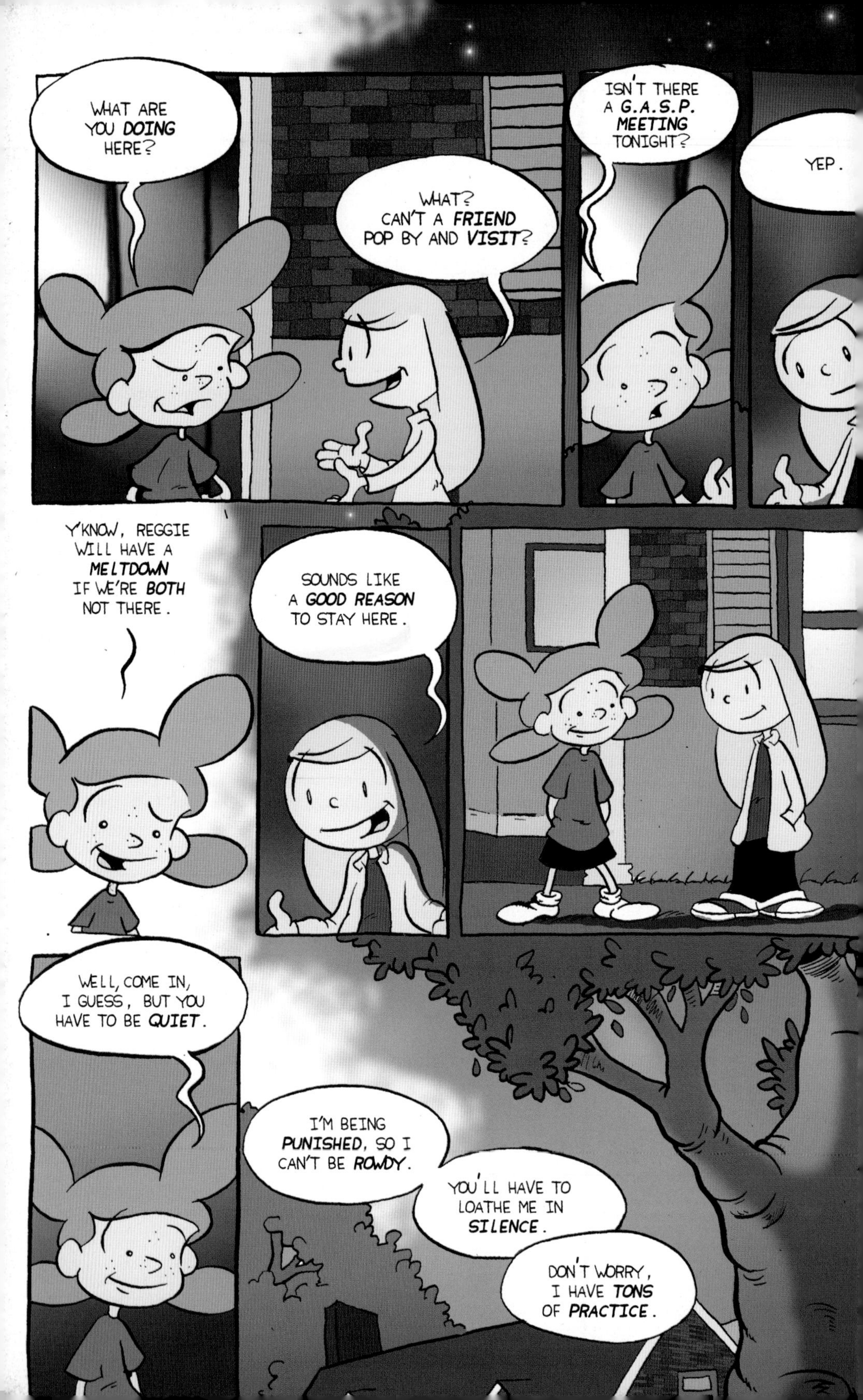

WHAT ARE YOU DOING HERE?
WHAT? CAN'T A FRIEND POP BY AND VISIT?
ISN'T THERE A G.A.S.P. MEETING TONIGHT?
YEP.
Y'KNOW, REGGIE WILL HAVE A MELTDOWN IF WE'RE BOTH NOT THERE.
SOUNDS LIKE A GOOD REASON TO STAY HERE.
WELL, COME IN, I GUESS, BUT YOU HAVE TO BE QUIET.
I'M BEING PUNISHED, SO I CAN'T BE ROWDY.
YOU'LL HAVE TO LOATHE ME IN SILENCE.
DON'T WORRY, I HAVE TONS OF PRACTICE.

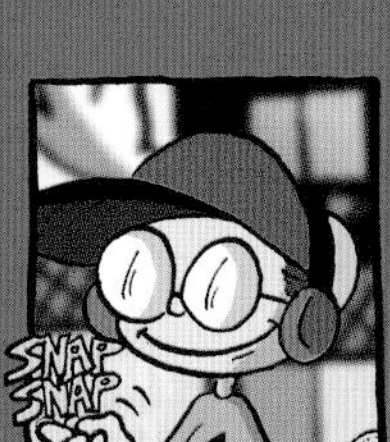
SNAP
SNAP

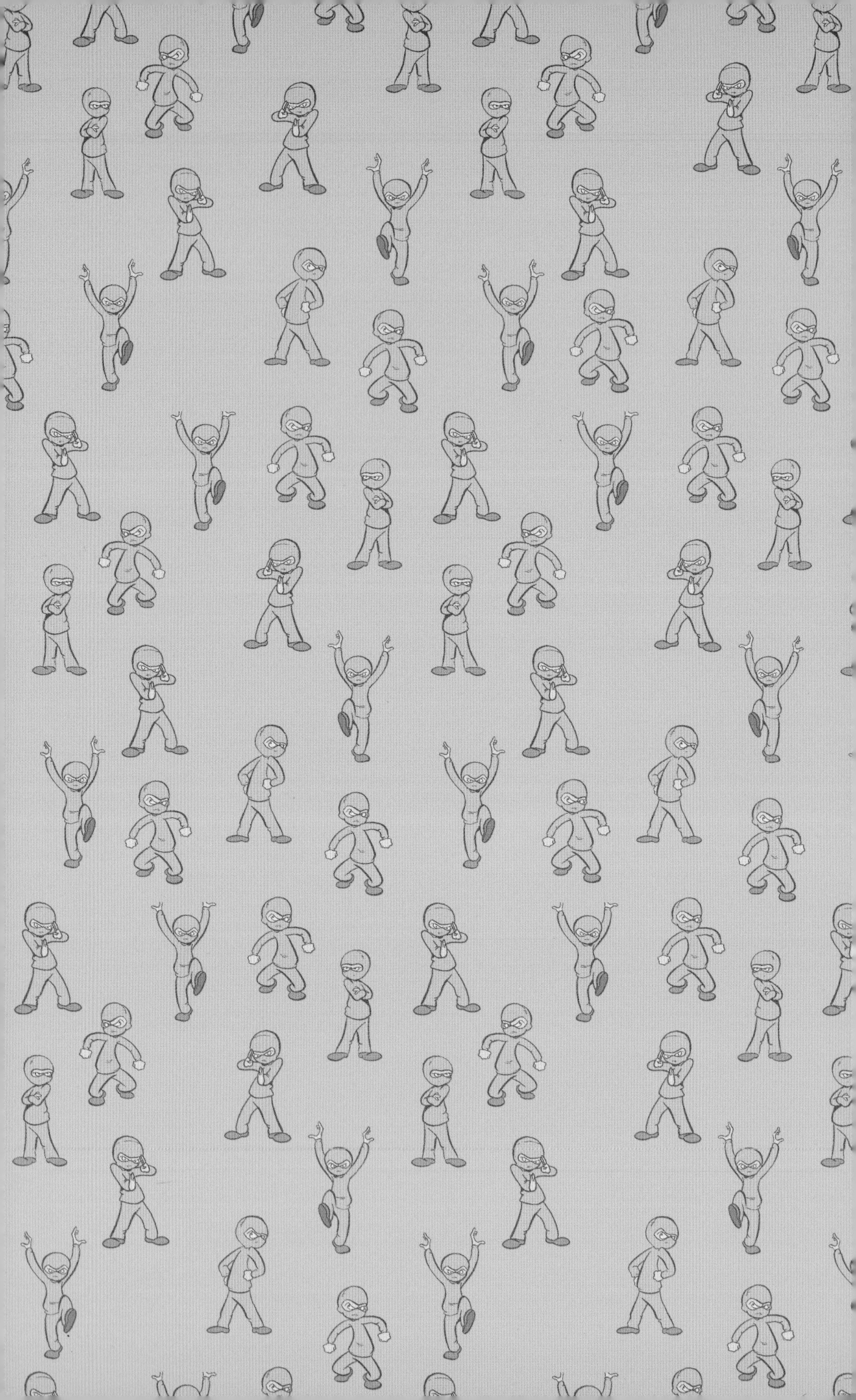

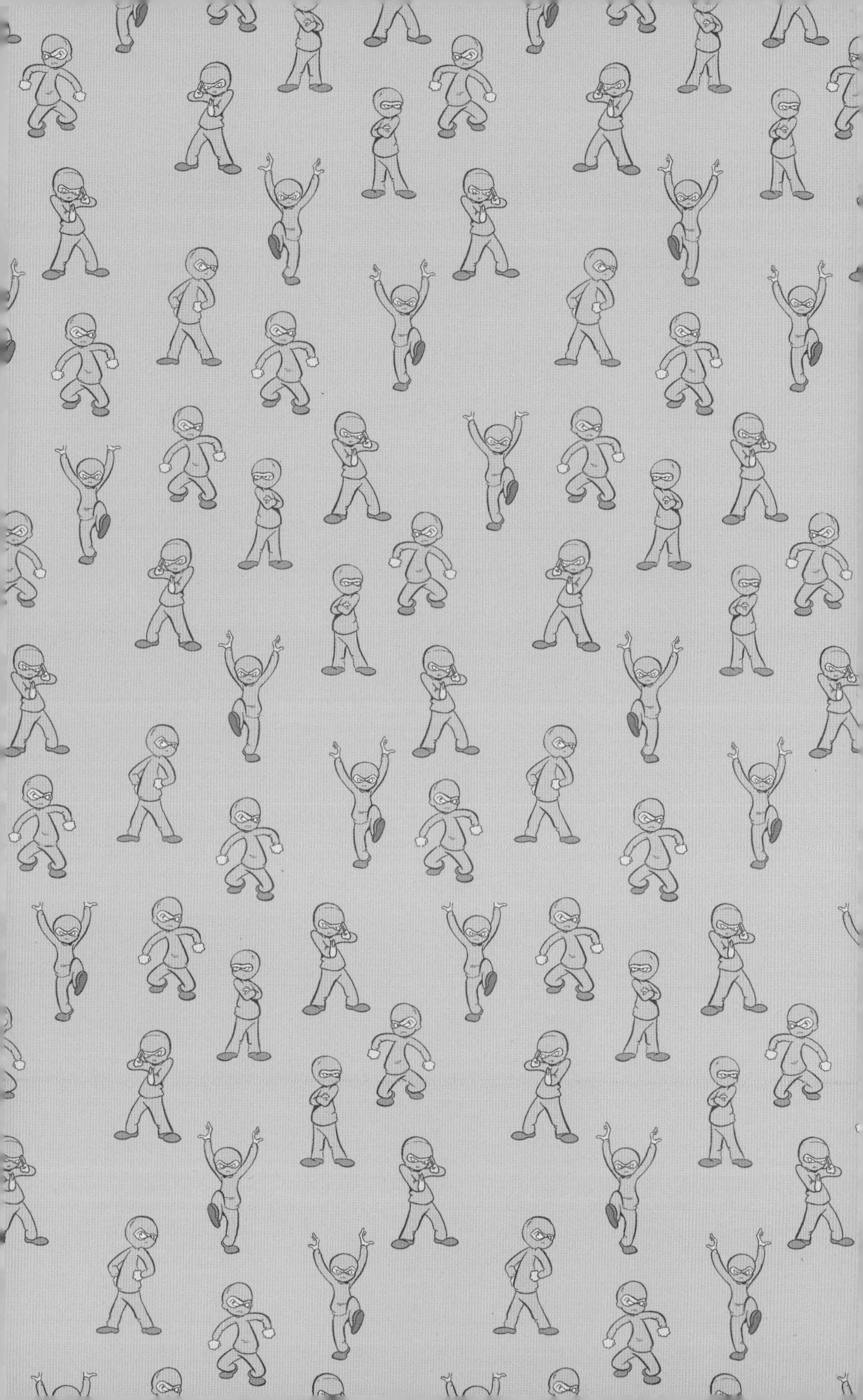

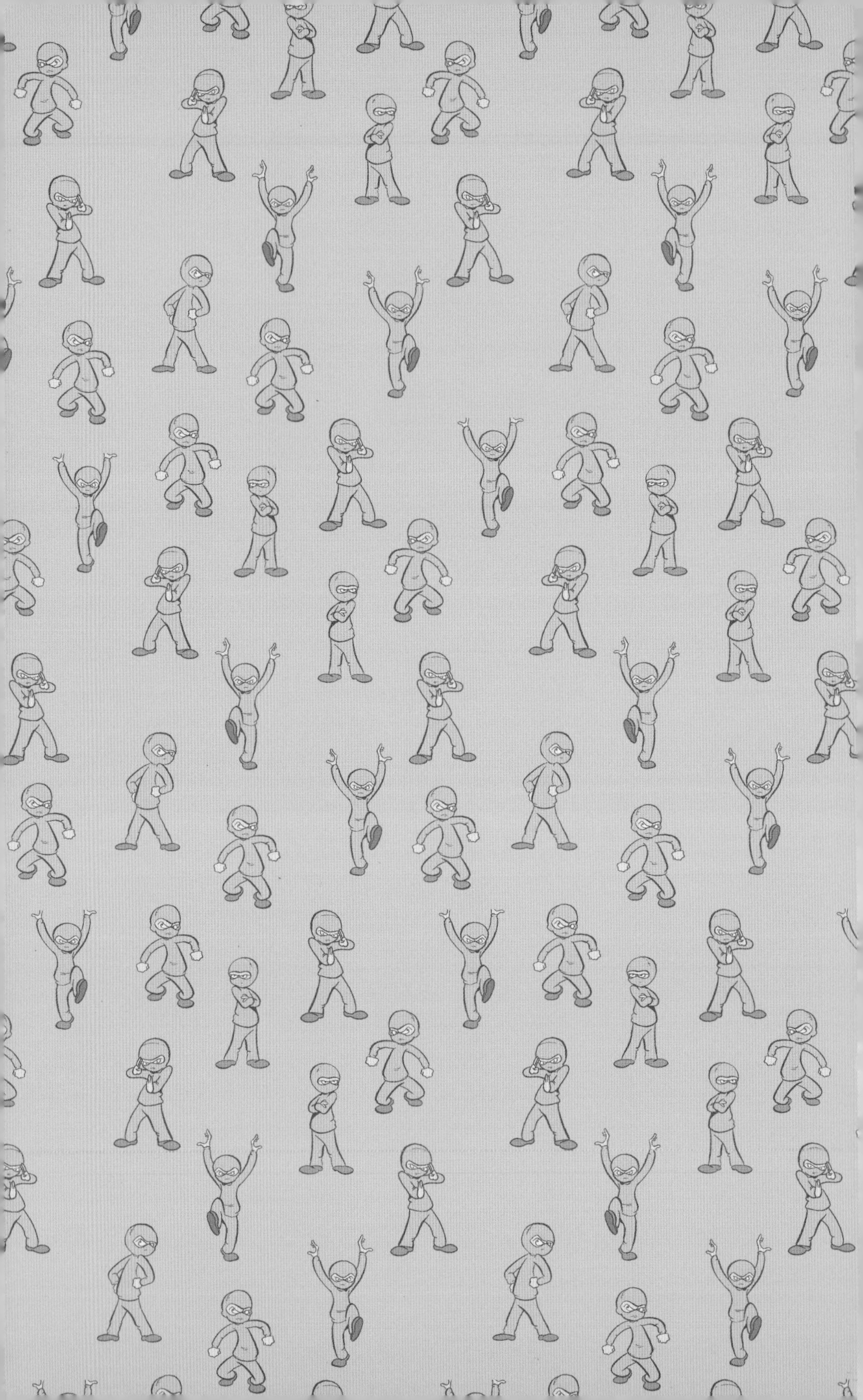